CAPTAIN'S KISS

Not in a thousand years could Meg have imagined that a mere touching of the lips could do such strange things to her. A slow heat invaded her limbs, as if she had just surfaced from a deep dive to feel the tropical sun, hot against her skin. She felt light-headed and dizzy, and there was a roaring in her ears like the boom of the surf pounding against the shore, and yet she was wonderfully, sensually aware of the captain's lips moving over hers, of his body, lean and hard, against her. Deep within, something stirred and awakened, something primitive and wild—like a storm at sea.

Glenmorgan held her, not ready yet to let her go. And then her arms wrapped themselves around his neck, and melting to his embrace, she returned his kiss—wildly, uninhibitedly, her body molding itself to his.

Bending down, he took her up in his arms and carried her to the bed.

A groan broke from Meg's depths as he laid her down. Dazed, she blinked up at him. He was breathing heavily and the eyes that looked into hers were fire-bright and glittery. Her lips parted—to what? Warn him? Tell him the truth before it was too late? She didn't know. And then he lowered his head to hers and she forgot everything but his lips drawing fire from her veins.

ANOTHER TIME . . . ANOTHER PLACE . . . ANOTHER LOVE—
Let Pinnacle Historical Romances take you there!

LOVE'S STOLEN PROMISES   (631, $5.99/$6.99)
by Sylvie F. Sommerfield

Mitchell Flannery and Whitney Clayborn are two star-crossed lovers, who defy social conventions. He's a dirt-poor farm boy, and she's a South Carolina society belle. On the eve of the Civil War, they come together joyously, and are quickly and cruelly wrenched apart. After making a suitable marriage, Whitney imagines that she will never feel the soaring heights of passion again. Then, Mitchell returns home seven years after marching away. . . .

VELVET IS THE NIGHT   (598, $4.99/$5.99)
by Elizabeth Thornton

To save her family from the guillotine, Claire Devereux agrees to become the mistress of the evil, corrupt commissioner, Phillipe Duhet. She agrees to give her body to him, but she swears that her spirit will remain untouched. To her astonishment, Claire finds herself responding body and soul to Duhet's expert caresses. Little does Claire know but Duhet has been abducted and she has been falling under the spell of his American twin brother, Adam Dillon!

ALWAYS AND FOREVER   (647, $4.99/$5.99)
by Gina Robins

Shipwrecked when she was a child, Candeliera Caron is unaware of her wealthy family in New Orleans. She is content with her life on the tropical island, surrounded by lush vegetation and natives who call her their princess. Suddenly, sea captain Nick Tiger sails into her life, and she blooms beneath his bold caresses. Adrift in a sea of rapture, this passionate couple longs to spend eternity under the blazing Caribbean sky.

PIRATE'S KISS   (612, $4.99/$5.99)
by Diana Haviland

When Sybilla Thornton arrives at her brother's Jamaican sugar plantation, she immediately falls under the spell of Gavin Broderick. Broderick is an American pirate who is determined to claim Sybilla as forcefully as the ships he has conquered. Sybilla finds herself floating upside down in a strange land of passion, lust, and power. She willingly drowns in the heat of this pirate's kiss.

SWEET FOREVER   (604, $4.99/$5.99)
by Becky Lee Weyrich

At fifteen, Julianna Doran plays with a Ouija board and catches the glimpse of a handsome sea captain Brom Vanderzee. This ghostly vision haunts her dreams for years. About to be wed, she returns to the Hudson River mansion where she first encountered this apparition. She experiences one night of actual ecstasy with her spectral swain. Afterwards, he vanishes. Julianna crosses the boundaries of her world to join him in a love that knows no end.

Available wherever paperbacks are sold, or order direct from the Publisher. Send cover price plus 50¢ per copy for mailing and handling to Penguin USA, P.O. Box 999, c/o Dept. 17109, Bergenfield, NJ 07621. Residents of New York and Tennessee must include sales tax. DO NOT SEND CASH.

JOHANNA HAILEY
SEA TREASURE

PINNACLE BOOKS
WINDSOR PUBLISHING CORP.

PINNACLE BOOKS are published by

Windsor Publishing Corp.
475 Park Avenue South
New York, NY 10016

First Printing: February, 1994

Printed in the United States of America

To Wendy, who has been such a good friend and who has taught me so much. Thanks.

A special thanks to Eastern New Mexico's Golden Library and staff, to the Portales Public Library and staff, and the Charleston, South Carolina, Chamber of Commerce.

Since once I sat upon a promontory,
And heard a mermaid on a dolphin's back
Uttering such dulcet and harmonious breath,
That the rude sea grew civil at her song,
And certain stars shot madly from their spheres,
To hear the sea-maid's music.
                    —*A Midsummer Night's Dream*

One

On Antigua, along a lonely stretch of coast not far removed from English Harbor, high-pillared cliffs stood sentinel above the steady rise and fall of the sea, while below, fountains of spray shot up against their sides. Overhead, a waxing moon, nearing its half-phase, darted in and out of clouds bearing the promise of rain before morning. It was November in the year 1747, past the season of the hurricane, and yet Meg, perched on the parapet atop the cliffs, felt uneasy inside, as if the stormclouds gathering out to sea came as a warning that some dire thing was about to happen.

It was not a new feeling. She had experienced premonitions before. But this time it was different, she mused, conscious of a prickling of nerve endings. Indeed, this time her skin crawled with the sense of something issuing from the island itself—a wrongness or a danger. And this time, too, she had something more to go on than mere feelings.

At once her forehead puckered in a wry little frown. Or maybe the wrongness came from inside herself, she thought, and the storm was in her own breast, the remnants of the tempest that had driven her to this barren, windswept place. Hugging her knees to her chest, she heaved a sigh.

She had never seen the old man angry before, let alone

furious with her. She supposed she could not blame him. Restless and brooding, her temper ready to snap without a moment's notice, she was all too aware that she had not been the easiest person to get along with of late. Indeed, there were times when she hardly knew herself anymore.

The way she had taken to prowling the beaches of Antigua at night, for example, or worse, the way she had dared to sneak up to the grand house perched atop the bluff overlooking the sea. In spite of the fact that she was tinglingly aware of the danger in being caught, she had peeked through the windows at the fine people inside. Only it seemed they were not really quite so fine as they had appeared.

She had been conscious of amazement mingled with awe as she beheld them. How odd was their raiment. Surely they did not choose of their own will to drape themselves with layer upon layer of heavy fabrics, no matter how rich or magnificent. To one who protested at having to cover herself even with the lightweight frock the old man insisted upon, such behavior seemed fantastic at best. She doubted they could draw even a breath when the heat of the day was upon them. Still, she could not deny that the woman in her voluminous gown, her shoulders, arms, and a large expanse of her white bosom bare, appeared to attract a deal of attention from the men in her attendance. She was beautiful, Meg supposed upon reflection, all small and white and delicate-seeming, and yet there had been something about her that made Meg think of the fragile-looking sea wasp with the fatal sting.

The other women present made little impression. From the very first, her eyes had been drawn to the golden-haired beauty.

As for the men, she found them to be quite different from what she had expected. How very strange they were, with their faces painted white and their lips and cheeks red.

They were not at all like the old man. Indeed, they some-what reminded her of crabs the way they were forever mincing and sidestepping or waving their arms about in the most extravagant fashion. She supposed such behavior was due to the constricting clothes and the absurdly high heels they wore. For the most part she found them quite bizarre and not a little amusing—save for one.

Slender and not above average height, he stood off by himself, patently bored with the antics of the others. A shapely hand bearing a great ring on the index finger toyed absently with a crystal goblet as his heavy-lidded gaze observed with a chilling lack of emotion the woman who was the center of all the attention. Not above forty, he was handsome, his features fine-cut and regular, but cold and, beneath the rouge, unnaturally pale.

In spite of herself, Meg shivered, repulsed by something she sensed in him, something indescribably dark and passionless. Every instinct cried out to her to flee and never look back, and still she remained, held there by some dread fascination she could not explain. Then a servant had come with a low-murmured message for the man. With a gesture, he had summoned the woman and another man out on to the verandah.

Meg had barely time enough to conceal herself behind a potted palm before they emerged from the house. Heartily regretting the impulse that had brought her to such a pass, she peeked cautiously through the leaves at the woman, who was regarding the slender man with haughty displeasure.

"I beg your pardon for drawing you away from your admirers, my dear," murmured the gentleman, his smile utterly devoid of anything but cold amusement at her obvious disdain.

"Then why did you?" she retorted acidly. "Somehow I do not think it was out of any desire for my company."

9

"No? How very odd. But then, who am I to argue, when you, of all people, know me so well."

"No doubt the two of you are finding this all very amusing," interjected the third of their party, a portly man above middle age with bad teeth and a ruddy complexion. "I, however, was on the point of luring Sir Alfred to the gaming table."

"Really, Father," snapped the golden-haired beauty. "How much must you lose before you discover that you have no talent for cards? You will not be satisfied until you have ruined us all with your gambling."

The object of her censure flushed a shade redder.

"Faith, Logan," he sputtered. "I had hoped when you wed my daughter that you would teach her to curb that damned unruly tongue of hers."

The man called Logan shrugged, apparently unmoved at the older man's protest.

"Be that as it may, my dear Thornton, all this has very little to do with my purpose in calling you both here. You will be pleased to learn, Clarissa, that an old friend of yours has been seen in English Harbor."

"How very interesting, to be sure." Clarissa lifted a white shoulder indifferently. "And does this 'old friend' have a name?"

"Oh, indeed. A name which, while not exactly illustrious, has attained a certain notoriety."

At this, Clarissa's temper snapped.

"Enough of your riddles. Come to the point, if you will."

"But of course. How thoughtless of me. You would naturally be all eagerness. I confess I myself was more than a little intrigued to discover a man we had thought dead to us is very much alive. Especially when that man is Captain Michael Glenmorgan."

Meg, from her hiding place, could almost feel the shock

that was generated by this revelation. While her father uttered a strangled cough, Clarissa paled alarmingly.

"Glenmorgan alive!" she exclaimed before she caught herself. "You must be joking. Why, even if he were alive, he would not dare to show himself here. Not after the way he humiliated the King's Navy. I doubt there is a king's officer who would not give his right arm to see him keel-hauled."

"Your logic, as always, is flawless, my dear," Logan smoothly applauded. "It would seem, however, that circumstances have changed. The rumor is that our enterprising young captain has earned the gratitude of the king."

"A pardon. Good God, you cannot mean it," ejaculated Thornton, drawing a square of white linen from his sleeve and mopping his forehead with it. "Then there will be nothing to stop him from coming after us. Or making public the cursed letters his father discovered before I could destroy them. Dammit, Logan, you swore this would never happen. You swore you would put an end to his existence."

"And so I shall, my dear Thornton. You have nothing to worry about."

Thornton, looking as if he had just eaten something that sorely disagreed with him, was anything but comforted.

"That's easy enough for you to say," he pointed out, waving the handkerchief about in an agitated manner. "You're not the one who will hang if those letters turn up in the wrong hands. This is all your doing, Clarissa. I never should have listened to you. Had I not, Turlough Glenmorgan would still be alive today, and I should not have his son plotting his revenge against me. I said from the very beginning that it would all turn bad in the end."

"Oh, do control yourself, Father," retorted the lady in disgust. "We don't know that Glenmorgan has the letters. And without them, it will be impossible to prove anything.

11

Lavoillet and Duval are dead, and the Frenchman is hardly likely to talk."

"*I* am sure of nothing. I tell you, I don't like it, Logan. We should never have killed Turlough. Now it isn't enough simply to put Glenmorgan out of the way. I warn you, I must have those letters. I shan't be able to sleep knowing they are out there somewhere."

"Then naturally you will have them," Logan replied. Meg, peering between the palm leaves, shivered at the man's cold-blooded self-assurance. "If the letters still exist, I shall make certain that, before he breathes his last, the captain will be only too glad to reveal their whereabouts."

Thornton's hand jerked in a gesture of impatience.

"And what makes you so sure?" he demanded in a shrill voice. "Glenmorgan's as slippery as a bloody eel."

"But it is quite obvious." Logan's lips curled in a chilling smile. "Now that the brave captain is a free man, he will undoubtedly come to us. We have, after all, the one thing he desires most in the world. We have the lovely Clarissa."

Meg, forced to listen to them lay their plans to lure the captain to a most certain death, went almost limp with relief when at last several young men swarmed the verandah in search of their vanished hostess. Bewildered and frightened by all that she had witnessed, Meg fled as soon as she was alone again.

Now, as she stared out at the restless bulge of the sea, she was miserable. Upon reflection, it had been a mistake to unburden the scene she had overheard to her grandfather, for it had triggered the argument between them.

She groaned and clutched her arms around her, haunted by the memory of the harsh words that had passed between her and the old man. He had been like a stranger, his usually kind and gentle features suddenly hard and closed to her. His voice had lashed out at her.

"I cannot understand you, Meg. You are not lacking in

intelligence. Nor are you ignorant of the danger. If you care nothing for yourself, you might at least think of me. Thus far we have been safe because we have kept to ourselves. What would become of me if something happened to you? Do you think I could stay here without you? I cannot live the way we did before we came here. I am too old, Meg. Too tired. Even if there were someplace else to go, I cannot, will not, run. Not ever again."

It was true. Why had she never seen it before? He had always been "Grandfather" or "the old man" to her, but somehow he had never seemed old. He seemed to possess an immutable strength upon which she might draw forever. It had never occurred to her that one day it would fail. But suddenly, in spite of the muscular leanness of his body, the bent, yet unbowed, shoulders, the inky blackness of his hair, touched by silver, but still as thick as ever in his youth; in spite of his eyes, steel-gray and keen-edged as a sword, he had looked old.

"I'm sorry, Grandfather," she had replied. "But I made sure I wasn't seen. Can it really be so bad?"

He turned abruptly away from her.

"What good is talking if you will not listen?" he said, his voice so weary that it cut her to the quick. Her hand went out to him, only to be snatched uncertainly back again.

"I am listening," she persisted, driven, as she always was, to gain knowledge of so much that lay beyond her constricted world. "I have always listened. But I must understand. Tell me, Grandfather, I beg you. What did their words mean?"

He stood, staring so long out the window into the night, that she had thought he meant not to answer. Thus she had started at the sound of his voice, low and heavy with a strange sort of weariness.

"I have tried to tell you, Meg. There is evil in the world.

What you have overheard is a plot to do grave harm to one of their own kind."

"Yes, but why? Why would they do such a thing?"

"Why is of no importance," he answered curtly. "Have you heard nothing of what I have said? They mean to kill this man. To lure him into a trap and then murder him. One excuse is as good as another to those who think nothing of killing."

Meg frowned, troubled and perplexed.

"I have seen sharks turn and kill those of their own kind who are wounded or ill," she persisted, though it was obvious the old man had meant that to be the end of the discussion. "But they are not creatures of great intelligence, and nor do I think it is evil for them to do only as their natures would dictate. With the whales, it is different. Whales will succor and protect, even call encouragement to another whale in need. Are men less than whales and more of a kindred with sharks?"

"Men are neither fish nor whale," the old man replied darkly. "Man alone of God's creatures has been cursed with the ability to distinguish good from evil, and thus only man is capable of rising above his own nature—or sinking below it, which is more often the case. And that is why I want you to promise you will not go back to that place again."

"No, I will not go back." She shuddered, remembering Logan's cold eyes. "Not there, ever again. But the man—somehow I must find a way to warn him. If only they had said when and where they intend to—"

"Enough! You will do nothing of the kind, do you hear me?"

Hurt, she had recoiled from the anger in his voice. He was, perhaps, understandably irate, for she had indeed risked a great deal in what she had done, and yet she seemed to sense there was something else beneath his agitation—something which had nothing to do with her.

"Yes, Grandfather," she replied stiffly. "I hear you. How could I not when you are shouting at me? But he is a man, and they intend to kill him."

"I will not listen to such nonsense! It has nothing to do with us, do you understand? You will forget what you heard. You will get down the books and we will do your lessons, just as we have always done, and you will forget everything else that has happened this night."

Her heart full of rebellion, she had reached for the books, but she had not forgotten. She did not believe that she could ever do that. Nor had she ceased to wander restlessly at night.

In a sudden fit of temper, she picked up a pebble and hurled it over the edge of the cliff. What was the matter with her? She felt all twisted up inside by terrible yearnings for she knew not what, yearnings that not all the boundless beauty and the teeming energy of the sea could assuage. It was not just that she was lonely, she told herself. She had always been that, and always it had been enough to seek out the old man, to sit for long periods on the floor by his knee and talk or read. But not that time. That time the books had served only to intensify the storm of discontent within her, and the old man's stoic calm to infuriate her. She had ended up lashing out at him with words meant to hurt and, flinging out the door, had left, swearing that he would never see her again.

In spite of the fact that she had stayed away for three days, it had yet been an empty threat. None knew it better than she. No matter how much she might have meant it at the time, she was bound to go back again. She could not stop herself anymore than she could have stopped the endless cycle of the moon tides. Their lives, the old man's and hers, were inextricably intertwined, and if it no longer was enough to completely fill the void in her heart, it was at least infinitely better than the alternative. She knew well

15

the difference between being lonely and finding oneself suddenly and unutterably alone in the world.

She shivered, as memories kept carefully locked away threatened to surface. But she would not think of that, she told herself firmly, her chin coming up. Rising lithely to her feet, she stared out over the shimmering sea. It did little good, after all, to dwell on what could not be helped. Tonight she would walk along the beach and try to still the tumult in her breast, and on the morrow, she would go and make her peace with the old man.

That much settled at least, she started for the trail that led down the cliffs, when something—a sound, perhaps, or a flash of movement below—caught her attention. Instinctively, she dropped flat on her belly to avoid being seen and peered down over the sheer drop of the cliffs to the sea.

Her heart skipped a beat as she spied a small boat skirting the headland. There was a safe mooring tucked away inside the curving arm of a small bay, but the way was through perilous waters fraught with hidden snags and jagged outcroppings of reef. Apparently the oarsman was no novice. He maneuvered his boat through the dangerous shoals with a cool daring that made her pulse race with excitement. Who was he, this reckless stranger who dared the headland in the wee hours before dawn? Why had he come?

She waited long enough to see him tie up his boat and come ashore. Then, making sure that he intended scaling the narrow trail that would bring him to the escarpment, she dropped quickly to the ground. For a moment she hesitated. All her instincts warned her to flee, but curiosity and a strange compulsion she could not understand urged her to remain. At last the latter won out, and she retreated behind the cover of an umbrella tree draped with vines, there to watch and wait.

* * *

The moon had set and a light rain was falling when the faint scrape of shoeleather against rock reached her straining ears. Her heart began to pound beneath her breast, and she blinked as a yellow light appeared where the trail emerged at the top of the cliff. Then at last she saw him, bathed in the glow of a lantern—a tall figure of a man with a strong, chiseled countenance and raven hair that reached to his shoulders.

A multitude of unfamiliar emotions rushed over her as she stared at him, not the least of which was an awed sense of wonder. This man had not the look of the mincing crab. He was lean and powerful, his magnificent body showing to advantage in a plain white shirt and black leathern breeches tucked into the tops of knee-high boots. While she sensed a certain recklessness about the stubborn cast of the mouth and the intimation of a strong will in the firmness of the jaw, there was yet the capacity for laughter as well and a strong proclivity for passion. But more than that, there was something about him that reminded her of tales told of the seafarers of old—men of courage and daring, who had had adventure in their hearts and the sea in their blood. Here was such a one as she had envisioned a man to be.

And then it came to her with a blinding flash of insight who he was and why he was here.

He was Capt. Michael Glenmorgan, and he had come to meet the beautiful, golden-haired Clarissa.

Impulsively, she started forward, to warn him that he had walked into a trap, when suddenly she froze, her heart gone suddenly cold.

All the old strictures, the ancient teachings, the sacred vows and warnings forbade her to show herself. Nothing but ill luck had ever come to those who had disobeyed or to those not of the blood who had had the misfortune to lay eyes on one of her kind. Were not her mother and father evidence enough of what could happen?

17

She drew back slowly, step by step, her eyes never leaving the man. Then suddenly she turned and fled.

She ran blindly, the breath sobbing in her throat, until at last she stumbled and fell. With a groan, she curled her fingers into the wet black earth and wept bitter tears.

She did not know how long she lay there before at last her weeping abated, leaving her drained and listless and yet filled with a bitter disgust of herself. Would she let the man die because of what she was? And then a new thought came to her. Perhaps what she was had nothing to do with it. Perhaps she was afraid to do anything to stop it.

Suddenly she sat up, a fixed expression on her lovely face. She came of a strong and peace-loving people who valued goodness and life above all else. Wasn't it a greater wrong to do nothing than to risk breaking the old strictures? Even if she dared not show herself, was she not gifted with other means of helping the man?

Buoyed, she rose to her feet and, with hands that trembled slightly, lifted the circular gemstone that hung on a chain around her neck. Its surface, transparent and smooth as glass, reflected the image of her face. The words of the old ones came easily to her lips as she gazed into the stone, like the clear, blue-green depths of her eyes, and began to sing.

Two

The day broke, still and gray, with a curtain of mist that hung in the air. In less than an hour the sun promised to burn through the low-hanging clouds, leaving the island prey to the merciless heat of the tropics, but for now it was pleasantly cool, the air redolent with the mingled scents of wet, black earth, fragrant blossoms, and rain. From somewhere in the distance came the sound of someone singing—the words indistinguishable, but the voice true and hauntingly lovely. The daughter of one of the fishermen, no doubt, who inhabited the huts along this side of the island, speculated Michael Glenmorgan. Oblivious to the clinging dampness of his shirt, he stood, apparently idly, beneath the spreading branches of an umbrella tree, a slender thumb and forefinger twirling the chain of a gold locket to and fro between them. Only the brooding crease between the dark slash of his eyebrows and the pale glint of piercing blue eyes seemed to tell a different tale.

The truth was he had made his way long before daybreak to Pirates' Bay, had climbed the winding trail to Lookout Point with long, quick strides, and had been waiting ever since, his impatience like a hard knot in his belly, slowly tightening.

His thin lips quirked in wry amusement at himself as he

19

slipped the chain over his head and thrust the locket inside his shirt. He was eight and twenty, hardly a callow youth to risk everything for a woman, especially this woman. And yet, with a king's pardon in his pocket and the rest of his life before him, here he was. Somberly he bent to pluck an orchid, delicate and white, from among the exposed roots of the umbrella tree. Undoubtedly Dick Chapin was in the right of it, he reflected, the sweet fragrance of the blossom triggering unwelcome memories: a moonlit garden, music wafting on the breeze, and a young girl as fresh and lovely as the orchid he had woven in her hair. He *was* a damned fool to come. Bloody hell! He had not needed his first mate to tell him he was allowing his obsession to overrule his head. And over something that should have been finished long ago.

Clarissa Thornton was lost to him. She was wed to Logan Tharp, the man who had sworn to see him hang!

Glenmorgan's head came up. The low rumble of carriage wheels sounded faintly above the steady wash of the sea against the rocks below then, with a creak of harness, came to a halt. A horse snorted and pawed the earth. His long frame strung like whip cord, Glenmorgan stepped forward to peer through a curtain of pink shower and woody vines trailing from the branches overhead.

The carriage, seen through the enshrouding mist, appeared insubstantial, and the coachman, hunched on the seat and garbed in black, looked like the driver of a bloody hearse, he thought. A sardonic smile played about his handsome lips. If Logan Tharp had learned of the tryst between his wife and his oldest enemy, it might well be the death coach come to bear Michael Glenmorgan to hell. Then the carriage door was flung open, and a woman, draped all in white, stepped down.

"Wait for me here. I shall call you if you are needed." Her words carried clearly on the breeze.

Glenmorgan crushed the flower in his fist. It was Clarissa. She had come. He could feel the blood flow, quick and light, in his veins like the first touch of a fever, and then—the cold brush of warning at the nape of his neck. He had lived far too long on the edge of uncertainty not to recognize the latter feeling for what it was. And yet if it was a trap, with Clarissa as the bait to draw him out, he could see no sign of Logan Tharp or his men.

His eyes gleamed recklessly. The devil take Logan Tharp. Glenmorgan would have risked more to be with Clarissa, if only for a few fleeting moments. After all, he had waited a long time for the answers to certain nagging questions.

Noiselessly he melted into the thick underbrush as she started down the path toward him, seeming almost to float through the mist.

She did not pause until she reached the umbrella tree. There she reached up to slip the flowing white mantle from her head and gazed uncertainly about her.

The breath whistled in Glenmorgan's throat at sight of her. Her beauty had not diminished in the seven years since he had seen her. Her hair shone like spun gold in the pale light, and the face was the one that he carried in the locket over his heart, the eyes, the clear transparency of amber, childlike, innocent-seeming, seductive. Silently he cursed those eyes. Even knowing she was as false as the love she had once sworn was his, he felt a small wrench beneath his breastbone, like the opening of an old wound that had never completely healed. At last, chiding himself for a bloody fool, he shoved such thoughts firmly from him.

"Michael?" she called in a low, thrilling whisper. "Michael Glenmorgan, where are you?"

"Here."

She wheeled, a hand pressed to her throat. An unwitting gasp burst from her lips as she saw the tall form detach itself from the shadows.

21

The thought flashed in her mind that he had changed. Oh, the broad shoulders and long, lithe frame, she remembered well enough, and the coal-black hair worn defiantly uncovered by either tricorn or wig. As rebellious as the man himself, the thick mane fell in unruly waves down to the shoulders, which served to give him the look of some wild Celtic warrior, she mused. But the blue eyes, dark-rimmed and piercing, were colder now, harder, as was the lean face. Indeed, what had once been boyish dimples in either cheek had deepened to sensuous creases, wholly masculine and undeniably intriguing. Even more telling, however, the unmistakable hint of recklessness in the slight curl of the lip was now tempered by the stern line of the jaw. There was little left of the wild youth who had courted her long ago, she realized with a shiver. Here was a man, coolheaded, fearless, hard—and utterly dangerous.

"Did I startle you?" he asked, the steel-flecked eyes unreadable. "Forgive me. It was not my intention."

For an instant something flickered in the pale oval of her face, something cold and calculating. Or was it only uncertainty? He could not be sure.

"Michael, it *is* you," she cried huskily, and flung herself against him. Her silk wrap slipped unnoticed from her shoulders to the ground, leaving bare her arms and her bosom above a daring décolletage.

Glenmorgan's powerful muscles tensed as the woman's soft body pressed close to his. His strong hands hesitated before they closed lightly on her arms.

Clarissa, waiting for their touch, let out a silent breath.

"My darling," she whispered. "I could not believe my ears when I heard you were here. Alive and well as I had thought never again to see you—and in English Harbor, of all places."

A hard glint of a smile flashed in the lean face, tanned by sun and wind.

"I imagine that *was* something of a shock," he drawled in the slow, cool accents which had led many to believe that Michael Glenmorgan was a man without nerves. "To more than just a few of the good people of Antigua."

"But then, it must be true, what is being said." She drew back to lift searching eyes to his face. "The king has granted you a pardon."

"Aye. 'Tis true enough. It seems the king was not displeased to be rid of a certain pirate chief and his lieutenants. And I was not loath to oblige him."

"Lavoillet and Duval!" Clarissa breathed. "Logan said it was the *Raven,* but Papa did not believe it. He said only a British man of war would have dared take on the pirate stronghold at Tortola." Suddenly she melted against him, her cheek pressed over his heart. "I might have known it was you. After the tales that have been told of your exploits. Seven years, Michael, and never in all that time a word from you. Why?"

The muscle leaped along his jaw line, but his voice, when he spoke, was dispassionate.

"Perhaps it never occurred to me that you would be interested. You were Logan Tharp's wife."

"Yes, I am his wife," she said with a bitterness that was not feigned. "Oh, why did you leave me? Was the Orient more important than what we had? One last voyage, you said. And then you never came back again. They—Papa and Logan—persuaded me that you had been lost at sea, and I-I—"

"You believed them," he finished for her. "And why shouldn't you? It saved you the embarrassment of having to break off your engagement to me, a man who had been so indelicate as to lose everything, including his fortune and his honor."

"Michael, you could not have thought that?"

"What was I to think? Then, or four months ago when

23

Logan laid his trap for me off Jamaica? I hear you gave a ball in honor of his victory. You will be glad to know that it was being talked about in practically every port in the Caribbean, a fact for which I am extremely grateful. Oh, don't look so surprised. It suited my purposes for the world to think Mad Mike Glenmorgan was permanently out of the way. And since it was Logan who branded me a pirate before I decided to take up the game for myself, it seemed only fitting that he should have the glory of ending my illustrious career. Are you trying to tell me now that you grieved over my supposed loss?"

"Oh, Michael." She trembled and clung to him with her small, white hands. "You have no notion of the anguish I have suffered. The ball, everything, was Logan's doing. I was a fool. I never dreamed what Logan was till it was too late. I should have waited for you as I promised to do, but I was weak, a-afraid to disobey my father. Then, when Papa at last convinced me you were never coming back from the Orient, I-I wanted to die, too. But I couldn't."

She did not see the flash of uncertainty in the stern features, quickly shuttered behind an expressionless mask. Careful, he told himself. He had been fool enough once before to fall for her cursed sweet air of innocence. And yet, what if she was telling the truth? She was only a woman and, like all of her kind, weak and vulnerable, at the mercy of the men who ruled her existence. At once he caught himself. Bloody hell! He was doing it again, succumbing once more to her spell, to the aura of fragility and helplessness that had first drawn him to her so long ago. Deliberately, he forced himself to remember.

"My poor Clarissa. Three whole months you waited, and then you sought solace for your grief in the arms of a man like Tharp." His fingers bit into her flesh, till she nearly winced with pain. "I suppose to some that might seem an eternity of suffering."

Gasping, Clarissa flung up her head to look at him.

She paled at what she saw in the chiseled hardness of his face. The thought came fleetingly to her that it was true—he knew everything. Then deliberately she quelled the cold clamp of fear that had gripped her. All was not yet lost. She had tamed Michael Glenmorgan once before. She almost laughed aloud at the memory of the daring sea captain so blindly in love that he had not seen what was going on beneath his nose. He was a man. How difficult could it be to arouse all his previous desire, to make him want her even more than he had before?

"If you know so much, then surely you must realize I was given no choice in the matter." As if her limbs could no longer bear her, she sank weakly against him. "Michael," she breathed, her eyes shimmering with unshed tears, "you're hurting me."

Still, he held her, the hard glitter of his gaze seeming to bore holes through her, and all the while the scent of her perfume teased at his senses. The warmth of her body, soft and pliant against his, made it difficult to think clearly. His glance seemed drawn against his will to the trembling of her lips, slightly parted, to the even white of small kitten's teeth. The droning of honeybees somewhere nearby seemed to fill the air, which was grown hot, stultifying. As if drawn against his will, he lowered his head toward hers.

From somewhere the sound of singing, high-pitched and resonant, a sweet, lilting voice, filled with innocence, shattered the spell.

Abruptly he released her, nearly flinging her from him. His breath lanced through his throat like a hot blade as he saw the marks of his fingers on her arms, livid against the ivory paleness of her skin.

"I find it difficult to believe you," he uttered, his breath harsh in his throat. "You, my dear Clarissa, have never been without choices."

25

"I—I do not understand you." Pressing a hand to her breast, she backed a step. "You are a stranger—hard and-and unfeeling. Michael, what has happened to change you?"

His short bark of laughter sounded harshly in the quiet, and unwittingly her cheeks grew flushed.

"You ask me that?" he demanded cynically. "I arrived home from the Orient to find myself outlawed, my mother and sister living in poverty and my father dead, by his own hand, and you marvel that I have changed? And where were you, Clarissa? Did you spare them or me even a passing thought when you climbed into bed with the man who helped ruin them?"

She winced as if he had physically struck her.

"I—I don't know what you mean. Indeed, how could I? There were business reversals. Papa told me your father was forced to borrow heavily. And then, when the ships on which all his hopes depended were lost at sea, he could no longer meet his obligations. The loss of the *Argonaut* and its cargo of Spanish gold finished him. What could he do, but take the honorable way out?"

She had blundered. She saw it instantly. Glenmorgan's eyes flashed terrible sparks of anger.

"Enough!" he said, his voice edged with steel. "Who are you to speak of honor? Do you expect me to believe you didn't know those 'business reversals' were contrived? You didn't know the man closer to him than a brother was secretly stealing him blind?"

At last a spark of fear shone in her face, quickly masked.

"No, it is a lie. All lies. Michael, how could you believe such things of a man who has always been your friend? How could you think such things of *me?*"

"I have Lavoillet's dying word. Logan Tharp arranged to have those ships plundered. Your *father,* my sweet Clarissa, betrayed my father, and the man who is your husband hounded him to his grave."

26

Clarissa hastily lowered her eyes to hide their fierce light of triumph. A pirate's word. That was all the proof he had. It had to be. Had it been otherwise, he would already have exposed Logan and her father to the port authorities. In a way it was too bad. Her eyes beneath the thick veil of her eyelashes swept the long, lean frame, the broad, masculine chest, the way the black mat of hair curled just above the V of his shirt, open at the throat, the narrow torso and slim waist, the muscular thighs beneath skin-tight breeches. So long as the possibility existed that the papers might yet be discovered, Glenmorgan could not be allowed to live, and his death would not be an easy one. Indeed, when Logan had finished with him, there would be very little of the brave sea captain left. What a pity to waste such a delectable figure of a man! Mentally she shrugged. Ah, well, it could not be helped. Perhaps, however, since there was little else to do now but keep him here until the trap was sprung, she might as well reap what pleasure she could in the short time remaining. No doubt she owed him that much at least.

Deliberately lifting her eyes to his, she clutched at the sleeves of his shirt with hands that clung. "Michael, you must believe me. I was never a part of what happened to your father. They forced me to marry Logan. But I have never loved him. I have never loved anyone but you."

Even as a cold clamp of warning tightened like a fist on his vitals, Glenmorgan felt himself drawn into the depths of those spellbinding orbs. Bitterly he cursed. He had thought to see her one last time, to prove to himself that she was as false as the vow she had sworn to him, and then to walk away, free of her haunting memory at last. He should have known better. No man was proof against her witchery.

Savagely his mouth closed over hers.

Her mouth opened wide to him, to the hard thrust of his tongue. Uttering a low moan deep in her throat, she clung

27

to him with her white arms and sank to the ground, pulling him down with her onto the thick cushion of grass. With her hands and lips, she devoured him, with her woman's supple body, kindled a fire that consumed him till there was nothing left but the savage need and, from somewhere, a song, faint on the breeze, like a memory.

Caressing the dark head bent to the white heave of her breasts, she whispered, "Michael, my darling. You are mine, now and always. You have always belonged to me."

The words, only half heard through the fever that raged in his mind, were like a cold touch of a wind across his spine. He stilled, the sweat pouring off his body as he raised himself to peer into the woman's half-slitted eyes.

The mist had lifted, and the sun filtered down through the tree limbs. In the golden shafts of light the amber orbs gleamed, hard and opaque, drawn in on themselves like the eyes of a cat. He turned his head away, a queasiness welling up inside him.

Her hands and her voice reached out to pull him back again. "Michael? Michael, love, what is it? Why have you stopped?"

But he was already shoving himself to his feet. His shirt open to the waist, his powerful chest rising and falling, he stood over her, drinking in the pure sweetness of the air, as if by that he might clear his head of her cloying scent. Only then, as the silence lengthened, did he become aware that the singing had stopped.

"Michael . . . ?" Her voice faltered and came to a halt as he turned his head to look at her.

For a long moment he stared at her, till she felt the color drain from her cheeks.

"You are remarkably beautiful, my love," he said at last. "A man would have to be blind not to want you. But you know that, don't you? That's what makes you so very dangerous."

28

"Dangerous! To Michael Glenmorgan? Forgive me if I find that hard to believe." She frowned, her lips puckering childishly in a beguiling pout. "When Logan hunted down your precious *Raven,* you laughed in the face of his guns. Surely you're not afraid of me?"

"That was a fight between men. Death is not a thing I fear, Clarissa. It is only death, after all. A woman's treachery is quite another matter altogether. Was it your idea, I wonder, or Logan's, to lure me here?"

At last twin spots of color—anger or perhaps pique—flared in the pale cheeks.

"Enough, Michael. I warn you, if you do not take the chance that is offered, there may not come another. I am not every man's for the taking."

"Are you not?" He laughed, a frosty glint in the steel blue of his eyes. "And yet you are remarkably adept at the art of seduction. It occurs to me that you and Logan are admirably suited to one another."

There was neither rancor nor bitterness in his voice, only a cold finality that should have chilled to the bone anyone less vain than she.

Clarissa laughed.

"Is that what is wrong? The thought that I must return to Logan? But Michael, my darling, I told you. The marriage means nothing. *He* means nothing." She rose to her knees and lifted her arms to him. Her eyes beneath the luxurious veil of her eyelashes were sultry with promise. "Do not fling away the short time that we have, I beg you."

But Michael was no longer looking at her. His gaze was fixed on a point beyond her lissome form.

"I find I must refuse your generous offer," he said. Sensing something inevitable in the way he looked at her then, she drew back. The next moment, he had dropped to his knee beside her and, with his hand at the back of her neck, pulled her relentlessly to him. His kiss, lingeringly and sensuously tender, was like nothing she had ever known before. A groan broke from her depths when at last he released her, and she swayed, feeling dazed. Pressing her fingertips to her lips, she stared into light, piercing orbs as if she had never seen him before.

"It comes a trifle late, Clarissa," he murmured. "Seven years too late."

Then he was on his feet again. His hand drawing the sword from the scabbard at his side, he pressed the hilt to his lips in a mocking salute to her.

"My congratulations, madam. For seven years I have pursued the uncertain existence of a pirate, and now, on the very day I was to have begun life as a free man, I have allowed myself to be ensnared by a woman." He grinned. "How amusing, quite ironic really, that you have managed to do what the entire King's Navy could not. And now, my dear, I suggest you cover yourself. Your husband awaits you."

Clarissa, he noted ironically, did not even bother to glance up as seven or eight men emerged from the depths of the jungle to cut him off from any possibility of escape. Neither did she make any more than a cursory attempt to cover her nakedness. She was staring at him with that same, peculiarly stricken expression.

"So," he breathed, "the pretense is over at last. No doubt I should at least be grateful for that. Tell me, is the pleasure greater knowing that the man you would make love to will soon lie dead by your husband's hand?"

"Michael, no." Jarred at last out of her seeming distraction, she clutched at his hand. "It is not too late. I know things. Logan would not dare to harm you if I forbade it. There is nothing else between him and me, nothing but the secrets I hold over him. Do you not see? You and I could have each other. We could be together as it was always meant for us to be."

30

Sickened, Glenmorgan marveled at his own blindness.

"I think not." Grimly, he looked away from her, to the slim, arrogant figure of the man who waited at the edge of the clearing. "I fear we have already had enough of each other to last a lifetime. It is at an end, Clarissa. Save your charms for him."

She swayed as Glenmorgan released her. Warily the captain began to back away from the men, closing in for the kill.

"*Damn* you, Michael Glenmorgan," she cried after him. Gathering her bodice together in front, she struggled to her feet. "He means to take you alive, but you will never walk away from his stronghold. You will beg him to end your life before he is done with you. Is *that* what you want? Are torment and death preferable to what you might have with me?"

But Glenmorgan had already forgotten her. He had but one chance, and that damnably slim—to make the escarpment before the pack surrounded him. He had almost reached his objective when he turned to meet the first of his attackers, foolish enough to charge in ahead of the others. With a blinding swiftness the captain's sword flashed. Hardly had the man dropped, a look of surprise on his swarthy features, than Glenmorgan had spun lightly on his heel and leaped to the top of the high stone wall embracing Lookout Point. There, his back to the sea thirty feet below him, he stood balanced on the balls of his feet, his sword in one hand and a dagger in the other held ready before him.

He had not long to wait. Spurred on by Logan Tharp, shouting orders at their backs, three of the men leaped in the face of his slashing sword, the others crowding in behind them. One of the foremost dropped, and another took his place, and still he fought on with a reckless disregard for the odds. More than once it seemed that he must be driven

31

from the wall, but somehow he managed to fell one more before a glancing blow to his sword arm sent his weapon flying from his grasp.

Emboldened to see him disarmed, one of the villains leaped to the wall beside him. Glenmorgan's lips stretched into a wild grin as he ducked beneath the thrust of the sword. Then, catching the man's collar and the broad leather belt at his waist, he hefted him above his head.

One instant Glenmorgan was standing, his would-be assailant squirming above his head in horrified anticipation of being hurtled on to the swords of his fellows, and the next, a blow, like a fist, slammed high up into the captain's chest, followed by the resounding crack of a pistol shot. Glenmorgan staggered and, heaving his burden into the remaining men, clutched a hand to his breast.

The hand came away, wet with blood. His brow creased with puzzlement, and it was only with the greatest effort that he was able to lift his head.

Strange that the sun should be blotted out as if a storm cloud were gathering overhead or that Logan's men had miraculously fallen back, buffeted by what seemed a raging wind. But in truth it had grown ominously dark, and it took all of his strength to remain upright in the fury of the gale that had sprung out of nowhere. Indeed, it was all he could do to make out the lone figure of the woman, standing where he had left her beneath the spreading boughs of the umbrella tree.

Realization like bitter gall in his throat, he saw her lips curve in a cold, pitiless smile and, in a gesture of finality, the pistol drop from her hand to the ground. Then the pain, like a white-hot iron, seared through his body. With the last of his fading strength, he flung himself out and away from the wall. A cry of despair welled up from his depths as he hurtled endlessly downward. And at last the sea rushed up to meet him.

His senses stunned and his lungs bursting, he felt himself sinking into the watery depths and could not help himself. Darkness, thick and velvety, was closing in on him when he thought he imagined the strong grip of hands on his shirt dragging him upward. A face floated before his eyes, the exquisite face of an angel, grimly determined. He was dreaming, he thought, and filled with a strange sort of contentment, he gave himself up to the waiting darkness.

Three

Nightmares washed over him like relentless swells in a tortured sea. Nightmares of pain and torment, of hands, lifting and turning him, holding him while they probed his chest with a red-hot brand. He fought them till the sweat ran from his body in rivulets and, mercifully, a final searing burst of pain plunged him deep into darkness. He resurfaced at last to the unyielding embrace of a bandage and to a face, like old, weathered oak, bending over him. He struggled to get up.

"Must get . . . to my ship. *Raven*. Mustn't . . . find me here."

The pain pounced out of nowhere, crushing the breath from him. Gasping, he fell back again.

"*Easy,* lad. By all rights you should be dead. And by God, if you do not lie still, you will be yet."

"No." Sick and reeling, he was yet driven by the need to get the words out. "You don't . . . understand. They'll . . . kill you if they find me here."

"No, Captain. I promise they will not."

The words came from behind him, and the voice was a woman's. He tried in vain to twist his head around to see, but the old man held him.

"It is all right, Captain," murmured the woman's voice,

low and vibrant with compassion. "No one will come look-ing for you. Don't you remember? You fell from the wall into the sea. She . . . the whole world believes you were drowned."

The voice, like a fragment of a memory, broke through the desperation. He went still, his body clenched against the pain. Struggling to hold off the swell of darkness wait-ing to engulf him, he tried to remember.

"Aye. The sea maiden. I remember. You were there"—a groan shuddered through him—"singing," he gasped, and felt the wave wash over him, dragging him into the depths.

He was unaware of the hand that brushed the sweat-dampened hair from his brow with infinite tenderness. Nor did he hear her voice filled with sadness.

"Oh, yes, Captain, I was there. I saw everything that happened. And now you must fight more bravely than you've ever fought before. It won't be easy. Not even magic could help you now, and the secret remedies from the sea can heal only the wounds of the body. Rest now. I will be here if you need me."

Time passed, measured in spells of cold, icy sweats, the fever running like ice water through his veins, or in the slow torment of stifling heat, consuming him from within. There were times as he lay, sweating and delirious with pain, that he heard himself cry out. Always the voice re-sponded, murmuring soothing words, while the cool touch of a hand against his fevered brow drove the nightmares away. He slept fitfully, never very far beneath the surface of despair, his tortured mind clinging to a calm strength he sensed somehow, hovering just beyond the impenetrable curtain between oblivion and awareness. Until at last the fever broke.

He did not know how long he slept. In the ebb tide of

his dreams, he lay, enveloped in a heavy blanket of lethargy, content to listen vaguely to the voices talking over him.

"Come, my child. It's daybreak—time you were going."

The answer came, sharp-edged with impatience.

"Not now, Grandfather, I beg you!"

"I cannot hold back the day, Meg. Or alter the tides, any more than can you. Look at you. You have put it off as long as you dare, and now your strength is nearly exhausted. What good will it do him or you if you needlessly destroy yourself?"

"Oh, why can't you leave me be? I am well enough, Grandfather!" Then, appearing to relent somewhat, she added in a voice dull with weariness, "Just a little while longer, and then I will go. I promise."

A sigh breathed through the stillness.

"Meg. Dammit, lass! You know the danger. You'll be seen if you wait much longer."

"I don't care." The impatience was back again, made sharper with stubbornness that hinted at a formidable will. "I won't leave him. Not yet. I gave him my word."

"And you have kept it. Now you must think of yourself, child. He'll be coming awake soon. Will you risk being seen by him?"

A frown etched itself in the captain's brow. "Risk being seen"? Bloody hell. The words made no sense.

"And why not?" came the answer, bristling with defiance. "Am I a monster too dreadful for his eyes to behold?"

"You know I did not mean it that way. It's far more likely that he would be bewitched by your beauty, and then what, Meg? Do you want him to love you, knowing what you are? Look at him, child. He's not of your kind. Think what you would be asking, not only of him, but of yourself."

"I *have* thought, Grandfather. Over and over as he lay so long near death. And still I don't know the answer!"

Glenmorgan stirred, troubled by the unmistakable anguish in that cry.

"Then go. He's over the worst of it, child. Leave him to me. Renew your strength, and perhaps then you will see things more clearly."

"Perhaps," Meg answered doubtfully. "Or perhaps suddenly I see things too clearly. You should have left me to die long ago, Grandfather. Because now *I* have seen *him*. And though you send me away, I know I will never be the same."

The bitterness and despair of that final utterance jarred the captain into wakefulness.

"Wait!" The word came out a faint whisper of sound. The realization that the old man was driving his angel of mercy away lent him strength, and heaving himself up on one elbow, he struggled to see through the blinding glare of light streaming in from the open doorway.

He was given a glimpse only of the tall, slender figure of a girl clad in a loose-fitting gown, and of hair, the burnished silver of moonlight on water, falling in silken waves down her back to a willowy waist. Her arms, clasped in a farewell embrace about the neck of the old man, slid down to her sides, then with a final salute, she turned and was gone.

He was struggling to get up, driven by the need to go after her and bring her back, when the old man's muttered oath sounded harshly in the room.

"Here, now." Hands, toughened to the bite of the net and the pull of the oar, gripped him hard by the arms and tried to wrestle him to the bed. "What do you think you're doing? You'll ruin everything with this foolishness."

He was sweating profusely, the pain grinding the strength from him, and at last the old man was forced to clasp him in a bearish hug.

"She is gone, Captain," he rasped, "and it is better so."

37

Something in the other man's voice reached through to his reeling mind, and he ceased all at once to struggle. "For seven days and as many nights she has hardly left your side," said the old man quietly. "Let her go, lad. She has given all she has to give."

For a long moment their eyes locked. Then the captain let out a shuddering breath.

"Aye," he nodded, feeling the strength ebb out of him. "I'll let her be—for now." He let the old man help him back on to the cot. Irresistibly, he felt his eyelids drifting shut. "When I'm on my feet again, that will be time enough to find her," he muttered to himself.

"Yes, and I've not a doubt that you'll do it, too," rumbled the old man, staring down at the worn face, the lines of suffering less pronounced in sleep. "You've a stubbornness about you no less than her own. God help you both."

With the fever gone, the captain began steadily to mend and soon he found his enforced stay in bed infinitely galling. Nevertheless, the pain, waiting to pounce on him without warning, and the persistent weakness that dragged at his limbs, obliged him to learn patience. How close he had come to dying was borne in on him with each interminable day spent fighting his way back to recovery.

For the first week or so, with his life still hovering in the balance and the girl gone, the old man was in constant attendance. Since the captain's waking hours were few and far between, they spoke little, at first only enough for Glenmorgan to learn that his host was Joseph Pippin, a fisherman, who lived on one of the countless, small, unnamed islands that dotted the Caribbean. Then later had come the memorable occasion when Pippin presented him with his sword and pistol. "They threw them after you—into the sea," said the old man, as spare with his words as a miser

38

doling out ha'pennies. "Meg saved them for you." Glenmorgan was grateful the old man turned away. Seeing the old, tarnished blade again had torn at his defenses. The sword had been his father's, handed down through four generations of Glenmorgans, all seafaring men. Losing it on that ill-fated morning had been rather like losing a piece of himself.

At last, with slowly regaining strength, the captain had little else to occupy him, but a growing curiosity about his sole companion.

Glenmorgan was not slow to surmise a great deal more about Joseph Pippin than his host was willing to divulge— the marks of the whip on his back, for example, glimpsed once as the old man washed himself in the pale light of morning, told a tale of their own, as did his hands. Those scarred and tar-blackened hands of a sailor, strong and thickened from labor, and yet long-fingered, dexterous, and strangely enough, shapely. They were a mystery, like everything else about the man.

He had seen scars like those before—on the poor bastards pressed into the King's Navy. Whipping was the favored punishment for those who earned the displeasure of their superiors. Was he a deserter then? It seemed likely. After all, he lived the miserable existence of a hermit on an unchartered island in the Caribbean, and he was as closemouthed as a bloody clam. That in itself seemed evidence enough that Joseph Pippin was possessed of a doubtful past, which was hardly remarkable. Only riffraff, the desperate or the adventurous, men either fleeing something or in pursuit of something, came willingly to the West Indies, where white men fell like flies to the fever. Far more intriguing was that he was obviously educated.

The two dozen or so books arranged neatly on a shelf on one wall were hardly what one would expect to see in a fisherman's hut. Few of the wealthy white planters could boast of a single volume among them, let alone a tome as weighty as Plato's *Republic* or Plutarch's *Lives*. That Copernicus and Galileo should find a place among them, as well as Dante and Boccaccio, along with a smattering of the great poets of antiquity, would seem to point to a classical education. Eton, perhaps, or Harrow? Oxford even, or Cambridge? On the other hand, a curious array of books devoted to pharmacology and anatomy would seem to indicate an interest, at least, in medicine. To go so far as to assume his host was a doctor stretched the imagination. The old man may have saved his life, but a physician with the scars of a sailor was too farfetched by half. Or was it?

The captain's gaze rested speculatively on the bent figure, working with flint and steel to light a tallow candle. Apart from the hands, there seemed little on the surface to suggest other than a common birth. Still, in spite of the humble attire, there was something about him that was neither lowborn nor common. Indeed, he wore his patched tunic and breeches with an unconscious dignity, which seemed an integral part of the man himself. The hut, too, showed the same pride. Neat and scrupulously clean, the single room boasted a wooden floor over which a braided rug was laid, a well-made table with two chairs for dining, an ancient wooden sea chest, which had seen a great deal of service, and a small wooden hutch, which contained dishes and utensils for cooking, that office being reserved for the lean-to, reached through a curtained door at the back of the house. He had been tall once, and powerfully built, and even now, weathered and spare, his shoulders bent beneath the burden of his years, he exuded an aura of enduring strength, which was reflected in the strong-boned features of the face and in the eyes, a marvelous, clear gray, like fathomless still waters beneath a clouded sky, and just as impenetrable, curse them.

Who the devil was he? What secret bound him here?

What fear drove him to hide his granddaughter away from the sight of men? Bloody hell! Where was she, the elusive Meg?

The memory of her presence, like some disembodied spirit without face or form, haunted him day and night. He had only to close his eyes to feel the touch of her hand upon his brow, to hear her voice as it had called to him from beyond the torment of his own private hell. There were times when he awakened in the night, certain that he had felt her near, only to find the room empty, a silvery beam of moonlight falling across the floor from the window where he had imagined he glimpsed her peering in at him.

Silently he cursed. He would drive himself mad if he did not soon leave his bed. Somehow he must get word to Dick that he was alive. If *Raven* had sailed without him, it might be months before he could escape this bloody island, indeed, the whole blasted Caribbean. It had been all over the Harbor that Logan Tharp was leaving Antigua for good. Michael Glenmorgan must not be far behind him. It was time he returned to the living. To Charles Town and unfinished business.

"You are thinking of the woman and what happened on the cliffs above the sea."

Glenmorgan glanced up, startled out of his somber thoughts, to find the old man studying him from the far side of the room.

Grimly he laughed. "Am I so transparent?"

The old man grunted, a flicker of amusement in the bronzed face. Pulling a stool up beside the cot, he set the candle on a rough-hewn table at the bedside and seated himself. "You've the habit of putting a hand to your chest whenever you wear a certain look. As if the pain of your wound and the memories were one and the same." One of the hands fumbled at a pocket in his leather jerkin. "Or as if you were reaching for something—this, perhaps?"

41

From his pocket the old man drew forth a shiny thing suspended on a gold chain and dangled it in front of the captain before dropping it into the palm of Glenmorgan's hand.

Glenmorgan drew a slow breath. The locket was flattened and mangled almost beyond recognition, pierced at its center with a round hole the size of the tip of his little finger.

"So it was not lost in the fall," he said, closing his fist around it. "I wondered."

"I thought you might. 'Tis a precious thing, or was once. It saved your life, and then nearly cost you dearly."

The captain's head came up, his eyes piercing on the old man's face.

"Aye, the pistol ball struck the locket, over your heart, and was deflected from its intended course. Otherwise, you should have been dead instantly. Even so, it drove deep, taking fragments of the locket with it. Even now I am not certain I recovered them all. However, I take it as a favorable sign that you appear to be recovering without signs of infection."

"Those are words a doctor might use," observed the captain, when he had had time to take in the irony of his luck. "So you are indeed a surgeon then—as well as a fisherman?"

The gray eyes never wavered.

"I have been many things in my lifetime. As I am sure you must have guessed. Oh yes, I have seen you observing me. You are, I should judge, a man of intelligence. I should be a fool to believe you would not note the seeming paradoxes around you and, having observed, would fail to draw your own conclusions. Am I naive to believe you will keep what you have learned to yourself?"

"No." The captain returned his look with a measuring one of his own. "I owe you my life, and I have always prided myself on paying my debts. Other than curiosity, which is natural in the circumstances, I have no interest in your past—save for one thing only."

"Yes, of course. Meg."

He said it with quiet resignation, which left little doubt that he had been waiting for this moment. Still, it seemed he had yet to come to terms with it, or perhaps with himself. His glance wavered at last and, hands on knees, he heaved himself to his feet. Glenmorgan said nothing as the old man crossed to the window to stand looking out into the night.

"I suppose it would not be enough simply to ask you to forget her—forget that she ever existed." He glanced over his shoulder at the captain. Apparently reading his answer in the other man's face, he turned away again. "No, I did not think so." He propped his hands against the window ledge and leaned his weight on them. "And what if I were to tell you that you will only do her irrevocable harm if you try to find her?" Abruptly he shoved himself erect and came about. "Together, we saved your life, Captain. She and I. You owe her no less than you owe me."

"Aye, I owe her," returned the captain levelly. "And I would repay her, but not by leaving without seeing her."

"Then you are a fool. And a danger to us all."

Glenmorgan's lips thinned to a grim line. How could he deny it, when all of his finely honed instincts for self-preservation were screaming that he had already remained far too long in one place? And yet something kept him from giving in to them—the anguish in a girl's voice, the secrets he sensed all around him, or mere stubbornness. He could not say what it was, but he was damned certain he was not ready to weigh anchor before he had a few more answers.

"And if I grant you that," he said at last, "it still explains nothing. What is it that you're really afraid of, old man— that I shall bring danger upon her? Or that I might take her from you?"

43

To his surprise, a spark of grim amusement leaped in the seamed countenance.

"That you will do only if there is no longer breath in this body. Do you think I hold her here against her will? Hidden away and jealously guarded from the eyes of any man like yourself, to whom she might lose her heart?"

"Are you saying that is not the case?"

"I am saying that Meg belongs to no man, least of all to me. She comes and goes as she wills. But she will never of her own choice go from me. It were better, Captain, if you accepted that. For your sake and hers, delve no further into what you cannot understand."

Feeling impotent and angry, Glenmorgan watched the old man stalk out into the night. Bloody hell. What had he expected? Pippin, if that was indeed his name, was as full of riddles as a blasted sphinx. He was hardly likely to bare his soul to a man who was little more than a stranger to him, especially where his granddaughter was concerned.

It must have been unsettling in the extreme to have the girl turn up with a wounded man on his doorstep. And not just any man, but Michael Glenmorgan, who had made something of a name for himself as a pirate captain, an adventurer, and a rogue with a violent past. The old man could hardly be blamed if he frowned on the notion of having her in the company of someone like himself, a sea rover who had all but bragged he would spirit her away.

The blue eyes hardened to steely points. Hell, who was to say Pippin was not in the right of it? He hardly needed a female to complicate his life, especially one who had the damnably unnerving habit of vanishing seemingly from the face of the earth, and not now either, when he was on the threshold of seeing everything he had worked for during the past seven years come to fruition. If he had the brains he was born with, he'd do just as the old man asked and simply walk away.

Aye, it made sense, he told himself. It was, in fact, the only thing that did make sense. Just count himself lucky that he was alive and get back to the more important matters that awaited him in Charles Town. And so he would, he vowed. Just as soon as he had no further need of a safe haven to hole up in. Another week, perhaps, or maybe two to regain his strength, and then he would be out of the old man's hair for good.

The decision, strangely enough, gave him little comfort. Indeed, it was long into the night before sleep came at last to claim him.

It seemed that he had hardly closed his eyes when he came awake with a start. The sweat cold against his skin, he lay staring into the moonlit night, wondering what had jarred him out of his sleep. He had been dreaming, he remembered, about Clarissa, the same blasted dream that had tormented him night after night when he lay with fever. Only this time it had been different. Seductive and beautiful, the amber eyes sultry with promise, she had woven her pale arms around his neck and pulled him to her, there, beneath the umbrella tree. Her name broke from his lips, husky with desire, when suddenly she had changed. Her hair the color of spun gold was gone silvery with moonlight, and her face was the face of an angel. Even as his arms had closed about her to hold her captive, she had vanished, the echo of her voice, crying out in warning, all that remained of her.

"There is danger in the night. Awake, Captain, and flee!"

Bloody hell, it had seemed real enough. Grinning sardonically at himself, he ran a hand through his hair and lay back, forcing his muscles to relax.

Suddenly he froze as a scream rent the silence. High-pitched and thin, as though coming from a fair distance, it

45

was filled with despair. Hells fire, that was no bloody dream.

Gritting his teeth, he heaved himself up on one elbow and peered through the mosquito netting at the Spartan room. It was empty, the pallet on which the old man slept a rumpled heap in the corner. Of the old man himself, there was no sign.

"Meg!" he breathed, knowing with bitter certainty that it had been she.

When the cry came again, he had already flung back the blanket and slid his legs over the side of the bed. Clenching his teeth against the dizziness, he shoved himself up. For what seemed an eternity, he sat on the edge of the bed, his head down, the sweat pouring over his body, while he waited for the room to cease its spinning. Bitterly he cursed. Christ, he was weak as a bloody infant. At last, anger, like a swelling tide, welled up inside him. Fighting off the dizziness, he pulled on his breeches and boots and lurched to his feet. He was vaguely surprised to find his hands steady as he buckled the swordbelt around his waist then reached for the pistol and, as an afterthought, the long knife Pippin used for scaling fish. He doubted in the circumstances the old man would mind, and a knife was better than a sword in a close fight. At last he stumbled out the door into the night, silvery with the light of a full moon.

The hut stood on a steep promontory overlooking a small cove embraced by jungle and a white, sandy shore. From where he stood, his breath knifing through him, he could just make out a dinghy on the beach and, beyond, a Spanish frigate, its sails furled as it rode at anchor. A chill hand closed like a vise on his innards. He knew that ship. The *Sea Hawk,* late of Tortola. If John Drago had loosed his men on the island, then no one was safe, let alone a beautiful young girl with only a stubborn old man to protect her.

Keep a clear head, he told himself. Think. More than likely the pirates were come in search of fresh water to fill their depleted casks. With the British Navy hounding them and the defenses at Tortola in a shambles, they would risk only a small landing party to discover if there were any springs to be had on the island. Naturally they would come at night, hoping to complete their mission and be well out to open sea before daylight and the chance of being surprised by a King's man-of-war. But what if they were led to believe they had stumbled into a peril even greater than the British navy? The *Raven,* for instance.

His lips stretched in a grim smile. The *Raven* had made a name for herself as a rogue ship and her captain as a man who played by his own rules for the sake of ambition and greed—though there were some who declared only vengeance could drive a man to take the risks he had taken or to deal with a vanquished foe with the cold implacability that he had done. Whatever the truth of it, there was not a pirate in the Caribbean who would willingly incur the wrath of the man who had hanged Jean Lavoillet from the yardarms of his own ship before sinking it to the bottom.

A desperate plan already taking shape in his mind, Glenmorgan began to make his way down the hill.

He made agonizingly slow progress, impeded as he was by the weakness that weighted his limbs and by the tangle of vines and jungle growth which seemed bent on tripping him up and dragging him down. More than once he was forced to hack his way clear with the sharp edge of the knife. His strength was nearly spent when suddenly he felt the ground give way beneath him. In a vain effort to save himself, he lost his balance and toppled forward, to plunge head over heels seemingly endlessly down a steep incline— till at last he came up hard against the trunk of a tree. With a groan, he sank into unconsciousness.

He did not know how long it was before he came to to

find himself staring up through swaying palm leaves at the pale glow of the sky. It could not have been more than a few minutes or so, judging from the position of the moon. A curse hissed through his teeth as he shoved himself up, every muscle in his body protesting the sudden movement. With relief he glimpsed the glitter of metal a short distance away and reached for the long-bladed knife. His luck was holding. Neither it nor the pistol had been lost in the fall.

The harsh bark of laughter froze him in his tracks. His grip tightening on the haft of the blade, he backed deeper into the shadows. His lips stretched in a cold little smile as he listened to the crash of cutlasses hacking their way through the underbrush. He was luckier than he could ever have dreamed possible. The bloody bastards were coming to him.

Crouching in the cover of a thick growth of silver ferns, he waited until they had worked their way past him.

There were four of them, which meant that two, possibly three, more waited on the beach—guarding the captives, if the blackguards had not already dispatched Meg and her grandfather, he speculated grimly. The dinghy was hardly large enough to have carried more of a crew.

Shoving the knife in his belt, Glenmorgan grasped the pistol by the barrel and crept up behind the man last in line. His arm rose and fell. The butt of the pistol struck the sailor a sharp blow to the back of the head. Glenmorgan caught the sagging man around the chest and dragged him into the concealment of the thick undergrowth. Cutting a length of vine, the captain bound the sailor and gagged the villain with his own kerchief before going after the next man in line.

Working silently, he disabled them, one by one, until at last, drawing his sword, Glenmorgan went after the single remaining pirate.

Four

John Drago's second-in-command scowled at the tangled mass of foliage pressing in around him. Swatting at a mosquito on a thick forearm, he muttered a curse.

"Bloody damned jungle. No fit place for a sailor," he grumbled, mopping the sweat from his forehead with the back of a cutlass-filled hand. "If there be a trail up here, then me name ain't Bill Moffit. What say 'ee, Toby, me lad? Which way does we go to find the wench's hut and the spring of fresh water she promised were there?"

"I'd say, Bill Moffit, that if you've a wish to go on living, you'll drop your blade," came the answer in soft, chilling accents. "No, no. Do not turn around. I have a sword at your back, and I'm hard put to find a reason not to use it."

The first mate froze at the touch of cold steel between his shoulder blades. His face working beneath the whisker stubs, he licked dry lips.

"Easy, mate." He swallowed carefully. "Let's not be hasty now. I ain't hankerin' to be spitted like a wild pig for the roastin'."

"Then you have my congratulations. If you play your cards right, you might even live long enough to see another day."

Moffit stiffened, his head cocked to one side.

49

"Damme if I doesn't know that voice. It ain't one I'd be like to forget, not after that brawl in Fitz's Tavern. Less'n I've lost me mind, 'tis Captain Glenmorgan I've the pleasure of addressin'."

"You've a sharp ear, Mr. Moffit, and a keen memory. And now that the amenities have been observed, I suggest you do as you're told. *Drop* it—*now*—before I forget we once shared a jug in Road Town."

At the bite of the blade into flesh, Moffit muttered an oath and let the weapon drop to the jungle floor.

"Very good, Mr. Moffit," commended that cursed soft voice at his back. "And now the knife and your pistol, if you please. Slow and easy, else I might be forced to find some other means of delivering a message to Drago."

"Am I to take that to mean I be the only one left alive to perform that little favor for 'ee?" queried the pirate lieutenant in a queer tone. Gingerly he removed the gun from his belt and let it drop before reaching for the dagger.

"Right again, Mr. Moffit," Glenmorgan lied glibly. "Unless, of course, you count the two with the prisoners below. They, unfortunately, have been foolish enough to lay hands on my woman. I wouldn't count on them to help you, if I were you. Their lives promise to be of damned short duration."

The pirate's muscles tensed at the chilling lack of emotion in that utterance.

"Ah, but, Captain, that ain't hardly fair." He spun around, the knife flashing in his hand. "How was we to know it were *your* woman?"

There was a sickening crunch of bone against steel as the hilt of Glenmorgan's sword connected with the other man's jaw. Moffit dropped to his knees and stayed there, the point of the sword quivering at his throat.

"That was foolishly done," ground out the captain between clenched teeth. The sweat stood out in beads on his forehead with the effort he had already expended on the band of pirates. He could feel his strength draining from him with every moment he wasted on the burly first mate. "Next time I won't be so generous. Now get on your feet."

For an instant longer, the other man hesitated, his face registering surprise at the captain's appearance. A look of cunning crossed the heavily jowled features as his glance lingered on the bandage, on the round stain that shown crimson against the white fabric high up on the left side of the captain's chest.

"We heard 'ee was dead," he grunted as he came carefully to his feet. The back of a filthy hand reached up to wipe the blood from the corner of his mouth. "From the looks of 'ee, the reports wasn't much exaggerated. Might be you should take it easy, Captain, and just let old Moffit go back to his ship."

The captain's lips stretched in a humorless grin.

"Looks can be deceiving," he replied coldly. "If I give the signal, you'll not *have* a ship to go back to."

He could see the sudden flicker of fear in the other man's eyes and had no difficulty guessing his thoughts. A man, half-naked and wearing a bandage about his chest, was a man who had been summoned from his sickbed. Obviously he had believed the captain's ship had left him ashore to recover, and a man, wounded and alone, was not an insurmountable obstacle, even if he was Michael Glenmorgan. The thought that the *Raven* might ride at anchor somewhere nearby had come as a blow.

"Yes, I see that you begin to understand."

Without warning, the captain's blade lashed out. A strangled cry broke from Moffit. Arms up to ward off the blow, he fell back, the breath sobbing in his throat. Sheathing the sword, Glenmorgan grinned mirthlessly and bent down to retrieve the vine he had severed. Seconds later, the pirate's wrists bound before him, Glenmorgan prodded the man in the side with the barrel of the pistol.

"Now get going, Mr. Moffit. And I suggest that you pray no harm has come to either the old man or the girl."

Surly and withdrawn into his own thoughts, Moffit said nothing as he sidled past the captain and began to pick his way down the hillside. Glenmorgan followed, a frown etched into his brow as he struggled against the fog that threatened to cloud his vision.

He was stumbling by the time they reached the edge of the jungle. Grimly it came to him that he could not hold on much longer, when he caught the other man staring at him.

"Keep your eyes to the front, damn you!" he growled.

"Whatever 'ee says, Captain. Though it seems to me 'ee's in no shape to be thrashing about in the jungle. Why not be reasonable and leave be? I give me word no harm'll come to your lady. Why, we'll just cut her loose and send her and the old man back to 'ee."

The ominous click of the pistol hammer going back left little doubt as to the answer.

"You, Mr. Moffit, will keep your mouth shut and do as you're told. Now, take me to her. Any attempt to warn the others, and I won't hesitate to put a pistol ball through the back of your skull. Do I make myself clear?"

"Aye, 'tis clear enough," growled the pirate, "and just what I might've expected from the likes of 'Mad Mike' Glenmorgan."

Mindful of the cocked pistol trained on his back, Moffit kept inside the cover of the jungle as he followed the contour of the cove south, in the direction in which the dinghy lay beached. Glenmorgan stayed close behind him, his senses strained for the sight or sound of the captives. Nevertheless, he was unprepared for the sharp stab of relief that went through him when her voice carried to him, hauntingly familiar.

"Please, I beg you. He is an old man and grievously hurt. Let me go to him. What can you possibly fear from me? I swear by all that I hold dear that I shall make no attempt to escape."

"You swear. Faith, I believe she means it, Gates."

At the gentle ripple of insinuating laughter, Glenmorgan's lips thinned to a grim line. He knew that voice well enough. So, John Drago himself had come.

Warningly, Glenmorgan's hand closed over Moffit's shoulder.

"Not a sound," he hissed into the first mate's ear. Only a thick tangle of brush and vines separated them from the pirates and their captives on the beach.

"She would swear to anything if she thought we were fools enough to set her free," Glenmorgan heard Gates reply, the man's voice venomous with dislike. "I'd sooner take the word of a sea serpent."

"Would you now," Drago gently murmured. "You make me wonder, Mr. Gates—indeed you do—if there isn't something you haven't told me. But I'm a reasonable man, wench. Only tell us where the treasure's hid and we'll see to the old man. Why, I give you *my* word upon 't."

"The word of a pirate," the girl answered, unafraid and yet bitter with certainty. "No doubt it is of the same substance as this treasure you seek. One is empty while the other is false. We are poor fishermen. The house on the hill and the spring behind it are the only 'treasures' we possess."

Behind the concealing thicket, the barrel of Glenmorgan's gun found the throat of his captive.

"So, it was not water only you were after," he murmured in a soft, steely voice.

"Well, now, I never said that it were, Captain. As a mat-

53

ter-of-fact, I don't recall sayin' one way or t'other why we was here."

He watched the man spit contemptuously into the sand and silently cursed himself for being a bloody fool. Moffit was right. Once he had drawn his own conclusions, he had never bothered again to question why Drago had come. A treasure. Bloody hell. It needed only that. True or not, it hardly mattered. It was enough that Drago believed the thing existed and, worse, believed that Meg and her grandfather knew where to find it. Suddenly the odds had shifted dangerously.

Steely-eyed, he shoved his captive to his knees and, holding the gun to the back of the villain's head, peered through the tangle of vines at the scene being enacted only a few feet from where he stood. A single glance revealed Pippin, sprawled facedown on the sand, blood oozing from a gash at the back of his head. He must have been pistol-whipped from behind as he rushed in to save his granddaughter. He tried to catch a glimpse of the girl, but in vain. Her abductors blocked her from view.

Glenmorgan smiled grimly. There were three of them— two between him and the girl and a third, a common sailor, standing lookout farther up the beach. Gates was a stranger. Tall and thin almost to the point of emaciation, he was severely garbed in black—like a vulture, or a spider, mused the captain. Obviously he was no sailor. Indeed, with his hair cut short and the tall hat perched precariously atop his head, he had more the look of a lawyer's clerk. As for the other, Captain Drago had always affected a flamboyant style, as was evidenced by the cloak of bright purple slung dramatically over a crimson-clad shoulder. The matching crimson silk breeches, trimmed in lace, embraced slender thighs above knee-high bucket top boots made grander still by three-inch heels and butterfly surpieds over the instep. The shoulder-length wig done in ringlets and topped by a plumed felt hat was powdered white, while the thin, aristocratic features beneath demonstrated a generous reliance on the rouge pot. In spite of his appearance of effete worldweariness, Glenmorgan was not fooled. John Drago might affect the guise of a fop, but he was possessed of a keen intellect and a cunning surpassed only by the ruthlessness with which he pursued his trade, which made him a dangerous man to have as an enemy, and yet invaluable as an ally. For years, Drago and Glenmorgan had entertained an uneasy bond of mutual respect between them and consequently had taken care not to provoke one another—until now. He would prefer to preserve the truce, if at all possible.

Glenmorgan's lean frame went suddenly taut as Gates drew Drago to one side, apparently for a conference.

Bathed in moonlight, the girl, Meg, stood revealed to him at last.

No doubt it was only an illusion occasioned by lightheadedness and the peculiar lucency of the night itself that made her resemble an ethereal creature from some other world. Mentally he pinched himself. In sunlight she would not look all silvery, as if she had been wrought from moonbeams by magic. She would appear simply what she was—a girl of flesh-and-blood, standing tall with defiance to hide the fear in her heart. Aye, it was in every line of her proud bearing—courage and strength, and a woman's vulnerability.

He had half convinced himself he had only dreamed the existence of the sea maiden who had drawn him up from the depths of the sea. But here she was, dressed in the same loose-fitting gown she had worn the day she had vanished from his life. She had the high-boned cheeks and determined chin which were reminiscent of her grandfather, but the long, straight nose and wide full lips were peculiarly her own, as was her hair, shimmery in the moonlight. Had she been a man, she would have been considered tall, but

55

for a woman, she was of Junoesque proportions. Indeed, he judged that his own considerable height would top hers by only a couple of inches or so. Still, there was nothing masculine in the willowy slenderness of her woman's body, made alluring with soft, feminine curves only imperfectly concealed beneath the thin white fabric of her dress. In spite of himself, he felt his loins stir. Long-limbed and lithe as a dancer, she was a woman who would arouse men to lust without even trying.

Silently he cursed himself for a bloody fool. The last thing he needed was to allow himself to be bewitched by a female, no matter how alluring. She was obviously an innocent, hardly more than a child—not the sort for Mad Mike Glenmorgan. His gaze went to her bound wrists, the end of the long rope made fast to the dinghy's bow cleat. A cold gleam came to his eyes at the sight of the tear in her gown which laid bare her shoulder, the pale skin marred by a black, angry bruise. And certainly not for the likes of a man like John Drago.

By all rights he should kill Drago for having laid his filthy hands on her, but not this day. He needed him alive and at the helm of his ship. Without him, there would be no one to keep his band of cutthroats from running amok on the island.

"She's lying, I tell you." Gates's voice, shrill with rancor, jarred the captain from his thoughts. "I've told you what she is—a creature of evil, the devil's spawn. Force the old man to talk. He can tell you. He called himself Phillip Belding when I knew him. I'll wager you've heard of him, the man who incited the men to mutiny on the *Argonaut*."

Glenmorgan's fist tightened on the pistol grip. Belding! Hellsfire! *He* knew the name well enough. His glance flew to the old man and froze as he saw one of the marvelous, tar-blackened hands move. His face grim, he watched Pippin, or Belding, or whoever the hell he was, sneak a pocket gun from its hiding place in one leather boot.

Drago's bloodless laugh lent a chill to the air. "But naturally I have heard of him and the *Argonaut*. Who hasn't? The unfortunate souls were run to ground by a King's ship off Barbuda. They would have hanged the lot of them—if a squall hadn't blown up and saved them the trouble." The curl of Drago's thin lips was suddenly devoid of all humor. "The *Argonaut* went down with all hands, Mr. Gates," he observed dispassionately. "Would you have me believe yonder lies the ghost of Phillip Belding?"

A savage look of triumph infused color in Gates's sallow cheeks.

"Hardly, Captain Drago. He was saved from a watery grave, as was I." A fleshless arm swept up to point a quivering finger at the girl. *"She* saved him. With her witchery."

"No," gasped Meg, her face paling alarmingly. "It isn't true. It wasn't I."

"I was purser on the *Argonaut*. I was there," Gates said with cold implacability. "With my own eyes I saw her. She is not like us. She is—"

Whatever the purser had been about to say was shattered by the crack of a pistol shot.

The girl's scream rent the air.

"Grandfather, no!"

As if by magic, a round hole had appeared in the center of Gates's forehead. For an instant the purser stood, his eyes fixed with a blankness, terrible to behold, on the old man, on the gun trailing smoke into the air. Then suddenly Gates's knees buckled beneath him.

As if freed from a momentary paralysis, Drago jerked his eyes from the dead man. The girl struggled against her bonds as, helplessly, she watched the pirate captain turn with ruthless deliberation toward her grandfather.

"So Gates was right, eh, Mr. Belding?" he murmured,

the surprise giving way to cold, malicious cunning. "Your error was in killing him instead of me."

"No doubt. But I had an old score to settle with Gates," ground out the old man, lifting his head. "And only one bullet." A wry smile twisted at his lips. "I'm afraid I was thinking only of finishing something that should have been ended a long time ago. Rather foolish in the circumstances."

"Aye," growled the pirate. Knocking the gun from the old man's hand, Drago closed a fist in Pippin's shirtfront and dragged him to his feet. "Exceedingly foolish. I am not without my own ways of making a man talk, as you are about to discover for yourself."

"I fear you are wasting your time, Captain Drago," Pippin said with an almost inhuman calmness. "My granddaughter has told you there is no treasure. Do what you will, you will learn nothing more from me."

Something in the still, gray eyes must have convinced him. Uttering a blasphemous oath, Drago released him. With nothing to hold him upright, the old man sagged to the ground. Head hanging, he drew in long, shuddering breaths while Drago paced before him.

"There was a fortune in Spanish gold on the *Argonaut*," said Drago, straightening the lapels of his coat with an impatient tug. "The spoils of war. But the holds were empty when the British searched her, just before she was sunk. You do know where the gold is hidden, Mr. Belding. And I intend to have it."

Glenmorgan's lips thinned to a grim line as he saw Drago's eyes go to the girl. The pistol shifted and held steady. Still, Glenmorgan stayed his hand, unwilling yet to interfere. He was most damned curious about the *Argonaut* and her cargo of gold. Like Drago, he had believed all hands went down with the ill-fated ship. If Pippin and his granddaughter held the secret of the Spanish gold, Glenmorgan, more than anyone, had a right to know. And thus far, even though the old man must have known exactly whom he was harboring these past weeks, Pippin had shown damned little inclination to confide in Turlough Glenmorgan's son.

Beyond Glenmorgan's leafy cover, Drago casually crossed to the girl. His hand on the rope that bound her, he began to pull her toward him.

"She's a fetching wench, wouldn't you say, Mr. Belding, for all she's your granddaughter?" Playing with the line like a man with a fish, he drew the girl inexorably toward him. "Aye, a rare piece for the taking. All soft and white and, from the looks of her, the rarest of all treasures—a maiden. Spirited, too, I should think. I fear she'll not be easily broken."

Glenmorgan, watching from cover, seemed frozen by the look on her face—the horror mingled with proud defiance. He could not take his eyes off her. Her head held high on the slender column of her neck, she appeared indomitable and yet fragile somehow, as if the dauntless spirit within were greater than the vessel of flesh-and-blood that held it. Then suddenly she turned her head and looked straight at his place of concealment.

Even as it came to him with startling swiftness that somehow she knew he was there, her gaze rendered him powerless. Huge in the pale oval of her face, her eyes willed him to be gone, and suddenly he knew what he had only sensed before. She had been trying to protect him when she was captured, and she was willing to submit to torture, perhaps even death, to protect him now. The realization shot through him like a lightning bolt.

Then, as if weary of the game, Drago gave a final jerk on the rope. Stifling a gasp, the girl stumbled to her knees at the pirate's feet.

"Aye, that's more like it. You will not be so proud when I am through teaching you the humility due your betters."

Flinging back her hair, the girl lifted her eyes to his.

59

"Doubtless I shall be dead. That is what you have planned for us." A strange gleam of a smile touched her lips. "I am not afraid to die, Captain. You will never bring me to beg for my life."

"Ah, but there are worse things than dying, my pretty," murmured the pirate, caressing her cheek with the back of his hand.

Without warning, he struck her, brutally with his palm. Her head snapped back, and she would have fallen had it not been for the rope, dragging her back again.

The old man's head came up with a jerk. "Stop it! Leave her be." A groan seemed forced from him at sight of the girl. The mark of Drago's fingers shown livid against the pallor of her face, but her eyes glittered defiance.

"Meg, don't be a fool," he uttered hoarsely. "Save yourself. There is nothing you can do for me."

What came next happened with bewildering swiftness. Drago's hand closed on the neck of the girl's gown to rip it from her. There was the flash of metal in the moonlight and the hollow thud of steel imbedding itself in wood. Drago froze, his eyes fixed and staring on the knife, quivering in the gunwales a bare inch above his arm.

Glenmorgan's voice cut through the silence. "Make so much as a move, Drago, and it will be your last." Then, as the lookout started at a run toward them: "Hold where you are, if you value your captain's life!"

The sailor froze, and the girl, stifling a sob, scrambled backward out of reach of the pirate captain.

Drago wrenched his eyes from the knife. "Who the bloody hell—"

"Perhaps you should ask your first mate, Drago," came Glenmorgan's steely-voiced answer. "He can tell you."

Dragging Moffit to his feet, Glenmorgan booted the pirate lieutenant unceremoniously into the open.

"They took us from behind, Captain," blustered the burly

seaman. Stumbling, he fell hard to his knees. "There must've been a dozen of 'em. Mebbe more. We never had a chance. I swear it!"

"Silence, you bloody fool!" Drago rasped.

Glenmorgan grinned mirthlessly. He could hardly blame Moffit for embellishing the truth. Drago had a reputation for dealing ruthlessly with those who failed him.

"Who are you?" demanded Drago, his glittering eyes trying to pierce the underbrush. "I've a curiosity to know the man with so little fear of John Drago. I suggest you are either a fool or a man with little wish to go on living."

"It would seem I am a man with a charmed life," Glenmorgan answered. "Like a bad penny, I keep turning up."

"'Ee's got to believe me, Captain," Moffit pleaded. "'Tis Mad Mike Glenmorgan himself. I seen 'im wi' me own eyes. 'Tis the woman he wants."

For an instant disbelief vied with something deadlier in the man's painted face. Glenmorgan tensed, ready to send a pistol ball through Drago's heart if he came to the wrong decision, but Drago did the unexpected. Propping a slim fist on either hip, he threw back his head and laughed.

"Mad Mike Glenmorgan, is it? Ecod, I might have known it would take more than the likes of Logan Tharp to bring you down. Tell me you've risen from the grave, Glenmorgan. That, I might believe, but not that you'd risk John Drago's wrath for the sake of a woman."

"I don't give a stone's toss in hell what you believe," Glenmorgan answered coldly. "You've come uninvited to my island and laid hands on my woman. I have every right to cut you down for that."

Drago arched an inquisitive eyebrow. "Indeed? Then why haven't you? Surely not because of the small matter of a favor I once did you? But my dear captain—you mustn't let that stop you. You have been a thorn in Logan Tharp's side. It amused me to spoil his plans to remove you."

"Nevertheless, you did warn me Lavoillet's men were lying in wait for me in Road Town. I consider us even now, and it's up to you whether you live or die. You have ten seconds to cut the girl loose. If you value either your ship or your life, I suggest you don't waste them."

The pirate hesitated, as if sensing a bluff.

"But be reasonable, Captain. How were we to know you'd laid claim to this abominable island? There's no need to be unfriendly."

"Seven seconds," announced Glenmorgan. "What's it to be, Drago?"

Dragging the knife free, Drago absently tested the point with the tip of a finger. "Come now, do you honestly think I don't know 'tis the treasure you're after?" Balancing the knife carelessly in his hand, he appeared to consider the matter. "John Drago and Michael Glenmorgan are men cut of the same cloth." Without warning, the knife slashed out and down, severing the rope that bound the girl. "Where lies the profit in pitting one against the other, when there's plenty enough for both?"

Hastily, the girl gathered up her skirts and, stumbling, ran to kneel beside her grandfather, who dragged the rope from her wrists.

Drago gave a broad sweep of the hand.

"There, 'tis done. Now what say you to a dram of good Jamaican rum—in the way of showing there are no hard feelings between us? It is possible we might even come to some sort of an agreement—partners with an even split of the gold? You could do worse than join forces with John Drago."

Glenmorgan felt a prickling of nerve endings. Something was wrong. Drago was stalling—why? On a sudden hunch he cast his glance beyond the beach to the cove, rippling with moonlight. There, no more than half a cable length away, he saw it—the yellow glow of a lantern bobbing up and down with the waves. It was a second boat. Drago must have been expecting it. Perhaps the pistol shot had served as a summons or perhaps the vessel carried the empty casks for water. Either way, it meant that his bluff had failed. In a matter of minutes Drago would have reinforcements.

He was not given time to consider a new plan of action, as Meg's voice sounded the warning. "A boat, Captain. There are more men coming!"

Drago's shout rang out. "Take him, fools!" Hurtling the knife in Glenmorgan's direction, he drew his sword and made for the girl. Glenmorgan's shot caught the lookout in the shoulder and spun him around. The next instant, Glenmorgan was in the open. Driving the hilt of his sword in Moffit's face, he felled him and without stopping lunged past him to cut Drago off from the girl.

"Back!" shouted Glenmorgan, driving the other man before him with a merciless slashing attack. "Back, damn you!"

Step by step, Drago gave way, till with a final twisting thrust of the blade, Glenmorgan sent his sword spinning.

Disarmed and staring death in the face, Drago spread wide his hands before him.

"Stay, Captain!" he panted. "I yield."

The point of the blade quivered at the pirate's throat as if still eager for blood, when suddenly strong young fingers closed gently about Glenmorgan's arm.

"Captain," murmured the girl. "He has yielded. Let him live, I beg you."

Only then did Glenmorgan's eyes falter, the wildness giving way gradually to returning rationality. A breath shuddered through him, and he felt the weariness closing in on him. Feeling him sway, the girl gave a small cry of dismay and hastily threw an arm about his lean waist.

"Your wound!" she exclaimed, her eyes on the stain spreading slowly on the bandage. "It's bleeding."

The words seemed momentarily to rouse him from the lethargy stealing over him.

He said thickly, "No matter. It can wait." With an effort, he straightened. His eyes, cold now and steady, went to Drago.

"Our time is short. So for both our sakes, I suggest you attend carefully to what I have to say. I'm afraid, Captain, that I must refuse your offer of a partnership. You will no doubt be gratified to hear that I have decided to give up pirating as a trade."

"Have you? But on the contrary, I confess I am disappointed. Your exploits have been, if nothing else, exceedingly entertaining."

"You will, I trust, find other sources of entertainment," observed Glenmorgan, smiling mirthlessly at the man's cool nerve. "As for the treasure, apparently you haven't been listening. Nor are you well informed. The Spanish treasure ship did not surrender her gold easily. She was all but sunk before she pulled down her colors. Which is why the *Argonaut* was conscripted out of St. Vincent's to transport the spoils home to England."

"How very interesting, to be sure," murmured the pirate in accents of boredom. "However, I confess I could not care less as to why the gold ended up on the *Argonaut*. All that really matters is that it was there."

"Aye, it was there. I myself can attest to that. What you don't know is that the *Argonaut* was fitted with a false bottom. No one did, save for a handful outside of the crew. Certainly, the captain of the King's ship that captured her was unaware of it. Which is why they failed to discover the treasure. The gold was never unloaded, Drago. It is still with the *Argonaut*—at the bottom of the sea."

Glenmorgan could see outright disbelief at war with the beginnings of uncertainty in the man's face.

"You make it all sound so very convincing. Perhaps you would care to tell me how *you* know so much about it."

"I know," answered Glenmorgan, smiling coldly, "because I helped design that hold. The *Argonaut* was one of my father's ships. And the men who sailed her were Americans, loyal to him. Is it any wonder that they should find naval discipline intolerable? Or that when the British commander ordered the ship's master hanged for insubordination, the men should be driven at last to mutiny? It was never the gold they were after. Only freedom from tyranny. They were trying to return the *Argonaut* to my father when they were taken."

Had he not been fighting the weariness that threatened to drag him down, he might not have failed to note the sudden tremor that shook the girl's slender body next to his. As it was, he was aware only of the time growing short, of the boat drawing nearer with every passing second.

"Meg—the old man," he said, without taking his eyes off Drago. "Get him up. It's time the two of you were leaving."

"But what of you? You are coming, too? I will not go without—"

"You will do as I say!" he cut in, his voice sharp with impatience. Sensing her draw up in protest, he softened his tone. "Trust me, Meg. I'll be along directly. Now go. And whatever happens, don't look back."

She went reluctantly, sensing, no doubt, the lie. He had not the strength left to make it back to the hut, but he might be able to buy her time enough to get herself and the old man to safety.

Drago knew. The pirate was staring at him, a peculiar expression in the shrewd eyes.

"The *Raven*'s nowhere near. You're alone on the island. Ecod, it really was the woman, wasn't it. You intend to die for her."

65

"You can believe what you like, Drago. But know this. There's nothing to stop me from running you through right now. By the time your men figure out what has happened, the girl will be safely hidden in the jungle. How long do you think they'll hang around for the dubious pleasure of getting even for the loss of their captain? In these waters, patrolled by the King's Navy, hardly long enough to find her."

He was bluffing, banking on the slim hope that Drago had kept his crew in the dark about the treasure. If they scented gold, the band of cutthroats would not stop until they had combed every inch of the island.

The sound of oars carried clearly to the two men. Drago frowned, a film of sweat breaking out on his forehead. The boat was only a few yards from shore. The game had played itself out. With a flip of the wrist, Glenmorgan reversed the sword and extended it, haft first, toward Drago.

"It's finished," he said, the weariness dragging at his voice. "If you take my advice, you won't waste your time scouring the island for the girl or the treasure. You won't find either of them. Take your men and get out while you still can. I left three of them tied up in the jungle close to where I encountered Moffit. He can tell you where."

Drago stared at him in disbelief.

"You'd surrender your sword when you had the drop on me? Why?"

"Perhaps I'm feeling generous. What does it matter?"

When the pirate still made no move to take it, Glenmorgan flung the blade contemptuously at Drago's feet.

"Do as you will," he stated flatly. "I don't give a bloody damn."

Turning, he started to walk away, but somehow he could not make his legs do as he willed them. He was falling even as a woman's cry sounded somewhere far away. Then darkness closed in around him.

* * *

It was a long time later before he came awake. Frowning against the sunlight streaming through the window into his eyes, he cursed the sun and the cry of seagulls swooping over the sea. He felt irritable and unrefreshed, as if he had spent the night pounding his pillow—or *being* pommeled, he amended with a wince as his body became sensible all at once to the sting of numerous cuts and abrasions. Now what the hell? In vain, he tried to shift his long length into a more comfortable position on the cot. It seemed every muscle in his body ached. Nor did it add to his comfort to feel gritty and in need of a shave. Bloody hell, bed was no fit place for a man!

At last he eyed with distaste the meal, laid out for him on the table by his bedside. He had drunk enough weak tea to last a lifetime, and he had no stomach for food, let alone for fruit and a slab of dry bread. What he needed was the feel of the wind in his face. Aye, and a deck beneath his feet.

Inexplicably the thought triggered his memory. There had been a ship, a pirate ship, lying off shore in the night. Or had it been longer? He could not be sure. He remembered the scream in the night and his wild plunge down the hillside. His eyes hardened. He had been like a wild man, driven by the singleminded need to save the girl and her grandfather.

Good God—Meg!

Remembering, he bolted upright in the bed, only to double up as a hard fist of pain struck out of nowhere. Retching and gasping for air, he waited until the pain had eased and he could breathe normally again. Bloody hell. He had forgotten the cursed wound.

Grimly he tried to assess what his wild foray into the jungle had cost him. He felt feverish and light-headed, and he was acutely conscious of the dull throb of a headache. And yet, surprisingly enough, he felt stronger than he had yesterday. The wound, while painful, apparently was no worse. The real wonder was that he was alive at all. It would seem that Drago had not thought it worthwhile to kill him. But what of Meg and the old man?

Hellsfire! Why was there no one around? Someone had brought him back to the hut and tended his wounds, had even thought to supply him with food and drink. Somehow he did not think it had been Drago. Then who? The old man? The girl? Surely they, too, must still be alive. Or maybe Drago had discovered the girl. Maybe, thinking to lure her into revealing the supposed secret of the treasure, he had offered her, in exchange for her freedom, the life of the man who had tried to save her.

Stricken with the all too plausible explanation for her absence, Glenmorgan flung off the coverlet and shoved himself heedlessly to his feet.

He had dragged on his breeches and was reaching for his sword when the room was flooded suddenly with sunlight.

"Captain, no," cried a low, vibrant voice. "You will only harm yourself."

Blinded by the light, he sensed rather than saw the tall, slender figure limned against the doorway.

Her name formed itself on his lips.

"Meg? Bloody hell, I can't see. Is it really you?"

No doubt the sudden unbearable pressure in his chest was due to the wound, he told himself, as he heard a light step coming toward him. The next instant, strong young hands reached out to help steady him.

"Yes, it's Meg. And you should not be out of your bed."

Glenmorgan, however, was not listening. He was still reeling from the sudden swift stab of relief that had gone through him at discovering she was alive. Silently he cursed himself for a bloody fool. She was a woman and, incredible as it might seem, the granddaughter of the man who, in instigating the mutiny on the *Argonaut,* had played no small part in ruining Glenmorgan's father. No doubt she was as steeped in artifice and intrigue as she was enshrouded in mystery, he told himself. Well, she would soon see that her game, whatever it was, would not work on him. He would have the truth from her, and he would have it now.

A startled cry burst from the girl's lips as his fingers closed ruthlessly on her arms.

"Aye, it is you, alive and unharmed," the captain uttered darkly. "And what price did you pay for our deliverance? Did you give Drago what he wanted? Tell me, Meg. Did you give him the gold?"

Five

Meg stood perfectly still in the captain's grasp. She was bewildered by his sudden change of manner and the accusation in his voice, but she was not afraid. After all, wasn't he Glenmorgan, the son of the man who had been her grandfather's benefactor many years before? And hadn't he risked his life to save hers and her grandfather's? He wouldn't harm her. He could not. It was only that he was hurt and ill, perhaps even a little out of his head, she told herself. And truly, his eyes burned with a feverish brightness, which worried her. If only she could persuade him to lie down and rest.

"I don't understand, Captain," she said as soon as she had overcome her initial surprise. "Don't you remember? It was you who convinced Drago there is no treasure."

"Don't play the innocent with me," Glenmorgan growled. His fingers tightened until unwittingly Meg winced. "It was all a bluff, and you know it."

"A—a bluff?" she echoed. Her brow furrowed in puzzlement as she struggled to make sense of the word. She had never heard it used that way before. But then, there were so many things of his world with which she was unfamiliar, she reflected with a sinking heart. He would think her strange indeed, a silly, ignorant fool. Embarrassed, she blinked and dropped her eyes from his. "I—I don't know what you mean," she faltered.

"Don't lie to me," snapped the captain, mistaking the blush on her cheek for guilt. "Your grandfather is Phillip Belding, isn't he? He knows where the gold is."

Meg's eyes lifted to his in troubled confusion.

"Yes," she replied. "He is Belding. But there is no gold. Last night you said—"

Glenmorgan cut her off with an impatient gesture.

"Bloody hell, I know what I said!" he answered harshly, and then, seeing the look in her eyes, immediately caught himself. "All right," he said. "All right. If that's the way you want to play it, I'll spell it out for you." He swallowed drily and ran his tongue over parched lips. Curse the blasted hut. The heat was stifling, and he had to force himself to think. "It's true, the British naval captain who captured the *Argonaut* may have been in the dark about the false bottom. But Belding and the other American officers on board knew. These waters are crawling with uninhabited islands. In the two weeks the mutineers were in charge of the ship, there was plenty of time to drop the gold off on any one of them. Maybe even on this one. Dammit, it's what I would have done."

"Yes, but—"

"No, listen to me, Meg. If you and the old man have made a deal with Drago—our lives for the treasure—then you're playing a fool's game. I know Drago. You can't trust him. He'd sell his soul for that much gold."

At last Meg's face brightened with understanding. He didn't know about Drago. He thought they were still in danger.

"No, Captain," she said impulsively, "you are wrong. The pirate ship has gone. Don't you see? It was Drago who had you brought here. He said since there was no profit to be gained, he saw little point in killing us. And besides, he

71

could not easily dispatch a man whose exploits served so greatly to entertain him." She paused, her brow wrinkling in a frown. "What a strange thing for him to say. I think you surprised him when you spared his life. Is it possible that a man of such brutality could yet be capable of acting with generosity? Grandfather didn't think so. He said it was a matter of honor among thieves."

Glenmorgan stared at her as if he hadn't heard her right. Meg felt the blood grow suddenly warm in her cheeks. Little knowing what else to do, she stared frankly back, until at last a rueful bark of laughter seemed torn from the captain. Abruptly he released her.

"Aye. Honor among thieves," he muttered gruffly. "No doubt your grandfather is right."

Turning away, he crossed to the window and leaned his hands against the sill. Gratefully he drank in the breeze flowing off the sea. Strange that it should feel so cold against his skin. Unwittingly he shivered. Christ, it was the fever, creeping up on him again. He could feel it, dragging at him, clouding his mind. Bloody hell, he had no time for it. Thanks to Drago, the whole world would soon know that Mad Mike Glenmorgan was alive and laid up on the blasted island. He must get the girl to talk—now, before it was too late. Then somehow he would get word to the *Raven*. The gold was out there somewhere waiting for him to find it.

Behind him Meg watched the brooding figure of the captain. Unwittingly her heart went out to him. How pale he looked, and thin. And yet she could sense the strength in him, the iron will that would not let him give in to weakness, the stubbornness that kept him on his feet when he should be resting. What was it that drove him so? she wondered.

At last her brow furrowed in perplexity. What a strange creature he was. When she had first entered the hut, she had been sure that he was glad to see her. And yet how

72

quickly he had changed. What had she done to make him suddenly turn on her? she thought, unconsciously rubbing her hands over her arms where his fingers had bitten into the flesh. She felt an unfamiliar weight settle upon her heart. More than likely she had done nothing. She didn't have to. He had probably sensed right away that she was—was "different" somehow, and that was why he had drawn away.

Glenmorgan's voice, sounding weary in the quiet, startled her out of her reverie. "He is all right, then—your grandfather?" he asked, without turning around.

Meg swallowed. It was very hard to lie. And yet what choice had she? Grandfather had sworn her to secrecy before he left.

"He is very stubborn—like you," she answered, saying what she had been instructed to tell the captain. "He insists there is no reason to stay in bed. He took the boat out to fish. There was nothing I could do to stop him."

Meg's breath caught as she saw the powerful leap of muscle across the captain's shoulders.

"But you did try," he said in a strangely quiet voice. "Aye, of course you did."

He brought a fist down hard against the windowsill, then without warning he came about to impale her with light, piercing eyes.

"Dammit, Meg," he said in that same quiet voice. "Don't lie to me. Do you think that I don't know the last thing the old man would do is go fishing and leave you here alone with me? Tell me where he is. If Drago has taken him by force, there's no time to lose. It's your grandfather's only chance. Tell me where they've gone, and I'll find a way to go after them and bring him back to you alive."

"But there's no need," Meg insisted, desperate to make him believe her. "He's not with Captain Drago." At least that much was true. She stopped and drew a breath to calm the ridiculous pounding of her heart. "He is not in any danger, Captain. You must believe me. After all, why shouldn't he leave me here alone? I am well able to take care of myself."

"Are you?" he queried dangerously. Meg had to force herself not to back a step as he loomed suddenly over her. "I'm afraid your grandfather entertains a slightly different notion. At least so far as I'm concerned. He warned me to stay away from you."

"Did—did he?" she stammered. Unsettled by his near-ness, she turned away to hide the tumult written plainly on her face. "Yes, I suppose he would. But not for the reasons you think. We are fugitives, he and I. We have spent our lives fleeing from one place to another for almost as long as I can remember." Steeling herself to meet his gaze, she came around again. "Is it any wonder that he tried to warn you away?"

Glenmorgan's glance narrowed sharply on the lovely countenance turned up to his. She returned his look steadily, with just the right hint of defiance. For a moment he was almost tempted to believe her. It made sense, after all, in light of what he had learned about the old man. Joseph Pippin had had a great deal to hide. Phillip Belding, on the other hand, was no great mystery. Or was he? Glenmorgan wasn't satisfied. The girl was hiding something, he felt it.

"No, I don't suppose it is," he answered at last. "And yet somehow I don't think that's what he had in mind. I remember once, when I was delirious with fever, he was arguing with you, trying to persuade you to leave. He was afraid I'd wake up and see you."

"There," she said a little too quickly. "That only proves what I said. He was trying to protect me. But now he knows I am in no danger from you."

Glenmorgan smiled, a faint sardonic curl of the lips that made her distinctly uneasy.

"Are you so sure?" His hands lifted to frame her face.

Meg froze, paralyzed by his look, which made her heart seem to stop, and by his touch, which made her feel strangely queasy inside. She swallowed and from somewhere managed to find the wit to answer him.

"I'm not afraid of you," she declared, though her stomach was churning and all the old strictures screamed at her to flee. "Why should I be? You saved my life."

"Aye, and you saved mine. For which I am grateful. Still, I wouldn't count on my gratitude, if I were you. I'm Mad Mike Glenmorgan, after all, and you . . ." His voice trailed off, and Meg stared, entranced, as he looked into her eyes. How long he held her like that, she did not know. Her heart had begun to do flip-flops beneath her breast like a fish out of water, and her breath to come in short, hurried gusts. She was suddenly acutely aware of the captain's nearness, of the controlled strength in the hands that held her, of the lean, powerful frame bending over her.

How very strange, she marveled distractedly. It was as if time had stopped and there was nothing in the world but the slow torment of waiting for something that she only vaguely understood. Like a warning from the past, the memory of her mother singing a song of the old ones drifted unexpectedly through her mind. It was the song of Callandra, whose heart had been captured and then broken by Yorath, a sailor. Suddenly, Meg knew she should be afraid. And yet somehow, she wasn't. Then Glenmorgan drew a breath and she saw a frown darken his eyes.

Without warning he let her go. "And you," he uttered darkly, "are the kind of trouble I can do without."

He lurched away to stand with his back to her.

"Get out," he ground out savagely between his teeth. "Get out before I forget that I used to be a gentleman."

Meg reeled, feeling weak and suddenly sick inside. Grandfather had been wrong. The *songs* had been wrong.

Far from falling victim to her supposed beauty, the captain had been repelled by her. Indeed, he could not stand to have her near. The truth hurt her more than she could ever have dreamed possible, and for a moment she did not know how she could bear it. And then pride came to her rescue. Who was Glenmorgan to scorn her, after all? He was a sea rogue, a man without feelings, a pirate, while she had been heir to a world the likes of which he could only dream about. A cold wave of anger, unlike anything she had ever felt before, welled up inside her. She would show him that he could not treat her like some insignificant thing to be brushed away in disgust.

"Who do you think you are," she uttered scathingly, "to order me from my grandfather's house?" Glenmorgan gave no sign that he had even heard her. Furious, she reached out to grab his arm. "Look at me!" she cried. "No one tells me what to do, and least of all you!"

At last he came around, his expression slightly bored, like a mask in which his eyes glinted with a steely intensity.

"No, I don't suppose they do," he said with a cynical twist of the lips. "You're pigheaded and spoiled, and judging from what little I've seen of you, I'd say you haven't a lick of sense in that pretty head of yours. You should be beaten, and often, something your grandfather has apparently omitted from your upbringing."

"Oh!" gasped Meg, hardly knowing what outraged her more—the fact that he obviously considered her a child or that he would suggest anything so humiliating as a beating. "You—you are no better than—than Drago. And I couldn't care less if you cannot bear the sight of me. Do you hear me? I am Meg, and I come and go as I please."

Head held high, she stood before him—lovely and dangerous and fairly scintillating with wounded pride.

"I hear you all right," Glenmorgan had the effrontery to reply. "It'd be damned hard not to. And now if you're finished . . ." Grabbing her by one arm, he spun her around and, with a hard hand applied tellingly to her behind, sent her stumbling toward the door. "Now run along like a good little girl—before one of us does something we'll both regret."

Never had Meg felt anything like the humiliation and anger that swept her then. No one had ever before laid a hand on her, not even her grandfather. He deserved to have the fury of the heavens unleashed against him. Or to be cast into the merciless depths of the sea. Or better yet, to be fed piecemeal to the sharks. As it was, she did the only thing she could in the circumstances. Coming about, she swung at him with all her might.

Muttering a curse, Glenmorgan ducked. The next instant found her pinned against his chest. Meg stiffened as the fingers of a strong masculine hand curled about her throat.

"You're right. I am no better than Drago," growled the captain, panting a little from his recent exertions. "I could take you now. Is that what you want?"

Meg gasped. "Take me—where?" Alarmed at what she had unloosed, she strained to break free. "I haven't the slightest wish to go anywhere with you."

A startled laugh broke from Glenmorgan. Only a fool or a total innocent could possibly have misconstrued his intent. Of course there was one other possibility: that she had not misunderstood at all. Maybe, just maybe, she was as accomplished an actress as one other woman he had known.

"What's the matter?" he said mockingly. "Do I frighten you? Well, you should be afraid. You should have run when you had the chance. But you didn't, and now you're going to find out what it means to be at the mercy of Mad Mike Glenmorgan. No more lies, Meg. Tell me what I want to know."

Meg's chin came up, her eyes sparkling with resentment and the tears that she barely held in check.

77

"Does it mean so much to you?" she demanded. "This gold that drives men mad with greed?" Her eyes searched his face. "If I am to die for it, surely I have a right to know why it is so important to you. And don't tell me it is out of concern for my grandfather. You have made it plain that it has nothing to do with him."

For an instant she was sure she glimpsed a flicker of grim amusement in his face. Then it was gone as quickly as it had come, leaving him staring at her with a singularly fixed expression. Inexplicably her pulse began to race.

"You're not going to die from it," he promised huskily. Meg gasped as he bent his head to her. "But you're right. It's not your grandfather who interests me at present." Then his mouth covered hers.

Not in a thousand years could Meg have imagined that a mere touching of the lips could do such strange things to her. It was like sustaining a shock from one of the rays that hide in the sand off the islands, she thought distractedly, only deliciously pleasurable. A slow heat invaded her limbs, as if she had just surfaced from a deep dive to feel the tropical sun, hot against her skin. She felt light-headed and dizzy, and there was a roaring in her ears like the boom of the surf pounding against the shore, and yet she was wonderfully, sensually aware of the captain's lips moving over hers, of his body, lean and hard, against her. Deep within, something stirred and awakened, something primitive and wild—like a storm at sea. She could feel it building within, driving all rationality before it. Frightened, she tried to pull away.

Glenmorgan held her, not ready yet to let her go. He wanted her frightened, scared enough to tell him what he needed to know. And if she learned a disgust of him in the process, all the better. He'd not let it go so far as to hurt her, only teach her a lesson about the dangers of placing herself at the mercy of desperate men—men like himself and Drago, sea rovers and brigands. Afterward, he could wash his hands of her with a clear conscience, he told himself, knowing that she would be as glad as he to see him go.

But then her arms wrapped themselves around his neck, and melting to his embrace, she returned his kiss, wildly, uninhibitedly, her body molding itself to his. Silently he cursed. Hellsfire, this was no innocent. She took his breath away, set his brain on fire. No bloody virgin could kiss like that. But then, that was all the better, wasn't it? he told himself, suppressing the unexpected stab of disappointment at discovering she was no different from the rest of her kind—no different from Clarissa, who hid her deceitful heart behind a lovely mask of innocence. He would take what she offered so delectably, and why not? It had been a long time since he had had a woman. And afterward there would be no tears, no recriminations.

Bending down, he took her up in his arms and carried her to the bed.

A groan broke from Meg's depths as he laid her down. Dazed, she blinked up at him. He was breathing heavily, and the eyes that looked into hers were fire-bright and glittery. Her lips parted—to what? Warn him? Tell him the truth before it was too late? She didn't know. And then he lowered his head to her, and she forgot everything but his lips drawing fire from her veins.

Glenmorgan kissed her ruthlessly, rousing her with his lips and hands until she writhed beneath him, her fingers clutching at his shoulders. Somewhere in the back of his mind, he knew it was the fever driving him, but he could not stop himself, had no desire to. Her body, lithe and supple beneath his touch, only served to inflame him more. Impatiently, he worked the gown up her slender length and over her head, nearly ripping it in his haste. The simple chemise underneath quickly followed suit, revealing the intriguing fact that she eschewed the usual underthings. Apparently she was a child of nature, but then, living in isolation as she did would hardly necessitate the niceties. His breath caught in his throat at sight of her. Whatever else she was, she was a magnificent creature. She was long-limbed and beautiful, like a healthy young animal, the muscles firm and well defined, like an athlete's. Her breasts were full and round and beautifully molded, her skin soft and silky smooth. All sinuous curves and sensuous valleys, she inflamed his senses. Hurriedly he stripped off his breeches and turned back to her, only to halt at the look in her eyes.

She was staring at him, her eyes wide and childlike. She had never seen a man totally naked before. How beautiful he was! In wonder she beheld the stark maleness of him, the broad chest bristling with its black mat of hair, which in spite of the bandage appeared perfect to her, the long torso tapering to a lean waist, the slim hips and muscular thighs. A small gasp escaped her lips at sight of his swollen member, which seemed to sprout from the curling mass of hair about his groin. Faith of her fathers, she marveled. Never had she seen anything like this. Like a child confronted with something new and wonderful, she reached out to enfold it carefully between her palms. She felt it leap beneath her touch, heard Glenmorgan's swift intake of breath. Startled, she glanced up into his face, into his eyes, burning with a feverish light.

And suddenly she understood what he had meant earlier, understood what he wanted of her. It was the mating rite her mother had told her about. The magical thing between a male and a female, which bound them forever as one. And it was forbidden to her! Only pain and unhappiness could ever come of giving the gift to one who was not of her kind. Had not her mother been proof enough of that? And still she felt her pulse quicken with the birth of feelings new and strange to her—a yearning born out of loneliness,

80

an overwhelming desire to unlock the secrets of this body which even yet was so strange to her. And why should she not? she thought rebelliously. Who was left to either know or care what happened to her? She might never have another chance to know what it was to be one with a male, *this* male, and she wanted it, more than she had ever wanted anything before.

Flinging caution to the wind, she rose to her knees on the bed and, taking his hands in hers, drew him to her. Unselfconsciously, she ran her fingers up through the black mat of hair on his chest and over his shoulders until her hands clasped behind his neck. Her eyes, blue-green like the sea, smiled up at him.

"I am ready, Captain," she announced with simple candor. "Please do take me now."

She saw his surprise and the hardening of his eyes with suspicion. Then pulling him to her, she kissed him fully on the mouth.

She felt his lips hard and unresponsive beneath hers, and she experienced a sickening sensation in the pit of her stomach. She was doing it wrong, she thought. He was not pleased. Mortified at her failure to arouse in him the keenly pleasurable sensations he had aroused in her, she almost drew away. Then some instinct, stronger than her fear, awakened within her. Refusing to give up, she released his mouth to begin a slow, tantalizing journey of discovery. Careful of his wound, she explored the broad expanse of his chest, the firm, powerful muscles, the thick mat of hair, bristling beneath her fingers. With her lips she made a trail of kisses, slowly, savoring him, storing in her memory the wondrous lean hardness of his male body, until at last curiosity led her to sample with her tongue one of the intriguingly masculine nipples. In wonder, she felt his nipple grow rigid beneath her touch. An answering thrill shot through her, leaving her breathless and eager to learn more of him. How

81

marvelous he was! The narrow torso and the abdomen, rippled with muscle, aroused in her a bewildering array of emotions. She felt giddy and warm, her breath hot in her throat. All of her senses seemed magnified, just as they did when she deliberately flirted with danger. Her pulse racing, she bent to press her mouth to his firm, flat belly, to the line of black hair that disappeared into the thicker mass about his groin, and finally the proud member, thrusting upward.

Glenmorgan let go an explosive oath. Driven beyond rationality, he forgot that she was Meg or that he owed his life to her. In his fevered mind, he was living the dream again, of Clarissa beneath the umbrella tree, a transformed Clarissa with silvery hair and the seductive face of an angel. His hand closed ruthlessly in her hair and dragged her backward onto the bed. This time he would not let her get away. This time he meant to punish her for her betrayal.

"Seductress," he growled, impaling her with eyes like burning embers. "You go too far."

Brutally, he kissed her, his tongue thrusting savagely between her teeth. Somewhere deep inside she felt a poignant shock of pleasure, a slow melting, like lava pouring through her veins. She moaned and opened to him, her hands clutching at his powerful shoulders. Releasing her lips, he devoured her—her eyes, her cheeks, the tender flesh along her neck.

Meg groaned and moved her head mindlessly back and forth against the pillow. Glenmorgan's lips tormented her and unleashed the storm within her. Helplessly she felt herself swept up in its fury. Deliriously, she reached out to him. Unafraid, she responded, giving of herself freely, generously, utterly without restraint. His mouth, molding itself to her nipples, hurt her, and yet the pain was as nothing compared to the sharp thrill of pleasure that ripped through her. With his tongue he caressed her, with his hands explored the secrets of her flesh. He was a devil and a madman, cruel and demanding. A keening sigh broke from her as his hands stroking her thighs at last found the intimate place of her greatest desire. She heard herself groan, felt herself arch against him. She felt herself borne upon the crest of a tidal wave and did not know what was happening to her. Frantically she called out to him, wanting him, needing him to end her torment.

Instantly he spread wide her thighs and, drawing up and back, plunged savagely into her depths.

Meg screamed as he ripped through her maidenhead. Her anguish shattered the stillness, ricocheted off the hillsides. The jungle erupted in a rush of wings and the screech of birds frightened into flight.

And then there was silence.

In some part of his brain, Glenmorgan heard, but lost in the dream, he knew no other reality but Clarissa and the need to finish what he had started. Feverishly he thrust, carrying Meg beyond the pain, beyond everything but a need so powerful, she thought she would die from it. With all her supple young strength, she responded, moving with him, striving for the thing that seemed forever just beyond her reach, until at last she felt carried on a swelling flood of rapture.

Glenmorgan plunged deeply, spilling forth his seed inside her. She heard him utter a name: "Clarissa." A sharp pang pierced her heart, and then she forgot everything as the billowing swell of pleasure burst forth within her to leave her shuddering helplessly with sigh after sigh of mindless release. Then with a groan, Glenmorgan collapsed on top of her, his breath harsh in his throat.

Meg lay beneath him, her heart pounding in the aftermath of their lovemaking. She felt stunned by the violence of their joining, dazed by the wonder of it all. Together, they had soared on the winds of a hurricane. And now it was over. He had called out to Clarissa in what should have been their shared moment of ecstasy.

Only then did the grim reality of her situation hit her. It had happened, the thing that was forbidden to her. She had given herself to him, a man who did not even know she existed, a man for whom there was only one woman—Clarissa, who had betrayed him. Mother of her mothers, what was she to do? For her, there was no turning back now. She had rendered up the gift freely, a gift which, to one of her kind, was more precious than life itself, because it was forever. And now was she to be like Callandra, forever pining for that which had been denied her, until finally there was nothing left of her but a longing for death?

The thought filled her with repugnance and an instinctive defiance. She was not Callandra. She was Meg. Somehow she would find a way, just as her mother before her had done. But unlike her mother, she would never regret what had happened. She could not. Everything that made her what she was—the spirit within her, the instincts, her heart, beating fiercely beneath her breast—told her that it was not wrong, this thing that she had done. And if in the end she could not win Glenmorgan's love, then she would find the strength to do what must be done. She would give him up for his own sake, no matter what the cost to herself.

In the wake of her resolve, she felt a fierce swell of tenderness well up inside her for the man who had awakened her to the wonders of her woman's body. Even now she could scarcely believe the fury of the storm that had swept over her. He wielded a magic more powerful than any she could ever have dreamed possible. It robbed her of all reason, transformed her into a creature of frenzy, and left her feeling vulnerable and yet sated, her entire being infused with a poignant sense of warmth that she had never known in her life before.

No wonder Callandra had pined for her lost love! Having

once tasted of so potent an elixir, how could one learn to live without it? Already she was thirsting for more. With all of her heart she wished to have him awaken to her with a hunger that was for her alone, to have him hold her and drive her slowly mad with his lovemaking. But alas! It was more likely that he would awaken hoping for Clarissa only to discover himself in bed with an impostor. How would he feel upon discovering the truth? Bitter tears welled up in her eyes as it came to her that it was all too likely he would have a disgust of her. No doubt he would hate and despise her for what he would see as but another woman's betrayal.

But what if he awakened to find her gone? Wouldn't he think it had all been a dream, a product of his fever? Perhaps he need never know what had passed between them. He was still weak and ill from his wound. It might be weeks before he was strong enough to leave the island. Might that not be time enough for her to make him forget Clarissa? Time enough to make him want her—Meg—for herself?

Yes, oh, yes. It was the only way. She must go at once, she told herself. Grasping at what suddenly seemed her only hope of ever winning his heart for herself, she tried to ease his weight off her.

Instantly Glenmorgan stirred. Meg froze, her heart pounding wildly, as he rolled over onto the bed beside her. It was done! She was free! Her heart in her throat, she started to get up. Too late! Glenmorgan's arm encircled her waist and, pulling her to him, pinned her against his lean length. She lay still, made weak by a soft melting pang deep inside her. Never had she imagined she could feel so wondrously snug nestled against a hard, muscular body. If only she dared remain where she was.

But she couldn't, she reminded herself firmly, not if she hoped to break Clarissa's hold over his heart. Slowly, carefully, she lifted his arm and slipped out from beneath it. In a flash, she was off the bed and searching for her clothes.

There was an ominous creak of the bedstead as Glenmorgan shifted his weight. Meg snatched up the gown and, tugging it on over her head, looked up to find him staring at her. The feverish brightness was gone from his eyes, and in its place was a faintly puzzled expression. She did not wait to see more. She fled wildly from the hut, her chemise left lying in a forgotten heap on the floor.

Behind her, Glenmorgan lifted himself on one elbow. Feeling something wet against his bare thigh, his glance went to the crimson stain on the bedclothes. His brow darkened with sudden, dawning comprehension.

"Good God," he groaned. "Meg!"

Six

Meg fled blindly, heedlessly, until her sides hurt and she couldn't run anymore. Then she walked, little caring where her wandering steps might take her. She felt lost, her heart torn between the overpowering emotions that Michael Glenmorgan had awakened in her and the bitter truth that she had given herself to a man who was bewitched by another.

How foolish her single small thread of hope seemed now in the stark afternoon sunlight! He had seen her. He knew it was no dream that he had lain with her. But even if she had been able to slip away unseen, she doubted that it would have changed anything. If Clarissa's treachery had not been enough to cure him of his former infatuation, then very likely nothing could. And what if by some miracle she, Meg, did manage to earn some measure of his affection? she reflected somberly, snapping a fragile blossom from a vine. Glenmorgan would never really love her, not the real Meg. He could not. The real Meg must remain hidden, a strange secretive creature beyond his comprehension. She shuddered to think how he would look at her should it ever be otherwise. What had Gates called her? A creature of evil, the devil's spawn. Glenmorgan would be no different. As surely as she lived and breathed, the truth would drive him from her in horror and disgust, and that she could never bear.

From her first glimpse of him in the lantern light on Lookout Point, she had felt drawn to him, and the days and nights of caring for him had only strengthened those feelings that she did not understand. She knew only that she wanted to be near him and that to be apart from him filled her with unbearable discontent. Indeed, she had been like one driven, as night after night she stole to the window in the hopes of catching a glimpse of the man while he lay sleeping. And then Drago and that other one had come, and in her panic to warn the captain, she had foolishly allowed herself to be captured. Not that she had been in any real danger. It should have been a relatively simple matter to escape, had her grandfather not unexpectedly blundered into harm's way.

Her brow furrowed with perplexity at the thought. How unlike Phillip Belding, the man of quiet strength and unfailing reason, to come charging wildly right into the middle of the pirates! Even now she had difficulty believing that the mere sight of his old enemy could drive him to do anything so hopelessly irrational. He had fallen on Gates like a madman, seemingly obsessed with the need to choke the life from him with his bare hands. Her grandfather had not stood a chance. With a single blow, Drago had knocked him senseless to the ground.

What a fine kettle of fish the old man had landed them in in his moment of madness! Afterward, he must surely have realized the dilemma he had made for her. To save them both, she was left with the grim prospect of having to reveal herself to the pirates, a thing that, even were it not forbidden to her, would have been fraught with dire consequences. She was sworn to die rather than to compromise the secrets of the old ones. Still, she might have brought it off, using some of the more timeworn techniques—a howling wind to douse the lanternlight and throw the pirates into confusion, or a sudden cloudburst might have served. Faith, a simple concealing veil of mist would probably have done the trick. But then she had sensed Glenmorgan hidden in the jungle a few feet away, had known with her whole being that he was there, and from that moment on, she had had no choice but to submit to whatever indignities might lie in store for her. Even death was preferable to revealing so much as a glimpse of her true self to him! And yet how close had Gates come to disclosing everything!

She shuddered with the memory. Another second and Glenmorgan would have known the truth. But then, the old man had made sure Gates would never tell his story again. Her blood ran cold at the thought of what her grandfather had done to keep her secret safe. Faith, he had killed for her! His one thought had been to silence the only witness to what had really happened that fateful day on the *Argonaut,* even if it meant Drago was left alive to exact his own vengeance.

How well the old man knew her, had known that she would not break her vow never to take a life. He had reasoned that no man, least of all Drago, could have held her did she not choose to be held, which meant that Gates, not Drago, was the only real danger to her. Ironically, the old man had not been aware of Glenmorgan's presence or that because of it she was indeed at Drago's mercy.

She would never know how she managed to hold her temper in check when Drago laid his hands on her. His touch had been as inviting as the caress of a sea snake, and his intentions just as venomous. Even now her skin crawled at the mere thought of it. Only her fear for Glenmorgan's safety and the need to keep her secret from him had given her the strength to play the part of a defenseless woman.

A fierce light flashed in her eyes. Nevertheless, not all

the strictures in the world, her sacred vow, or her own belief in the sanctity of life would have been enough to preserve Drago if he had harmed even a single hair on Glenmorgan's head. She had known that with bitter certainty as she endured the torment of waiting for Glenmorgan to make his move.

She need not have worried. She should have known Glenmorgan, even in his weakened state, was more than a match for Drago. She had witnessed the fight on Lookout Point, after all. Faith, but he had been terrible and magnificent, like the ancient Celtic warriors in the songs sung by the old ones. No wonder such tales were told of him as to inspire fear in the hearts of men.

She knew now without a doubt, however, that he inspired something quite different in the hearts of women.

"A curse on him!" she muttered out loud. "I should have left him to Clarissa's loving care." But it was too late. And even if it hadn't been, even if it had been possible to go back and do everything all over again, she knew she would have changed nothing. His spell over her was too powerful. She would have risked anything to keep him safe, done anything to have him hold her in his arms, given anything to have him unloose the storm within her, if only for that single, glorious moment in time. By the faith, she did not know herself anymore. Where was the Meg who prided herself on ruling her own life? The Meg who, having long ago accepted that she must be a solitary creature, had pledged never to allow her freedom to be taken from her? In a single moment of abandonment she had jeopardized everything she had ever held sacred. Mother of her mothers, she was indeed lost!

Uttering a groan, she started to run again, as if by that she might escape the torment of her thoughts.

How long she wandered or how far, she was never quite sure, or when the sun finally dipped toward the bulging horizon. Twilight found her standing on a high promontory looking out to the sea. No doubt it was instinct which had led her there—to the cliffs with their secret caves below, to the pounding of the surf—to the sea!

A lump rose in her throat. She could end it here. Glenmorgan need never see her again. Would it not be better that way? As if in answer, she let her gown trail to the ground at her feet and stepped to the edge of the cliffs. For a single breathless moment she stood limned against the fading brilliance of the sky, savoring the feel of the wind in her hair, its caress against her skin. Then she lifted her arms above her head and launched herself outward over the water. Her back arched, and for an instant she seemed to hover between earth and sky before at last she plummeted toward the sea.

A whisper of thought flashed through her mind: *"Bethuinmuir. Dainaon."* Then she plunged deep beneath the surface.

No sooner had the water closed over her, than she felt the familiar shock of change, like an electrical current shooting down her backbone, extending her spine, fusing her body from the waist down into a single unit of supple strength. She drew in deep draughts of seawater, her altered lungs extracting oxygen from the water as easily as they had done from the air. Her sluggish heart quickened. Revitalizing energy flowed through her veins. Her weariness dropped away. She felt powerful and wondrously clearheaded, no longer doubtful as to who or what she was. She was Meg, and she was home.

The metamorphosis was complete. She was as she was meant to be—a creature of the sea, neither fish nor human, but *dainaon,* something of both. A marvelous silvery green tail had taken the place of her land legs, and pulsating within her were the magical powers bequeathed to her by her sea-dwelling ancestors.

With a quick undulating movement, she rose through the watery depths to the surface.

And now what was she to do? she wondered, feeling suddenly very small and very much alone beneath the dazzling brilliance of the tropical night sky. She could not go back to Glenmorgan.

Faith, her grandfather had been right to warn her away from the sea captain! She saw it all so clearly now. There could never be anything lasting between them—he, a landsman, and she, a mermaid, who would die if she were ever parted from the sea. Had her mother not taught her that it was both the promise and the price—the gift and the punishment?

The Tale of the Beginnings as her mother had taught it to her came back to her with somber significance. Once, long ago, her people had enjoyed the freedom of the land and the sea, the favored offspring of a god who had built for them the city of three concentric circles on a solitary continent at the center of the ocean. Both clever and curious, they had mastered the secrets of power that reside in earth, fire, water, and air, the continuums of time and space, matter and energy and the music that binds them, and finally the songs of command. It was too much power, even for the offspring of a god, and knowledge without humility and wisdom had always been dangerous. In learning to command, they forgot that they were one with the continuum, their existence as much a part of the cycle of being as any other, and that the phenomenon of life, with its capacity for ever renewing itself, was the greatest marvel of all. It was a thing of the god. The power, in their hands, became a weapon of destruction, which threatened the existence of all things. They used it to kill and to conquer other living creatures, other peoples. Whether it was the god who intervened before they could disrupt the universal harmony or whether they brought retribution down upon themselves remained a matter for speculation. The reality was that the continent and its magnificent city of circles was swallowed up by the sea and the children of the god banished to the watery depths. They retained the songs of command and the power to transform themselves into creatures capable of walking the land, but their life forces were inextricably bound to the sea, to which they had always to return to renew themselves or die.

They had life and power, just as the god had promised they would always have, and finally wisdom and humility, but they were no longer human. They had evolved into creatures suited to their environment, and so long as they remained apart from those who dwelt on the land, they lived lives of peace and contentment, at total harmony with themselves and their watery world. Nothing good had ever come to any who allowed themselves to be seen by the land dwellers. Nevertheless, there were always a few who were drawn to the land out of curiosity or a longing for something they themselves did not understand. Sheela, Meg's mother, had been one of those.

A lump came to Meg's throat at the thought of the gentle creature who had mothered her and taught her the songs of the old ones, the strictures and taboos, which she, Sheela, had broken when she stole onto the land one night and was seen by a young man walking alone on the beach.

Her mother had been very young, hardly past the age of Becoming, which marked the passage of a mermaid into sexual maturity. She had gone to the island to be alone, to think and dream. She had been to the island before, and it had always been deserted, and so she had thought nothing of lifting her clear, pure voice in song as she fashioned a necklace out of seashells. Her singing drew him to her, or perhaps it was the god.

He had come in a small sailing boat to explore the island, to escape the society of planters, merchants, and traders on

St. Vincent's, which was no different from the one he had left behind in Charles Town. He was a physician, like his father, but he was a poet and a dreamer, too. He had hoped to recapture the dream of adventure that had brought him to the West Indies three years before, the dream that had eluded him.

The song wafted on the breeze, the words indistinguishable, but the voice hauntingly lovely. At first he thought his ears were playing tricks on him. The island was small and insignificant, the soil thin and unsuited to growing sugar. He could think of no reason why a woman should be there. He followed the sound of singing, thinking to discover it nothing more than the wind playing through the trees. What he found was a slender girl with hair the color of moonlight glancing off water.

He had come on her, unawares, and though she half turned toward the water, she had not fled. Something had held her—a sudden quickening of her heart, a flooding of awareness, a feeling that this was why she had been drawn to the island, that whatever was to happen was somehow meant to be. She had known without understanding that the landsman was her chosen lifemate. As for Richard, *he* had been captivated by her beauty from the first moment he laid eyes on her, and not even the ultimate discovery that she was not what she had at first appeared to be could alter the fact that he had fallen hopelessly, irrevocably in love with her.

That night they lay together, and Sheela gave the gift of love freely, withholding only the final rite of *hrum,* which would have made them truly one. That, she was forbidden to do with one who was not of her kind. Though the ancient Song of Muirgheas told of a landsman who had been tested by the god and found worthy to receive the rite of joining, there had never, to Meg's knowledge, been another.

How different things might have been had Sheela trusted

her own heart enough to perform the final rite! Richard might never have succumbed to the fever. He might be alive and Sheela with him. But Meg could hardly blame her mother for refusing to defy the teachings of the old ones, not in light of what had come after that first night of love. Returning to her home beneath the sea, Sheela had found the Dwelling Place buried beneath an avalanche of earth and rock, her mother and father—her people—dead or gone. Ironically, her love for Richard, the landsman, had saved her from whatever fate had befallen her kindred: she was with him when it happened. The god had spared her— why, if not to go on living and, in living, preserve and pass on the gifts of knowledge and power? For all she knew, she was the last of her kind. And because she was, she dared not risk the further anger of the god by joining with her lifemate in the forbidden rite of *hrum*.

It was one of the lessons Meg had been required to learn by rote: only ill luck can come to those who fail to heed the strictures.

And now she, like her mother, had given herself to a landsman and, in giving him the gift, had bound herself to him forever. What, then, was she to do? Use the forbidden spells of magic to bind his heart to her for all eternity? No, not even to save her life! Glenmorgan was not meant to be shackled. He was a sea rover, an adventurer. He must always go where his restless spirit willed. She would not be the one to take that from him. Indeed, she must not. With her whole heart she knew that Glenmorgan would grow to hate anyone who tried to take his freedom from him, and she— she would rather die than see his heart filled with loathing for her! She must not make the same mistakes her mother had made.

At last she saw clearly what she had to do. She must make a sacred vow never to do anything to hold him against his will. It was the only way she could be certain she would not weaken in her resolve.

The very thought of losing him created a great, aching void within her far worse than anything she had ever felt before. Not even when she had lost her mother and father had she felt such inconsolable grief. Then, she had had her grandfather to fill the terrible aching emptiness in her heart. There was no one, however, who could ever take Glenmorgan's place. He was her chosen lifemate, and without him, she would die, just as Sheela had done at the loss of Richard and as Callandra had done at the loss of Yorath. Separated from one's chosen lifemate, one of her kind was fated to pine away of grief and inconsolable yearning. It was to be alone and incomplete after having known the supreme joy of being one with another.

Instantly her chin lifted. She would not be so craven. She would be stronger than that, stronger than any curse of death, stronger than Glenmorgan's spell over her. She would lose herself in the sea. She would play with the dolphins and the whales. She would explore places she had never seen before. She might even look for sunken treasure, maybe even Glenmorgan's precious Spanish gold. Or then again, she might not, she thought with a flash of her eyes. If time dragged, she would practice the old songs, and if she were really bored, she might even call up a storm to play havoc with the passing ships. That was, after all, the sort of thing landsmen expected of her kind, she reflected bitterly. But then, they were such fools—especially one landsman in particular!

With an angry flick of her tail, she shot through the water, away from Glenmorgan and the island, away from the pain and uncertainties. She was Meg. She would find a way to survive, she told herself. She would stay away until long after the captain was safely gone from her life, and then she would return to her old, uncomplicated existence.

* * *

Morning had hardly dawned when Glenmorgan was driven from the stifling confines of the hut into the fresh air and the slowly strengthening sunlight. He had spent a wholly unrewarding night, tossing and turning and fighting his pillow, till he had finally fallen into an exhausted sleep scarcely an hour before sunrise. Even then, he would have been better off pacing the floor, he thought wryly, jamming Pippin's knife under the leathern belt about his waist. Better that than to have his peace cut up by confused snatches of dreams about a silvery-haired female with eyes that could bewitch a man's soul.

Out of habit, he slipped the strap of a small leather pouch over his shoulder. Then fastening the sword about his waist, he picked up his pistol, already primed and loaded. At last, restless and heartily weary of the miserable hut, he began to wend his way down the hill along a barely discernible path through the jungle. It was not long, however, before his thoughts returned to Meg.

"Damn her!" he cursed aloud. No woman should look the way she did, seductive and beautiful and yet with the innocent aspect of an angel.

He could remember with stark clarity the way his breath had caught in his throat the first time he had really looked into her cursed orbs. He had been about to demonstrate just how dangerous it was for her to be alone with a man like him. Was it only yesterday? It seemed like a lifetime ago. Egad, he had had the most damned unnerving sensation that time itself had stopped. He had never looked into eyes like those before, though he could not have said what made them so paralyzingly unique. Heavily lashed, they slanted beguilingly upward, giving her face an exotic cast that was both intriguing and breathtakingly lovely. But that was not enough to explain the spellbinding effect they had on him.

Perhaps it was their color. They were neither blue nor green, but a subtle blend of both, like turquoise, or the translucent blue-green depths of the sea. Or perhaps it was their strange mixture of innocence and secrecy, the impression they gave of hiding nothing and everything. There had been loneliness there, too, poignant with yearning. And still, it was more than all of those. It was something he sensed, but could not explain. It was like being drawn down into fathomless blue-green depths into a secret, solitary world beneath, a world he could not hope to comprehend.

It was all very ironic. He had meant to intimidate her and instead she had unnerved and unmanned him. That first time, only his strong sense of self-preservation and his own well-defined notion of honor had given him the strength to break the spell her eyes had cast over him. Damn the chit and her stubborn pride! Why had she not run when he had given her the chance? Not even his sense of honor had been enough to preserve him a second time. She had been magnificent when she turned on him, her glorious eyes scintillating sparks of anger. But that was as nothing compared to the feel of her in his arms, the sensations aroused by her lithe, warm body pressed to his.

The fresh clean scent of her had filled his nostrils. The smell of the outdoors clung to her, to her hair, which felt as soft and silken against his cheek as he had so often imagined it to be. He had felt her strength. The resistance in every glorious inch of her had aroused in him the primitive male urge to conquer and possess.

Good God. What an understatement! No man could have resisted the feverish madness her capitulation had aroused. And yet somehow he should have done.

Hellsfire! The last thing he had wanted was to ravage an innocent. And she *had* been innocent. He could not delude himself on that account. Even if he had been too delirious with fever at the time to realize he was bedding a virgin, the telltale signs of blood he discovered on the bedclothes afterward had left little room for doubt. The truth was, however, that he had *not* been too far gone to realize it. Bitterly he acknowledged that he had known the moment he entered her and heard her cry out. And still he had not stopped himself. The dream had been too intoxicating, his need to punish too great. It was as if all the pent-up fury at Clarissa's betrayal, the years of bitterness and exile, the wearing weeks of fighting to regain his strength had been unleashed in that single overmastering moment of madness. Yet through it all, ironically, in some part of his brain that still functioned, he had somehow been keenly aware of the supple young body beneath his, had known all along that it was Meg. And therein lay the true source of his present torment.

Never in his wildest imaginings could he have dreamed a woman—nay, an untaught virgin—could arouse him to such mindless, uncontrollable lust. Egad, she had inflamed his senses beyond anything he had ever experienced before. Not until it was over and he had awakened to see her pulling on that cursed absurd gown, which was too small for her and clearly intended for a much younger girl, had he been struck with the full significance of what he had done.

As long as he lived, he would never forget the look on her face just before she turned and ran away. He had seen mortification in those huge eyes, and something of panic, but not the slightest sign of accusation. That had been the hardest to bear. It was obvious she blamed herself for what had happened.

But it was not her fault. He was all too aware of the fact that the blame all lay with him. He was no inexperienced youth, but a grown man who had had his share of women. He should have been able to control his animal lust. Bloody hell! He should have known she was nothing like Clarissa. There had been nothing of the practiced harlot in her response to his lovemaking. Far from it! She had been wild and sensual, gloriously uninhibited, just as one might expect of a healthy young female who had never been taught to fear or hold in disgust what came naturally between a man and a woman. Damn her! It would have been far better for his peace of mind if she had been as coldly calculating as the false-hearted Clarissa, and a hell of a lot simpler.

What was he to do now that he had dishonored the chit? Marry her? Take her with him to Charles Town and plunge her into the middle of the deadly game that waited for him there? There was only an even chance that he would come out of it alive. If the worst happened, what would become of her? In Charles Town, even with his mother and sister to look after her, Meg would hardly stand a chance. She was far too beautiful not to attract a deal of notice and far too young and unworldly to know how to defend herself against the unscrupulous attentions of some of the so-called gentility. His mouth thinned to a grim line at the thought of Meg at the mercy of a man like Logan Tharp—or of a woman like Clarissa. Egad, she would be safer in the Carolina backwoods than in the fashionable salons of Charles Town without a man to protect her.

No, he would not be doing her any favors if he took her away from everything she knew here on the island only to leave her unprotected in a world in which she would be out of place. The best thing he could do for her was simply to go away.

The thought gave him no comfort. If anything, he was left with a sour taste in his mouth. Bloody hell! He had had plenty of women before and left them without so much as a thought. Why should this one be any different? He tried to tell himself it was because the others had all been women of the world, fully knowledgeable of the rules of the game, and that Meg was nothing like them. But he was not fully satisfied. By God, the truth was he did not know what Meg was.

There were times when she had the proud look of a bloody queen about her. And others, when she appeared an unruly sprite. In spite of her childish naiveté, she was every inch a woman. And what a woman! She was dauntless and headstrong and maddeningly elusive, and yet beneath the facade of impregnable strength, she was all too obviously vulnerable. Where did she come from? Who were her parents? When she was away from the old man's hut, where did she go? What did she do? All of which brought him to the thing that had really been nagging at him and which he had refused to face squarely before. Meg's grandfather was an old man near the end of his life. When Pippin was gone, what the devil would become of Meg?

A steely glint came to his eyes at the thought of the exquisite Meg left alone on the godforsaken island. By God, she deserved better than that. She deserved better from him. He muttered a blistering oath. What a bloody damned mess he had gotten himself in!

Immersed in his less than rewarding thoughts, Glenmorgan was taken by surprise when the jungle gave way, leaving him dazzled by sunlight. Shading his eyes with his hand, he gazed out over a crescent-shaped cove, set like a jewel within the curving arm of a barrier reef. Palm trees cast weird shadows across a sandy beach, a dazzling white in the sunlight, while in the distance rock cliffs, molded into bizarre shapes by the sea, marched in lonely procession down one end of the crescent. It was a wild and lonely spot, with the breakers spewing white plumes of water into the air with every pulsating crash against the sentinel rocks. And yet within the protected boundaries of the barrier reef, aqua-marine waters lapped tamely against the shore.

Glenmorgan, no stranger to the startling gems of beauty encountered on tropical islands, was nevertheless struck by something peculiarly arresting about this one. He experienced an odd prickling at the nape of his neck, as if he were not alone, or at the very least as if someone had been there before him. And then inexplicably he knew.

This was Meg's secret place. It was here that she came when she was not with her grandfather.

He could not have explained even to himself what drew him unerringly toward the distant cliffs. Perhaps unconsciously he sensed that it was the sea, restless and boundless, which would appeal to Meg's passionate nature, and not the peaceful tranquility of the cove. Whatever it was, his step quickened, and he was wryly aware of an old, familiar tingling of nerve endings, something he had not felt since that morning he had gone to Lookout Point for his tryst with Clarissa.

When he reached the jumble of boulders at the base of the cliffs, he was sweating freely, and he had to stop to catch his breath, but the feeling that he was on the track of something was even stronger than before. He was convinced as soon as he glimpsed the yawning mouth of the cave, partially concealed behind a pinnacle of lava rock, that his instincts had led him truly.

His disappointment was consequently keener when he came close enough to see it better. Half-submerged beneath the water, it was obvious that the cave would be totally inundated at high tide. Chiding himself for a bloody fool, he sank down on a boulder. Cynically he wondered if the fever had affected his reason. What sort of female, after all, would choose to frequent a dank, miserable cave when the island offered any number of more pleasant hideaways? It hardly made any sense. But then, nothing had since he had first regained consciousness to find himself marooned on the blasted island. It was time he turned his energies to finding a way back to the *Raven* and more important matters.

Shoving himself to his feet, he became aware that his shirt was sweat-soaked and clung to his body. What was more, he felt gritty after his sleepless night and sorely in need of a bath. On an impulse he stripped off his shirt and boots and, leaving them with his weapons in a pile, dove headfirst into the water.

The salt stung his half-healed wound, but the cool depths cleared his head of any cobwebs. He surfaced, only to dive deep again. Idle curiosity led him toward the mouth of the cave.

It was bigger than he had first supposed. The entrance at the surface was perhaps a dozen feet or more wide and arched over the water about the height of a tall man. But underneath, it broadened and extended downward another good ten feet or more. Surfacing, Glenmorgan dragged in a deep breath.

He could feel the first renewed stirrings of excitement. The entrance allowed more than enough room for a large dinghy to pass through, and it had the added benefit of being virtually undetectable from the seaward. If he were a man with a large cache of gold to hide, he could hardly have found a better place for it.

Quickly, he left the water and, working swiftly, gathered some of the coconuts that lay on the sand where they had fallen. One by one, he split them open and dug out the kernel. Then, with the handle of the knife, he pounded the kopra into an oily pulp, kneading thick strands of coconut fiber into the mess until he had enough for two sizable torches. He was sweating again by the time he had finished wrapping the fibrous strands about the ends of two pieces of driftwood, but he did not stop to rest. Retrieving flint and steel from the leathern pouch, he removed their oilskin wrapping and carefully bound it about the head of one of the torches before kneeling to light the other. Finally, he

103

secured the pouch and his other things in a place well above the tide mark.

Moments later, a burning torch held high overhead and the second one to be lit later strapped to his back, he slipped into the water.

This was not the first time Glenmorgan had ever been in a cave. In his pirating career, he had found various caverns along barren strips of shore useful for secreting stores of ammunition or even plunder from ships that had had the misfortune to cross his bows. And each time he had entered the beckoning maw to gaze down the murky entrails leading into the depths of the earth, he had felt the stirring of a boyish sense of adventure quite different from the serious business that brought him there. This time was no different. If anything, the feelings were stronger than ever.

Perhaps it was only that for the time being he could leave behind the dark business that had been driving him for too long. Or perhaps it was because he was alone and consequently was relieved of the necessity of being Capt. Mad Mike Glenmorgan. For a short time he could revert to the old Michael Glenmorgan, a man with a simple love of adventure.

Or perhaps it was the cave itself.

The cave delved into the cliffs, a tunnel, neither narrowing or broadening, until the gaping maw was little more than a faint aperture of light behind him. He had the sensation of having entered a tomb, haunted by the macabre flicker of torchlight against the walls, which were black and rippled by the endless wash of the sea. And then the tunnel turned, and the opening was lost from view.

With nothing to give him his bearings, he soon lost all sense of direction. There was only forward or backward, and he began to wonder if he was on a fool's errand. Perhaps fifteen minutes had passed since he had entered the cave. In short order he would have to light the second torch. And then he would have no choice but to turn back before it, too, burned out, leaving him to find his way in total blackness. The thought was not a pleasant one, but he had faced worse perils and lived to tell of them. Of perhaps greater danger was the inevitability of the tides. He had perhaps an hour before the tide turned. Certainly no more. But then, he told himself, he would be forced to head back long before that. Doggedly he kept on.

The sudden splay of light across the water had an unreal quality about it. Thinking at first that his mind must be playing tricks on him, he rubbed a hand over his eyes, but the shimmer in the distance refused to vanish. A shiver ran down his spine, and he could not shake the feeling that, here, he was an intruder. Even so, he was hardly prepared for the sight that greeted him as he rounded a final bulge of rock.

A great vertical gash, which appeared to have been blasted out of the bowels of the land mass by some primeval cataclysm, reared up before him, and beyond, bathed in light, yawned a magnificent vaulted chamber.

Glenmorgan gave a low whistle. The chamber of light was bigger than a king's ballroom. It had to be at least a hundred fifty feet in diameter, while the vaulted roof rose maybe thirty-five feet or more. He guessed it had once been a dry cave, carved out of the land by an underground river. Now the sea filled a depression at one end of the chamber, forming a pool. Worn shelves of lava rock, each roughly waist-high to a man, climbed out of the water like a primitive stairway, which ended at a ledge at the bottom of a sheer drop of perhaps fifteen feet or more. There, where the river, long since dried up or diverted, had once flowed in a great cascading fall, a rift had been formed in the ceiling, letting sunlight flood the lower reaches. Pink shower and woody vine, spilling through the rift from above, draped over the rock, itself covered with red and green algae. Everywhere there was color, from the turquoise blue of the pool to the iridescent green of the algae-encrusted rocks. It was beautiful, spellbinding, timeless. Once again Glenmorgan tried to shake off the feeling that he was trespassing.

Grateful to leave the water, the captain pulled himself onto one of the worn outcroppings of rock just as the torch began to sputter and go out. Hurriedly, he retrieved the second torch and lit it off the first. All of which left him damned little time to explore, he reflected wryly, as he let his glance sweep around the cavern.

If he were of a fanciful bent, he might have persuaded himself that the chamber, interspersed with columns of lava rock, was some nobleman's great hall, built on a grand scale. Except, of course, for the tangle of tree roots dangling from the ceiling. He shrugged. So much for fancy. The real question was, where would a desperate band of mutineers conceal a huge cache of stolen gold? If the treasure was there, he could see no sign of it. It was unlikely that they had buried it, not a vast treasure trove and in solid bedrock at that.

Without really knowing what he was looking for, he began to search along the walls for something, anything, that might have led to a place of concealment. His explorations led him to the far reaches of the cave, and still he found nothing. He was on the point of giving it up for another day, when the sound of trickling water lured him back to the falls. Spurred on by curiosity, he began to climb.

It was hardly a marvel that he had not earlier glimpsed the narrow crevice well above the tide line. Not only was it hidden in deep shadows cast by an overhang of rock, but it was further concealed by a thick curtain of vines.

His pulse quickening, he thrust eagerly through the vines, only to come to a startled halt once on the other side.

He was not sure what he had expected. Caskets of gold, certainly—enough to fill the hold of a sizable ship. What he found was a cozy cell, comfortably, if somewhat crudely, furnished. He had little difficulty in recognizing Pippin's handiwork in the hand-fashioned couch and dressing table complete with bench and mirror or in the rude table and single chair. Fresh water, seeping through a rocky crevice, gathered in a natural basin before trickling over the lip to seep underground again. A linen towel hung near the basin, along with a simple cotton frock like the one Meg had worn in Pippin's hut.

So, he mused. He had stumbled onto Meg's hideaway after all.

Using flint and steel he found on the table, he lit one of three oil lamps set about the chamber, then smothered out the torch for later use.

Like sunlight glancing off water, the thing of polished blue-green transparency caught the light and reflected it back again. As if drawn, Glenmorgan went to it.

It lay on the dressing table along with a comb and a simple necklace of seashells. His lips pursed in a low whistle. Perfectly round and roughly the size of the palm of his hand, it was like nothing he had ever seen before. He picked it up and saw his face reflected on its surface, the mirrorlike smoothness of glass or unruffled water. But it was not glass. He was not sure what it was. It was like a crystal without planes, transluscent and having a blue-green heart of flame. Whatever it was, it was exquisitely beautiful.

The comb, too, was curious—a mixture of seashells and something that resembled coral, polished to a fine smoothness. Yet it had nothing of the fragility of the coral with which he was familiar. It was beautiful, more like fine ivory.

Curiously reluctant to let go of the mysterious gemstone, he at last set it aside, and even then he was somehow aware of it as he made himself look elsewhere.

An old sea chest, similar to the one in Pippin's hut, next caught his attention. Kneeling down, he lifted the lid. Strange, he thought, finding nothing inside, but a few leatherbound books, charcoal and sketchpad, a slate of the sort used by schoolchildren, and materials for writing. Except for the gemstone, the comb, and the necklace, there was nothing in the cell of a personal nature, any more than there had been in Pippin's hut.

The girl, Meg, remained as much of a mystery as before.

Relighting the torch, he left the cell just as he had found it and climbed down to the pool. He had stayed longer than he intended, and much of the torch was already used up. Mentally he cursed. It looked as if he would have to find his way in the bloody dark after all.

Sitting down at the edge of the pool, he made ready to lower himself into the water.

"Captain—wait!" The low cry echoed off the walls and died away.

Glenmorgan turned and glanced upward. Above him, poised on the ledge at the bottom of the sheer drop, stood Meg, looking down at him.

Seven

"Meg!" exclaimed Glenmorgan, coming quickly to his feet. "Where the devil have you been? I've been looking for you."

"Have you?" Meg suffered an involuntary pang at the sight of the tall masculine figure clad only in breeches. How good he looked! She had to remind herself firmly of the vow she had sworn so that she would not forget the captain must be allowed to return to his own world—without any interference from her. Besides, she told herself grudgingly, the only thing he wanted from her was the Spanish gold from the *Argonaut*. "Why?" she shrugged, her first quick surge of joy at seeing him effectively squelched at the bleak reminder.

Glenmorgan's lips curled in a wry grin. Obviously she was not disposed to make things easy for him.

"Because I was worried about you," he answered. "Why do you think? You shouldn't have run away like that."

Frowning, Meg sat down and, folding her knees to her chest, propped her chin on them. "I see," she said. "You mean it was rude of me? Yes, I suppose it was. Do you expect me to apologize? I warn you, I don't think that I will."

"No?" Glenmorgan swallowed his impatience. "Then

109

you may be sure I won't expect it of you," he answered dryly. "Perhaps, however, it would not be too much to ask that you come down from there?" He spread his hands in front of him. "Simply that I may see for myself that you're all right."

Meg stared doubtfully at him. She would not be fooled into believing he had really been the least concerned about her.

"I assure you I am perfectly fine," she replied, as if she could not imagine why he should think otherwise. "But *you* won't be for long if you try to go back the way you came. In a matter of minutes the tunnel will be flooded and the chamber along with it."

Glenmorgan glanced down, made suddenly aware that the water, rising rapidly, was already level with the ledge on which he stood. He had put it off for too long. The tide had turned.

"You're right. I'll never make it that way," he said, not greatly displeased at being spared the necessity of traversing the tunnel in the dark. "Well, then. I guess I'll just have to come to you."

Meg could not quite subdue the quickening of her pulse as she watched him climb effortlessly toward her. Powerful and light on his feet, he moved with an easy, supple grace that sent a thrill of excitement through her. Just as strong, however, were her feelings of misgiving. She should never have come back, she told herself, already keenly aware of the effect he was having on her, had had from the first moment she had seen the tall figure emerge from her secret retreat and realized it was he. All in an instant she had felt a shock course through her body, a slow heat invade her limbs, and a dizzying sensation set her head a-spin. Her first instinct had been to duck into the shadows, and only the realization that Glenmorgan would be drowned if he attempted the tunnel had given her the courage to call out to him.

Oh, if only she could have remained hidden as she had planned to do, waiting to perhaps catch one last glimpse of him from afar! And yet, how foolish to think she could ever be satisfied with only a glimpse. In spite of all her fine resolves, the longing to be near him had drawn her unerringly back to the island.

She experienced a slightly queasy sensation as it was borne in on her just how close she had come to appearing before him revealed as a sea maiden in truth. Only the necessity of retrieving her gown from the cliffs above had prevented her from coming in as she normally did—through the sea passage that emerged at the bottom of the pool.

Perhaps it would have been better had she come that other way. Then all the agony of wishing for something that could never be would be over. He would have known the truth at last.

But already it was too late, she realized, her heart fluttering, as she went to meet the captain halfway.

Glenmorgan, panting a little from his climb, stood over her, gravely studying her. He was relieved to see none of the havoc in her smooth, young countenance that he had half expected to see. On the contrary, she looked calm and rested. Her eyes, clear and as hauntingly beautiful as he remembered them, returned his look steadily. Little did he realize the turmoil they hid, or how helpless she felt against the involuntary glow of warmth that spread through her as he took her hand in his.

"Meg," he said simply. Then, finding himself curiously at a loss for words, he squeezed her fingers and smiled. "I'm sorry if I've intruded where I had no right to be. I had no idea what lay at the end of the tunnel. If I had, I—"

"You wouldn't have come," she interrupted in a strangled

111

voice. Nervously she pulled her hand free. "It's all right. I know it was the gold you were after."

Glenmorgan gave an impatient gesture.

"Yes, it was the gold. I won't deny that I hoped to find it here."

"No, how could you?" Her laugh sounded unnatural in the brooding stillness of the cave. "But you didn't find it," she observed in a brittle voice. "How very disappointed you must have been. Instead of a treasure, you found only me."

"Dammit, Meg. I was worried sick about you."

Feigning indifference, Meg shrugged.

"Yes, I suppose you were." She frowned, as if giving the matter her serious consideration. "It must have been extremely unsettling when you thought I might not come back—with my grandfather gone, I am your only link to the *Argonaut* after all."

Meg's heart nearly stopped at the grim flash of his eyes.

"The gold had nothing to do with how I felt," he said. "But you're right to hold what happened against me." His lip curled cynically. "Hard as it may be for you to believe, I don't make it a practice to bed young and inexperienced girls—not even for gold. Meg, I never meant for it to go so far. The last thing I wanted was to hurt you."

Meg stared at him, unable to believe her ears. He thought she had been hurt because he made love to her? No, worse. He thought of her as a child too *young* to be made love to. How dare he! She would show him that he understood nothing about her!

"Does that mean you don't want to know where it is?" she asked innocently. "Are you going to tell me you are no longer interested in the gold?"

The muscle leaped along the hard line of Glenmorgan's jaw.

"I didn't say that."

112

"No, you didn't, did you? You said you never meant to make love to me. Then you *do* want it. Enough to try again to make me talk?"

He was tempted to try fingerscrews at that moment. And if that didn't work, maybe slow strangulation. She was playing with him and enjoying it. "Would it do me any good?" he asked, amused in spite of himself.

"I don't know. Did it ever occur to you that that might be why I came back? To find out?"

For a moment their eyes locked, his, hard glints of steel, and hers, limpid pools, innocently questioning.

The latter won out. Glenmorgan suddenly broke into reluctant laughter.

"It occurs to me that if that's what you had in mind, then I don't stand a chance," he said with a wry gleam of humor. "In which case, this discussion might be better put off for a later time. Sometime when I am not at a disadvantage." He paused, a bemused expression on his face. "I don't know about you, but suddenly I find that I'm hungry. I hope I'm not wrong in assuming there is a way to the cliffs above."

"Beside the falls—a concealed passage that leads to the top," she murmured somewhat distractedly. She could not recall ever having seen him laugh before. Magically, the hard lines about his eyes and mouth had vanished. He looked younger, less the daunting sea captain and more the reckless youth he must have been long ago, when he had lost his heart to Clarissa. Oh, if only she might have known him then.

"Meg?"

At the sound of her name, spoken in quizzical accents, Meg was made suddenly and uncomfortably aware that she must have been staring at him for some moments. She blushed, something she had never done before Glenmorgan had come into her life. Indeed, he was responsible for a great many changes in her previously uneventful existence, some of which she was not sure she liked at all.

Mentally shaking herself, she frowned irritably up at him. "You—you said you were hungry," she reminded him, more than ready to escape to the open air. "There is nothing here to eat. If we are going to gather fruit, we should go now, while there is still enough daylight to see."

A startled giggle broke from her at the sight of his comical grimace. "The idea displeases you?" she asked.

"I am heartily sick of fruit," he admitted frankly. "And dry bread. This is the Caribbean. Don't you and your grandfather ever have anything more palatable to eat?"

"I believe my grandfather's tastes are rather simple," she hedged, naturally reluctant to divulge that, since her sustenance came entirely from the sea, she seldom if ever had occasion to dine with the old man. The truth was, she had very little notion what people ate on the land. "Was there something in particular that you wished?"

"I wouldn't haggle at *acras de morue,* followed by *callaloo, crabes farcis, langouste, pain-boise,* and for dessert, a coconut custard," he answered whimsically. "But I'd settle for fresh clams, baked on the beach, along with lobster and any of the local substitutes for potatoes." At her blank look, he laughed and, taking her hand, began to climb. "Never mind. I'm hungry enough to eat anything we can find."

"No, please. Tell me," she insisted. "I've never heard of such things."

Something in her voice, a longing perhaps, made him look at her.

"You've lived all your life in the islands, and you know nothing about Creole food?"

Embarrassed, she dropped her eyes. "No, nothing." But almost immediately she lifted them again. "I told you, we are exiles, my grandfather and I. Until you and Drago came here, I had never spoken to a man other than my grandfa-

114

ther." She did not mention her father. There hardly seemed any point. He was little more than a vague memory to her now.

Mentally, Glenmorgan kicked himself for his tactlessness. He had known her life was isolated and lonely, but bloody hell, never to have spoken to another human being?

Turning and starting to climb again, he began to tell her about fish fritters, soup made of the leafy greens of the taro plant, stuffed crabs, spiny lobster, and finally breadfruit, which was prepared like a potato.

"No wonder you are weary of the fare in my grandfather's house," she exclaimed, "if that is what you are used to having." They had reached the ledge at the foot of the steep drop, and Meg took the lead, showing Glenmorgan the narrow entrance to a side passage, clearly a branch of the underground falls. Less sheer, it was a relatively easy climb over the boulder-strewn falls. "Are all your meals so lavish?"

"Lavish?" Glenmorgan laughed. "Maybe, compared to ship's food. It would hardly be considered an appetizer at some of the feasts I remember as a boy on my father's plantation."

He was never quite sure afterward how he went from a dissertation on French cuisine to the subject of his boyhood in Carolina. Nevertheless, as they emerged from the passage into broad daylight and stood on the cliffs overlooking the open sea on the left and the tranquil cove on the right, he found himself describing the moss-draped trees that touched over the lane leading up to Marigold, the home Turlough Glenmorgan had built for his bonny wife, Mary.

"The house stands on a bluff a little way off the Ashley," he said, seeing in his mind's eye the great square house with its pillared porch, shining whitely in the sun. "My father wanted me to take my place among the landed gentry, but I hated farming. I wanted to be with him, in the Town

115

House, overlooking the wharf where the Glenmorgan ships rode at dock. I lived for the spring, when the entire family traveled down the river to Charles Town on cypress canoes. They were big enough to carry fifty or sixty barrels of rice in a single load, and it took a dozen strong men to ply the oars. We'd stop along the way to visit friends along the river." At his harsh laugh, Meg stared at him in wonder. "What a fool I was to begrudge my mother and sisters the pleasure of those stopovers! I couldn't see then what such things meant to them. I could only think of getting back to the sea, to the ships and the men who sailed them."

"And why shouldn't you?" queried Meg, puzzled by the bitterness in his voice. "You were only a boy, who wished to be like his father."

Glenmorgan's piercing glance flew to her in something like surprise.

"You sound like my mother," he answered, smiling a little in amusement. "My father used to bellow like a bull whenever he discovered I had snuck out again. It was always left to my mother to smooth things over. 'He's a Glenmorgan, Turlough,' she used to say. 'Where should he be but down at the wharf, learning his father's business?' Well, I learned the family business all right. And while I was about it, my mother and sisters lost everything—including my father and Marigold."

Meg winced at the hard glint in his eyes as he gazed, unseeing, out over the sea. He was thinking about Logan Tharp again, she knew, and the vengeance that awaited him in the place called Charles Town. Oh, if only she could make him see how pointless it was to waste his life brooding over what could not be changed. Turlough Glenmorgan was gone, and there was nothing his son could do to bring him back again. But *she* was here. She could make him forget the past, if only she dared and he gave her the chance!

116

She started as Glenmorgan, appearing to shake himself, came out of his thoughts in time to catch the fierce flash of her eyes. A single eyebrow shot toward his hairline.

"Now what, I wonder, have I done to make you look at me like that?" he said quizzically.

"I—I beg your pardon?" Meg stammered, uncertain how to take the humorous curl of his lips.

"For a moment, there, it looked as if you could eat me alive."

"Eat you?" Meg gasped at the thought. "Is that what you think of me? By the faith, I should rather die than eat human flesh."

Glenmorgan's eyes leaped with amusement.

"You cannot know how relieved I am to hear it."

Meg eyed him doubtfully.

"You—you are laughing at me," she said. "Why? Because I am too stupid to realize that people do *not* eat one another where you come from?"

Her voice broke at the end, and furious with herself, she turned abruptly away.

She heard him sigh. "No," he said.

She sensed him draw near, nearly winced as his fingers closed firmly about her arm. Gently, he turned her to face him and, with a hand under her chin, forced her to look up at him. In spite of herself, Meg trembled at his touch.

"You are," he said, "undeniably stubborn, short-tempered, and quick to jump to conclusions. But you are far from being stupid." He shook his head in apparent bafflement. "I can't begin to grasp what you are. I have the feeling a man could travel all over the world and never find another like you. Or maybe it's me. Maybe I've lived the life of a pirate for so long I've forgotten there are people who don't prey on the weaknesses of others. It's the one thing that's kept me alive—knowing it's a hell of a lot safer not to take loyalty or trust for granted. They have to be

117

earned. I'd lay my life on the line for a man like Dick Chapin because he's done the same for me on more than one occasion. But there are damned few like him." Suddenly he stopped, a wry gleam in the look he bent upon her. "You don't understand a thing I've said, do you?"

He was wrong. She understood a great deal more than he had put into words. It was all there to read in the stern lines of his face—the bitter lessons that had been forced on him by a woman's betrayal and the treachery of evil and greedy men. But those were not things she could tell him.

Making herself smile, she lifted her eyes to his.

"I understand," she said simply, "that I have a great deal to learn."

Glenmorgan nodded, satisfied.

"Good," he said. "Now, if you are ready, I suggest we go down to the beach and see what we can forage for supper."

In normal circumstances, Meg would have taken the easy way down—a high dive off the cliffs. This time, however, she had to be satisfied with showing the captain the long way around. By the time they had retreated from the cliffs and worked their way down the hillside to the cove, the afternoon was nearly spent.

Glenmorgan went straight to the place where he had left his sword and the other things and donned his boots and shirt before initiating the search for whatever was edible. The island abounded in coconuts, avocados, papaya, guave, and a myriad of other fruits, which were readily available. It took more ingenuity to locate the tuberous malanga, some wild onions, vegetable pears, and native "yams" found in the jungle.

He was amazed to discover how little Meg knew about the edible plants on the island. Charles Town abounded in imports from the West Indies, as well as immigrants, so that he had been familiar from earliest boyhood with most of the delicacies that came from the Caribbean. He had been forced to learn even more when his survival had depended on it. His jaw hardened at the memory of another deserted island and the weeks spent plotting his revenge against the man who had put him there. That had been seven years ago, and the man had been Logan Tharp. Fortunately, he had escaped, and he had made it a point after that to familiarize himself as much as possible with everything pertaining to the islands, a practice that had helped him elude capture by the King's Navy on more than one occasion. It was perhaps little wonder, then, that he should find Meg's almost total lack of familiarity with anything but the most elemental foods more than a little puzzling.

She was, however, to prove an apt pupil, delighting in being the first to spot the leafy greens of a malanga, once he had introduced her to them, or the drooping flowers of the wild onion. She was somewhat less enthusiastic about searching out land crabs and absolutely refused to venture into the water to harvest various mollusks that clung to the rocks.

"I am in no mood for a swim," she declared, unable to tell him the real reason for her refusal to enter the water. She had never learned to swim in her human form. After all, there had never been a reason to until now. "Besides, I cannot think why you should want shellfish," she added, making no attempt to hide her abhorrence. "They are living creatures, no less than you or I."

Glenmorgan laughed, clearly amused.

"On the contrary," he replied, "they are *only* creatures, which makes them a great deal less than you or I. What's more, prepared properly, they are extremely pleasing to the taste. As you, my girl, are soon to discover for yourself."

"You are mistaken, Captain," she shouted after him as he dove into the water. "I shall never be induced to do anything so utterly barbaric."

119

Stubbornly holding to her word to have nothing to do with eating anything that swam or crawled, she withdrew a short distance up the beach and sat down on the sand with her knees folded to her chest. And there she remained while the captain gathered shellfish, laid wood for a fire, and readied the vegetables and mollusks for cooking. Pretending a total disinterest, she nevertheless could not keep herself from watching curiously out of the corner of her eye as Glenmorgan placed several large stones in the center of the fire and then lit it. At last, plopping down on the sand, he pulled his boots on and shrugged into his shirt before settling with his back against a large piece of driftwood to watch the fire burn.

In all that time he had not spoken a word to the girl, nor did he now. Pleasantly tired after his rather long day, he was content to soak in the slow heat of the fire. Folding his hands behind his head, he let his muscles go lax and waited.

He said nothing when Meg finally came and sat down stiffly beside him, though a keen observer might have noted a faint twitch at the corners of his handsome lips. There was something irresistible, after all, about a fire on a clear night, with the gentle lapping of waves in the background. After a moment or two, he reached out and pulled her, unresisting, into the cradle of his arm.

Glenmorgan felt a quiet peacefulness steal over him as they sat and silently watched the flames. It was rare to find a female who apparently knew when words would have spoiled the moment. Most of the women of his acquaintance would have found any prolonged silence intolerable. He was ruefully aware, in fact, that any other female would already have accused him of gross neglect. But not Meg. Curled up beside him, her cheek resting against his chest, she appeared dreamily unaware that the evening was slipping by without a single exchange of clever conversation. She was a strange creature, he mused. Restful rather than boring, she filled the lonely void by her mere presence. Suddenly he realized that he had not for a very long time felt so totally relaxed and at peace with the world.

By the time the fire burned down, leaving the rocks sizzling hot and ready for cooking, a full moon stood high overhead. Meg suffered a sharp pang of disappointment as Glenmorgan withdrew his arm and left her. A few moments later, however, she felt a trifle sickened as, in the light of the moon, she watched the captain place the shellfish and vegetables on the rocks and cover them with wet seaweed before burying them with sand.

"Why did you do that?" she demanded, dismayed that he had ruined the seaweed, the one thing in the entire meal that was remotely palatable to her.

Glenmorgan turned from completing his task, struck by the sharpness of her tone.

"I beg your pardon?" he said.

"Your supper," she answered, pointing to the mound of sand. "You have buried it. Why? Have you decided not to eat it after all?"

"Would it make you feel better if I had?" he countered.

Meg blushed and dropped her head, keenly aware that, earlier, she had behaved rather badly. Grudgingly, she even went so far as to acknowledge to herself that Glenmorgan had a right to his own preferences, just as she had a right to hers. The sea had taught her long ago that, in the cycle of things, there was a place for both.

"It is a matter of indifference to me," she ventured at last, "what you choose to put in your stomach. On the other hand"—Lifting her head, she looked at him squarely—"You, I trust, will grant me the same tolerance. I will not, indeed cannot, eat an animal."

After only the briefest hesitation, Glenmorgan nodded.

"Fair enough," he agreed, but inside he was troubled. It

was not simply her abstinence that bothered him. That, he supposed he could attribute to a sort of squeamishness on her part. Not everyone relished the idea of eating something they had seen living only moments before. No, it was something else. In fact, it was more than any one thing. It was the realization that he had never seen her take any sort of sustenance in his presence or her grandfather's. Nor had he seen any sign that she partook of any meals in her cavern retreat. There were no dishes, no utensils, not even a drinking cup. Those things, of course, while somewhat odd, might have had a reasonable explanation. It was not really her eating habits that bothered him anyway. It was the unstated assumption that lay underneath. Obviously, she abhorred the taking of a life, no matter how small or insignificant. How, then, must she view a man like himself, who was notorious for the men he had killed?

It was not a comfortable thought, and he didn't like the direction it would seem to be leading him. He had never felt the least compunction for the things he had done either for survival or vengeance, and he was damned if he would start now. The men he had killed had met their just deserts. Of that, he had not the slightest doubt. *Or* that he would one day meet over drawn swords the one man left alive who deserved more than any of the others to die. Why, then, should it matter *what* the girl might think of him or his affairs? The answer, he told himself, was that it didn't, and yet somehow he was not totally satisfied.

"Captain?"

The girl's voice, questioning him, brought him out of his reverie.

"Yes? What is it? I'm afraid my thoughts were elsewhere."

"I know," Meg said, well aware from his brooding expression the general vicinity of his musings. "I'm sorry if I disturbed you."

Glenmorgan smiled and shook his head.

"Don't be. You were right to recall me." Stretching out on his side next to her, he propped his head on one elbow so he could look at her in the moonlight. "One day you will learn that a beautiful woman never apologizes for what is due her. You deserve better company than I have been tonight. But perhaps I can still make it up to you, if you let me. Tell me, what was it that you wanted to know?"

Meg shifted nervously. She wished that he would not look at her that way. It made her feel all quivery inside. He almost made her believe that he really did think she was beautiful.

"It—it was nothing," she stammered, her eyes on her finger drawing wavy lines in the sand. "I was simply curious. You never really answered my question earlier. Why did you bury your supper?"

"So that it can cook," he explained, concealing his amazement that she apparently knew as little about cooking as she did about food. "Burying it holds the heat in. Don't worry. I haven't ruined it. Besides improving the taste, the seaweed keeps the sand off. The steam from it helps everything to cook slowly, with the result that the food practically melts in your mouth."

"I see," said Meg, who did not understand at all why he should wish to go to all that trouble. Sea plants were made to be eaten in their natural state. But perhaps it was different with those that grew on the land. As for the poor creatures, she would not let herself even think of them.

Glenmorgan, well aware that her mood was rather more subdued than before, set about to woo her back again. This was not a particularly difficult task. He was possessed of a keen intellect, a vast store of experience, and a compelling sense of humor. Meg listened spellbound as he described the far lands he had visited, laughed at his humorous anecdotes about people and places, and felt her blood run hot then cold as he related a few of his more harrowing adventures.

The one thing he could not do was draw her into talking about herself. Whenever he tried, she always changed the subject, turning it back to him with an adroitness that was surprising, considering her previous lack of social intercourse. Obviously she was intelligent. What was more, she demonstrated that she was not only willing, but more than able, to match him in exchanges of wit. His singlemost advantage lay in his greater knowledge of the world in general, something that she more than made up for with a penetrating insight into particulars. She was like no one he had ever known before.

Refreshingly natural and displaying an artlessness that was wholly captivating, she reminded him of a lovely, precocious child. And yet not a child, he decided, keenly aware of her woman's body beneath the clinging gown as he bent to retrieve their supper from the sand. Firmly banishing such dangerous thoughts, he handed her a cooked malanga on a palm leaf.

Her brow wrinkled as she concentrated on balancing the tuber, the size and shape of a small potato, on the makeshift plate. Then, smiling uncertainly at the captain, she sniffed the steamy fragrance. He was just on the point of humorously apologizing for the lack of tableware, when, to his startled amazement, she popped the steaming hot vegetable into her mouth and took a generous bite out of it.

Her reaction was inevitable and wholly excusable in the circumstances. Uttering a strangled cry of pain, she spewed the mess out with a violent gust of air. Instantly she leaped to her feet and started toward the water, only to halt in painful confusion as she realized that she dared not take that avenue of escape. It was left to the captain to come to her rescue. Hacking the top off a coconut with his knife, he forced her to drink its sweet, soothing milk.

Hardly knowing whether to be grateful for his having come so swiftly to her aid or whether to call down the fury of a storm on him for having been the cause of her discomfort, she drew in a long, shuddering breath.

"You—you did that on purpose," she gasped, staring accusingly up at him out of watery eyes.

"Don't be a fool," he retorted brusquely. "Any child knows you can't eat a potato before it cools." Angry with himself for not having foreseen and thus prevented what had happened, he drove the knife into the sand.

Meg swallowed and blinked her tears away.

"*I* didn't," she said quietly.

Glenmorgan, sensing a slight tremor in her voice, glanced sharply up at her. Expecting to see tears, he was startled to find himself staring into green eyes, shimmery with barely suppressed mirth. Their glances locked in sudden, mutual understanding. The next instant they both burst into laughter.

"I think," gasped Meg, when she had sufficiently regained her breath to talk, "that I shall never forget the look on your face when I screamed and spat out that awful stuff."

"I would be lying if I said you did not take me by surprise." Hellsfire! "Surprise" did not begin to cover what he had felt. Astonishment was more like it, and the inevitable realization, no matter how farfetched, that tonight she had been introduced to her very first hot meal. Good God, he could not begin to explain that one away! Grimly he wondered if Pippin could. Reaching out, he took her hand and laid it in his palm. "I'm sorry, Meg. It simply never occurred to me to warn you."

Meg blushed, suddenly wanting nothing more than to run away and hide her embarrassment. "No, why should it?" Nervously she pulled her hand away. "It is I who should beg your forgiveness. I'm afraid I have quite ruined your supper."

125

"Oh no you don't," Glenmorgan warned. "Don't think for a moment you're going to use this unfortunate incident as an excuse to escape. I'm still hungry enough to eat a whale. And you, my girl, are going to stay and dine with me."

Meg, who could not have found the will to resist him even if she had wanted to, allowed herself to be led back to her seat beside the charred remains of the fire. Reluctantly, she accepted another of the detestable malangas, along with freshly cut avocado halves, guava, and the juice of a coconut, drunk from the shell. Wanting to please him, she was determined to at least pretend to enjoy the meal, only to discover, to her surprise, that she did not have to pretend at all.

No doubt the captain had more than a little to do with her enjoyment. Gently teasing, he soon made her forget that she had not dined with anyone since the death of her mother when Meg was twelve, let alone with a landsman. It was all very pleasant. So much so, that she found herself wondering how she would ever be able to go back to the way it was before he had come into her life. How clearly she could see now how lonely that life had been!

She had been born *dainaon,* which literally meant "two-in-one," and *muirsiol,* "a child of the water," and though metamorphosis was instinctive and therefore involuntary, based as it was on certain life-preserving triggering mechanisms, a mermaid learned the words of command to gain control over the process. Otherwise, a rain shower on land would have been enough to trigger the transformation from human to mermaid. Until she was old enough to control the basic instinct of metamorphosis and to understand that she must not reveal her true form to others, she was kept hidden from her father's people. And later, when she might have formed friendships with other children, her mother never ceased to remind her that she was different from them and that they would turn on her if they ever discovered what she was. From afar, she watched the human children play and wondered if, inside, she was truly so different from them. Then one night, when she was in her ninth year, she met the boy, Caleb.

There was a storm, and she was having difficulty concentrating on the book her father had given her to read. She sat in the window seat, the book propped on her knees, but her gaze wandering more often than not to the rain-spattered window and beyond, to the palm trees writhing in the wind. All day she had had the exhilarating sense that something was going to happen, had glimpsed on the gemstone's surface clouded images of a carriage, the anxious face of a woman, and a boy, his eyes dark with pain. She was not surprised when the knock came at the door.

They laid the boy in the bed in the guestroom, which was never used. No one noticed Meg slip into the room behind them. The boy had fallen and struck his head and was already deep into the coma from which there would be no calling him back again. As her father gently led the weeping woman from the room, Meg crossed to the bed. He was young, no more than seven or eight, and he had brown hair that lay in curls against his forehead. Compelled by some instinct she did not understand, she touched her hands to either side of his forehead and began to hum.

Afterward, she could not explain what happened. It was as if for a time she merged with the boy's essence, melding her strength to his and drawing him back with her to consciousness. She blinked and opened her eyes. The boy was awake, his gaze wide and knowing on hers. He smiled. Then slowly his eyelids drifted down over his eyes.

Quietly, she stole out the French doors on to the terrace, while behind her, her father reentered the room to find his patient sleeping quite normally. The next day they took him home, and she never saw him again, but the boy, Caleb,

127

remained a part of her, for in that brief moment of joining, she had known everything about him and he about her. It was not the same as *hrum*. They were both too immature for that, but it was akin to it. She knew when the ship bearing him to London two years later foundered in a storm and went down. She knew when his spirit left him.

And so the pattern of her life continued as it had before. Her mother and she came at night to be with Richard in the house that stood alone on the edge of a small, secluded bay, but before dawn, they returned to the sea. She had loved her father, who had taught her to read the books of his people and had instilled in her a yearning for adventure. But it was her mother who gave her an understanding of who and what she was.

Sheela taught her the songs of the old ones and the strictures that protected and bound her people to the ways of the god. While mastery of the songs came easily to Meg, understanding seemed something she was born with. By the age of two she could summon the whales with a thought, by three, wind and storm. At four, she fashioned the gemstone from earth, fire, and water.

Meg never forgot the look on her mother's face when Sheela found her on the beach one night molding the liquid flame that was the heart of the gemstone. Every mermaid could sense the vibrations in solid matter and especially in crystals, but the art of crystal binding had been lost when the city of circles was swallowed up by the sea. When Sheela asked Meg what she was doing, the child replied that she was crystal-singing. She had not known how to explain it any other way. She knew now that the song had come from inside herself, a song of her own essence, her own being. The gemstone was a crystallization of that song, and through it, she could channel powers that not even her mother could command. The least of these was the power to see, if the god willed it, images reflected on the gemstone's surface of past, present, and future events. The greatest, she dared not even think about. It was the power to disrupt the bonds of energy and matter, the same power that had nearly destroyed the old ones.

With awe in her voice, her mother had said Meg was *celede*, "one chosen to serve the god." But Meg had watched first her father die and then her mother and had been powerless to save either of them. For the first time in her life, she had known what it was to be truly alone, for with her mother gone, there was no one to know and understand what it was to be *dainaon*. Not even her grandfather, as much as he loved her and tried to make up for the loss of her parents, could go where she went, do what she did, feel the bewildering yearnings awakening within her. Bitterly she wondered how one could serve the god of a people who had apparently vanished from the face of the earth.

And then Glenmorgan had come into her life and given her a glimpse of the happiness that might have been hers if she only dared to snatch it to her. She could have asked for no greater joy than to be joined with Glenmorgan in the way of the old ones, their minds melded so that, though they were free to think their separate thoughts, they shared an apprehension of each other's total life experience and an empathic awareness of one another. One so joined with another was never alone. And yet it was more than that. When she had given herself to Glenmorgan, a bond of sorts had been established, a bond that would have grown stronger with time. But the empathic awareness was one-sided. She was joined to him, but he remained *uileun* and *sgarid:* "alone" and "apart." Only in *hrum* could they be made *gnath*—"knowing." Only in *hrum* could their thoughts and physical vibrations become a harmonic oneness, a song. And only through *hrum* could Glenmorgan share the magical powers that were an integral part of her, become as she was.

It was something she and Glenmorgan could never have. *Hrum* was forbidden between a mermaid and a landsman, and tonight must be their last night together. Somehow she must find the strength to let him go.

Firmly, she banished such sobering thoughts from her mind, telling herself that she would not let anything spoil the brief time that they had. Then, suddenly, she found it difficult to think at all as the captain reached up to wind a silvery lock of her hair about his finger.

"Meg," he murmured, his eyes speculative on her lovely countenance, "what the devil are you doing here? In the middle of nowhere, with no one to talk to but an old man. Where do you come from? Who are your people, your parents? Have you no one except your grandfather to care what happens to you?"

Instantly Meg stiffened, alarmed at having been caught off guard. She had known the time would come when he would start to ask questions, had been warned of it by her grandfather before he left. Nevertheless, she was woefully ill prepared.

"No," she exclaimed on a sharply expelled breath, "please. You mustn't ask such things. I have no parents, and I live here with my grandfather because there is no place else for us. That is all I can tell you."

"All that you can tell me—or only what you are willing to divulge? Dammit, Meg. I have to know."

Instantly she bridled, the spell of the evening totally shattered.

"Why must you know?" she flashed passionately back at him. "Why must it always be what *you* want or must have?"

"Because," he said, "I have lain with you. I took what

130

was not mine to take. And now whether you like it or not, I am responsible for you."

Meg went pearly white.

"Responsible for me? How?" she demanded, her stomach suddenly queasy. "I fail to see how the one is related to the other."

"You may be sure that your grandfather will not fail to see it," Glenmorgan noted dryly. Meg frowned, uncertain as to his meaning. Immediately the captain softened his tone. "Meg, you are a young female without knowledge or experience of men. I, unfortunately, have not that excuse."

"No, how could you?" she was quick to point out. "You are a man."

Glenmorgan's teeth clenched.

"Dammit, Meg! Don't play games with me."

"I will not play games, if you will not shout."

Glenmorgan choked. Good God, this was going to be more difficult than he had thought.

"Very well, you're right," he said, drawing a deep, steadying breath. "I shouldn't have shouted. In fact, let's just forget I said anything."

Meg's hands clenched into fists at her sides.

"Now you are angry with me," she said, wondering how everything could change so quickly.

"I'm not angry." Shoving himself to his feet, the captain gazed speculatively down at her. She looked incredibly beautiful in the moonlight, and in spite of the defiant tilt of her chin, very young and uncertain. Glenmorgan sighed. "You really don't have the least idea what I've been trying to tell you, have you? Never mind. It's probably better that way." Turning, he started for a pile of driftwood with the intention of building a new fire to drive the chill of night away.

"You have been trying to tell me that it was wrong—what happened between us," Meg stated without warning in a

131

very clear voice. Glenmorgan halted in midstride. "And that because of it, you feel an obligation toward me. I think in another minute or two you would even have proposed marriage to me." Glenmorgan came around, an expression of disbelief on his face. She was standing very tall and very straight, looking at him. "That is what my grandfather told me to expect from you," she said.

Eight

Glenmorgan's voice cut across the silence.

"The old man told you that, did he?" he demanded, coming a step toward her.

He appeared unnaturally calm, and yet Meg had little difficulty sensing the same hard glitter of purpose about him that he had had the night he faced Drago. Why? she wondered. What had she done to make him look at her one moment out of eyes that had spread a slow warmth through her veins and the next with such cold, piercing intensity that she felt frozen by it?

Unconsciously she pressed a hand to her heart.

"Yes," she said.

"What else did he tell you?"

"Nothing." Nothing, anyway, that mattered now, she reflected, her grandfather's words ringing in her mind—a warning that she had understood too late: "Mark me well, child. In spite of his reputation, Glenmorgan was born a gentleman. It'll do neither of you any good if he's put in the position to think he's honor-bound to marry you. Think, Meg, what would you do then?"

The old man had been trying to warn her to keep Glenmorgan at a distance, for the captain's sake as well as her own. It hadn't made any sense to her—all his talk about

133

honor and a gentleman's code. How much less had she understood his attempt to explain a landsman's concept of marriage. Among her kind, after all, one didn't ask to be joined. It just happened. As it had with her and Glenmorgan. Only something had gone terribly wrong. *She* was joined heart and soul to the captain, while he felt nothing at all! Even now, it hardly made sense. Nothing had—until the captain had spelled it out for her in blunter terms. Then she had suddenly realized what her grandfather had been trying to tell her. To Glenmorgan, this thing called "marriage" was an arrangement, an agreement, which apparently had nothing at all to do with the intimacy of bonding one with another. On the contrary, she thought, as everything began to come together for her, it was obvious the captain saw it as a price one paid for having given in to such intimacy!

Glenmorgan ran a hand through his hair and then looked at her as if he were putting a few things together as well.

"Where is your grandfather?" he asked in a voice that left little doubt that the conclusions to which he had come had put him in a dangerous mood. Meg felt her mouth go suddenly dry. "How long did he plan to stay away before he decided he'd given you enough time to do your part?"

Meg blinked, stunned and bewildered at the contempt in his voice. Worse, she hadn't the least idea what he was talking about.

"How long?" she repeated. "He didn't say. How could he? He didn't know how long it would take to—to . . ." Realizing what she had been about to reveal, she stopped and bit her lip.

Glenmorgan's laugh was decidedly unpleasant.

"No, of course he couldn't." Suddenly he cursed. "Good God, you took a lot for granted! What the devil made you think I'd give a bloody damn that I'd bedded a virgin?"

"I—I didn't—" Meg started.

Glenmorgan cut her off with a savage gesture.

134

"That's right. You didn't. If you had thought, you might have known all you had to do was ask for my protection." A shadow that might have been bafflement passed over his hard features. "I would have taken you and your grandfather anywhere you wanted to go. Set you up in a house. Given you money or anything else you needed. Dammit, Meg. You didn't have to climb into bed with me for it."

Meg's eyes widened in startled disbelief.

"You think that's why I did it? Because I wanted a house and—and money?" The notion struck her as indescribably funny. Perhaps it was the unbearable tension or the sudden relief of discovering the absurdity of the delusion under which he was laboring. Whatever it was, she found herself overcome with an irresistible urge to laugh.

"A—a house?" she said unsteadily. "And—and money?" Whatever would she have done with either? She choked. Then at sight of Glenmorgan, grim-faced with amazement, she broke into uncontrollable laughter. "O-oh, it is too absurd," she gasped, dashing tears of mirth from her eyes.

Glenmorgan, who did not see anything the least amusing in what he had said, stared at her with narrowed eyes. Now what the devil? he reflected, beginning to wonder if he had missed something along the way. The girl was either demented or totally lost to any sense of decency. Whatever it was, he was bloody damned well going to find out.

Propping a booted foot on top of the driftwood, he leaned an elbow on his knee and grimly set himself to wait.

At length, Meg's paroxysms gave way to a last convulsive hiccup. Feeling a trifle weak, she sank down on the sand and, leaning on one hand, drew in long shuddering breaths. It was not till she had got her breathing back to normal again that she became aware of a brown leather boot planted ominously in the sand almost beneath her nose.

Whimsically, she let her gaze travel slowly up the calf

135

to a muscular thigh, a lean waist and narrow torso, and finally a pair of steely eyes.

Glenmorgan's lips curled in a smile that was singularly devoid of humor.

"Feeling better?" he asked.

Meg smiled demurely back at him—a demureness, he noted ironically, belied by an irrepressible sparkle of mirth dancing in her eyes.

"Oh, much," she answered, looking like a mischievous imp. "I can't imagine what got into me. I can't recall ever having laughed like that before."

"Odd," he commented in acerbic tones. "I had no idea I was such an amusing fellow."

Meg gasped. "Oh, please don't remind me. I don't think I could bear it."

Glenmorgan's eyebrow sardonically arched.

"Unfortunate, to say the least," he murmured silkily. "But you see, the joke totally escapes me. Perhaps you would be so good as to explain what you found so *blasted* amusing."

Meg carefully lowered her eyes. Oh dear, she thought, he *was* in a nasty mood. But then, he deserved it. It had been bad enough to discover he was thinking of Clarissa when he made love to her. That he thought she had done it for ulterior motives was simply beyond belief. And now he had the audacity to demand that she explain herself to him! Really, it was too much.

Deliberately she sat up, straightened the fabric of her gown sedately over her knees, and smoothed back her hair before deigning to reply.

"I'm sorry, Captain," she said composedly. "The fact of the matter is that I simply can't explain it."

Glenmorgan's foot came down off the driftwood.

"Oh, can't you?" he said ominously. Dropping down on his knee before her, he took her by the arms. "If it's not money, what are you after? Where is your grandfather? Dammit, Meg, I *will* have some answers."

Uncomfortably reminded once more of the deception her grandfather had forced upon her, she glanced guiltily away. Maybe she should tell him, she thought. In spite of what her grandfather had said, didn't Glenmorgan have a perfect right to know? Especially now that there was nothing the captain could do to stop the old man?

Determinedly she lifted her chin.

"He's gone to try and find your ship," she answered, flinging caution to the wind. "To warn her. Drago told us Logan Tharp has put a bounty on her. He will pay a handsome reward for any ship that can blow her out of the water."

Letting Meg go, the captain settled back on his heels. Good God, he thought. He should have known. Tharp was taking no chances on leaving anyone behind who had witnessed Lavoillet's confession. He wanted them all dead.

A grim smile touched his lips. No wonder Drago had been content to spare Mad Mike Glenmorgan's life. With the bounty on the ship, not her captain, there really had been no profit in killing him. But more than that, it would amuse Drago to take Tharp's blood money, knowing Tharp had failed to rid himself of Glenmorgan. Aye, he thought, Drago would be after the *Raven*. And how many others would there be, waiting for the day the ship sailed from English Harbor—if she had not sailed already?

Then it hit him. Dick Chapin and the others were free men now. They wouldn't be looking for it.

Grimly he shifted his eyes to Meg.

"Why didn't you tell me before? I should have been the one to go."

"You were hardly in any shape to go," Meg reminded him. "Besides, what chance would you have had if one of Tharp's men had recognized you? No one will know my

137

grandfather. He made me swear not to tell you. He said there was no need for you to know what you could not help. You would only wear yourself down with worrying."

Glenmorgan gave an impatient gesture.

"That was not his concern. *Raven* is my ship. Bloody hell, he doesn't stand a chance of finding her."

"Oh, but you're wrong," Meg hastened to assure him. "He will find her. She is still anchored in English Harbor."

It was a mistake. She realized it as soon as the words left her mouth. Glenmorgan realized it, too.

"How could you possibly know that?" he demanded with a sudden steely intensity that quite took her breath away.

"I—I don't, of course," she lied. She could hardly tell him, after all, that she had been to English Harbor the night before and seen the truth of it for herself. "At least I cannot be certain. Drago told us the ship was there the last he had heard, and I simply assumed it would be still. It is rumored your first mate refuses to believe you are dead. He has sworn to remain at anchor until—how did Drago phrase it?—'until hell freezes over, or until he finds proof you won't be coming back again.' "

"The crazy fool," muttered the captain, turning away to hide the sting of emotion in his eyes. "I might have known Dick would pull some fool stunt like that. The question is, will he believe the old man's story?"

"Very likely he will—when he sees your locket." She watched with interest as the captain clutched, in the old, instinctive habit, at his chest. "It's gone," she said, struck by the fact that he had not missed it till then. "Grandfather took it with him."

Slowly Glenmorgan let his hand drop.

"He's welcome to it, if it does the trick. And even if it doesn't"—he turned to look at her—"I'll be grateful that he tried."

She could see in his face that he was thinking of the risk

138

the old man had taken, and more—that he had been wrong about her. All at once she felt strangely uncomfortable.

"It's getting late," she said, climbing nervously to her feet. "I think it's time I took you back. Now, while there's still moonlight enough to show the way." She started toward the trail that led to her grandfather's hut. "You must be tired, and I—"

"Meg."

Whatever she had been about to say remained frozen on her lips. Motionless, she stood with her back to him, her heart pounding as she sensed him draw near. Then his hands closed gently on her shoulders. Feeling herself begin to tremble, she clenched her hands into fists and willed herself to be still.

"Meg," Glenmorgan murmured. "I misjudged you—and your grandfather. I was a fool to think either of you could have planned what happened. I'm sorry for that. Unfortunately, the fact that I was wrong doesn't change anything."

Meg stood very still. "I don't know what you mean," she said in a voice hardly above a whisper.

"Don't you?" Glenmorgan answered. "Meg, look at me."

Meg's stomach twisted into a knot at what she sensed was coming. He was going to leave her, and she must do nothing to stop him. Steeling herself to do what she must, she lifted her head and turned to face him.

"Meg, I—"

She did not give him the chance to finish.

"You don't have to say it, Captain," she blurted all in a rush, hoping that he could not sense the panic in her heart. "I know you don't want to marry me, and you needn't worry that Grandfather will hold you to it, for he won't. Nor will I. It's a—a silly custom, anyhow."

Glenmorgan's eyebrows swept up in his forehead. A silly custom, was it? He had heard marriage described in many ways before, but never quite like that, and certainly not by any female he had ever known before. Damn the chit for trying to make it easy for him to bow out! Not for the first time he experienced an uncomfortable twinge of conscience. It wasn't a feeling that he liked.

"What I want or don't want has nothing to do with it," he snapped. "I've done things I'm not proud of, but I have never made it a practice to ruin innocent females."

"Haven't you?" she queried to his amazement. "What a shame. Personally, I found it not at all displeasing to be ruined by you. It's the prospect of marriage that troubles me. I don't think I should like being tied to a man who asked me to be his wife simply because he felt obligated to do it. Very likely it would take all the enjoyment out of what caused him to marry me in the first place. And then where would we be? In such a case, I should much rather be ruined than wed, wouldn't you?"

Glenmorgan stared at her, apparently much stricken by her unconventional point of view. Good God, she was trying to be noble, a bloody damned martyr. If she had meant to scourge his conscience, she could have found no better way. At last he appeared to shake himself.

"Don't think," he warned, "that I don't see what you're trying to do. If circumstances were different, there wouldn't be any question. I would do the honorable thing. As it happens, however, honor is not the only consideration. I have to take into account that, married to me, you would be in constant danger."

"Then don't think of it," Meg suggested. "Marriage is obviously out of the question."

A scowl darkened Glenmorgan's masculine brow.

"*Dammit,* woman. I don't need you to make excuses for me. The simple fact is I cannot take you with me where I'm going."

Meg made an impatient gesture, irritated at his refusal to accept her acquiescence in the matter.

"I know," she agreed testily. "Better than you. I wish you would cease to let it concern you."

"Concern me! Is that what you think?" The captain paced a step, turned, and came back again. "Well, you're mistaken. It doesn't concern me at all."

"I'm relieved to hear it," Meg retorted, her voice rising in volume to match his. "In which case, I wish you would stop shouting!"

It seemed that she had at last and irrevocably gotten his attention. Pale-faced and steely-eyed, he stepped in front of her.

"Do you now?" he queried softly.

"I do," answered Meg.

For a moment they stared at each other, neither willing to retreat an inch. Then before she could stop him, Glenmorgan reached out and snatched her to his chest.

"Damn you," he muttered, his eyes twin points of flame boring into hers. "All the women in the world, and you had to be the one to save my life."

Meg stiffened with indignation.

"You are indeed to be pitied," she bitterly retorted. "If I had known the consequences, believe me I would have spared you that annoyance."

A hard gleam of a smile flashed across his lean countenance.

"On the contrary," he said, "you would have done just as you did. More's the pity."

Sensing something in that look that she did not trust, Meg belatedly broke into a struggle. Glenmorgan's arms tightened around her. The next instant, his mouth covered hers.

Glenmorgan in a fever had been one thing. Glenmorgan with his wits about him, Meg quickly discovered, was quite another.

He kissed her slowly, deeply, his mouth moving over hers

141

with sensual deliberation. He caused her thoughts to scatter before an onslaught of powerful emotions only he could call up in her. He conquered her will, melted her resistance. With a groan, she gave in to him, with her arms, clung to him. She knew she was utterly lost as his tongue, exploring the sweetness of her mouth, unloosed a swelling tide of arousal which she was powerless to stop.

Forgetting everything—Clarissa, her grandfather's warnings, her own resolve not to allow Glenmorgan to sacrifice his freedom for a moment's forbidden passion—she returned his kiss with a wild, uncontrollable hunger that took even Glenmorgan by surprise.

Taking the initiative, she turned it back on him, running her hands feverishly over his chest beneath his shirt, devouring him with her lips. And still it was not enough. She wanted more of him, all of him—his hard, powerful body with nothing to keep her from him.

Covering his mouth with hers, she kissed him, while with her hands she pulled the shirt down over his shoulders and arms.

Glenmorgan's hands stopped her as she reached next for the waistband of his breeches. Dazed, she looked up at him—into his eyes, glittery and dark in the moonlight.

"Meg, I . . ." he said in a voice husky with passion. At the look in her eyes, he stopped. She saw the muscle leap along his jaw, and then his mouth set with a sort of grim finality. "Bloody hell," he muttered to himself.

Holding her with his eyes, he undressed her and then hurriedly disrobed himself. Quickly, he knelt in the sand and, using their discarded clothing, made a place for them to lie. Then at last he came back to her.

Naked and unashamed, she stood waiting for him.

Glenmorgan felt a shock go through him at the sight of her. Tall and slender, her hair falling in silken waves around her back and shoulders to a willowy waist, she shone silvery in the moonlight. Indeed, her eyes were shimmering pools of reflected light in the perfect oval of her face, her skin soft and smooth, like ivory-colored satin. Long-limbed and beautiful, she was magnificent, every glorious inch of her. His loins ached to possess her.

Going to her, he drew her into his arms. She went willingly, her eyes huge and unafraid on his. Then at last with a groan he kissed her.

Meg hardly knew when he lowered her to the ground, his lips never leaving hers. She was lost in the magic of his hands moving skillfully over her body, stroking her, teasing her, mastering her and the secrets of her flesh. Feeling herself rising on a swelling sea of arousal, she clutched at his shoulders and arched against him. Mercilessly, he held her off. His mouth molded itself to the upthrust promise of her breasts, first one and then the other, until she writhed beneath him, her blood on fire with need for him. And still he was not satisfied. Spreading wide her thighs, he bent over her, trailing delirious waves of pleasure down her torso with his lips and tongue, until at last he came to the swelling bud of her desire.

At his moist caress, a keening sigh broke from her lips. Never had she known a woman's body could ache with such sweet torment. She felt herself rising, peaking on a swelling wave of rapture and cried out to him, not wanting to be alone.

Quickly, he came to her. The muscles of his neck and shoulders stood out as he poised above her, his own need an aching torment, and still he held back. Pressing his manhood against her swollen orifice, he teased and tormented her with shallow forays until her loins were moist and aching with desire. Meg groaned and reached out to him, and at last he entered her, slowly, carefully, the muscles of his neck corded with the effort to control his almost ungovernable need to plunge deeply, violently into her flesh.

In spite of his care, the pain came like a searing hot flame inside of her. Gasping, Meg clenched about his member.

Instantly, Glenmorgan stilled.

"Easy," he murmured. Leaning his weight on one elbow, he smoothed the hair back from her forehead and pressed his lips gently to her eyes, then her cheeks and finally the corner of her mouth. "Don't be afraid. It won't always hurt, I promise. Trust me, Meg. Let go of the pain."

In her anguish, the words meant nothing to her. It was the tone of his voice, low, gentle, reassuring. Fastening her eyes on his, she let herself be carried away from the pain. He began to move slowly inside her in gentle, pulsating thrusts, patiently building the rhythm, patiently arousing her again, until at last, lost in the slow sensuality of the cadence, she was moving unconsciously with him.

Never had she thought she could feel anything like the slow-building ecstasy of their climax. It engulfed her with a rippling explosion of sensations—his seed spewing forth within her, the shuddering burst of her own rapturous release, her flesh constricting in wave after wave of pleasure so intense it left her trembling and weak.

They collapsed together on their bed on the sand, Glenmorgan nuzzling her hair as she lay, wondrously sated, in the warm cradle of his arm. How she wished she might remain there forever! But at least there would be tonight, she consoled herself, her eyes growing heavy as she drifted irresistibly toward sleep.

Consequently, she was not aware how long Glenmorgan lay awake, staring somberly into the night.

The sun had hardly come up when she awakened to the chatter of birds in the trees and the chuckle of a laughing gull swooping down over the water. For a moment, she blinked in bewilderment, wondering how she came to be sleeping on the beach. Then instantly it all came flooding back to her. A soft pang of tenderness went through her as she became aware that she lay with Glenmorgan's arms around her, her cheek nestled against the hollow of his shoulder.

How strange and wonderful to wake up and find she was not alone! To feel the warmth of someone next to her! It was like nothing she had ever imagined before. How different from the sea, where it would have been difficult to embrace, let alone sleep in the arms of a loved one. And even if it were feasible, it could never be as wondrously sensual as on land with only the air to impede the sense of touch. Perhaps that was why her people had developed other means of achieving intimacy—the use of sound, for example, to create finely tuned vibrations, which not only gave pleasure, but communicated a wide range of nuances of feeling. A mischievous imp danced in her eyes as she speculated how the captain might respond to the *zhandeem,* which, culminating in the *hrum,* formed a major part of the ritual of courtship.

Of course, she herself had never seen or taken part in the love dance. She had only her mother's account, as it had been told to her by *her* mother, of the sensual fluidity of motion between male and female, the touching without touching in which pulsewaves transmitted from one to the other stimulated sensory organs within. It was a liquid stroking in which male and female approached and met, skimming past one another and back again in spiraling circles that grew smaller and smaller until at last they glided in slow, synchronous, intertwining swirls around and around each other. Their bodies, though never separated by more than an inch or two, never came in contact and yet were linked in ever-heightening sensory arousal. As they became lost in the ritual of arousal, the dance swelled, gaining mo-

145

mentum, reaching toward an overpowering need to achieve oneness. It was at the frenzied peak of physical desire that the final rite of *hrum* was initiated. Only then did they actually touch, coming together to achieve mental and physical rapture in the ultimate joining of bodies and minds.

Carefully she lifted herself on one elbow so that she could see Glenmorgan as he lay sleeping. He was dreaming, his eyes moving back and forth beneath his eyelids. Whimsically, she wondered if he was dreaming of her. How stern he looked, with the shadow of a beard along the lean line of his jaw, and yet younger, too, somehow. Perhaps, she mused, it was because in sleep the hardness was gone from his face. Suddenly it came to her that she might never see him like this again—vulnerable, his defenses down. Fiercely, she told herself that she must remember everything, every detail—like the way his hair shone blue-black in the sunlight filtering through the palm leaves.

Her eyes seemed inevitably drawn to the broad chest and the terrible scar, livid against the pallor of his skin. Against her protests, he had discarded the bandage the day before as they hunted land crabs and the elusive malanga plants, saying that it had served its purpose. The wound, while well on its way to being healed, still needed time, and he had not helped it in his reckless dash to rescue her and her grandfather. Regretfully, he would carry the scar with him forever, a grim reminder of how close he had come to death, indeed, how greatly he had been made to suffer. Eventually, however, as exposure to the sun banished his sickroom pallor and tanned his skin to its former deep golden brown, it would become less appalling in appearance.

With a sigh, she laid her head down over his heart and closed her eyes. His heartbeat, strong and steady against her ear, brought a bittersweet smile to her lips. She should go now, before he awakened, she told herself. She had already stayed too long.

Sternly, she quelled the ache in her heart and, forcing herself to do what she must, lifted her head. A startled gasp broke from her as she found herself staring into Glenmorgan's eyes.

For what seemed an eternity, but was only a second or two, he appeared to study her face. At last his lips twisted in an oddly rueful smile.

"Strange," he murmured. "I half expected you to be gone when I woke up."

Furiously, Meg felt her cheeks grow warm.

"I meant to be," she admitted. "I—I should have been. Grandfather warned me to stay away."

"On the contrary," he replied. Rolling over on his side, he pinned her neatly to the ground. "You should be exactly where you are."

Grinning at her squeal of surprise, he bent his head to nibble at her ear. "But your grandfather was right about one thing." Sampling next the tender flesh below her ear, he sent a delicious wave of pleasure shuddering through her. "You are far too beautiful to be left unchaperoned with any man, let alone one like me."

"Am—am I?" she quavered, hardly aware of what she said. "I know nothing of such things."

"Liar." His hands punished her for her supposed deceit, ruthlessly seeking out and finding places of exquisite sensitivity that she never knew existed. "Women are born knowing such things." He kissed her above the soft swell of her bosom, slowly working up to the rapid pulsebeat at her throat. Breathing a delirious sigh, she tipped her head back, baring her neck to his lips. "How to drive a man to madness with a look." Meg trembled as he kissed the side of her cheek and then her eyes, first one and then the other. "How to torment and beguile."

"You are—are wrong," she whispered unsteadily. "You—

you are thinking of Clarissa. I'm not like her. I'm not like anyone you have ever known before."

Her heart gave a small lurch as she felt him go suddenly still against her. She had been right. He had been thinking of Clarissa. Oh, how she would like to entrap the evil creature in a web of enchantment. Or better yet, confine her on some forgotten island for what she had done to him.

Glenmorgan released a low expulsion of breath.

"No," he said after a moment, "you aren't like her."

Meg searched desperately for something to fill the sudden, ensuing silence. Finding nothing, she pulled away from him and sat up.

"I must go," she said. "I shouldn't be here with you like this."

Before she could get up, Glenmorgan caught her by the wrist.

"No, stay." Sensing the resistance in the slim member, he gentled his grasp. "Meg, we need to talk."

"No. I can't," she murmured. "I—it was a mistake for me ever to have come back."

"Why?" he demanded, more harshly than he had intended. "Because of something your grandfather has told you about me?" Abruptly he let her go. "Aye, that's it, isn't it? Well, he was right to warn you away from me. I am, after all, hardly different from Drago and his men. But then, you witnessed that for yourself, didn't you? You heard what they called me—'Mad Mike' Glenmorgan. You saw for yourself the power of that name. It inspires fear in the hearts of men like Drago. And I have been at great pains to make it so."

"No!" she cried, flinging back her hair to look at him with tumultuous eyes. "You are *not* like Drago. And my grandfather has told me nothing about you. He—he did not have to."

Her voice faltered at the end. Biting her lip, she turned her head away.

Glenmorgan stared at her, conscious of perplexity and a growing sense of exasperation. With an effort he quelled his impatience.

"Then why?" he asked. "Tell me what you're thinking." Grasping her by the arms, he shook her gently. "Meg, look at me."

She swallowed and at last lifted her head.

"Tell—tell me why you want the gold," she said, her eyes searching his face. "Please. I must know. I truly do not understand your obsession."

"Don't you?" Mirthlessly, he laughed. "Very well, I'll tell you. The blame for its loss was laid on my head by those who ruined my father, and I was forced into piracy. My father took his own life because of it. Surely that's reason enough."

"Reason enough to hate it perhaps," Meg answered doubtfully, "but not to want it. If it has caused so much grief, wouldn't it be better to leave it where it is—where it can never hurt anyone else again?"

A single dark eyebrow swept up in the captain's forehead.

"Come now, you must know that's why I want it. Because it can cause a great *deal* of grief for those who hounded my father to his grave. Can you blame me?" His hand reached up to trace the line of her cheekbone as he gazed speculatively into her face. "The gold rightfully belongs to me—and to your grandfather, if he wants a share of it. You see, I am not an unreasonable man. All you have to do is tell me where it is." Meg's breath caught as he pressed his lips to her hair. "You can, can't you, Meg?" he whispered, his fingers trailing liquid fire down her bare arm. "You do know where it is, don't you?"

"Y-yes." The answer seemed forced from her. Indeed, she could no sooner have resisted the compelling force of his hands weaving their spell over her than she could have stopped herself from breathing.

Glenmorgan's breath sounded harshly in the quiet.

"Then tell me, Meg. Tell me, and I promise to do right by you. We'll even get married, if that's what you want."

The spell was shattered. Meg lifted her head in alarm.

"You are worse than Drago," she choked. In a swift blaze of fury, she shoved with all her strength against his chest. "He is only savage, like a—a moray, but you—you have no heart."

Glenmorgan bit off a blistering oath at the sudden rending pain in his wound. In a flash Meg was free and on her feet.

"Meg," Glenmorgan gasped, "wait!"

In spite of herself, Meg paused, quivering, where she stood. Nevertheless, she fixed her gaze stubbornly on the sea, refusing to look at him. Consequently, she did not see Glenmorgan's eyes harden or his lip curl in bitter self-mockery.

Drawing in a long, steadying breath, he told himself to be careful. One wrong move would send her bolting. But then, perhaps it would be better so, he mused cynically. At least he would be saved whatever final shreds of honor were left him.

"You're right to run from me," he said at last, weary of himself. "Yes, I want the gold. And I'd do anything to get it, even use you, just as I've used others to get what I want. But I'll not lie to you, Meg. I have nothing left to offer a woman. Clarissa put an end to all that—to whatever remained of what I once was. Now there's only a man with a single purpose in life—to destroy those who ruined Turlough Glenmorgan. I need the gold from the *Argonaut* to finish what I've started, and only you can give it to me. Tell me where it is, Meg, and I swear you'll never be troubled by me again."

At last Meg turned to look at him, and for the space of

a single heartbeat he thought she meant to give him what he wanted. Then deliberately she squared her shoulders.

"I'm sorry, but I'm afraid that it will do you little good," she said with a strange mixture of pity and proud defiance. "The gold is in the *Argonaut* off Barbuda, Captain. On the bottom of the sea."

At the last, her composure broke ever so slightly. Bending quickly down, she snatched up her dress and straightened before looking at him again.

"And now there is *nothing* to keep you here," she uttered in frozen accents. "You may sail to Charles Town whenever you choose. Look there—your ship has come for you."

Glenmorgan, wrenching his eyes from her, looked where she was pointing. It was true. A ship was rounding the headland. Long and trim and built low to the water, her three tall masts square-rigged, the corvette skirted the reef and made farther north toward the small bay where Drago had anchored only three nights before. For a moment his vision blurred, but in that instant he knew her. It was *Raven*, and in tow behind her, a small sailing vessel of the sort used for fishing off the islands.

When he looked back again for Meg, she was gone.

Nine

Meg heaved a small metal coffer up onto the rock floor of the secret cave, then pulled herself from the sea onto the shelf beside it. In no mood to return to her human shape, she did not think the words that would have changed her. She was all too aware that there was little chance that she would be discovered. After all, she had been away for five whole days and nights. The captain would be long gone by now. Sighing, she opened the coffer and took out one of the gold coins from inside it. Then, settling on her belly, she propped her chin on the back of one hand and curiously rolled the shiny thing back and forth between her thumb and forefinger.

The Spanish doubloon glinted gold sparks in the morning sunlight streaming in through the rift above. It was pretty, Meg decided, but what good was it? She could see little use for something that only weighted her down and wore her out with trying to carry it through the water. It was a mystery to her why anyone would want a whole ship full of the stuff, and yet in the *Argonaut* there had been chests too numerable to count, all of them filled with gold and silver. She could see nothing in it worth dying or killing for.

Petulantly, she tossed the coin back into the box and

slammed the lid shut. What did it matter anyway? It had nothing to do with her. She could not even remember clearly now why it had seemed so important to find the sunken ship or why she had dragged the box of coins back with her. Something had been driving her—perhaps the need to see for herself what made men like Glenmorgan want it. And yet now that it was done, she knew no more than she had before. She was left feeling irritable and listless, wearier than she had ever felt before. With a sigh, she laid her cheek down on folded arms and closed her eyes. If only she could sleep for a little while—a sleep without dreams.

It was no use. No sooner did she feel her mind relax and start to drift than the image of a stern, handsome face with piercing blue eyes crept in. She was losing herself in the dream of Glenmorgan, his hands weaving their magic spell over her, his lips drawing fire from her veins. His name was a groan welling up from deep inside her, a liquid storm building, ready to be unleashed, when suddenly she cried out and jerked awake.

"No!" She shuddered, finding herself transformed into her human shape without remembering having pronounced the words of the spell. Groaning, she covered her face with her hands. Faith, what was happening to her?

The next instant, she was on her feet. Picking up the box, she started to climb. As if pursued, she did not stop to catch a breath until she had reached the safety of her hidden retreat. Then slamming the box down on the wooden table, she leaned over it, her shoulders heaving.

Her first awareness that she was not alone was the feel of a blanket being draped around her.

"So," pronounced a deep voice with a strange sort of finality, "you decided to come back after all."

Instantly Meg relaxed.

"Grandfather," she sighed. Holding the blanket around her, she turned into his arms.

153

"Come. Sit down," said the old man a few moments later, when Meg showed the first signs of pulling away. "Let me look at you." Leading her to the cot, he saw that she was seated before he turned to light one of the oil lamps with flint and steel.

For a moment he said nothing. Only looked at her. At last drawing up the stool, he sat down in front of her.

"When was the last time you slept?" he demanded brusquely. "Or ate anything?"

Meg lifted an indifferent shoulder.

"I don't remember. Why? What difference does it make?"

"None, I don't suppose," he answered, his eyes never wavering from her face. "Just an old man's curiosity. Tell me about the box, then. Where did you get it?"

"I got it," she said evenly, "from the *Argonaut*."

"So you've been to Barbuda, have you?"

"Eventually. I just wandered at first. Then yesterday, I found myself at the wreck," she said with a strange sort of vacant look. "I'm not even sure how I got there."

"I see," murmured the old man dryly. "I suppose that explains something. Why, you look ready to drop. And did you find what you were looking for?"

Meg glanced at him suspiciously. She knew him of old. He was not asking all these questions out of idle curiosity.

"I found the treasure, if that's what you mean."

"Ah, yes. The treasure." He nodded. "No doubt that is what I meant. Did you have any difficulty locating it?"

Meg shivered, feeling the cool dampness of the cave, and hugged the blanket more tightly to her.

"No," she answered, "it's where you said it was, little more than two hundred feet below the surface. Even you could swim down to it."

The old man laughed.

"No, I'm afraid you're the only one who can do that for us. The question is: How are we going to do it without letting the captain in on your little secret?"

Speechlessly, Meg stared at him, her mind reeling with the significance of what he had just said.

"No," she whispered hoarsely. "I won't. It's out of the question. Surely you can't expect me to—"

Leaning quickly forward, the old man caught her wrists and held them in a strong, steadying grip.

With his hands and his voice, he forced her to look at him. "You must see we no longer have a choice in the matter," he said."I will *not* let you die, Meg."

Meg froze, her face assuming a deathly pallor.

"You know," she said with bitter certainty. "How? Did *he* tell you?"

"He didn't have to." Releasing her, he stood up and paced a step before coming back again. "I knew as soon as I saw him. I've known, in fact, from the moment you brought him here that it was practically inevitable. I did try to warn you." He coughed to clear his throat before giving her a long look out of the corners of his eyes. "He's offered to give you his name," he said bluntly, "if that's what you want. To see that you're cared for. But it will be a marriage in name only. Until he is certain his enemies can do you no harm, you would remain here with me. He won't leave, Meg, until he has your answer."

"You mean he is still here?" Meg impaled him with her eyes. "But why, Grandfather? When you should already have sent him on his way? A marriage such as you have described is as meaningless as his reason for offering it. He has not dishonored me by accepting a gift I freely offered any more than he is obligated to put it right by making me his wife. *I* am not human."

155

Hastily Meg turned her head away, but not before the old man glimpsed the anguish in her face.

"I have no need of his name, Grandfather. It will not save me." Defiantly she looked at him. "I will find a way. I do not intend to die because of what has happened."

Her grandfather's fierce gesture quickly put to the rout any such notion.

"You're dying already," he said, his voice harsh with grim reality. "Do you think I don't have eyes to see it?"

Meg turned away from him. It was true, it was pointless to deny it. She *was* dying, little by little with each passing hour. And how not? Her days and nights were a living torment, an endless nightmare of aching emptiness. She had no desire for food and dared not sleep for fear of the dreams that would not leave her be. Nor could she rest; her thoughts would not allow her any peace. She was driven by the yearnings she could not control, haunted by visions of happiness that could never be hers. But worst of all was the empathic bond that only death could sever.

She was aware of him always, could sense his life force, his energy, his every change of mood. The bond she had shared with the boy, Caleb, the grief she had experienced as she felt him dying, was as nothing compared to this. This was the primal instinct to mate, to bear offspring in order to preserve the race. It was akin to the instinct that drove salmon to return to the river pools where they had been spawned, only in her people it was intensified by the emotional bonding between mates that joined them for life. It had been born out of a need to preserve sanity and to ensure the perpetuation of the race in a vast, hostile environment. Lifemates, joined empathically, were better equipped to protect and care for each other and their offspring. It was a means of instant communication of needs and danger, and it was a buffer against loneliness. It was not enough for sentient, thinking beings to mate. They must

156

be fulfilled emotionally as well. And that was why the gift was not given lightly. Once given, it could not be taken back or given to another. Had Glenmorgan been one of her kind, he would have been bonded to her as she was to him. *Hrum* would have followed naturally, and they would have been made truly one. For the first time she understood the "Song of Callandra," her mother's disconsolation and pining death. Even without *hrum,* Sheela had had Richard's love to sustain and fulfill her. Without him, she was like Meg, incomplete and yearning for the one who would have made her whole.

Her grandfather, in his own way, understood what was ailing her, but he could never be made to accept that Meg would rather die than condemn Glenmorgan to a life of secrecy and hiding, of isolation from his own kind. That was the price her father had paid for loving her mother. In stony silence she listened as her grandfather paced about the small cell and talked.

"I have had my doubts about the wisdom of giving in to the attraction you have for this man, I grant you. But now that it has happened, we have no choice but to make the best of it. It will mean disregarding the taboos your mother taught you. In the circumstances, it simply can't be helped. I'll go with you to Charles Town. If you don't want to go through the formality of a marriage, you don't have to. We'll have our own house on the sea, but away from the town itself. He'll come to you. You needn't worry about that. He won't be able to help himself. In time you'll win him. Don't you see, Meg? All you need is time—and this way you'll have it." When Meg said nothing, but only continued to stare at the floor, the old man felt his patience snap. "Or maybe you don't have what it takes to fight for him, is that it?" he demanded harshly. "Maybe you'd rather leave him to the woman who has already come within a hair's breadth of ending his life. And maybe you're right to bow out. He's going up against a dangerous lot, after all. The chances are he won't make it out alive. But you won't be around to see it, will you?"

He stopped, feeling as if he were ramming his head against an immovable wall. In exasperation, he studied the set cast of her face for some sign, no matter how small, that he was getting through to her. It was no use. She was remote, untouchable, a cold facsimile of the Meg he knew.

"Very well," he said on a note of grim finality. "If you won't do it for him or for yourself, then at least do it for me. I *owe* Glenmorgan. It was his father who gave me a chance to reclaim something out of the mess I had made of my life when no other man would. Surely that's worth *something* to you?"

Meg reacted as if she had not even heard.

Defeated, the old man sank down on the stool. He wondered if she knew what the past seven years had meant to him. He was already an old man when his son Richard had sent word to him in Charles Town, pleading with him to come to the West Indies—old, and embittered, his life wasted in a futile effort to drown his memories in drink. But Richard had needed him. For the first time he had sobered up long enough to take a good long look at himself. He hadn't liked what he had seen, and neither, it seemed, did anyone else, with the exception of Turlough Glenmorgan.

The *Argonaut,* bound for Saint Vincent's, had needed a ship's surgeon, and in spite of the fact that Phillip Belding had not worked at his chosen profession for better than ten years, Glenmorgan would have him in no other position. It was a kindness that Pippin would never forget. The voyage to Saint Vincent's Island had given him a new lease on hope—too late, if he had only known it. Richard was already dying.

A wave of anguish swept over the old man's weathered

features. Richard had been dead hardly a week when the *Argonaut* made port at Saint Vincent's. Even the unexpected news that his son had left behind a wife and daughter was not enough to keep him from resorting to old habits. By the time he sobered up enough to wonder about them, they were nowhere to be found, and the *Argonaut* was preparing to weigh anchor for England.

Even now he found the ensuing events a strange mixture of bizarre fate and unholy luck—the voyage that had been doomed from the start, the unreasoning cruelty of the British captain and his officers, the disastrous culmination of events that might have been avoided had the British captain been less arrogant and more knowledgeable of Caribbean waters.

It was the hurricane season. Josiah Roth, the sailing master, had commanded merchant ships in the West Indies for longer than most men lived. When he ignored the British captain's orders to heave to before the sweeping onslaught of the storm, he had only done what had to be done to save the ship and crew. For that, the British had hanged him from his own yardarms, an example, they had said, to a rebellious crew.

Isaiah Gates had only been partially right when he accused Phillip Belding of inciting the men to mutiny. The truth was the crew was already ripe for it. The hanging had been the spark that ignited the powder keg of resentment, a fact the purser had been more than eager to deny two weeks later to their British captors. In order to save his own worthless neck from the noose, he had even implicated Turlough Glenmorgan and his son in the mutiny, implying there had been a conspiracy to do away with the British officers and steal the gold for themselves. It was the only thing that *had* saved him. In order to prevent his murder by his former mates, he had been transferred to the British warship just

159

before the gale struck that sent the *Argonaut* with all hands to the bottom.

All hands, that is, except for Phillip Belding. *He,* miraculously, had been saved by a mermaid. Not Meg, as Gates had believed, but Sheela, Richard's lifemate.

He had often wondered if Sheela had called up the storm that delivered him. Mermaids had a certain power over the elements, and she, it had developed, had been following the ship since its departure from St. Vincent's, knowing that he was on board. But somehow, as he had watched the gentle Sheela pine away for loss of her beloved Richard, he had come to doubt her capable of killing for any reason. How much less could he believe it as he had found himself growing ever closer to Meg!

In a year's time, Sheela had succumbed to her grief, and Meg had become his sole reason for living. They had been hounded from island to island by Isaiah Gates, who never gave up the notion that Phillip Belding had recovered the *Argonaut*'s gold with the help of a mermaid, until at last, led by some deep-seated instinct, Meg had brought them here—the one place where they should have been safe. Only, Glenmorgan's presence had rendered them vulnerable, opening the way for Pippin's old enemy to stumble by accident on to their secret haven. He supposed he had gone a little mad upon discovering Gates once more on his doorstep. But that was all past. Fate had seen fit to present him with a new twist.

Had it been anyone other than Turlough Glenmorgan's son, he would not have hesitated to take his unasked-for guest, even wounded as he had been and on the brink of death, to Antigua and leave him. But Joseph Pippin was a man who believed in fate. And suddenly it seemed that Providence had seen fit to provide him not only with the means of securing the future well-being of his granddaughter, but of paying his debt to Turlough Glenmorgan as well.

Michael Glenmorgan, after all, had already proven himself to be a man of courage and resourcefulness. In his fight to survive the terrible wound he had received, he showed a strength of will that matched even that of the irrepressible Meg. It had taken only his willingness to risk his life to save the lives of others to whom he had felt an obligation to demonstrate that he was a man of honor as well. It had been that which had convinced the old man that here was the man to succeed him in making sure his granddaughter should never be left alone. It appeared, however, that he had miscalculated the strength of the mutual attraction between the two of them. And now Meg looked to be set to pay the ultimate price of his error.

Breathing a sigh, the old man heaved himself to his feet and stood for a moment looking down at Meg, who had sunk down on her side, her eyes closed. Carefully, the old man lifted her feet onto the cot.

"Aye," he said wearily, "you sleep. There'll be time enough later to make up your mind. When you're ready, we'll face him together—you and I, the way it was meant to be."

Leaving the lamp burning, he left her and made his way up the tumble of rocks that formed the dry falls.

The sun was nearly overhead when he emerged from the rift at the top of the cliffs. In the distance, he could see the *Raven,* her sails furled as she rode at anchor awaiting her captain's orders. His own little ketch the *Mirabel* looked frail and insignificant in comparison to the sleek corvette, which carried thirty guns and a hundred-fifty-man crew. But they would need her, too, if they were to accomplish the difficult task before them.

Striking out with long, brisk strides for the hut, he set his mind to work on the final details of the plan that had begun to take shape in his mind almost from the moment he had arrived home to find Meg gone and the captain obviously troubled.

Actually, "troubled" was putting it mildly. Glenmorgan displayed all the signs of a man on the horns of a dilemma, a fact which the old man had viewed with a mixture of grim satisfaction and vague disquiet. Obviously, the captain was not indifferent to the girl. The problem was Meg's unexplained absence. He had expected to find upon his return a cozy pair of lovebirds, and instead he had found a man, grim-faced and brooding, and Meg seemingly fled from the face of the earth. The succeeding five days had taxed his patience to the limit. But even they were as nothing when compared to the sharp stab of alarm he had suffered at sight of the indomitable Meg, hollow-eyed and lackluster.

All too plainly, something had miscarried, and there seemed very little that he could do about it. Everything, in fact, now depended on Meg and her ability to resolve whatever it was that was driving her to reject her chosen lifemate.

As the old man emerged in the clearing a few minutes later, he was afforded some small comfort on discovering that Glenmorgan appeared in very little better state than the girl sleeping the sleep of exhaustion.

In spite of the fact that his broad-shouldered, slim-hipped build showed to advantage in a clean white shirt and buckskin breeches, and though he appeared fit enough, his lean, freshly shaved jaw and cheeks already returned to a semblance of their former healthy complexion, the captain yet wore the look of a man possessed. If his thunderous brow and the pale glint of his eyes were not evidence enough that it was better to tread lightly in his presence, the aspect of studied indifference worn by his second in command as he lounged against the trunk of a red manjack tree would have left little room for doubt.

Dick Chapin was a man who gave the immediate impression of enormous size coupled with prodigious strength. Standing a good five inches over six feet, thick-bodied and barrel-chested, he was built rather on the lines of a stout English oak. Still, there was unmistakable intelligence in the keen blue eyes, and about the wide mouth, a good-natured stubbornness. He might be slow to anger, but once aroused, he would wreak havoc in a fight. Thick forearms and bulging biceps only added to the overall effect. Toward his captain, he displayed a strong inclination toward the protective, weathering the other man's flashes of temper with stoic patience and a simple pride. He was sandy-haired and ruddy complected, and looked to be in his late twenties.

The old man could not doubt the strength of Chapin's loyalty to his captain. He had seen it in the sudden brightness of Chapin's blue eyes at learning Glenmorgan was alive, in the way his huge hand had snatched the gold locket in an elated fist. In between giving orders to muster all hands and prepare to weigh anchor, the old man had heard Chapin exclaim softly to himself, "I knew it! I *knew* it!"

He had been less certain in what light Glenmorgan viewed his subordinate—until, that is, he had witnessed their reunion. Chapin had been out of the launch before it hit the beach, wading with long strides to meet the captain on the shore. For a moment it had appeared as if Glenmorgan was in danger of sustaining a renewed injury to his wound as Chapin caught him up in a bearish hug that lifted the captain off his feet.

Laughing, Glenmorgan pounded the big man on the back. "Put me down, you great oversized oaf. Before you break every rib in my body."

"It'd only be what you deserve, Captain, for walking into a trap with your bloody eyes open. Have you any notion of the trouble I've had keepin' the lads from sailin' to Charles Town to do for Tharp what he tried to do to you?"

"I'm all sympathy. Now put me down, and maybe I won't

have you flogged for disobeying my orders." Set on his feet again, Glenmorgan eyed his lieutenant squarely. "It was your idea, I hear, to remain idle in English Harbor, when I distinctly remember giving you instructions to sail without me." His hand went out. "For that, I owe you my thanks, old friend, and more."

Their hands clasped wrists and held in a strong grip.

"I expect you'd have done the same for me, Captain," rumbled Chapin, his rugged face reddening, nevertheless, with pleasure. "Besides, I didn't have the first idea where to go now that you've made honest men of us."

That had been all there was to it, and yet the old man had had little difficulty discerning the strength of feeling running like an undercurrent between the two men. He might almost have called it affection, though between two strong men, that was not a term easily used. Indeed, he was aware that it went much deeper than that.

In the days that had followed, Glenmorgan divided his time between pacing the quarterdeck of his ship and roaming the shores of the island, until Chapin had at last been moved to complain that the captain was wearing himself to exhaustion. Little good it had done. Chapin had earned a blistering reprimand for his efforts, and Glenmorgan had continued to drive himself toward the limit of his inner reserves.

Little wonder, then, that the captain appeared something less than cordial as he glanced up from his charts laid out on a table beneath the trees to see his former host approaching. In an instant he was on his feet.

"Well? Have you any news to tell us?"

"She is back," the old man announced without preamble.

"Is she now indeed?" rejoined the captain, the first, swift flash of relief giving way to a darkening expression that boded ill for the object of his emotion. "And did she tell you where she has been for the past five days?"

164

The old man shrugged. "I told you. She often goes to the other side of the island. Whenever she feels restless or has something she wants to think about. I did not question her. She appeared in no state for it. I left her sleeping, and if you take my advice, you will let her be. Either she will come when she's ready, or she won't. In either case, to disturb her now will only do more harm than good."

Glenmorgan's fingers closed in a steely grip on the old man's arm.

"What are you saying, man?" he demanded. "Is she ill?"

"I have seen her better," the old man tempered. "Something is obviously deeply troubling her."

For an instant it seemed that Glenmorgan would ignore the old man's advice. Behind him, Dick Chapin straightened, his eyes worried as he watched his friend's lean frame tense with some powerful emotion. Then the moment was past. Letting his hand drop to his side, Glenmorgan appeared to withdraw into himself.

"Very well," he murmured, more to himself than to them. "I'll wait." His piercing eyes lifted to the old man's. "But only till dusk. Then I go see her for myself. Either way, I intend to sail in the morning—for Charles Town."

"Charles Town?" interjected a cool voice from behind them.

As one, the three men turned.

Dick Chapin's lips pursed in a soundless whistle at sight of the girl looking like a bloody vision in a plain white gown, her ankles and feet bare. No wonder the captain had been acting like a man possessed by a devil. She had the kind of look about her that would haunt a man all his days.

For an instant she appeared to falter, her glance wavering before the sudden fierce blaze of the captain's eyes. Then instinctively her head lifted. "Did I misunderstand you, Grandfather?" she continued, with only a slight catch in her voice. "I thought that we were going to Barbuda—to fetch the captain his gold."

"It's quite simple, Captain," said the old man a few moments later. Going to Glenmorgan's charts, he placed a finger on a point a short distance east of Barbuda. "The ship lies about here, perhaps a hundred feet or more down." Mentally he shrugged, telling himself that the small lie was necessary. "With a single diver, using block and tackle, we should have little difficulty salvaging the ship's cargo. Provided, of course, that the weather holds and we do not run into any unforeseen obstacles."

"Like Drago or any one of a dozen or more other pirate ships that would like to sink us to the bottom," commented Dick Chapin dryly.

"As I see it, we have a greater obstacle than Drago to contend with," said Glenmorgan, who had not taken his eyes off the slender girl, her face nearly as white as her gown. "Even if we do manage to locate the wreckage, where do we find a diver who can reach it?"

"I've heard of pearl divers off Sainte Margarite who could go a hundred," Chapin supplied doubtfully.

"Aye, but unfortunately, Sainte Margarite lies four hundred miles out of our way," Glenmorgan pointed out. "Better than eight hundred by the time we make the return voyage." He turned to Pippin. "Even if we are willing to make such a detour, I'm afraid it would be pointless. You say the ship lies in more than a hundred feet of water. I doubt there's a man alive capable of descending, let alone working, at such a depth."

Until then, Meg had refrained from entering into the discussion. Now she stepped forward.

"You're right, Captain," she said quietly. "It would be pointless to go all the way to Sainte Margarite for a diver.

166

Fortunately, however, you don't have to, since I will be making the dive for you."

"You?" Glenmorgan exploded. "What sort of jest is this?"

"It is no jest," Pippin assured him. "It is by no means beyond my granddaughter's capabilities. You might say she has been making such dives practically all of her life. I'm afraid, however, there are some conditions to which you must agree before I can allow her to commit herself to such a venture."

"Conditions?" echoed Chapin incredulously. "Captain, surely you aren't taking any of this seriously."

"On the contrary," Glenmorgan answered in such a tone as left no doubt that he was anything but amused. "I am in deadly earnest. Name your conditions."

"My granddaughter and I will require the privacy of our own vessel. Consequently, we will make the journey in the *Mirabel*."

"But that's absurd," choked Dick Chapin. "That old fishing smack cannot possibly keep up with us."

"Then we will take pains not to lose her," Glenmorgan observed coldly. "What else do you require?"

"For the sake of modesty, no one, not even you, Captain, can be allowed to view my granddaughter while she is diving. You will stand off at a distance while the gold is being raised from the bottom. At suitable intervals we will transfer our load to the *Raven*, is that understood?"

"It is clearly out of the question!" Glenmorgan snapped, his patience at an end. "This is not child's play we are talking about. Any of a number of things could happen to her while she is below. You cannot expect me to stand idly by while a female younger than my kid sister takes risks I would not ask any man to take?"

"I not only expect it, but demand it. If you cannot agree, then there is little point in discussing any of this further."

"I could not agree more," Glenmorgan replied with chilling finality. "I have listened this long only because I was curious to see how far you would go in this wild scheme. I've heard enough. As far as I'm concerned, the matter is closed."

"Then, Captain," Meg interjected, her eyes challenging, "you leave us little choice. Grandfather and I will do it by ourselves—or with the help of someone less squeamish. I cannot imagine that John Drago would turn down such an offer."

Glenmorgan's lips thinned to a grim line. Dick Chapin groaned and rolled his eyes skyward.

"Ask him and be damned," said the captain, steely-voiced. "If you're fool enough to go through with it, I'll not be around to save you a second time."

Suddenly as their eyes clashed across the table, it was as if there were only the two of them.

"Does the gold suddenly mean so little to you?" demanded the girl, refusing to be intimidated by the captain's forbidding expression. "That was not the impression you gave me the last time we met."

"You, on the other hand, have demonstrated a decided lack of interest in gold or anything else of material value—until now," Glenmorgan was odiously quick to point out. "Why the sudden change of heart?"

"Perhaps I have decided it is time I saw something of the world—Charles Town, for instance. Or that it might not be so bad to have a house and money, after all—"

"Enough!"

Her heart nearly failed her as the side of Glenmorgan's fist crashed down against the tabletop.

"I'm not a *fool*, Meg," he said. "Do you think I don't know why you're doing this?"

"It makes no difference why I'm doing it." She shrugged. "The point is that I intend to go after your Spanish gold."

"Like the devil, you are." Glenmorgan's eyes flashed steely sparks. "You're going nowhere. I'll make sure of that if I have to sink your grandfather's boat."

Meg gasped, her face going pearly white. "You wouldn't dare."

Glenmorgan's taut frame leaned toward her across the table.

"You can count on it. I've taken enough from you, Meg. I'll be bloody damned if I'll have your life on my head, too."

White-faced and trembling, Meg at last turned the full force of her eyes on him.

"You have taken nothing that I did not give willingly," she said proudly. "At least grant me that. *And* the right to govern my own life. You don't owe me anything, least of all concern for my well-being. Believe me, Captain. My life is in no danger from the sea."

A slow eternity seemed to pass as Glenmorgan stared at her, his eyes seemingly trying to pierce the proud mask of her face. Then at last he appeared to give in to something inevitable he sensed in her.

"Very well," he said grimly. "If that's the way you want it, then so be it. At least I'll be there to keep the vultures at bay. And don't think that they won't come. Because they will—Drago and Malpas, Sainte Claire and half a dozen more that I can think of who would take on the devil himself for that much gold. Word will already be out that the *Raven* has sailed. Only our proximity to the British at English Harbor has kept them at bay this long. They'll be looking for us. Never doubt it for a moment."

Tearing his eyes away from Meg, he shot a glance over his shoulder at Chapin.

"Alert the men. We'll weigh anchor at first light." To Pippin, he said: "Mr. Chapin will see that you have whatever stores you need from *Raven*. I suggest you send over to the ship any personal items not required for the task at hand. There is little enough room as it is aboard your boat. You do realize," he added, his gaze returning with grim significance to Meg, "that you cannot come back here. Once we make the attempt, successful or not, word of it will spread to every port in the Caribbean and beyond. And thanks to Drago, every pirate within a five hundred-mile radius will know about you and this island."

Meg bit her tongue to keep from retorting that it mattered little how many pirates heard Drago's story. None of them would ever lay eyes on the island.

"Yes, I—I suppose you're right," she faltered. "I hadn't thought about that."

"There seem to be a lot of things you haven't *thought* about," Glenmorgan replied coldly. "As for you, sir," he added, deliberately swinging his attention to the old man, "I understand your motives behind this. In your place, I might do the same." A long look passed between them, leaving little doubt in either man's mind that they, two, at least, understood one another. "Nevertheless, I suggest that you have not fully considered the potential risks to your granddaughter's welfare, what it will mean to her to be suddenly uprooted and placed in a world that is totally foreign to her. You may believe that I have thought about it, with the conclusion that Meg is better off here."

"So you have said before, Captain," Pippin answered gravely. "I'm afraid, however, that I have no choice but to disagree with you."

The muscle leaped along Glenmorgan's jawline.

"We all have choices, Mr. Pippin," he suggested somberly. "It is not too late to back out. If in the morning, however, you are still set on this madcap scheme, you force *me* to lay down some conditions of my own. Should we come through this alive, you will place yourselves under my protection. I will establish you and your granddaughter in a house in Charles Town where I can be reasonably sure of your safety. I will do my best to do nothing to harm your granddaughter's name or reputation. Further than that, I can make no promises. In the event that something should happen to me, Mr. Chapin will have instructions to take you wherever you would wish to go. Those are *my* conditions. Take them or leave them."

Meg's lips parted, but Pippin did not give her the chance to utter the protest that he sensed was coming.

"Very well, Captain," he said, extending a strong right hand. "I suggest we shake hands on it."

"Aye," rumbled Dick Chapin, "and the devil bedamned. Belike it'll take a bloody miracle to see us through this one."

Ten

Meg stood in the stern of her grandfather's fishing boat, her legs braced against the pitch and fall of the deck. Shading her eyes against the dancing reflections of sunlight on the water, she stared aft at the island, receding slowly into the distance. She had the strangest sensation that it was moving while she remained still, as if it were slipping away from her, like so much driftwood carried on a current. She had to fight the sudden urge to dive in and swim after it, as if by that she might halt the flow of circumstances that were altering her life forever.

Instead, she resolutely turned her face forward, toward the ship, pulling the *Mirabel* steadily through the water.

It was the captain who had decided in the end to tow the fishing ketch behind the *Raven*. She could see in his face as he informed them of the change in plans that he would have liked nothing better than to go one step further and order her and her grandfather aboard the ship. But he had kept his word to allow them their way in the matter, little as he had liked it.

"He appears in a fair taking—the captain," commented her grandfather, glancing up from a line he was reinforcing for the work that lay ahead of them. "Any more sail, and the ship will fly through the water. At this rate, we'll make Barbuda before the morning's over."

"It cannot be too soon for me," Meg answered shortly, her gaze never leaving the lone figure of the captain, who stood at the weather rail staring out to sea. At last, frowning a little, she tore her eyes away. "How far is it to Charles Town?"

"A long way," the old man replied. "Over a thousand miles. If you went the distance between Antigua and Barbuda forty times, you would still have a small distance to go to reach Charles Town."

"So far?" Meg's voice trailed off, filled with uncertainty.

"It is not too far for you to find your way back, if that, in the end, is what you want," he said quietly.

Startled, Meg glanced up at him. A reluctant smile tugged at her lips.

"You always know what I'm thinking," she accused.

The old man shook his head.

"No, not always." He cocked a sapient eyebrow at her. "I have been racking my brain trying to figure out why you were so set on sending the captain on his way. So far, I haven't come up with an answer."

"And I've been wondering why you didn't tell me Glenmorgan's father was your benefactor," she came back at him. "I never guessed the truth till he told Drago about the *Argonaut*. But you knew the instant you heard Tharp's plans who was meant to walk into that trap, and yet you said nothing. You did nothing. Why? You might at least have tried to warn Captain Glenmorgan. Then none of this need have happened."

"That would have been the *most* I would have done, and it would have been too much at that." The old man smiled mirthlessly. "Then and now, my only consideration has always been for your welfare. So long as no one knew anything about us, I could be reasonably certain you would be

173

safe—or so it seemed. It was an ironic twist of fate that landed the captain on my doorstep. Followed by Gates, by God. I have begun to think a man truly can never escape his past."

A look of anguish crossed Meg's face.

"Then why are you doing this?" she cried. "You are Phillip Belding. They will hang you if you are recognized."

"Come now. Surely that isn't what's keeping you from going after your captain. Because if it is, Meg, I won't stand for it," Pippin warned her. "The captain and I have already discussed that possibility, and we agree that I must remain out of sight. Glenmorgan will spread it about that I am a recluse afflicted with a melancholic disposition. It will be assumed by most that I am sitting at home drowning my sorrows, which will earn you a deal of sympathy and will allow me to remain undisturbed. In the meantime, I will do my best to disguise myself. What do you think? Shall I look a gentleman in a powdered wig and with white paint and rouge on my face?"

Meg said bitterly, "You make everything sound so easy, when it isn't at all. I would be doing everyone a great favor if I simply vanished when we have finished at Barbuda."

"That's utter nonsense, and you know it," her grandfather snapped, fast losing patience with her. "What *is* it, Meg? It isn't mere happenstance that you gave yourself to him. You were drawn to him from the first moment you laid eyes on him. Before, if I recall correctly. Why are you fighting it now that it's clearly too late to change matters?"

"Because it *is* too late! Oh, why can't you understand?" she exclaimed, a look of desperation in her eyes. For an instant it appeared she would dive over the side into the sea. Then her grandfather's hand caught her and held her where she was. Meg drew a deep breath. "My father willingly bonded with my mother, and they knew great happiness together," she said. "But in the end my mother died cursing everything they had ever meant to one another. You know well enough that it was the fever that killed him. If a white man stays long enough on the islands, he is bound to come down with it."

"Is that what you're afraid of?" Pippin demanded. "That you'll be left alone one day, like your mother? Meg, it's the chance everyone takes in life."

"No, you don't understand," she insisted. "They loved one another—a mermaid and a landsman—and because of what they were, they created a prison neither of them could escape. She was bound to the sea, and he to the islands so that he could always be near her. In the end, it killed them both. The old songs are true. It is death for a landsman to love a mermaid."

Deliberately, she lifted her head to look at him out of tormented eyes.

"He doesn't love me," she uttered in a strangled voice. "If fate is merciful, he never will."

Pippin, unable to find the words to answer her, sighed as she turned away to stare blindly out to sea.

In spite of her troubled heart, Meg could not long remain immune to the healing effects of sunshine and a brisk wind in her face. The sky was a clear, unmottled blue, the sea rumpled and white-capped. From out of nowhere a school of dolphins appeared, skimming through the water, leaping through the wake of the ship. Smiling a trifle mistily, Meg called to them. She was young, and the day was far too lovely to resist. Inevitably she was drawn out of herself.

In fascination, she watched the powerful corvette claw to windward. She marveled at the swarming figures on deck as they pulled the braces to, or scrambled up the rigging to trim the sails. In awe, she watched the yards swing in unison as the ship paid off on the starboard tack, the prow forging through the swells in a white curtain of spray. The white-canvassed ship was like a living thing with a spirit of its own, she marveled, as she watched the men's constant struggle to make the *Raven* do as they willed.

The weather made for an easy crossing, the wind holding steady out of the northeast so that they arrived off the southeast shore of Barbuda, just as Pippin had predicted, a little more than an hour before noon. With the tow line cast off, *Raven* drew away to make a last sweep up the coast while Meg and her grandfather dropped anchor and prepared to begin the search for the sunken vessel.

Hardly had the ship pulled off to a safe distance, than Meg flung off her gown and dove straight down into the water. As if they had been waiting all along for her, the dolphins swarmed around her, six in all. Their grinning faces bobbed up and down, an invitation to join them.

In an instant Meg was off, darting through the water with the dolphins chasing after her. Surging upward, the supple animals breached the surface in unison. Beneath them, the mermaid, content this time merely to watch, laughed in pure enjoyment as they swept a high arc into the air, then plunged into the clear depths again and circled around her, chattering in their strange tongue. It was glorious fun. Meg could not remember the last time she had played. But at last, regretfully, she turned her attention to more serious matters.

Curious, the dolphins followed her as she descended into the blue depths, searching for and finding familiar landmarks—crags of rock and brilliant blue coral, a garden of star-shaped anemones, red sea fans, and blue-fingered sea urchins clustered on a sand bank. The familiar landscape led her deeper, through a forest of kelp and along a coral-encrusted ridge, until at last a school of fish, like a brilliant yellow cloud, darted en masse away from her and she saw the wreckage at last.

It was just as she remembered it—a great hulking mass,

its shape blurred by a thick crust of barnacles and coral and great tentacles of weed swaying in the current. It lay half-buried on its side in sand on a shelf of rock, its bare masts seemingly suspended over a yawning canyon. It was a broken, lifeless thing, haunted by swarms of small fish and the occasional shark or moray. The other, exposed, side was broken and battered where British cannonballs had ploughed through the thick timbers—mute evidence that the mutineers had not allowed themselves to be taken without a last, desperate fight. Coupled with the fury of the storm that had swarmed unexpectedly over the stricken ship, they had proven fatal wounds.

Drawn by a curiosity that had been lacking in her earlier visit, Meg swam along the quarterdeck to the companion-way leading down into the dark interior. Pausing to allow an exiting manta ray to swim past her, she entered the murky passage.

She had never been in the belly of a ship before. When she had come to the wreck that other time, she had entered through a large rupture in the side and had immediately found herself in the exposed hold filled with Spanish treasure. She had not explored further. She had not had the heart for it. It had felt too much like intruding on the dead. Even now, the rotting timbers of the ship groaned and creaked all around her as if warning her away.

Quelling the urge to bolt back the way she had come, she glided through a gaping doorway into a large, spacious cabin. It could not have been other than the master's quarters, she guessed instantly. At the stern of the ship, it had once been comfortably fitted out. Now, the stern windows were vacant, gaping holes, and save for a great carved cabinet bolted to the deck, the cabin was empty, swept clean by the inrushing water as the ship had sunk to the bottom. Curiously, she crossed the canting deck to the cabinet and ran her hand over its carved swirls and gold leaf design, chipped, but still shiny in the dim light filtering down from the surface.

It was time she was heading back, she told herself, glad for an excuse to leave the wreck behind her. *Raven* very likely had completed its sweep of the coast and would be starting back for the rendezvous soon.

Meg rose swiftly toward the golden shafts of sunlight slanting through the water. She broke through the surface, grateful to feel the sun against her face, and looked around her for her grandfather's ketch.

The *Mirabel* bobbed in the swells less than a cable length away. Beyond the anchored boat, the island hovered, squat and flat, an oasis of green, swaying trees and white beach, while to the north, small in the distance, her sails a white patch against the blue horizon, the *Raven* tacked away from the headland across the wind in a pattern that would eventually bring her back to Meg and her grandfather.

Meg heaved a sigh of relief. She was not too late. The captain was taking his time, making a thorough search of the shoreline.

The old man must have been watching for her. She could see him, bent over the stern, already dragging in the anchor. In short order, the sails billowed out from the masts, and the old man could be seen working to bring the nose around into the wind. The weathered fishing smack bucked against the swells, dipping into the troughs and lunging out again as Pippin brought her about upwind from Meg. Then setting the rudder, he sprang forward to brail in the sails, letting the boat drift toward Meg.

"It's here," she called to him, as the *Mirabel* came alongside her, "directly below us."

Nodding, the old man lowered the anchor overboard before tossing a rope ladder over the sides for Meg.

* * *

178

When the *Raven* arrived and made anchor off their starboard bow, Meg and her grandfather had secured the ketch with moorings fore and aft and had begun the task of fashioning a hoist. With one end of a boom secured at the base of the mizzenmast, they were attempting to suspend the other end out over the water by means of hoist ropes running from the point of the boom to the top of the mast and down again to a windlass secured on the forward deck. It was no easy matter working on the pitching deck of the thirty-foot boat, just the two of them, and though neither might admit it aloud, they were both secretly relieved to see the corvette's return.

As a boat was lowered over the side, Meg's grandfather ordered her to go below. Meg went without an argument. She had no wish to be ogled by the eight sturdy seamen manning the oars. Giving the tall figure of the captain, seated in the sternsheets, a last, lingering look, she ran quickly down the ladder into the small sleeping cabin below deck, but she left the door ajar.

At the sound of the captain's deep voice, hailing the boat, she could not suppress a small tingle along her spine.

"Mirabel, ahoy."

Her grandfather's answer boomed across the water, "Welcome, Captain. Perhaps you would care to come aboard?"

The ketch lurched and swayed as the ship's boat came alongside. Through the small crack, Meg glimpsed the flash of a breeches-clad leg. Then she heard the splash of oars and knew the other boat was pulling away, leaving the captain on board the *Mirabel.*

The captain's voice carried clearly to her: "I see you have been busy, Mr. Pippin. A hoist, is it? Very ingenious. What do you intend to use for ballast?"

"I am in hopes the anchors will suffice to counterbalance the weight of the load."

There was a slight pause while Glenmorgan appeared to

consider the possibilities. Then he said, "It might be enough, so long as the weather holds. We are fortunate it is not the hurricane season."

"Still, I detect that you are not satisfied," Pippin observed. "What is troubling you, Captain?"

Glenmorgan's answer, when it came, was couched in measured accents. "The *Argonaut* was carrying sixty tons of gold bars when she went down, and nearly that much in silver. Add to that, several chests of Spanish doubloons, and you might begin to grasp the enormity of the task you have taken on yourselves. One diver, Mr. Pippin, and a girl at that. And yourself. At thirty-three ounces a bar, you will have over one hundred thousand of them to transport from the wreck. Even with a hoist, it would seem an impossible task, or does your granddaughter plan to carry them up to you one bar at a time?"

"Perhaps you should ask her that for yourself, Captain." Meg sensed her grandfather turn toward the companionway. "It's safe now, child. You can come out."

Meg pulled the door open and stepped up on to the short ladder. Her eyes met Glenmorgan's, piercing blue and unreadable in the glare of sunlight.

Masking her confusion behind a disdainful front, she stepped coolly into the open. "Captain," she murmured.

She thought she sensed Glenmorgan's long frame tense. Then folding his arms across his chest, he leaned negligently against the coaming, his legs crossed at the ankles. His eyes deliberately took in her long hair, flying unfettered about her head and shoulders, her slender figure, held straight-backed and defiant beneath the thin white gown.

"You would appear to be very certain of yourselves," he observed matter-of-factly, "to have done all of this." The sweeping gesture of his hand indicated the anchors, the half-completed hoist—all the work they had done. "How do you know the wreck is even down there?"

She answered with a composure she was far from feeling, "I have been to see it." She saw his eyes narrow on her face and gave a small shrug. "You don't believe me? I will describe it to you, if you like—the battered hull, the side caved in by the British cannon and finally the storm, the master's quarters, empty save for a carved cabinet which is trimmed in gold." She watched the leap of muscle along his lean jaw at mention of the cabinet and wondered at it, before adding, "The ship is there, Captain. As for the treasure, it will take time to recover it, but it can be done, I promise you."

"Can it?" His eyes challenged her. "How?"

"Perhaps with a little faith, Captain," she answered stiffly.

"And ropes and tackle," Pippin dryly added. He glanced from the captain to Meg, feeling the tension running rife between them like sparks of electricity in the air. He said, "And for that we need a hoist. If you'd care to lend a hand, Glenmorgan, perhaps we can have this finished before dark."

The captain stared a moment longer at the girl, ironically aware of the aloofness in her proud bearing. Damn the fates that had brought them together in the first place! Never had she seemed farther removed from him than she did at this moment in the cramped quarters of the fishing boat, not even when he had believed she had gone from him for good. He wished that she had not come back. Better that than to see her risk her life on some damned foolish gesture.

He felt the anger stir, like hot coals in the pit of his belly—anger and frustration at his failure to stop this madness before it was too late. His lips parted to refuse the old man's invitation, but unwittingly his eyes fell on the rapid pulsebeat at the base of the girl's slender throat. Suddenly it struck him that she was not quite so detached as she appeared to be.

"Very well, Mr. Pippin," he said in spite of his better

judgment, "I will stay—since that appears to be the only help you are willing to accept from me."

Later, that night, Meg sat curled up in the stern of her grandfather's fishing boat, her eyes fixed on the yellow glow of light from the *Raven's* stern windows. Therein lay the captain's quarters, she knew. The moon having yet to come up, it was all she could see of the ship, riding at anchor half a cable length off the *Mirabel's* port bow. Apparently the captain found sleep as elusive as she did, she thought with faint satisfaction.

A picture of Glenmorgan as he had looked earlier that day came back to haunt her. His shirt open to the waist, his skin shining with sweat and salt spray as he labored with her grandfather over the boom, he had seemed to fill the boat with his presence. Obviously well on the way to regaining his strength, he seemed to enjoy the physical labor as well as the challenge of tackling and solving each problem they had encountered as the hoist slowly took shape. She could recall with perfect clarity the way he had of throwing his head back when he laughed, something which he had done with surprising frequency as the afternoon wore on. For a while he had seemed to let the barriers down so that she had seen him again as he had been that night on the beach when he had cooked supper for her and enthralled her with tales of places he had seen, things he had done. He had disarmed her today no less than that other time, so much so that she had forgotten to guard her heart against him.

She groaned and hugged her arms around her, remembering.

All afternoon they had worked to finish the hoist so that countless impressions of the captain whirled in her brain. The time she was sitting, cross-legged, on the deck working to tie the ends of two lines together. Glenmorgan's voice said at her back, "Not like that." Bending over her, his hands reached for the rope ends. "Here, let me show you." How swift and sure those hands had been! She had been tinglingly aware of his nearness, his face so close to hers that when she, blushingly, turned her head to thank him, her lips had nearly brushed against his. Thinking about it now brought a hot flush to her cheeks, and she ducked her head just as she had done earlier that day, when his eyes had sought hers with sudden paralyzing intensity.

Another time she had watched with her heart in her throat as he climbed to the masthead to secure the lines. Standing negligently on the spar, one arm curled about the mast, he appeared totally oblivious to the dizzying heights or the swaying boat below. His dark hair ruffled by the wind, his teeth flashing white against his tanned skin—the images seemed permanently etched in her mind, as were the final moments before their parting.

The sun, a huge, burning ball melting into the horizon, shed a brilliant orange light over a fading sky as it went. On the island, the palm trees had stood out, still, black silhouettes against the flaming backdrop of color. The work was done, and Glenmorgan had signaled the ship for his boat, when the old man, mumbling something about fetching the lantern, went below, leaving them alone together.

She had been standing with her back against the mizzenmast as she watched the last remnant of the sun slowly vanishing, when suddenly Glenmorgan loomed over her, one hand against the mast next to her head.

He had smiled faintly, sensing, no doubt, the sudden leap of her pulse, she thought, and she felt a knot tighten in the pit of her belly at the memory. Like a witless fool, she could do naught but stare into his eyes, glittery in the half-light, when she knew well enough the power they had to hold her spellbound and helpless. Not even when his hand lifted to embrace the side of her neck had she found the wit to make even a feeble attempt at escape. She had just stood there, powerless, her breath quick in her throat. His shoulders moved toward her, blocking the island from her sight. For a moment he stilled, his eyes deliberately searching her face. Then his eyelids closed, and drawing her to him, he kissed her.

Meg, alone now in her silent vigil, nearly groaned out loud. It wasn't fair! She had no defenses against him. His lips had moved over hers with a slow, searching deliberation that drove everything else from her mind. One more link forged in the chain that bound her to him. Her senses were reeling when at last he released her, and she was grateful for the mizzenmast at her back.

His voice husky, he murmured, "Meg, you don't have to go through with this. Come with me to the ship. Tomorrow I'll take you wherever you want to go. Someplace where you'll be safe from Tharp and anyone else who might want to hurt me through you. Later, I'll come for you."

"Don't!" The word felt wrenched from her. "Don't make promises you can't keep, I beg you. It would be one oath too many." Carefully, she drew in a deep breath. "You will have your gold and your vengeance." She said it flatly, without emotion. "It will have to be enough."

She could feel anger sweep through his body as his hand leaning against the mast clenched into a fist. His voice came at her as hard as his fist.

"I have commanded a pirate ship for seven years. I could take you across with me, and there would be no one to stop me."

"Yes, but you won't."

The sound of oars, suddenly loud in the still of night, had somehow given her the strength to look at him.

"Please go, Captain," she said, surprised at the steadiness of her voice. She saw the leap of muscle along his jawline,

184

the sudden, hard glitter of his eyes. It was all she could do to stand there, but she made herself go on. "There is your boat, and I have no wish to be seen."

She had sensed his muscles tense and knew that he was about to argue with her, but then her grandfather had come on deck. She remembered Glenmorgan's mouth thinning to a hard line, and his hand falling away from her.

The next minute he was gone.

Alone in the stern of her grandfather's boat, Meg swayed beneath the press of doubts and uncertainties. Perhaps she had been wrong to listen to her grandfather. What could she do anyway to protect Glenmorgan either from himself or his enemies? For a while she had believed that with the gold he might finish his revenge and be done with it. It was that hope that had brought her here to Barbuda, or at least that is what she had told herself. Now she was not so certain. Perhaps she had come for more selfish reasons. To prolong the moment of parting? To gain the time her grandfather had said was needed to win the captain to her? To bind him to her, if not with love, then with a debt of gratitude? Was everything she had sworn to herself a lie?

She did not know anymore why she was doing it, only that she would not rest until it was done. Glenmorgan would have his treasure and his revenge, and afterward? She drew a long, steadying breath. Afterward she would just have to wait and see.

Meg awakened with a start to find her grandfather kneeling beside her, his hand on her shoulder.

He said quietly, "Nearly sunup. Time we were stirring."

Meg groaned and stretched her aching limbs. She had fallen asleep sitting in the stern, she realized, her head propped on her knees. She could feel it in every inch of her body. Struggling to untangle her mind from its cobwebs

185

of sleep, she realized that the thick curtain of darkness was rapidly thinning, revealing the outlines of rigging and spars. As if drawn, her eyes went to the corvette.

In the gray light of the slow-breaking dawn, she could see that the ship, too, was awake, her shrouds and swaying yards swarming with men as she prepared to up anchor and begin her slow patrol to the northward. It had all been pre-arranged between Glenmorgan and Pippin two days before, when they had first laid their plans. While the *Raven* kept an eye out for marauding ships, Meg would be given the privacy she needed to carry out her tasks below.

Stiffly, she shoved herself to her feet and watched the ship's headsails breaking from the yards. The corvette appeared to curtsy as the canvas billowed and swelled. Moments later the topsails followed suit, the yards swinging in unison as the braces were hauled. Tilting sharply, the *Raven* paid off into the wind and began her starboard tack, northeast, out and away from the far tip of the island. As more and more sails broke out, gleaming whitely in the first pale shafts of sunlight, she gathered headway. Soon Glenmorgan would bring her about again on the larboard tack to weather the headland. Then the little *Mirabel* would be alone until the ship beat its way back again, sometime later in the day.

Meg's glance fell on the boom suspended out over the water, the block and tackle swaying with the movement of the boat. She swallowed dryly. By then they would know if the hoist was adequate to the task at hand, she thought, or more importantly, if she was.

Eleven

Ignoring the boom of canvas and the scream and clatter of blocks as the ship was forced about on a new heading, north by northeast, Glenmorgan raised the glass to his eye and made a slow sweep of the endless stretch of sea. All morning they had stood well off the island as they worked their way around the northern reaches of Barbuda, then back, and now north again, swinging in an arc that kept them a goodly distance from Pippin, but close enough to dash in should a sail have been sighted. It was slow, tedious work, especially in light of the fact that they might have been just as well employed anchored off the island aiding Pippin and the girl with the salvaging.

His lips thinned to a hard line as he slammed the telescope shut. He had no patience for this sort of thing. While he crawled back and forth, the girl might already have come to grief, and he was too far away to do a thing to help her.

Blast Pippin and his misplaced sense of propriety! There should have been no objection to allowing him, Glenmorgan, to remain on hand to be of what assistance he could. Obviously she could not dive in a dress and petticoats, but if she wore nothing at all, it could hardly matter. He, after all, already had an intimate knowledge of her undeniable charms.

A mirthless smile twisted at his lips as he recalled his last image of her, her cheeks pale, but her eyes shimmery with defiance. "You will have your gold and your vengeance," she had said. The words had been like a rapier thrust. Damn her impertinence. Vengeance was only a part of it. There was such a thing as honor. But then, he was not ready to tell her the gold was not for him. The stakes in the game he was playing were far more complex than that.

Restlessly, he began to pace the weather deck, his mind only half aware of the sights and sounds of the ship around him, as he turned his thoughts to Charles Town and what awaited him there. By now Sutton had received his instructions and had had sufficient time to set things in motion. With any luck the refurbishing of the house would be completed by the time of his own arrival and his mother and sisters already comfortably settled. Briefly the hard lines about his mouth softened. How he would have liked to be there, to see the look on his mother's face when she stepped across the threshold. But then, returning the Town House to its former state was only the beginning. He would still have the pleasure of escorting Mary Glenmorgan to Marigold before the new year was out—if, that is, he was still alive.

All of which brought him back to the problem of Meg and her grandfather. Once again his features took on their granite hardness. If they still insisted on settling in Charles Town instead of someplace far removed from danger, he would have to make arrangements for suitable accommodations. A house, Pippin had said, overlooking the sea and yet somewhat apart from the town itself. No amount of reasoning or argument could dissuade him from what Glenmorgan considered a wholly impracticable arrangement. At least in the Town House they might have been assured of

Glenmorgan's protection. On their own, in a house on the outskirts of town, he could assure them of nothing.

At the nettings he stopped and lifted the glass to his eye. The island loomed off the port bow, a green shifting mass crouched against the sky. Carefully, he moved the glass and found the ketch. In the distance, it looked little more than a tiny bobbing toy boat. In spite of the fact that everything appeared peaceful enough, he could feel the uncertainty clawing at him, fueling his impatience to know what was happening.

Closing the telescope with a snap, he glanced at the sun. Meg and her grandfather had had six hours, he judged. Six hours to discover if they could indeed salvage the wreck. It was enough for a beginning, and he would wait no longer to find out for himself what progress they had made.

"Mr. Chapin," he snapped, "prepare to come about on the larboard tack."

"Aye, aye, sir."

As the formality of their exchange registered, Glenmorgan's eyes went to the burly form of his first mate, watching him noncommittally from the lea rail. Uncomfortably he was reminded of the argument that had flared up between them only the night before.

It had been over the girl and the seeming pointlessness of patrolling the area off the island.

"Out there, we'll be like sitting ducks, Captain. In plain sight of any ship that happens by. Why not do like we've always done and hole up in one of the bloody coves? We'd not be so easily spotted, and we'd be closer to hand if the old man and the girl fell into a pot of trouble. It'd make a helluva lot more sense to my way of thinking," he had ended grudgingly.

"Sense has little to do with it," Glenmorgan had snapped, in no mood to discuss what must have been obvious to anyone—anyone, that is, but an obstinate old man and his equally stubborn granddaughter. "It's the way *they* want it."

He remembered Chapin's frown. He had sensed, no doubt, his captain's own uncertainty beneath the show of anger. Dick Chapin was his oldest friend and closer to him than a brother. As boys, they had gone to sea together on a Glenmorgan trading ship and had been together ever since. Nothing could shake Chapin's loyalty. He had not even hesitated when Glenmorgan informed him of his intention to arm *Raven,* the last of the Glenmorgan vessels, and make it the most feared pirate ship in the Caribbean, a weapon to strike back at his father's enemies. He had sworn an oath to follow wherever Glenmorgan might lead, and so he had, with tenacity and an unflagging courage. Glenmorgan, consequently, was not surprised when the first mate had stubbornly persisted in questioning Pippin's eccentric behavior.

"Yes, but why, Michael?" Chapin had exclaimed, leaning forward as though to emphasize his words. "Doesn't it strike you as the least bit strange? Think, man! The idea of a female doing what she claims she can do is farfetched enough, but insisting on doing it without any help puts a damned odd light on things."

It had not helped that Glenmorgan could not deny it. Chapin had, with his usual hardheadedness, gone straight to the bone of the matter. It *was* odd, as were countless other unexplained pieces of the puzzle that surrounded Meg. But whether or not he understood the girl little mattered. For now, he had no choice but to adhere to the terms of the bargain. Meg had made sure of that.

He had made no attempt to keep the bitterness from his answer: "And if I agree with you, it changes nothing, Dick. The truth is I don't know the answers any more than you."

That was not to be the end of it. Of that Glenmorgan was certain. He could see it now in Chapin's plain, honest face. His first mate was not happy with what he must consider his captain's newest infatuation. After Clarissa, he could hardly blame him. And yet, in his own mind, Glenmorgan knew he could trust Meg and her motives. He was, in fact, all too aware that Meg was incapable of anything selfish or base. If she had any ulterior motives in what she did, they would not be intended to harm him or gain anything for herself. On the contrary, he strongly suspected that, in spite of the bargain they had struck, she would risk her life to help him achieve the one thing he had claimed he wanted, and in exchange, would resist accepting anything from him, including his money, which he had in plenty, his name, or his protection.

Damn her and her stubborn pride! What did she expect of him? He could not go on taking from her without giving something back in return. And yet, she had made it plain there was nothing she wanted from him. He could feel his frustration no less than his bafflement chafe at his nerves, driving him to pace the deck again as the ship came about on her new course. Even as they had worked together on the hoist, physically so close that there was not a moment he was not aware of her, she had maintained her aloofness like a barrier between them. More than once he had found himself having to forcibly restrain himself from taking her by the arms and actually shaking her. And so, instead, he had kissed her.

It was the one thing that offered any ray of hope in the whole bloody mess, he decided, smiling with a singular lack of mirth. There had been fire beneath the ice. Of that, he was certain.

Gritting her teeth, Meg forced open another of the rotting chests with an iron bar and, without stopping to rest, began to transfer its contents of gold to the fishing net. She had lost count of how many times she had filled the net and sent it topside with a tug on the signal line. In six hours she had managed to empty only two of the chests. How much easier it would have been to send the gold up in their oaken coffers! Their sheer weight, however, made that an impossible feat for her grandfather, working alone at the windlass. Once the gold was topside, the empty chest was lifted to the surface, where, working together, Meg and the old man placed the bars back inside.

It had been a long, wearing day, and she could feel herself growing more tired with each passing hour. Stubbornness and the certainty that Glenmorgan believed she would fail kept her at it when she knew she would otherwise have taken a rest.

An hour later, Meg struggled to secure the tackle to the now emptied chest. Pulling the signal line, she waited for the slack to go out of the cable, then, guiding the chest through the jagged rent in the *Argonaut*'s side, she rose swiftly to the surface ahead of the load. Wearily she climbed up the rope ladder and over the coaming.

Her grandfather was bent over the windlass, his shoulders hunched as he turned the crank.

"Better take time to slip something on," he cautioned without looking around. "We've company coming."

Only then did she see the corvette bearing down on them. It would take the ship another thirty minutes or so to draw near enough to drop anchor, but a sharp lookout, with the aid of a telescope, might be able to see more than she would have liked. Hurriedly, she slipped into her gown before going to help her grandfather swing the chest inboard.

"Well, I'll be buggered," exclaimed Dick Chapin, staring at the three wooden chests stored forward of the sleeping cabin, each one weighing at least nine tons or more. By any standards, it was an astonishing achievement. But considering who had done it and under what circumstances, it seemed to Chapin nothing short of the miracle he had claimed they would need.

Glenmorgan was studying the girl's face, his own eyes enigmatic, as he said, "Mr. Chapin means you have done better than any of us could have expected." Ironically, he noted the slight flush invade Meg's cheeks. It was the first sign she had given that she was not totally indifferent to his presence. He was conscious of the desire to have her to himself in order to further test that hypothesis and impatiently shoved the thought aside. To Pippin, he added, smiling, "It would seem that we have not made our arrival any too early. You've damned little freeboard showing. Had we put it off till nightfall, I'm afraid your little ketch might have foundered."

Pippin rubbed the sweat from his neck and face with a rag and grinned in wry agreement.

"We have had better luck than even I had thought possible. It is, at least, a fair beginning."

Glenmorgan barely nodded. Meg looked tired, he thought, and wondered suddenly what it was like to delve so deeply beneath the sea. He could imagine the pressure on lungs which must already feel near to bursting. And then to remain below long enough to secure the load. Such moments must seem like hours. How the hell did she do it?

Dragging himself from his thoughts, he realized the others were watching him and said brusquely, "Signal the boat crews, Dick. We will begin transport at once."

"In the meantime, Captain," Pippin suggested, "perhaps you would care to come below to quench your thirst. The port you had sent over from your ship is a good deal better than the island wines I am used to. It should be enjoyed in company."

"You go ahead, Captain." Chapin's huge grin banished the tension that had lain between them as if it had never been. "I'll handle things up here. I expect the young lady and her grandfather have earned a rest."

"Only as long as it takes to move the chests," Meg answered gruffly, thinking of the dozen or more that still remained below. "I see no sense in wasting the daylight we have left."

Moving toward the cabin hatch, she did not see the quick exchange of glances between Glenmorgan and his first mate. Both of them were thinking of the number of descents she must already have made that day. Egad, thought Chapin, the girl wasn't human.

After the merciless heat of the sun, the dark interior of the cabin felt almost cool. Meg found a place on a cot forward, leaving Pippin and Glenmorgan the bench seats on converging sides of a small table. Sitting with her chin propped on her knees, she watched as the old man poured two glasses of wine.

Handing one to Glenmorgan, he lifted the other and said, "To a successful endeavor."

"If it's to be a toast, Mr. Pippin, then surely your granddaughter should join us." Glenmorgan let the suggestion sink in before adding, "After all, any success we might hope to enjoy depends almost entirely on her."

Meg's voice cut across the sudden uneasy silence.

"I do not drink, Captain."

"Yes, I have noticed that about you." Glenmorgan settled his shoulders against the bulkhead and stretched his long legs out before him. "Or that you never seem to eat. I'm reminded of the Oriental custom of refusing food and drink in the presence of an enemy." Deliberately he lifted his eyes to hers. "Am I the enemy here?"

Meg stared at him, caught off balance. He was goading her. Why?

"There are no enemies here, Captain," Pippin was saying smoothly. "Only a young girl with no experience of spirits. It would not do to cloud her mind when she—"

"Grandfather, I am not a child," Meg firmly broke in. "A glass, if you please."

Pippin glanced from one to the other, keenly aware of the heightened tension in the close confines of the cabin.

"As you wish," he shrugged, "though I hardly think it wise."

Briefly he considered diluting the wine's rich potency with water, but on a sudden impulse discarded the notion. A faint gleam of a smile hovered about his lips. What was the worst that could happen? Perhaps it was what was needed to bring them both to their senses.

Pouring the drink, he handed it to Meg and once more raised his glass. "To us, then," he said, "and good fortune."

Glenmorgan drank, watching Meg over the rim of his glass as she tentatively lifted hers to her lips. A dark flush stained her cheeks at the sight of his smile, faintly mocking. The next instant she tossed her head back and drained the glass.

Pippin exclaimed, "Here, now, child. Wine's to be sipped, not guzzled."

It was all Meg could do to keep from gagging. Faith, but it was abominable stuff—sickly sweet, followed by a bitter aftertaste. It turned her stomach, but she would rather have died than let Glenmorgan know. Her chin lifted in unconscious defiance, she held out the glass for more.

The old man made only the briefest hesitation. "Yes, well," he murmured, filling the glass, "I think I shall just go and see how your Mr. Chapin is coming along with the boats. You two, feel free to enjoy yourselves."

Judiciously ignoring the startled look of dismay on his granddaughter's face, he made his way up the ladder, taking care to close the door behind him.

Meg shot a single glance at the lean masculine figure, sprawled carelessly on the bench, his sea-dampened shirt open to the waist, then dropped her eyes with something like desperation. She was suddenly and acutely aware that not only was she alone with the captain, but that his long legs, stretched out before the narrow companionway, blocked her only avenue of escape. Without thinking, she nervously swallowed some wine, hiding her grimace of distaste behind her hand.

She could sense Glenmorgan's eyes on her. He was probably laughing at her discomfort.

She nearly jumped when, holding his glass up to the light, he said casually, "You should go easy on that. You're not used to it and what it can do."

Meg felt a hot flush stain her cheeks. Why must he always be telling her what or what not to do? Just once she would like to be allowed to make up her own mind without his help. Instinctively her head came up, her look challenging.

"Then maybe," she said, "it is time I learned." Lifting the glass, she drank its contents without stopping to take a breath.

Surprisingly, it went down more easily than before. So much easier that she was beginning to think perhaps it was not quite so bad as she had at first imagined. She felt a delicious warmth steal over her, accompanied by a peculiar giddiness that was not all that unpleasant.

She found, in fact, that she was buoyed by an exhilarating sense of well-being, which she wished somehow to share with the captain. She was acutely aware of his lean masculine presence and for the life of her could not recall why it had previously seemed so important to maintain a rigid guard against him. On the contrary, she found that she wished nothing more than to have him take her in his arms, to feel his strong body next to hers, the magic of his hands weaving their spell over her. And why should she not? It might be the last opportunity she would ever have to be one with him.

With slow deliberation she slid off the cot and, casting what could only be construed as a provocative glance over her shoulder at Glenmorgan, reached for the bottle.

Glenmorgan's eyebrow went up at that look. "I think," he murmured dryly, "that you have had enough wine for one day."

"I, on the other hand, do not," she retorted, resisting the urge to giggle as, in her attempt to refill the glass, she sloshed wine over the table. Faith, what magic was this? She had never felt so gloriously light-headed or so marvelously reckless before. She did not even care that Glenmorgan was watching her, his blue eyes beneath drooping eyelids, maddeningly unreadable. Indeed, it was as if all of her cares, along with her inhibitions, had suddenly just vanished.

At last picking up her glass again, she favored Glenmorgan with a disapproving glance. "But what's this, Captain? I thought we were celebrating, but you are not drinking."

There was a sardonic twitch at the corners of Glenmorgan's lips as he noted the faint slur in her voice. "I beg your pardon. I was not aware we were in a contest. To what would you have us drink?"

Meg paused to consider. An image of Clarissa as she had looked on the verandah of the grand house in Antigua flashed in her mind—haughty, proud, even disdainful as she had plotted Glenmorgan's death. It was her fault Meg now found herself hopelessly in love with a man who could never love her back. A bittersweet smile curved her lips as she lifted the glass in an eloquent gesture.

"To the treacherous heart," she pronounced, staggering a little as the deck canted beneath her feet. "And its inescapable webs of entanglement."

197

Suddenly she was swaying badly, and her face had gone alarmingly pale. Frowning, she concentrated on raising the glass.

Glenmorgan's hand closed around hers on the glass before she even realized he had moved from his seat. He was too tall to stand upright and had to bend his head even between the deck beams so that his face was within inches of her own. Dazed, she stared into his eyes glittery in the dim glow of the skylight.

Quietly he said, "Enough, Meg. You don't have to prove anything. I was wrong to goad you to it."

Meg frowned, trying to make sense of his words through an enveloping haze that was clouding her mind. She let him take the glass from her hand and set it down on the table. But when he turned back to her, she slid her hands with sudden determination around his waist and up his back.

"If I have nothing to prove," she murmured, deliciously aware that she was flirting with danger and not caring what it might cost her later, "then why did you do it? What do you want from me that I have not already given?"

"The truth. The answers to a hundred unasked questions." He shook his head. "It doesn't matter now. Marry me when we get to Charles Town. Let me give you what protection I can."

"No." She felt the muscles of his body tense. Daringly, she lifted her head. "I have all the protection I need, Captain," she whispered, her lips within a tantalizing inch of his. "I would much rather give you the answers to your questions."

At the pale glint in his eyes, she felt a heady sense of danger, more potent than the wine she had drunk. It robbed her of all caution, imbued her with an intoxicating recklessness. She could feel the power pulsating within her veins, power which could awaken the winds or call forth the raging fury of a storm. What need had she for protection? Only Glenmorgan could destroy her—Glenmorgan and her own treacherous heart.

Deliberately she turned her face into the curve of his neck. "You once asked about my people," she said, her voice sounding detached, dreamy, as if someone else were doing the talking. "Richard Belding, my father, came from Charles Town to the West Indies in search of adventure. He found it—and Sheela, my mother, and never went back again. He died on St. Vincent's of the fever when I was eleven, and my mother . . . well, she soon followed him. I have lived with my grandfather ever since." Giving in to temptation, she brushed her lips against the pulse beating at the side of his neck. "What else would you know? That long ago I lost all contact with my mother's people? As far as I know, I am the last of them. They were a sea people, drawing from it their sustenance and their strength, and I am like them. I could not survive away from the sea, any more than you could, I think. It is a part of me. I know its secrets, which is why I am able to do what no one else can do." Deliberately she lifted her eyes to his. "I can retrieve your treasure for you. And if you wish it, I can love you. But I cannot marry you."

God knows, it should have been enough, thought Glenmorgan ironically, as he became aware that her hands had worked their way beneath his shirt and were running with sensuous deliberation up his back. Clearly the wine had unloosed more than her tongue. Yet in spite of the fact that she had revealed a great deal more about herself than she ever had before, he was keenly conscious of a need to know more. And he could not do that if he allowed things to go too far too fast.

Reaching out, he pulled her arms from around him.

"Perhaps we should sit down," he said—like a fond relative humoring a troublesome child, Meg thought in wry amusement. "Then you can tell me all about these secrets."

Meg, however, had different ideas. Due to the effects of the wine and her own weariness, she was feeling imbued with a wonderful feeling of languor. Laying her hands flat against Glenmorgan's chest, she leaned precariously against him. "They would not be secrets anymore if I told them," she whispered with an exaggerated air of confidentiality.

Glenmorgan grinned conspiratorially back at her. "They will be our secrets then. Just between you and me. Somehow I don't think the sea will mind sharing them."

Meg frowned as she appeared to think the matter over. "Perhaps not," she agreed uncertainly after a moment. Tilting her head back, she looked at him out of eyes that shimmered like water in moonlight. "There are things in the sea that you cannot even imagine. Wondrous creatures so delicate that it seems a miracle they can exist at all. And others so deadly that even the fer de lance pales before them." With her fingertip, she traced the puckered scar on his chest. "There is a power of healing in the sea—plants which your physicians can know nothing about. Some of them saved your life, Captain."

"For which I am grateful . . ." Glenmorgan began, only to break off as Meg pressed her lips with infinite tenderness to the scar. Unwittingly he stiffened, the muscle leaping across his chest. He felt his loins stir as he became keenly aware of her warm, yielding body against his. Once again his hands caught her wrists as she began to explore his bare torso beneath the shirt.

Meg's face lifted questioningly to his. Her eyes, those shimmering blue-green pools, took his breath away. She would never know the effort it cost him not to give in to the temptation to crush her lips beneath his.

"Tell me about these plants," he said, cynically aware of the oddity of the role he was playing—like a bloody maiden out to protect a jealously guarded virtue. It was no less surprising that he found the notion of taking advantage of

Meg's intoxication revolting somehow, especially in light of the fact that he had cold-bloodedly prodded her to it in the hopes of breaking down her reserve. Now that he had succeeded, he felt only a disgust with himself.

Meg's eyebrows lifted in astonishment.

"You cannot really wish to hear me talk about plants, Captain?" she queried archly. There was the muffled thud of a boat coming alongside and the clatter of men clambering on board the ketch. Meg's arms went around his neck, her lips finding his, at the very same moment that the *Mirabel* dipped and swayed sluggishly with the added weight of the boarding party. Caught off balance, Glenmorgan was thrown back a step. His head cracked against a deck beam overhead, and the next instant found him sprawled on the bench seat, Meg lying on top of him.

Glenmorgan let forth with a blistering oath.

Meg choked on a gurgle of laughter. Then at sight of the captain's wry expression, his hand massaging the back of his head where it had hit, her mirth instantly vanished.

"You've hurt yourself!" she exclaimed. Without thinking, she reached up to place the palm of a hand on either side of his forehead and began to hum, the low, throbbing song of the *hrum,* just as her mother had taught her so long ago.

Glenmorgan went suddenly still, the breath going out of him, as gentle pulsations of sound vibrated like a soothing caress through his entire length. With a sense of unreality, he felt the throbbing pain in his skull ease, then dissipate, leaving him dazed and staring into eyes which were dreamy, unfocused, distant.

No sooner had the pain left him than the humming stopped, and with a long sigh, Meg laid her head down on his chest. Instinctively he knew she had fallen asleep.

For a long time, Glenmorgan lay where he was, his hand

201

gently stroking Meg's hair, soft and silken beneath his touch. A frown etched itself between his eyebrows as he tried to make sense of what had happened. He might as well try to explain the wind, he thought wryly. He was reminded of other times, when he had lain delirious and in pain, when he had felt her hands upon him, heard her voice reaching through the anguish. She had driven the nightmares away, soothed the agony of despair. Was this how she had done it?

No, he thought, this was something different. Even now he could remember with vivid clarity the currents of pleasure throbbing through his body, pleasure that might soon have intensified to something else had it been allowed to continue. His lip curled in a bemused smile. By God, he did not know if he was relieved or sorry that it had ended when it did!

The squeal of blocks and tackle and the muffled shouts of his men working to transfer the treasure to the boats alongside the ketch broke into his thoughts, and at last he began to ease off the bench, carrying the limp body of the girl with him.

Meg murmured some incoherent protest as he bent down and lifted her into his arms. For a moment he stood still, keenly aware that he held something rare and beautiful and totally incomprehensible. Like one of the sea creatures she had described, he mused humorlessly. Unwilling yet to relinquish her, he savored the fresh, clean scent of her, the feel of her body against him. Her head lolled back against his shoulder so that he could see her face, vulnerable in sleep and breathtakingly lovely.

Bitterly he cursed himself as, unbidden, the image of another Meg, standing naked and unafraid on the beach, her beautiful body, her hair shimmering like silver in the moonlight, rose up not for the first time to haunt him. He had taken her once in a feverish madness. He had not meant to take her again. But even with his wits about him, he had not been able to control his desire. Good God, he doubted that any man could, presented with similar circumstances. But the realization did not lessen his guilt. He was cynically aware that it was an uneasy conscience that had made him deliberately belittle Meg and what had passed between them, when in truth it was himself that he detested.

In the succeeding five days of waiting in inactivity and uncertainty for Meg's return, he had had plenty of time to torment himself with the truth. He had not wanted her to come back, had not wanted the distraction of a woman who could so thoroughly inflame both his mind and his senses that for a brief moment as he had awakened to her that next morning on the beach, he had found himself tempted to give up his mission, his vengeance, even his honor—everything that had made him what he was. It was a sobering realization, one that he did not like. Had he been certain she was safe, he knew he would not have hesitated to sail without ever having to see or speak to her again.

How neatly she had turned the tables on him! From the moment he had turned and seen her, beautiful and elusive, her eyes coolly indifferent, as she came toward him from the corner of her grandfather's hut, he had not been able to keep his mind off her. The very fact that she held herself aloof had made her only the more maddeningly desirable. He had felt it working on him, on his already uneasy conscience, like salt to the wound.

Hellsfire! He should have been relieved to find her apparently indifferent to him. But the nagging suspicion that she was making some noble sacrifice for him would not leave him alone. He wanted none of her selfless generosity. He would far rather have had her curse and revile him. That he could have dealt with. As it was, he had been driven nearly to distraction at the thought that she could so easily dismiss him and everything that had happened between them. Nor had it mattered in the least that that was exactly what *he* had contemplated doing to her.

Was it his cursed pride that made him seethe inside at her coldness? Or something more. Whatever it was, he had known suddenly as he watched her here in the cabin, curled up on the cot and secure in her self-imposed shell of indifference, that he would stop at nothing to break her reserve and the devil with the consequences.

He had succeeded far better than he had expected, but it had been an underhanded trick, and he knew it. A second later, his teeth flashed in a smile at the memory of Meg's lips soft against his scar. Underhanded or not, he knew he did not regret it; indeed, given the chance, he would have done it all over again.

Carefully, then, he carried her to the cot and laid her on it.

Twelve

Meg awakened in darkness to the gentle swaying of the boat and her grandfather's snoring. For a moment she lay still, trying to remember how she had come to be there in the sleeping cabin. Ruefully, she recalled Glenmorgan's arrival at the mooring, her own feeling of irritation at being interrupted in her work when there was still sunlight left. She remembered going below and her grandfather's offer of a toast, Glenmorgan mocking her, goading her into behaving with a foolish disregard for the consequences. Suddenly she bolted upright, recalling something else. A gasp was forced from her lips as her sudden movement awakened a throbbing pain in her head. With a groan she sank back again.

Since she had never been sick before, it did not take her long to deduce that the wine was responsible for her present discomfort, and truly she had never felt so miserable in her life. Aside from the pounding in her head, her tongue felt swollen in a mouth so dry that she could hardly swallow, and worse, she knew with utter certainty that if she did not soon reach the fresh air, she was going to be disgustingly sick to her stomach.

Carefully, so as not to worsen the throbbing of her head, she shoved herself off the cot. Bitterly she cursed the devious Glenmorgan and her own stupid recklessness as she made her way unsteadily to the companionway and finally out into the blessed relief of the night air. Leaning shakily over the side, she drank in deep draughts of the cool breeze blowing inboard from off the island until she felt somewhat restored. Only then was she able to think about the thing that she had done.

She had resorted to the *hrum* to stop Glenmorgan's pain. Faith, how *could* she have been so foolish! This was not something she could simply explain away when the captain demanded answers to the questions he was bound to ask. It was an expression of the most intimate feelings between male and female, a thing that was enshrouded in mystery until one passed over from childhood into sexual maturity. Not until her mother had realized she was dying had she revealed the secret rites of joining to her daughter and only then because she knew there would be no one else to instruct Meg later. Meg went very cold, then very warm, with the realization that had she not fallen asleep when she did, Glenmorgan would have experienced a great deal more than the relief of a headache. With a groan, she sank her head into her hands and wondered dully how much more she had betrayed to the captain while her brain was clouded by the effects of the wine.

Oh, it was all *his* fault. How cleverly he had laid his trap for her, and how blithely had she walked into it. She could not bear to think of it, and yet she could not stop flashes of memory from rising up to torment her. At last, unable to stand herself anymore, or her thoughts, she flung off her gown and dove over the side into the water.

For once the transformation from human into mermaid did nothing to relieve her inner turmoil. If anything, it served only to exacerbate it. For suddenly she saw with utter clarity what she had so carefully kept hidden from herself in her human state: she had *wanted* to complete the rite of *hrum* with Glenmorgan, and if she had not succumbed to the intoxicating effects of the wine and fallen asleep, she was quite sure she would have.

Mortified, she lunged through the water, swimming full tilt farther and farther out to sea. On land, Meg was only as strong as a strong woman. In the sea, she was a magical creature with phenomenal strength and endurance. Even so, she managed to exhaust herself.

Rising at last to the surface, she drifted aimlessly with the current, her body tired but her brain active. Wearily she acknowledged to herself that she had no choice but to return to the boat and to the work of salvaging the wreck. She would do it for her grandfather's sake and because she had given Glenmorgan her word, but most of all because she could not help herself. No matter how far she fled, she would always go back to him. She would even go to this place called Charles Town in order to be near him.

Having given herself up to the inevitability of her attraction to Glenmorgan, she next accepted with equal fatalism the impracticality of pretending to be indifferent to him—especially in light of what she had already revealed of her true feelings. She groaned, wishing she were dead. Oh, how he must be laughing, she thought miserably, then immediately called herself to task. There was no dignity in feeling sorry for herself. From now on, she would simply follow her heart, no matter where it might lead her.

Suddenly she felt as if a tremendous burden had been lifted from her and, with it, all sense of weariness. Feeling considerably more at peace with herself than she had for a long time, she began the long trek back to the *Mirabel*.

In the next few days, Meg saw little or nothing of the captain. She did not know whether to be relieved or disappointed that he sent Chapin in charge of the boats at each of their daily rendezvous. It was enough for the time being that she was too busy to think about anything but the salvaging of the wreck.

The work had gone well. They had been fortunate that the weather remained calm with only the occasional cloudburst to disturb the long days of sunshine and tropical heat. Nor had they spotted any sign of a sail, not even so much as a Barbuda trading vessel. It was beginning to feel as if they were the only people left in the entire Caribbean, but Meg's grandfather and undoubtedly the captain as well knew how vain such a hope was. Gradually Meg became aware that her grandfather kept a sharp eye on the island. Only then was it borne in on her that they were probably being observed with a great deal of curiosity by more than one pair of eyes from ashore, though at two miles out, it was doubtful an observer could tell very much what they were about.

It was not until dusk of the fourth day that Glenmorgan deigned at last to leave the confines of his ship. As usual, Meg was below in the sleeping cabin. Preferring to remain out of sight, she never came topside when the boats were near. She had just finished drying her hair and was busy combing out the tangles in front of the small square of mirror her grandfather had hung on the bulkhead for shaving, when the hail reached her ears.

"Mirabel ahoy!"

Instantly her head turned, her mouth going suddenly dry. She would have recognized that voice anywhere. Hard upon the realization that Glenmorgan himself had come, she was shaken by uncertainty. How could she possibly face him after she had made such a fool of herself? Indeed, how was she to answer when he demanded to know what she had done to him that dreadful day in this very cabin? And he would ask her, she knew, probably with an oath and with eyes that would look at her as if she were some strange creature, a monster, a horrid freak of nature. Or perhaps, having no wish to see her ever again, he would not come below at all.

She experienced a sudden surge of hope at the thought. Perhaps he would be satisfied with her grandfather's report of their progress. The old man would inform him that, with only three chests left to salvage, there was every chance they would be through with the entire business by this time tomorrow. Glenmorgan would thank him, and there being no reason for Meg's confirmation, he would return with the first load to the ship.

That hope quickly faded as, straining to hear above the clatter and squeal of block and tackle and all the other sounds that accompanied the transfer of a nine-ton chest of gold to a waiting boat, she thrilled to the sound of a light footstep on the companionway, followed almost immediately by a rap on the door.

The next minute, the door opened, revealing Glenmorgan, limned against a dazzle of sunlight, though she could not recall having called out permission to enter.

He was alone. Ducking his head beneath the coaming, he came in and shut the door behind him.

"Good afternoon, Captain," Meg managed in a voice that was reasonably normal. After a single glance, she continued combing her hair as if she were not acutely aware of the man standing with his head slightly bent between the deck-beams, his eyes unreadable in the thick shadows. "This is an unexpected pleasure. I was beginning to think you had taken a dislike to us."

A gleam of a smile shone against his tanned cheeks. "Now why should you think that?"

Meg made a comical grimace. "You know very well why. I did fall asleep in the middle of your last visit, after all. When you didn't come back the next day, I was convinced I had chased you away." She gave him a long, searching

209

look from beneath her eyelashes, but there was nothing in his face to indicate he thought anything untoward had happened on his previous visit. At last, turning back to the mirror, she said, "Why *have* you come here?"

As if taking his cue from her, he sat down on the bench seat and watched her draw the comb through her long hair. "Your grandfather tells me that you are nearly finished below."

"Yes." Meg glanced at his reflection in the mirror. "There are three chests, smaller than the others. I think they contain coins, or jewelry perhaps. It's my hope that we will be able to bring them up as they are, without having to empty them first. If so, it will take a fraction of the time."

His sudden low exclamation took her by surprise.

"So that's how you've been doing it! Good God, Meg. It must have taken you hours—"

Meg bit her lip, realizing her mistake. "It—it was not so difficult as you might think," she interrupted in an attempt to retrieve her error. "Not with the—er—breathing tube," she finished lamely. Before he could have time to question the feasibility of a breathing tube over a hundred feet long, one, moreover, which was nowhere in evidence on the crowded fishing boat, she laid down her comb and came about to face him. "But that isn't what you came to discuss, surely, Captain."

Glenmorgan eyed her grimly. Clearly he realized she was deliberately changing the subject, but for the moment it seemed he meant to let her get away with it.

"No," he agreed, "that isn't what I came to discuss." For an instant he appeared to hesitate as if considering the best way to phrase what he had to say. "That first day," he said slowly. "you described the master's quarters. The cabinet. Do you remember?"

Of course she remembered. There was hardly any reason why she should forget it—or the expression on his face when she had described it. "What about the cabinet?" she prodded, curious now.

"Could you tell anything about it? What sort of shape it's in."

"It's in perfect shape, considering it has been under water for seven years. The wood is rotting, the gold leaf pealing off. What sort of shape do you expect it to be in?"

"Dammit, Meg, that's not what I mean." He got up, ducking his head beneath the deckbeams, and came toward her. "There was a secret panel. With any luck it is still intact. And behind it, a metal box. I need that box and what's inside it. Tomorrow I want you to go after it."

"Very well, if you can tell me how to work the panel." Meg shrugged. "It should be easy enough after I've taken care of the chests to—"

"Forget the other chests! They don't matter. We've got enough of the blasted treasure to satisfy even the cursed Admiralty's pound of flesh. It's the box I want." At the startled look in her eyes, he immediately relented. His hands closed on her shoulders. "It's important, Meg, or I wouldn't ask you to go down there looking for it. God knows you've done enough."

There were a myriad of questions that she wanted to ask, but before she could get out even one, he was already describing the mechanism and how it worked.

"There's every chance that it was damaged when the ship was sunk," he ended. "You might have to break into it. Whatever you have to do, do it in as little time as you can. It's time we were getting out of here."

Her heart lurched as his strong supple fingers wove themselves through the hair at the back of her neck. "Take care tomorrow, Meg," he murmured, then kissed her, lingeringly, on the mouth. His head lifted, and she saw his eyes glittery in the dim light. "I have the feeling that our luck cannot last forever."

Her lips tingled with the feel of his kiss long after he left her, standing dazed and staring fixedly at the door he closed carefully behind him.

Glenmorgan was right, Meg told herself a good deal later as she leaned with her elbows on the gunwale and gazed out at the island ablaze in the brilliant glow of sunset. Their luck had lasted longer than they had any right to expect. And yet in the still beauty of approaching dusk, it did not seem possible that danger might be waiting for them somewhere out there.

Unwittingly she shivered and turned her gaze away from the island to the sea, painted blood red in the last flare of the setting sun. Suddenly she stilled as, out of the ruffled crest of a wave rose a white pillar of spray and then, a short distance away from the first, another and yet another. She felt her pulse quicken with excitement. Whales, seven of them in all, their tall, pointed dorsal fins slicing through the water like swords.

She was hardly aware when her grandfather emerged from the cabin at her back and came to stand beside her.

"So they found you, did they," he said. "I was wondering when they would show up."

Meg laughed. It was one of the things he could never understand about her and her mother—the bond between her sea-dwelling people and the killer whales. But it was as old as time immemorial.

"You're going out there, I suppose."

Meg nodded. "It may be the last time I see them for a very long time. I have to make them understand that they must not follow where I am going."

"Yes, well, try and see if you can persuade them not to play too close to *Mirabel,* will you?" he remarked as Meg

212

stepped back into the shadows to slip out of her gown. "The last time, they nearly capsized the old girl."

He waited until he heard a splash then, shaking his head, returned below for a last pipe of tobacco before going to bed.

Hral, the young bull, was the first to come to her. Twenty-five feet and nine tons of sheer speed and power, he came streaking out of the darkness straight for her, as if he had mistaken her for a seal or a porpoise, which he intended taking for his supper. Just as it seemed he would scoop her up in his mouth, gleaming with sharp, pointed teeth, he dove neatly beneath her, giving her a light tap with the tip of his powerful tail as he passed. Meg, borne up on a surging backcurrent, darted after him, matching him in speed, if not in brute strength. It was an old game. One they had played often, and in spite of their differences in size, the young bull had never once harmed her.

She was quickly made to feel at home among the hunting clan. These few had left the larger pod, which numbered thirty or forty, and would soon rejoin it for the seal hunts farther out to sea. But for now they were content to renew an old acquaintanceship. It had always been like this, for as long as she could remember. One day they would appear without warning as if curious to see how she was getting on, and the next they would be gone. She had often told herself that one day she would follow these friends to the pod in the hopes that they might lead her to others of her own kind. But she never had, and now it looked as if she never would.

A bright half-moon had already traced its course across the sky toward the far horizon when Meg finally finished saying her goodbyes. Not that there were any words exchanged. It was a silent communication, difficult to explain.

They were bonded, she and the whales. She could summon them with a thought, the way she summoned the winds. Or she could send them away again. When she was with them, there was a sense of communing, so that at the end of her time with them, she was aware that two new young were due to be born within the time of the next full moon and that Jem, one of the older females and an old friend, would never again hunt with the pod.

Her heart heavy with the knowledge of Jem's passing, it was not till she was on the point of climbing on board her grandfather's ketch that her nerves prickled with the sudden warning of danger.

Carefully, Meg pulled herself on board the swaying vessel and crouched in the stern, her senses strained. A gasp rose to her lips, quickly stifled. There it was again—the muffled splash of an oar, closer this time than before.

Without waiting to hear more, she slipped noiselessly down the companionway and groped through the darkness toward the sound of her grandfather's gentle snores. Her hand found and covered his mouth.

"Hush," she whispered softly as she felt him jerk awake. "Quickly, we must get you away. We are about to be boarded."

With barely a nod, Pippin was already moving to get up.

She stopped him as he reached for his clothing. "There's no time for that. Hurry. They're almost upon us."

Topside, the old man's white nightshirt, fluttering about his lank frame, shone ghostlike in the moonlight. Wordlessly, Meg motioned him toward the side, away from the approaching boat. The oars could be heard distinctly now as Meg slipped silently into the water. She could feel her heart pounding as she waited for her grandfather to join her, afraid at any moment to see the ketch swarmed by pirates.

The crack of a shot shattered the silence. From somewhere came the sickening thud of a pistol ball striking flesh, followed by angry shouts and the hollow thump of the boat coming up hard against the ketch. Then her grandfather was over the side.

Her heart in her throat, Meg saw him go under. It was a long-standing joke between them that, in all his years at sea, he had never learned to swim. But Meg had him. Dragging him, choking and sputtering to the surface, she headed away from the ketch. More shots rang out. Pistol balls pelted the water all around them. Meg gasped as a searing pain cut across the top of her shoulder, but somehow she managed to keep her grip on Pippin, her arm across his chest, holding his head out of the water.

It was only then that she realized she had not stopped to consider what her next course of action should be. Until that moment, it had been enough simply to get Pippin off the ketch.

She felt her grandfather try to twist his head around. "The ship," he gasped, choking as a wave crested and broke over them. "Must warn 'em. Glenmorgan's only chance."

Instantly, she knew he was right. There would be other boats. There had to be. And it would not be *Mirabel* they were after, but *Raven* and the treasure chests. But her first thought must be for her grandfather.

Grimly she headed for the island in spite of Pippin's protests. Her grandfather would be safe on shore, and there still might be time for her to do what she could to help the captain. With any luck the gunshots had already alerted Glenmorgan to his danger, just as her grandfather had meant them to do. It was undoubtedly why he had taken the risk to fire that first, warning shot.

Setting her teeth against the fire in her shoulder, she

swam with all her strength away from the ketch and the gunshots.

At the first cry of alarm from the masthead, Glenmorgan was already bolting up the companionway to the quarterdeck. Unable to sleep, he had been on deck for most of the night. It was ironic that he had just managed to doze off on the padded bench seat beneath the stern windows when the faint sounds of gunfire jerked him awake.

As he stepped out from beneath the poop on to the quarterdeck, his eyes automatically swept over the ship, which had lain cleared for action all through the long night—the men crouched at their gun stations, the boarding nets hung to repel boarders, chain slings rigged to the yards to protect the men from falling timbers or spars. He felt little comfort in the thought that his instinct for danger had been proved right. He had felt in his bones that the attack would come, and now that it had, he was left with a bitter taste in his mouth. He had failed in one aspect of his strategy—in believing that the pirates would overlook the tiny *Mirabel*. Those shots had come from the direction of the ketch. Against his better judgment, he had left Meg and her grandfather to face capture and possible death alone.

Chapin's voice, taut with excitement, jarred him away from such thoughts. "Galleys, Michael, off the larboard bow. At least half a dozen, maybe more. Hellsfire, there must be a force at least as big as when we faced Lavoillet and all of his lieutenants put together."

"You may be sure of it," said Glenmorgan grimly. "There's a king's ransom in gold below." Going quickly to the rail, he trained a telescope to the leeward. In the pale glow of moonlight, he could just make out a cluster of square, single-rigged sails, one for each of the galleys. He thought he could see a white froth along either side of the lead boat where the sweeps dipped and dug into the water, but perhaps he only imagined it. There was little doubt, however, that they were making good headway.

"Load and run out," he said tersely over his shoulder. "They'll be in range in another ten minutes."

For a moment he toyed with the idea of slipping the cable and trying to outmaneuver them, then immediately discarded it. The wind had laid, leaving little more than a feeble breeze that plucked desultorily at the pennant atop the foremast. *Raven* was a good sailor in a light wind, but the galleys would be swifter, more maneuverable. He would be better fending off the attack with a stable deck for his larger guns. Nevertheless, they would be on him, like wolves tearing at his flanks, unless he could disable at least some of them before they drew near enough to use their bow chasers. After that, they would try to board, and with each galley carrying fifty men at the very least, it would be over for *Raven* and her men in a matter of minutes.

"Mr. Chapin, prepare to fire at will. And make sure that every shot counts. They will scatter at the first volley and try to board us."

"Aye, aye, Cap'n. All right, lads," Chapin shouted down at the gun crews. "You heard the captain. An extra round of rum to the first crew to sink one of the bastards. What do you say to that?"

"I says bring 'em on," shouted one of the men back at him. "I've a powerful thirst an' waitin' don't help it none!"

Glenmorgan, watching the steady approach of the closely packed galleys, lowered the glass and drew his sword.

"Ready, lads. We'll give 'em a welcome they won't soon forget." The meaningless words elicited some cheers at his back as he waited an agonizing few seconds more. Then he brought the sword slashing down. *"Fire!"*

Even as the *Raven*'s decks recoiled from the crashing salvo, the shout to sponge out and reload was already echoing from gun captain to gun captain. In two minutes, the guns were being run out again with a shrill squeal and thunder of the gun trucks.

Glenmorgan, straining to see through the smoke, saw the lead galley plunge and disappear behind a sheet of water. Seconds later, it reappeared, the mast gone and the bow smashed from the force of a direct hit. But already the others were sheering away from the damaged craft, spreading out in a wide line before turning to advance again.

The second volley was ragged and less evenly timed, as the gun captains aimed independently and fired. A mast toppled, and Glenmorgan could visualize the frantic scramble to cut the rigging away as the trailing spar dragged the galley around to the leeward. Moments later, the dismasted vessel took three direct hits broadside in a ragged salvo and broke in two as if snapped by a giant hand. A frenzied cheer went up from the men behind him. In that light and at that distance, they had been lucky to hit anything at all, and still they had managed to disable two of the enemy craft. But Glenmorgan could see the galleys on either end were pulling ahead of the others and in another few moments would bring their cannon to bear.

He had seen it all before, had even led one or two such attacks himself. They would come in at the stern where *Raven*'s guns could not be brought to bear. With their powerful bow chasers they would smash the ship into subjection, and then they would board her. But he still had a trump card to play.

Chapin loomed suddenly near, as if he knew what his captain was thinking. "They'll be on us like flies at a slaughter, Cap'n," he said, shouting to be heard above the din of firing.

"Aye, unless we can knock a few more of them out of the water." Glenmorgan felt his lips stretch in a grin. "I think it's time we evened the odds a little. Up anchor aft. And prepare to haul in the kedge line."

"Aye, aye, Cap'n."

Glenmorgan's hand caught Chapin by the arm and stopped him as he started to turn away.

"We'll have to be quick about it, Dick," he shouted, giving his first mate a meaningful look. "Once they see what we're about, we'll only have one chance at them."

Chapin's answering grin was like sunlight streaking through a stormcloud. "With our lads, Cap'n, one chance is all we'll need."

With the order to cease firing, the ship fell into an unnerving silence. The silence before doom, thought Glenmorgan grimly, watching the galleys closing in for the kill. He nearly winced at the sudden boom of a gun, felt the ball striking the hull close to the larboard bow as if he had received the blow himself. The corvette's fragile beams were not made to take a pounding. She was built for speed and maneuverability and had never been meant for standing to in an exchange of broadsides.

With an effort he shook off such morbid fancies and turned his mind to gauging the time left before the cursed galleys closed in for the final attack. He had ordered the kedge anchor dropped after dusk, when the boat pulling aft would not be observed from the island. Now the men at the capstan were dragging in the kedgeline, warping the ship around to bring the guns once more to bear.

Another ball cannoned into the hull, this time close to the stern, followed by another and another.

Chapin's voice cracked with strain. "Pull, damn you! Pull!"

"Mr. Chapin," said Glenmorgan in a voice that carried to the main deck in spite of its unnerving calm. "Let's see what we can do with the swivel guns."

He listened as the order was relayed, his mind registering

the fact that his men still had spirit left to lay wagers on the accuracy of the swivels fore and aft. The galleys would have to be almost on top of them for the guns to do any good at all, but at least it might keep the pirates guessing long enough for the kedge line to do its work. And it would keep the lads' thoughts off the merciless bombardment at the stern.

As Glenmorgan waited while the ship lumbered and wallowed about, dragged, seemingly against her will, to present her broadside to the enemy, he allowed himself to think about Meg and Pippin, captives, perhaps, out there in one of the galleys, waiting to be blown to bits by his own guns. He had been a fool to think they would be safer in the ketch than in a ship about to battle for its life. Or that the very insignificance of the ketch would somehow protect it from harm. Well, it was too late now. His arrogance had more than likely cost them their lives, even as it was about to cost the lives of the men who, in trusting him, now found themselves facing impossible odds.

Then *Raven* was about.

"Swivels, cease firing. Have the starboard and larboard batteries run out, Mr. Chapin. We'll take them on both sides at once."

In vague surprise, he realized the dark had sufficiently cloaked their painstaking maneuver. The galleys, having failed to guess their intent, were now on either side of the ship.

"Fire!" The *Raven* bucked and shuddered with the simultaneous broadsides. In the blinding smoke, Glenmorgan could only guess at the damage to the galleys. The guns ran out again, and again spewed their deadly defiance. Then with a sense of inevitability, he saw men with boarding spikes and axes hacking through the boarding nets.

"To me, lads!" he shouted, waving the sword over his head. "Repel boarders!"

He was carried to the larboard gangway in a mass of heaving bodies. Even as he slashed a wild-eyed seaman across the neck with his sword, another lunged at him, only to be hacked down by one of the *Raven*'s men wielding an axe. All around him men were fighting and dying. There would be no quarter on either side. But it was hopeless. Two of the galleys had grappled with the ship. Soon the others would follow, and then they would be overrun.

It began as a low rumble, uncertain at first, and then swelled to a wild tidal wave of cheering.

"They're falling back! By God, the bastards are drawing off!" With an effort Glenmorgan realized Chapin was shouting into his face, his arm gesticulating wildly as he tried to make his captain understand.

Glenmorgan leaped to the netting and peered over the side. With a start, he realized he could see them clearly, the wild scramble of men back into the boats, the two that had grappled, frantically shoving off to join the confused retreat of the two other remaining galleys. Vaguely, he realized they had sunk two and disabled a third. During the heat of the battle, the sun had broken over the horizon. It was morning. But that could not explain the unexpected rout. The boarders had been on the point of winning.

Once again, Chapin's voice broke through the din.

"Good God, would you look at that!" He was pointing excitedly at one of the galleys, listing drunkenly to the leeward, its oars along one side shattered and useless.

It was only with the greatest effort that Glenmorgan could make himself understand what was happening. They came at the galleys, sometimes singly, sometimes in pairs, smashing into the sides with the force of battering rams, driving the galleys before them like wolves harrying a terrified flock of sheep.

"Jeezus, they're whales!" uttered a hoarse voice behind him.

But Glenmorgan hardly heard it. He was staring hard at the shimmering crest of a wave where for a fleeting instant he thought he had glimpsed something—a pale flash of movement, like an arm lifted out of the water, or like hair, shining silvery in the sunlight. It was gone now, and strangely enough the whales, too, were retreating. Surely one had nothing to do with the other.

Then he was turning away, his eyes going to his ship to assess her wounds. He could hear the pumps going below and felt her listing somewhat more heavily astern than was normal, which meant that some of the shots had hit below the water line. But the masts were all intact, and that in itself was something of a miracle. More grimly he noted the number of men lying dead or dying on the decks, the blood flowing from the scuppers in crimson streams.

The wounded must be separated from the dead and their injuries cared for. And the dead must be buried. Work must be begun immediately repairing the hull. There was an endless array of things to be done to make his ship seaworthy, let alone ready to fight again, should the need arise. But first he *had* to know what had become of Meg and her grandfather.

Bitterly he quelled his first impulse, to order the gig lowered. No matter how much he needed to go himself, needed to ease the aching torment of not knowing if Meg were alive or dead, his duty was to his ailing ship.

His mouth opened to order Chapin to send a boat when an excited cry went up.

"By Jeezus, it's the old *Mirabel*," shouted one of the seamen, pointing and staring over the side. "She's coming alongside, Cap'n."

Glenmorgan dragged himself to the nettings to stare with disbelieving eyes at the weathered ketch, looking none the worse for wear, as it hove to under the lea of the ship. For a moment his vision blurred as he saw Meg, standing in

222

the stern, her hair hanging wetly about her shoulders. With a great effort he realized she was alive and apparently unharmed.

Then he was shoving his way through his men to meet her as she came in through the entry port.

Thirteen

Meg helped to support a wounded seaman as her grandfather wrapped a bandage about his shoulder. She marveled at the old man's hands, steady despite all that he had already done. Long ago she had lost track of the number of men those hands had worked on—extracting wooden splinters or lead, sewing up jagged wounds, amputating a shattered limb. She shuddered, dazed at the remembered horrors.

The old man glanced sharply up at her.

"Go and rest, Meg," he said bluntly. "I can handle this."

Numbly, she shook her head. She had used up nearly her entire store of healing plants and would have to go down for more before the day was out, or some of these men would die who might otherwise live. The poultices would have to be changed, the healing draughts only she knew how to prepare replenished and doled out. Her grandfather could not do it alone.

Vaguely she was aware of a shadow falling over her.

"You will do as your grandfather says." Startled, she glanced up at the captain, his face unsmiling. She had not realized he was there. In the glare of sunlight, he looked tired, the lines about his mouth taut with strain. But his eyes were as piercing as ever.

MORE PASSION AND ADVENTURE AWAIT... YOUR TRIP TO A BIG ADVENTUROUS WORLD BEGINS WHEN YOU ACCEPT YOUR FIRST 4 NOVELS ABSOLUTELY *FREE* (AN $18.00 VALUE)

Accept your Free gift and start to experience more of the passion and adventure you like in a historical romance novel. Each Zebra novel is filled with proud men, spirited women and tempestuous love that you'll remember long after you turn the last page.

Zebra Historical Romances are the finest novels of their kind. They are written by authors who really know how to weave tales of romance and adventure in the historical settings you love. You'll feel like you've actually gone back in time with the thrilling stories that each Zebra novel offers.

GET YOUR FREE GIFT WITH THE START OF YOUR HOME SUBSCRIPTION

Our readers tell us that these books sell out very fast in book stores and often they miss the newest titles. So Zebra has made arrangements for you to receive the four newest novels published each month.

You'll be guaranteed that you'll never miss a title, and home delivery is so convenient. And to show you just how easy it is to get Zebra Historical Romances, we'll send you your first 4 books absolutely FREE! Our gift to you just for trying our home subscription service.

BIG SAVINGS AND FREE HOME DELIVERY

Each month, you'll receive the four newest titles as soon as they are published. You'll probably receive them even before the bookstores do. What's more, you may preview these exciting novels free for 10 days. If you like them as much as we think you will, just pay the low preferred subscriber's price of just $3.75 each. *You'll save $3.00 each month off the publisher's price.* AND, your savings are even greater because there are never any shipping, handling or other hidden charges—FREE Home Delivery. Of course you can return any shipment within 10 days for full credit, no questions asked. There is no minimum number of books you must buy.

4 FREE BOOKS

TO GET YOUR 4 FREE BOOKS WORTH $18.00 — MAIL IN THE FREE BOOK CERTIFICATE T O D A Y

Fill in the Free Book Certificate below, and we'll send your FREE BOOKS to you as soon as we receive it.

If the certificate is missing below, write to: Zebra Home Subscription Service, Inc., P.O. Box 5214, 120 Brighton Road, Clifton, New Jersey 07015-5214.

FREE BOOK CERTIFICATE

4 FREE BOOKS

ZEBRA HOME SUBSCRIPTION SERVICE, INC.

YES! Please start my subscription to Zebra Historical Romances and send me my first 4 books absolutely FREE. I understand that each month I may preview four new Zebra Historical Romances free for 10 days. If I'm not satisfied with them, I may return the four books within 10 days and owe nothing. Otherwise, I will pay the low preferred subscriber's price of just $3.75 each; a total of $15.00, *a savings off the publisher's price of $3.00.* I may return any shipment and I may cancel this subscription at any time. There is no obligation to buy any shipment and there are no shipping, handling or other hidden charges. Regardless of what I decide, the four free books are mine to keep.

NAME

ADDRESS _____ APT

CITY _____ STATE _____ ZIP

TELEPHONE
(   )

SIGNATURE _____ (if under 18, parent or guardian must sign)

Terms, offer and prices subject to change without notice. Subscription subject to acceptance by Zebra Books. Zebra Books reserves the right to reject any order or cancel any subscription.

ZB0294

GET
FOUR
FREE
BOOKS

(AN $18.00 VALUE)

ZEBRA HOME SUBSCRIPTION
SERVICE, INC.
120 BRIGHTON ROAD
P.O. Box 5214
CLIFTON, NEW JERSEY 07015-5214

Brooking no argument, his hand went out, palm up, waiting.

With a sigh, she took it and let him pull her to her feet.

"Very well, for a few minutes," she conceded, then, smiling down at the wounded sailor, added, "You take care of yourself, Tollet. I shall be back later to make sure that you do."

The homely face split into a pleased grin. "You doesn't need to worry none about me, miss. I'll do fine now. I'm obliged for all that you done."

Meg nodded and let the captain lead her away toward the poop deck, then down into the shaded relief of the cabin hatch. She glanced curiously up at him as she heard a steady clanking coming from below.

"The pumps," he said, standing aside to let her enter the stern cabin ahead of him. "We took some hits below the water line. They'll be repaired soon enough. I'm afraid I must apologize for my quarters," he added as he saw her staring wide-eyed at the devastation wreaked by the galleys' heavy cannon—the gaping hole near the transom, the wood splinters where a ball had gouged a long furrow in the deck, one of the two twelve-pound guns, one on either side of the cabin, upended. Miraculously, the windows had been left intact. "My servant has not yet had the opportunity to return the furniture from the cable tier."

Only then did she realize the bareness of the cabin must be due to the fact that the furniture had been removed before the attack.

In astonishment, she raised her eyes to his. "You knew there would be a fight. Else there would not have been time to clear the cabin."

He shrugged, his face unreadable.

"I guessed. It was overdue, and I knew we were being watched. They must have been gathering on the far side of the island almost from the first day of our arrival. When

225

they believed we had had time to complete much of the transfer, they came for us. My mistake was in believing they would have no interest in you."

Meg stared, entranced, at the look in his eyes, the piercing intensity in their depths that seemed to burn her tiredness away. She nearly jumped at the sudden rap on the screen door.

"Beggin' your pardon, Cap'n." A small, bent man with bowed legs and a face that looked as if it had never seen the light of day shuffled into the cabin, a tray balanced on one hand. "I was able to retrieve only this one bottle of brandy, the lower deck being in somewhat of confusion, what with the fixin' goin' on. Some of the lads'll be here directly with your table and chairs."

"Thank you, Teel. You may set it here." Indicating the bench seat beneath the stern windows, he waited until the servant had withdrawn before taking a glass from the tray. Filling it, he came toward Meg, ducking his head beneath the deck beams.

"Drink it," he ordered when she opened her lips to protest. Then more gently, "It is not enough to affect your senses, but it will help to restore your strength."

Doubtfully, Meg took it. When still he stood over her, she hesitantly lifted it to her lips and drank. Her eyes watered as the fiery liquid burned her throat, but somehow she managed not to disgrace herself by choking.

"Good." Taking the glass from her, he led her to the bench seat and made her sit down. "Now, tell me how you managed to escape being taken."

"We swam for it," she answered simply. "When they left the ketch, we climbed back on board again." It was half the truth. Rather than go to the island, she had waited until the ketch was safe. But only her grandfather had gone on board. "I imagine they thought we had drowned."

"I see." It was almost more than she could do not to

fidget beneath his searching glance. Nor did it help that she was keenly aware of his nearness. His shirt, rumpled and damp with salt spray and sweat, clung to him in such a way as to make her keenly aware of his masculine body. As from a distance she heard him say, "And that was all there was to it?"

"Y-yes," she stammered, jerking her thoughts back to the present. "Except for the warning shot my grandfather fired before we jumped over the side."

"Aye, we heard it." She watched the grave restlessness in his eyes harden to a steely glint. "It was a brave thing to do. But for that, it might have been a lot worse for us. But it was foolish nonetheless. You might both have been killed."

"But we weren't." She gave an impatient gesture. "I wish you would stop blaming yourself for what was not your fault. Here, we would only have been in the way." And she would have found it difficult to summon the whales, she added grimly to herself. "As it turned out, we were better off where we were."

For what seemed a long time, he said nothing, but only looked at her with those eyes that seemed capable of boring holes through her. At last he breathed a sigh. "Meg . . ." He reached out to lay his hand lightly on her shoulder.

A sharp gasp burst from her lips and she could not keep herself from shrinking from beneath his touch.

Glenmorgan cursed, his hand coming away as if burned. "You're hurt!"

It sounded like an accusation, and embarrassed, Meg bolted to her feet. "It's nothing. Really. I—I should go now and help my grandfather."

"Meg!" His voice, flat, uncompromising, brought Meg rigidly to a halt. Deliberately he came around in front of her. "You will stand still while I have a look."

A single glance at his unyielding expression, his lips

compressed into a thin line, convinced her of the futility of arguing.

"As you wish, Captain," she answered stiffly, "though you are making a great deal out of nothing."

"Nevertheless," he said, gently laying her hair back as she stared rigidly in front of her, "you will allow me to judge for myself what is nothing." She could feel her heart start to pound at the light touch of his fingers undoing the bow at the front of her gown. Then, carefully, he was baring her shoulder.

A harsh breath hissed through his teeth at sight of the shallow gash, blackened with dried blood, the bruised, angry swelling of the flesh around it.

"Teel!" The servant must have been very close by. Hardly had the captain's stentorian shout died away than he came scrambling through the doorway. "You will fetch clean linen and hot water from the galley at once. And then you will send word to Mr. Pippin that I require his presence as soon as he is able."

"Aye, sir. Right away, sir."

Teel was so comical in his hasty retreat that Meg could not quite restrain a giggle.

"Poor little man. You have frightened him half out of his wits," she said, grateful for a distraction, no matter how small, from the captain's forbidding expression. "Must you be so harsh with him?"

"I don't care a tinker's damn what you think of my treatment of Teel at this moment. A pistol ball did this. Why the devil didn't you tell someone?"

She shrugged her uninjured shoulder.

"It is a small thing, compared to the wounds I have seen today. I would have taken care of it myself when there was time."

"The time is now. Sit *down*," he ordered harshly, but his anger was only a mask to hide the cold chill that still

228

gripped his heart. Had the ball hit a few inches lower or to the left . . .

His shout shattered the silence. *"Where the hell is that water?"*

"Here, sir," gasped Teel, nearly stumbling through the door in his haste. "Mr. Pippin sent word he will be down shortly. If you will pardon me, sir, the lads are here with your things."

Meg had only barely enough time to decently cover herself before the cabin was filled with men and furniture. In a surprisingly short time the cabin was made orderly, the table, chairs, wine cabinet, and desk returned to their proper places, the upended gun set right on its trucks, and both guns concealed beneath canvas. It would take longer to repair the jagged hole near the transom and smooth the splinters from the deck, but for the moment, it was almost possible to forget that a battle had been fought here.

"And now," Glenmorgan said pointedly to Meg when everyone else had been cleared out, "it is your turn."

The interruption had been fortunate in one respect, he thought wryly as he made Meg return to her seat beneath the stern windows. It had given him time to settle his nerves. With cynical detachment he noted that his hands were steady as once again he bared Meg's shoulder.

"This is bound to hurt," he said grimly, dampening a cloth in the bowl of tepid water before turning back to the girl.

Meg's muscles tensed, more in anticipation of Glenmorgan's unsettling touch than in dread of any pain. Nevertheless, she could not stop a gasp as she felt a searing stab, like a hot blade against her skin.

Glenmorgan's lips thinned to a white line. He had seen far worse wounds in his time, men with limbs severed by cannonballs or smashed to pulp by canister. Still, when it came to sponging the dried blood away from the shallow gouge on a soft white shoulder, he had to grit his teeth to do it. He thought of the twenty wounded left topside to take advantage of the healing breeze and of the girl's quiet determination as she had knelt beside one injured sailor after another, offering comfort, sharing her strength. She had been better than a tonic to men accustomed to the grim realities of battle and sudden death. Perhaps Meg's healing draughts had had something to do with it, and certainly Pippin's skill as a surgeon had gone a long way to tip the balance, but he had been at sea long enough not to underestimate the healing power of a beautiful woman's compassion. Men who would have perished under the crude care normally available to a ship's crew were prospering, thanks to her, while the passing of others had been made easier. And he had almost brought her to her death.

"You are very quiet, Captain," Meg spoke up, unable to bear the silence any longer. "Is it because you are worried that the pirates will try again?"

"They *will* try again," he answered shortly. "You can count on it. But this time it will not be boats in a night raid. It will be ships in broad daylight." He turned to lay the cloth in the bowl. "When that happens, I don't want you or your grandfather on board or anywhere near."

"I see." Meg watched his still face, the eyes troubled in a way she had not seen them before. "And where should we be? Do you intend to leave us here—on *Mirabel?*"

Glenmorgan carefully wrung out the cloth and laid it gently on the livid wound, noting as he did so the girl gamely trying not to wince.

"We will be outnumbered," he said gravely. "Our only hope will be to outrun them, and that is a slim hope at best. After we have sailed, you and your grandfather can make for Anguilla. I have friends there who would welcome you."

"Anguilla is not Charles Town, Captain," Meg calmly pointed out. But inside, her stomach had clenched into a hard knot at the realization that he meant to leave her behind while he faced death alone.

"And this is not Antigua. If it were, this discussion would be academic at best. Dammit, Meg. Look around you. Last night's battle was as nothing compared to what we will face if those ships find us. You yourself said it. There will be no place on board this vessel for a woman."

"Then you must forget that I'm a woman and allow me a place with the wounded. Surely I have proved of some little worth where they are concerned?"

She saw the leap of anger in his eyes, along with something like despair.

"You know without my telling you what you have meant to them," he said. His eyes swung deliberately to hers. "And to me. I haven't forgotten that you saved my life, too. But that is only one more reason why I cannot let you stay."

"On the contrary, that is no reason at all," Meg insisted stubbornly. "You will take us with you, Captain, if for no other reason than because you gave us your word."

Their eyes clashed and held for a seemingly endless moment. Then, when it seemed that neither would give in, a knock sounded briskly on the door.

Glenmorgan wrenched his gaze away. *"Yes?"* The word, seemingly yanked from him, reverberated through the cabin.

"Captain?" Pippin stuck his head through the door. "I was told I was needed here."

Glenmorgan gave a weary gesture toward the girl, the anger seeming to drain from him.

"It's your granddaughter," he said shortly. "She requires your attention. When you are finished, I shall have my men see that your things are transferred to the ship." Once more his glance sought Meg's and for a moment held. "We weigh anchor as soon as the repairs to the hull are completed."

Meg smiled gravely. "Thank you, Captain. We shall try to make sure you do not regret your decision."

For a moment longer he hesitated. Then grimly he said, "I hope we may not all live to regret it."

The next moment he was gone, closing the cabin door firmly behind him.

Meg slipped noiselessly into the water so as not to attract attention from the men working feverishly on *Raven*'s decks and dove deep beneath the surface before heading in the direction of the wreck. She had not gone far when she was joined by the six dolphins that had remained almost her constant companions since her arrival off Barbuda. One, turning over on his back, scudded through the water less than a foot beneath her, inviting her to join him in a game.

Meg grinned in spite of herself. No two dolphins were ever exactly alike. They were as varied in temperament as people, some spiteful and mean, like cantankerous old men of the sea, and others as mischievous and playful as children. But she had found most to be stimulating companions who never failed to relieve her feelings of loneliness. In fact, her memories of the few children she had known on St. Vincent's were less real than those of her many dolphin friends.

Today, however, she had no time for their frolics. Her grandfather had made it plain that she must be back aboard the *Mirabel* before she was missed. She wasted little time gathering the plants she would need, and it was not long before the net scrip she carried was full. Only then did she head purposefully for the *Argonaut,* the dolphins still tagging along behind her.

The stern cabin was just as forbidding as the last time she had been there, she decided, suppressing a shiver as she entered through the gaping stern windows. Perhaps more so now that she had been made to realize how close *Raven* had come to joining her sister ship on the bottom.

Eager to have the thing done so that she could leave the hulk, she went straight to the cabinet and tried to recall Glenmorgan's instructions.

Again and again, she ran her hands over the carved swirls of the cabinet, searching for the catch that would release the secret panel, but to no avail. Either Glenmorgan was right and the mechanism was too damaged to work properly or she was simply too tired to recall his directions accurately. Stubbornly she tried again, determined not to return topside until she had the cursed box in her possession.

Suddenly, without warning, a long gray shape hurtled out of nowhere straight at her. Her heart leaping to her throat, she threw herself backward. A sharp pain shot through her elbow as she dashed it hard against the cabinet. Then she saw the face grinning at her through the water and nearly sagged with relief.

Oppressed by the ship around her, its hollow groans and eerie, undulating shadows like ghosts of the dead, she had not noticed the dolphin following her into the stern cabin.

As she shooed the playful animal away, she glimpsed a flash of movement out of the corner of her eye and turned to see a door sliding open in the framework of the cabinet. When her elbow struck, she must have triggered the mechanism that released the panel, she realized. With a prickle of excitement, she reached into the dark interior of the secret compartment. Inside, she found a rectangular metal box perhaps the size of one of her grandfather's leatherbound books. Curiously, she lifted it out and ran her fingers over the brass plate bearing the initials, "T.M.G." Odd, she thought, frowning. Those were not the initials of the *Argonaut*'s sailing master. His name had been Josiah Roth. She was quite certain of that.

Her curiosity piqued even more than before, she gathered up the net filled with plants and, grasping the box to her breast, left the ship by way of the stern windows.

When she surfaced in the lea of the fishing boat several minutes later, her grandfather was watching for her, his face set in worn lines of disapproval.

"About time," he commented dourly as Meg thrust the box out of the water and waited for him to take it from her, followed by the net scrip filled with dripping plants. "I've had the devil's own time convincing Mr. Chapin we could not be transferred aboard the ship till you had finished your 'nap.'"

She saw his brow crease in a frown at sight of the initials on the lid. Then, assuming her human form, she pulled herself up the ladder and over the coaming while her grandfather turned to stand with his back to her, blocking her as well as he could from view of the ship.

She didn't bother to dry herself, but slipped the gown on over her wet body before flopping carelessly down in the stern of the boat. Flinging her hair back from her forehead, she glanced expectantly up at her grandfather.

The box was still in his hands, and he was staring at it with a peculiarly fixed expression. "Well?" she said. "Aren't you going to open it?"

"No." He glanced up, as if suddenly recalled to her presence. "No, I think we must leave that for your captain. See these initials? They're his father's. The box and whatever is inside rightfully belong to him now."

Meg stared at him, her brow puckering into a frown. "You know what's in it, don't you? At least tell me that."

"I think," Pippin answered slowly, "that it is something more important than gold to the captain. I suspect, in fact, that this may be the real reason he wanted to find the *Arqonaut*."

Meg felt her heart skip a beat.

"The letters!" she exclaimed, leaning suddenly forward in her excitement. "The ones Clarissa and her father were so afraid of. Grandfather, that must be it!"

"Whatever it is, it is no concern of ours. The captain would not thank us for meddling in his affairs." He glanced at her, a wry gleam in his eye. "Any more than he will thank me for allowing you to go back to the wreck. We can hardly explain to him that you heal faster in the sea, after all." He gave her a pointed glance. "How is it, child? You seem to be favoring it."

Meg gave a small toss of her head. "My shoulder will heal soon enough. And as for the captain, he is mistaken if he thinks he can order me about like one of his sailors." Her eyes sparkled at the memory of their last brief encounter, his voice, booming out from the quarterdeck as she was on the point of returning to the fishing ketch.

"Where the devil do you think *you're* going?"

She had found herself preparing for the storm she sensed was coming as, indifferent to the stares of his men, he had crossed the deck toward her in long purposeful strides.

"I am going to the *Argonaut*," she answered, forcing herself to stand very straight beneath his searing scrutiny. "I have one last dive to make before we quit this place, or had you forgotten, Captain?"

"You have already made your last dive," he stated unequivocally. "Yesterday. It's finished, Meg."

"It is nowhere near *finished*, Captain," she countered waspishly, the ache in her shoulder and her tiredness leaving her in no mood for a senseless argument, "and we both know it. Now please stand out of my way. You are wasting precious time."

She made as if to go around him, but his hand on her arm stopped her.

"I warn you, Meg, I'll not have you going against my wishes. You will return to the *Mirabel* and rest until we are ready to weigh anchor. And that is *all* you will do, do I make myself understood?"

Pippin had smoothly intervened before she could voice

the angry retort that rose instinctively to her lips. "The captain's right, Meg." The look he flashed her had been potent with meaning. "It's time you thought of yourself. Don't worry, Glenmorgan. I shall see that she does what is necessary to renew her strength."

Now, Meg shot a fond glance after her grandfather as he went below to sort the freshly gathered plants. They had both known that only the sea could restore her.

Smiling to herself, she followed him down to prepare a poultice for her wound. The salt water had done much to ease the pain, and had there been time to remain in her natural element, the wound would have been well in a day or two. As it was, she must wait for the slower recuperative powers of her human form, aided by the healing properties of the plants as only she knew how to prepare them.

"Perhaps Glenmorgan is right," Pippin suggested sometime later as he applied the fresh poultice to Meg's shoulder. "An hour in the sea, and the swelling is already gone. Why risk infection and an unsightly scar when you could be done with this in a few days where you belong? A leisurely trip to Anguilla, and then board a packet to Charles Town. It makes sense, Meg."

Meg grimaced irritably. "Why don't I just swim to Charles Town, and you can join me by way of Anguilla? It would be a whole lot simpler, and I would not have to eat any more cooked malangas."

"It would be better than having to worry about you in the middle of a battle between Glenmorgan and the cursed pirates."

She laughed at his dour expression. "But that is exactly where I most want to be if it happens." Then on a more sober, if somewhat wistful, note, "It's where I belong whether *he* knows it or not."

Pippin finished fastening the bandage in place with strips

of court plaster before easing the neck of Meg's gown up over her shoulder.

At last he looked at her, a curious expression in his gray eyes. He said, "Then you've changed your mind about things?"

Restlessly she moved away, her fingers fumbling with the fastening at the front of the gown. "No, nor will I. The captain has his revenge to occupy him. To him, that is all that really matters. Once we reach Charles Town, he will have little time *or* thought for me. He should be safe enough from any further entanglement. And I, at least, will be near him until . . ." She smiled ruefully and shrugged. "Until it is no longer possible to be near him."

Pippin smiled ironically to himself. He doubted that any man, even one obsessed with vengeance, could long remain indifferent to Meg. But then, she didn't know the first thing about men or the effect she had on them. He doubted that there was a sailor on board the *Raven* who was not more than half in love with her already. He had seen it in their faces as she moved among them, the mere sight of her enough to help make easier their fear and pain. And if he was any judge, he doubted that their captain was any different. Without effort he recalled to mind the look in Glenmorgan's eyes earlier that day in the captain's quarters. Pippin had seen at a glance the torment behind Glenmorgan's careful mask, his realization of how close Meg had come to death. The captain might not know it yet, but he was going to find it hard to dismiss Meg from his life, very hard indeed.

No sooner had that thought crossed his mind than a curt hail cut across the silence.

"Ahoy, *Mirabel*. One to come aboard."

Pippin saw Meg's shoulders jerk, her eyes flying involuntarily upward toward the skylight. There was no doubt it was Glenmorgan, and from the sound of his voice, he had not come to make a social call.

"I'll go up," said the old man, moving toward the companionway. "Meantime, you might at least pretend that you have been in bed."

"There would hardly seem any point," Meg answered. "He will know as soon as we give him the box what I've been doing." Her lips curved faintly in a smile, which seemed to reflect something like grim amusement and a calm acceptance of the inevitable. "Ask him to come down. We might as well get it over with."

Pippin's eyebrows swept up in his brow. This was not the Meg who had come bursting in on him only a few weeks ago, frightened and bewildered because she had been given her first glimpse of the evil of which mankind was capable. This was a new Meg, one more certain of herself and yet more elusive, difficult to understand. There was a mystique about her, which he hesitated to put a name to. Then suddenly he smiled. It was the mystique of a woman, a woman, moreover, who was coming to grips with the yearnings of her own heart. He thought of the captain, waiting impatiently abovedeck. Suddenly he both envied and pitied him. A Meg in command of her own destiny would be a formidable Meg indeed.

With that thought, he scrambled up the ladder to the deck above.

Meg listened to the muffled sound of voices drifting down through the skylight and was conscious of a growing feeling of impatience. She little doubted that the two men were discussing her and her future as if she had nothing to say to it. But they would soon learn that neither she nor her own wishes could be so easily dismissed. She would sail on *Raven* to Charles Town or she would die with Glenmorgan here in the Caribbean, but she would not be left on some island and forgotten. She had earned the right to decide her own fate.

Grasping that thought firmly to mind, she failed to hear the light fall of footsteps on the companionway. She almost gasped aloud as Glenmorgan's tall frame seemed suddenly to fill the small cabin.

Meg forced herself to stand perfectly still as Glenmorgan's eyes raked over her, taking in at a glance her damp hair, the rigid set of her shoulders, the jut of her chin, unmistakably defiant. At last the muscle leaped grimly along the lean line of his jaw.

"It would seem you chose not to heed my advice," he observed coldly. "Obviously you haven't been asleep. Maybe you'd like to tell me what you *have* been doing."

"Perhaps," she retorted, refusing to give in to her wildly palpitating heart. "Where is my grandfather?"

"With his patients. Don't try to change the subject."

"Very well," Meg shrugged. "I have been to the *Argonaut.*"

She saw the sudden flicker of disbelief in his face and had little trouble guessing his thoughts.

"Oh, you needn't bother yourself as to how I managed it," she said, amazed at her own temerity. "The important thing is that I found the box. It's over there." She gave a brief gesture with her head toward a shelf on the far side of the cabin. Assuming an air of detachment she was far from feeling, she watched Glenmorgan go to the box, saw his fingers run over the plate with his father's initials.

Meg let out a deep breath. "Now that it is yours, what will you do with it?"

"Use it." She shivered a little at the stark brevity of his answer. Then he was moving purposefully toward her, a pale gleam in his eyes. "You went below again against my orders. Why?"

Meg's chin went up a fraction of an inch higher, but inside, she could feel her stomach start to churn. "Who are you to give *me* orders?" she countered, backing warily before him. She had seen that look in his eyes before.

Glenmorgan's lips curved in cynical amusement.

"No one, it seems," he answered, coming another step toward her. "But that doesn't answer my question, does it? Why did you go after the box?"

Suddenly the cabin seemed stiflingly small as Meg found herself backed into a corner. Somehow she quelled the impulse to lick dry lips. "What difference does it make?" she said, an edge to her voice. "It's yours. It's what you wanted, isn't it? You—you said it was important."

With something like panic, she tried to shove past him. Glenmorgan stopped her, a hand planted firmly against the bulkhead near her face.

"Aye, it's important," he said in a voice with a razor-edged softness. "More than you know. But that isn't why you went after it." She winced as she felt his fingers, feather-light in her hair. Instantly he stilled. "Dammit, Meg! What are you afraid of?"

Meg turned her face away. How could she answer him, when it was herself that she feared, the longing which lay ever just beneath the surface, ready to leap forth at a touch? What a fool she had been to think she could control it!

"Nothing," she uttered in a strangled voice. "I'm afraid of nothing. Please. Just take your precious box and go. My grandfather and I will not trouble you anymore."

There, she had freed him. And still, it was not enough, she thought wildly, as his arm closed about her waist and drew her inexorably to him.

"And if I refuse to leave without you?" he murmured huskily. Meg shivered helplessly, his lips against her ear sending cold chills down her back.

"You won't," she gasped. "It—it's what you want." With

240

her hands against his chest, she tried to push away from him.

His arm tightened around her, his voice harsh in the quiet.

"Don't tell me what I *want!*" His hands closed ruthlessly about her waist and shoved her hard against the bulkhead. A gasp broke from her lips as, deliberately, he let her feel the hard bulge of his manhood against her, the desire like a raging torment within him. "Tell me it's what *you* want! Tell me, Meg, and we end it here and now."

She stared into the fiery glitter of his eyes between slitted eyelids and tried to summon the words that would end it.

Glenmorgan uttered a blistering oath.

"Bloody hell, Meg! Tell me what you want from me."

"I want—you—to go," she gasped.

But already it was too late. Even as she voiced the words that should have sent him from her forever, he read the lie in her eyes, sensed the betrayal of her body awakening to a desire no less than his own. A hard gleam of a smile touched his lips.

"Then show me," he uttered thickly.

Summoning anger to her defense, she struggled in his grasp, turned her head away as he sought her lips. Furiously, she struck at him with her fists. With an oath, he caught her wrists in his hands and pinioned them to the bulkhead at either side of her head.

"Now . . ." Glenmorgan panted. His eyes like light piercing points of flame searched her face, noted grimly her own eyes, shimmering with tears of anger. ". . . the truth."

With the last of her flagging strength, she fought to remain impervious to his mouth closing over hers, to his lips, breaking down her will to resist. But she could not fight him and her own traitorous heart. She wanted him. Her whole being cried out to be one with him, and her heart knew, if her head did not, that anything else was a lie.

With all of her fierce pride, she embraced the truth, giving herself to him and returning his passion with the pent-up fury of all the long days of denial.

Never had she known such hunger. She felt starved for his touch, for the feel of his body against hers. Her lips could not get enough of him, nor could her hands, running feverishly over him. Mindless with need, she tugged at the fastenings at the front of his breeches, nearly ripping them in her impatience to release him from their confines. And then it was done. A groan shuddered through him as she caressed him with her hand.

In a fever to possess her, Glenmorgan lowered her onto the table, her knees folded to her chest. His hands thrust the gown up over her waist and savagely he entered her.

A keening sigh welled up inside her as he thrust ruthlessly, driving her to a delirious peak of rapture. She heard her name, uttered like a groan from a very great distance, felt his seed burst forth within her. Then she gasped with the ecstasy of her own release, like an explosion of pulsating heat inside her. As sigh after sigh broke from her depths, she clasped her legs about Glenmorgan's waist, holding him deep inside her as her flesh constricted in blissful ripples about his.

Then at last with a shuddering sigh, Meg collapsed, feeling breathless and weak.

Glenmorgan stood over her, his arms braced against the table, and dragged in deep breaths of air. When he had his breathing under control again, he reached down and gathered Meg to him. With her legs still wrapped around him, he carried her to the bench seat and sank down with her astraddle his lap. Meg breathed a contented sigh, savoring the feel of his member, still inside her. For a little while longer they would be one, she thought dreamily. Laying her head against his shoulder, she fell asleep with Glenmorgan's hand moving over her hair in long, steady strokes.

Thus she did not see the peculiar expression in his eyes or know the thoughts running through his head.

He felt stunned by the fierceness of her response, the fury of their lovemaking. It was the sort of thing a man only dreamed about in his wildest fantasies. But at least he had the answer to one of his questions. He had just made certain of that. He knew why she had made that final dive today, and all the other dives before that, and it had nothing to do with any debt, real or imagined, which she felt she owed to his father. He had been all too keenly aware long before this that she had done it and everything else for him and for him alone. But until now he still had not been sure *why*.

He had known too many women to believe she would go to such lengths for a man simply to enjoy the pleasure of sharing his bed. After today, he could not doubt that it went much deeper than that. No woman could make love the way she had unless her heart were involved. And if that was not enough to convince him, he had only to consider what seemed her single-minded determination to help him at every turn since she had first dragged him, more dead than alive, from the sea. Bloody hell, she had risked her life for him! No, she displayed all the characteristics of a woman in love, except for one—her adamant refusal to marry him. And that, he found with no little surprise, he was firmly resolved to overcome—if, that is, they survived the next forty-eight hours.

One thing was certain, he decided with a wry twist of the lips. With Meg at his side, his life would never be dull.

Fourteen

Meg came slowly awake to the steady creak of timbers and the uneven lurch of her cot, which seemed to have grown considerably in size since the last time she had slept in it. Feeling absurdly lazy and somehow inordinately pleased with herself in a way which she could not readily define, she stretched her arms deliciously over her head and yawned.

It was only gradually that it sank in on her sleep-befogged mind that it was the dead of night and that she could not remember how she came to be in bed. Unalarmed, she waited until her eyes adjusted to the darkness, relieved only dimly by moonlight, which appeared to be spilling through four tall windows beyond the foot of the bed.

Then suddenly she sat bolt upright, the last vestiges of sleep wholly swept away.

This was not her grandfather's fishing smack. It was the *Raven,* and she was in the captain's cabin. She could recognize now the shapeless mass of the two guns huddled beneath their canvas covers, the indistinct shapes of table and chairs, the wine cabinet set against the bulkhead. Flinging the blankets aside, she left the bed and hurried to the stern windows.

Spume surged below the counter, glinting sparks of

moonlight, as the ship tilted to the wind, and she could feel the bite of the stem as it cut through the swells. They were under way, she realized with a quickening of her pulse, and Glenmorgan had not left her behind!

A sleepless night, the strain and excitement of the battle, the days of salvaging the wreck—all must have taken their toll on her at last, she thought, for he had carried her on board as she slept, and laid her in his bed, and she had known none of it. Wryly, it came to her that she would not sleep anymore that night. She was wide awake, her senses attuned to the noises of the ship around her, the steady pitch and fall of the deck beneath her, the scents of tar and fresh paint.

Suddenly the walls seemed to draw in on her and she felt stifled in the close confines of the cabin. After only the slightest hesitation, she slipped through the door into the main cabin, which was deserted. No doubt her grandfather was on the orlop with the wounded sailors and Glenmorgan above overseeing his ship, she thought as she found her way to the companion and climbed the ladder to the poop.

The wind against her cheek as she stepped out onto the quarterdeck was sweet to her, and she stood for a moment feeling its caress through her hair and against the fabric of her dress as she searched for and found Glenmorgan, standing at the taffrail with his back to her.

As she started toward him, a solid figure detached itself from the shadows near the binnacle and intercepted her.

"Welcome aboard, Miss Pippin." It was the *Raven's* first mate, baring his head to her. "I hope you are comfortable below?"

Instantly Meg relaxed. "Indeed, yes, Mr. Chapin," she replied, a smile coming easily to her lips. She had liked him from the first—this gentle giant of a man with his plain, honest face and keen blue eyes. Instinctively she trusted him.

245

"I'm glad to see you looking a tad better than when the captain brought you aboard." Awkwardly Chapin shifted the tricorn clutched between his big hands. "You appeared plum tuckered out, which is hardly any surprise after all that you've been through. I—I wish I had the words to thank you for what you did for the lads." His gaze shifted toward the tall figure at the weather rail. "And for the captain," he added softly, "I know what you did to save his life."

Meg shrugged, embarrassed by his gratitude. "Fortunately," she said, "he would seem a hard man to kill."

The big man's startled chuckle rumbled pleasantly. "Aye, he is that. I expect it's his stubbornness, and the Irish in him. But I reckon he'll need more than luck in this new game he's playing." She felt his eyes on her, unreadable in the thick shadows. "Maybe he's even found it, though I doubt that he knows it yet—a dash of magic to even things up a bit."

"I—I beg your pardon?" Meg stammered, taken aback at this new tack. "I'm afraid I don't understand."

Chapin lifted a ponderous shoulder. "I'm not sure I do either, miss," he replied simply. "But I reckon it doesn't make any difference whether I understand or not. The important thing is, if anything should ever happen, if you ever need anything, you can always count on me. I just wanted you to know that."

For a moment she could not speak for the lump that had risen in her throat. She could only guess what lay behind his surprising speech. She felt her stomach constrict with the thought that he must have stumbled on to the truth of her identity. Then immediately she calmed herself. Even if he had discovered the truth or only suspected she was not exactly what she appeared to be, he was obviously not disposed to hurt her with the knowledge. She sensed that, from a man like Dick Chapin, a declaration of friendship was tantamount to an oath of loyalty and not one given lightly. He would be as good as his word.

Somehow she managed to summon a wavery smile as she held out her hand to him. "Thank you, Mr. Chapin," she murmured softly. "It is a friendship that I shall always treasure."

Chapin's huge hand swallowed hers and gave a gentle squeeze before letting go. Then, setting his hat on his head, he stepped back to let her pass.

"I expect you'll be wanting to speak with the captain now. But I'm glad we had time for this little chat."

"As am I, Mr. Chapin," she returned quietly, and strode past him toward the tall figure standing by the rail.

Meg almost faltered in her resolve as she came up behind Glenmorgan. In the pale gleam of moonlight she could see his shirt, wet from spray and clinging to his body, and could sense that he was oblivious to it or to the chill touch of the wind in his face. He was obviously deep in his own thoughts and probably would not thank her for breaking into them. She was on the point of turning and stealing away again when, without warning, he spoke to her.

"I never grow tired of the sea at night. It helps a man to see things more clearly—to look at where he's been and where he's headed." He twisted around to peer at her over his shoulder. "I seem to be doing a lot of that of late," he said, his face grave as he appeared to study her.

"Have you?" Meg moved to the rail beside him. "And have you come to any conclusions?"

"The answers always come out the same." His hands gripped the rail. "I'll finish what I started. Even if I wanted to, it's too late to change things now."

She accepted it in silence. She had not really expected him to say anything different, though in her heart she had hoped. Instead, she looked up at the stars. With the moon out, they appeared small and unattainable, like tiny pinpricks of light. Vaguely, she wondered if they would look different in Charles Town. Out of long habit, she began to pick out familiar formations. It was something her mother had taught her long ago—to use the sky as a map for the sea—when suddenly her mouth went dry. Her heart felt frozen inside her as she turned to face Glenmorgan.

"And what conclusions have you reached about me?" she asked, struggling to keep her voice steady. "Now that you have what you wanted."

Glenmorgan glanced at her sharply. "I haven't changed my mind, if that's what you mean," he said. "I've never pretended to agree with your grandfather or his demands."

"No, you've made that abundantly clear." Meg swallowed and looked away. "And now that you have the treasure, you can have Clarissa, too, can't you? She will be glad to take you back. With so much gold, you can give her anything her heart desires."

In spite of her effort to appear indifferent to such a dismal prospect, she could not keep her voice from breaking at the end. Mortified, she started to turn away. "I must ask you to excuse me, Captain. It's time I went below to—"

Glenmorgan's hand on her wrist stopped her. His low-pitched voice had a steely edge. "Whatever you have to do below can wait. You seem pretty damned eager to toss me to the sharks. The least you can do is stick around long enough to explain why."

Instantly Meg's head came up, her breast heaving with resentment at his high-handed manner. "I don't know what you're talking about. I said nothing about sharks. And I have nothing to explain."

"Oh, yes you do. You can begin by telling me what made you sore enough to wish me to the devil—or to Clarissa, which, in light of what she tried to do to me, amounts to pretty much the same thing."

Meg glared at him, furious that he could think her either so stupid or so naive as not to realize everything he said was a lie.

"It's very simple, Captain," she retorted in accents meant to freeze his very soul. "We're going *south.*"

Glenmorgan looked at her with an air of expectancy. "Yes," he prompted, when it seemed she did not mean to expand on the statement, "we're going south. Any fool can see that. What has that to do with anything?"

"Perhaps you can explain why you've chosen such a course," she answered scathingly.

"What course would you suggest I take to reach Antigua?" he demanded, his patience clearly strained. "I'd have made it a point to consult you beforehand, *if* I'd known you had an aversion to traveling in a southerly direction, but unfortunately, the thought never occurred to me."

Meg, however, was not listening. She had, in fact, gotten no further than the declaration of their intended destination.

"Antigua," she gasped. "But I thought . . ." Immediately, she stopped herself, mortified at the conclusions to which she had so readily jumped.

Glenmorgan eyed her from beneath a cocked eyebrow.

"You thought what?" he coaxed dangerously.

Furiously, Meg blushed. "I—I thought you were taking me back to the island, now that you have no further use for me. It is, after all, what you said you did with people—use them."

A gleam of wry amusement sprang to Glenmorgan's eyes.

"Very true," he admitted. "However, I'm not in the habit of discarding them on deserted islands." Grabbing her by the wrist, he pulled her to him. "At least, that is," he added, imprisoning her firmly in the circle of his arms, "until I am absolutely certain they can be of no further use to me."

249

Startled, Meg gazed doubtfully up at him. "Are you saying that you have some further need of me?" she asked, her brow puckered in a frown.

Glenmorgan's teeth flashed in a grin. "I am very nearly certain of it," he assured her. "And as for your next question—oh, yes, I can read it in your eyes—we are going to Antigua because I have no intention of being saddled with a king's ransom on board all the way to Carolina. The British Navy can figure out how to get the cursed treasure to England."

"To England?" exclaimed Meg, more bewildered than ever as she pictured the British island as it appeared on her grandfather's maps, on the other side of the ocean. "But why?"

"Where else should it go? It belongs to the King, after all, a healthy addition to his war chest. And since King George's war shows no sign of ending anytime soon, he will need it." Suddenly he threw back his dark head and laughed at the look on her face. "You didn't expect me to keep it, did you? That would be the act of a pirate, and I am an honest man now, with a King's pardon to prove it." Just as quickly, he sobered, his eyes probing hers with a blazing intensity she had never seen in them before. "The last of my father's debts will have been paid in full when we reach Antigua, thanks to you. His name will be cleared and the mark against his honor wiped out. Without that, bringing his murderers to justice would have meant next to nothing. Meg, I—"

The lookout shouted from the masthead: "Deck ahoy! Sail astern! It's the *Barracuda,* Cap'n. I'd know her anywhere."

His hands on Meg's arms, Glenmorgan put her from him and strode quickly to the nettings.

"Two more sail! On the starboard bow!" shouted the

250

lookout, his voice crackling with excitement. "It's the *Devil Fish*. And the *Sea Hawk,* by God."

Only then, as Meg watched Glenmorgan lift the telescope to his eye, did she realize that the darkness was lifting, giving way before the first golden shafts of sunlight. It was morning, and before them, death waited to greet them.

"Pipe the hands up, Dick. And have the galley fires doused," Glenmorgan said quietly to Chapin as his first mate joined him at the weather rail. "I want the ship cleared for action."

"Aye, Cap'n." Chapin shifted his weight. "Then you intend to fight?"

"It would seem our old friends out there have given us very little choice in the matter." He glanced meaningfully at Chapin's impassive features. "If we try to turn tail and run, the *Barracuda* will cut us off. She'll delay or disable us till the others can come in for the finish. And beyond her, to the north or west, we run the gamut of every pirate in the Caribbean with a hankering for gold. East there is nothing between us and landfall, but thirty-five hundred miles of open sea and no hope of replenishing our fresh water or supplies. If, on the other hand, we can get past *them,*" he said, inclining his head toward the two ships forward, "we can make a dash for Antigua, four hours or five at the most to the southward, with the wind at our back."

"Dammit, Michael. You're talking about taking on two ships at once. And Drago's is a bloody thirty-six-gun frigate. We've done some crazy things before, but this! What chance can we possibly have against odds like that?"

"Practically none, my friend." Glenmorgan grinned. "It should make for an interesting morning, eh?"

In spite of himself, Chapin felt his own lips stretch in an answering grin. He knew that look of old. The reckless acceptance of impossible odds, the deliberate disregard of danger, the first leap of fire at the prospect of battle, and the restlessness as Glenmorgan's mind began to grapple with and formulate a plan of action. It was all there, and it was useless to resist. Glenmorgan would lead, and the rest of them would follow. It was as simple as that.

Or was it? he thought, as his glance fell on the girl, watching them with her unfathomable eyes. What was it he had said to her—a dash of magic to even things up a bit? Suddenly his grin broadened, and touching his hat to Meg, he turned to carry out his captain's orders.

As the pipes shrilled and men began pouring on deck from the hatchways, Meg watched Glenmorgan with an impending sense of doom. She had heard every word of his exchange with Chapin, had seen the look on their faces as they cold-bloodedly discussed their chances. It was as if they wanted to die, she thought, clutching her hands into fists at her sides.

Then Glenmorgan was before her, his fingers closing about her arms. "I want you to go below to the orlop and stay there, no matter what you hear going on up here. Do you understand?" he said, giving her a small shake.

"Ye-es," she answered, understanding all too well the futility of trying to argue with him. He wanted her someplace safe while he remained topside in the thick of danger, and she had promised she would not get in the way.

"Then give me your word you won't do anything foolish. Help with the wounded, if you will, but *stay below.*"

Forcing her head up, she met his eyes unflinchingly. "I— I will, I promise," she said as steadily as she could.

"Good girl." For a moment, he hesitated, his eyes lingering on her face as if memorizing each detail. Then he was talking again, hurriedly, his eyes willing her to understand.

"The last thing they want is to sink us," he said, preparing her for what was going to happen in the hopes that it would help her in some way to deal with the fear. "They'll try to dismast us, and then they will board us—if they can." His lips stretched in a smile that sent a chill down her back. "I don't intend to give them that chance." Then the moment was gone, and she could sense that his thoughts were already with his ship and the coming battle. Deliberately he put her from him. "Go below now," he said. "You'll be safe enough there."

Helplessly, Meg watched him turn away. What could she do? She could not call the whales to her aid this time. They were of no use against ships. And she could not call down the fury of the winds against Glenmorgan's enemies. Even if she could put her oath aside, a storm would be as great a danger to the *Raven* as to the others. If only she could call back the night again and its concealing cloak of darkness! That, however, was beyond her power.

Suddenly she stilled, her heart pounding wildly beneath her breast. If she could not call back the night, perhaps she could do the next best thing.

A determined gleam in her eye, she went below, but not to the orlop. She must find a place where she could be alone and unobserved.

Bracing his legs against the pitch and roll of the deck, Glenmorgan raised the glass to his eye. In the strengthening sunlight, he could easily make out the two ships, the tiny figures swaying in the rigging as the courses were taken in. They were little more than two miles off and sailing close-hauled to the wind, would take perhaps thirty minutes to draw into range. If the wind held, he could be dead or a prisoner in another hour.

Grimly, he shook off the thought and the one that had come immediately after—that Meg and her grandfather

253

might soon be at Drago's mercy again. Instead he forced himself to study the approaching ships.

The brigantine, the *Devil Fish,* was French-made, a trader that had fallen to Big Joe Drummond some years before. She carried thirty guns, but she was an old vessel, her timbers rotting from her years at sea, and she was dragging enough barnacles and seaweed beneath her keel to make her slow and sluggish in answering the helm. While Drummond was a formidable fighter, he was noted more for his ferocity than his intelligence. Drago would be the real threat.

A grim smile played about Glenmorgan's lips as he noted the *Sea Hawk*'s trim hull, the high poop and ornately carved bow. Under her previous, Spanish masters, *El Halcon del Mar* had patrolled the Spanish Main. Drago had taken her with galleys in a night raid off Panama, and though no country's ships were ever safe from Drago's greed, she had remained like a red flag in the face of the Spanish ever since.

Most of her thirty-six guns were eighteen pounders while the *Raven*'s were only twelve pounders or less. The *Sea Hawk* was bigger, heavier, built for pounding an enemy her size or smaller into submission, while the *Raven,* like the sloop *Barracuda* stalking her from behind, was a lightweight, designed for hit-and-run tactics. The *Sea Hawk* would carry a complement of two hundred men or more, to the *Raven*'s one hundred sixty hands. And she would have Drago's cunning behind her.

Glenmorgan grimaced. He could almost wish for an unseasonal hurricane to come tearing down on them. They would stand a better chance of weathering that than beating off the pirate ships. He would have to depend on his one strength—the *Raven*'s greater speed and maneuverability. It was damned little, but it was all he had.

His mind made up, he closed the telescope with a snap.

"Mr. Chapin, you may load both batteries and prepare to run out—but you will run out only the larboard on my command. The starboard battery I want double-shotted, then left manned and ready. Do you understand?"

Chapin gave him a probing glance, but held his tongue. He had learned long ago that Glenmorgan always had a good reason behind every order, no matter how odd the order might seem at the time.

"Aye, Cap'n," he rumbled. "The larboard loaded and run out, the starboard double-shotted and ready."

But Glenmorgan had already turned back to the approaching ships. Drago's three-pronged attack was meant to drive the *Raven* into a closing fist. Either he would be forced to sail between the two in front of him, taking a raking on both sides, or he could choose the safer course, tacking to starboard in order to place the slower, clumsier brig between him and the deadlier frigate.

With any luck, Drago would be expecting him to take on the less formidable *Devil Fish,* and when he did, Drago would swing around the bows of his slower consort and, taking the windage, would rake the *Raven*'s stern. While the *Devil Fish* fired to dismast the corvette with chain shot, the *Sea Hawk* would overtake and disable Glenmorgan's foundering vessel with a single, well-aimed broadside. At least that was what Glenmorgan hoped Drago was thinking.

To Brindle, the sailing master, he said, "Be prepared to come about to windward on my order. It will have to be quick, Brindle, if we don't want them to guess what we're about."

"Aye, aye, Cap'n," came Brindle's response, though the master eyed him worriedly. To the windward would take them across the Spanish frigate's bows, and against Drago's blasted guns, they wouldn't stand a bloody chance in hell.

Glenmorgan read all that and more in the man's weathered face, but he forced himself to ignore it. The master had been with him as long as Chapin and was too seasoned a veteran to question an order from his captain, at least not in the matter of taking on an enemy.

From somewhere he thought he heard the sound of singing as he drew his sword and laid it in readiness along the rail. For a moment, time seemed to stop as he realized it was Meg and that she must be trying to show him in the only way she knew how that her trust was in him. He shot a glance along the groups of men huddled at their guns on the main deck and could see that they heard it, too. Their faces wore varying expressions of disbelief, simple awe, and dawning realization.

"Hear that, lads?" called out Chapin, his homely face splitting in a wild grin. "It's the captain's lady. She's not afraid of those buggers because she knows they don't stand a chance in hell against Mad Mike Glenmorgan!"

"A cheer for the cap'n, lads!" shouted another voice. "And another for the lady!"

Taken off guard by the response as the whole ship seemed to erupt in a wild frenzy of cheering, Glenmorgan turned his face away. It was all there—the reckless acceptance of danger, the rising lust for battle, hope, where before there had been despair. She had done that for them—for *him!*

Meg sat curled up on a cot in one of the tiny cabins in the wardroom, the door safely closed against prying eyes. Holding the gemstone in one hand, she ran the comb through her long hair with the other. But her eyes were unfocused, dreamy, as she sang the song of the old ones. And on the gemstone's surface, she did not see the reflection of her face, but a constantly changing panorama of sky and rapidly moving clouds.

She was so engrossed in her song that she heard nothing of the sudden din of cheering. Nor was she aware moments later of the sudden careening of the ship to one side as it was forced about on to a new tack. Not until the first jarring explosions of the broadside was her concentration shaken. And by then she had finished the song.

Knowing she had done all she could to help Glenmorgan against the pirates, she hid the gemstone, hanging on its chain about her neck, inside her dress and slipped the comb in the green belt about her waist. Then, glancing up and down the companionway, she quickly made her way down to the orlop.

The knuckles of Glenmorgan's fingers shone white as he gripped the sword hilt and watched the approach of the two ships. Sailing on parallel courses and separated from one another by little more than two cable lengths, they had drawn to within a mile of the corvette—in range for a bow shot, or a broadside if either should choose to tack across *Raven*'s bow.

"Not long now," he flung over his shoulder at Brindle. Gauging the moment when it would appear he was committed to his present tack, he felt the adrenaline pumping in his veins. Any second he expected Drago to see through the ruse, expected to see the ships veer on diverging tacks and take him on either side.

Lifting the sword overhead, he brought it down in a quick slashing movement. "Now, Dick," he shouted, "run out the larboard!" He heard Chapin relay the order. "Steady now," he murmured, more to himself than to Brindle. "Steady." Ignoring the din as the guns rumbled outboard, he allowed himself a quick glance at the men, waiting at the braces, then another at the pennant, streaming from the mainmast. The wind was holding steady out of the northeast.

"The bastards are running their guns out," Chapin observed, his voice sounding clipped with tension.

257

Glenmorgan felt a sudden elation as he saw the *Devil Fish* shorten sails and realized Drago had taken the bait. Both ships had run out their larboard batteries, and as the *Devil Fish* dropped behind her larger consort, Drago's *Sea Hawk* appeared to surge forward to the attack. But already, Glenmorgan could see her yards swinging in unison as she made to come about in the wind.

"Now, Mr. Brindle. Point your helm! Dick, get those guns in, and run out the starboard."

For an agonizing moment, it appeared that he had waited too long as the *Raven* shuddered and fought against every effort to bring her around. Then her sails were filling and the stem was biting with new determination on the larboard tack. Not so the *Sea Hawk.* Thrown into confusion by the *Raven*'s unexpected maneuver, Drago was trying to beat back to windward.

"By Jeezus," groaned Brindle, "she's going to ram us!"

Glenmorgan clenched his hands on the rail until his knuckles ached as he watched the other ship's jib pointing straight at them. But already the *Raven* was proving his faith in her. Coming about, she was passing down the frigate's unprotected side.

"Prepare to fire as you bear," Glenmorgan shouted, feeling the excitement coursing through him like the effects of a potent wine. Then once again his sword flashed in the sunlight. *"Fire!"*

The explosion of the guns hurtling their broadside into the enemy ship was deafening. As Glenmorgan braced himself against the recoil, the other ship vanished in a thick cloud of smoke. Behind him, the gun captains were already shouting above the din of squealing tackles and rumbling gun trucks, "Sponge and reload!"

As the smoke rolled away, he saw the *Sea Hawk*'s mizzenmast begin to sway and slowly topple. Her side was pock-marked and riddled with shot holes, her decks littered with carnage. She vanished again in a new pall of smoke as another broadside hurtled into her. Then the *Raven* was pulling away from her stern.

"You've crippled him, Michael! And he never got off a shot!" Chapin was shouting excitedly. Along the main deck the men were starting to cheer. "By God, we can still rake him across the stern!"

"There isn't time." Glenmorgan squinted against the smoke, searching for the *Devil Fish*. As the smoke cleared, he saw the brigantine wallowing about in an attempt to cut them off. And from the north, the *Barracuda* was sweeping down on them.

"Get the courses on her, Dick," he said, feeling the madness slowly draining out of him. "Put every stitch of canvas on her that she'll take. Brindle, bring her around two points to starboard." He glanced meaningfully from one to the other of the two men. "We're not out of this yet, my lads. Not by a long shot."

For a moment it seemed as if the wind must have shifted, blowing the smoke back in their faces. Glenmorgan stared incredulously along the quarterdeck as the sun was suddenly blotted out by a thick mass of black, roiling clouds. Even as he looked, the ship was enveloped by an impenetrable curtain of mist.

In seconds the *Sea Hawk* was lost from view, swallowed up in the freakish storm, along with the three pirate ships.

"What the devil?" Glenmorgan swore softly to himself.

But Chapin was grinning hugely. In fact, Glenmorgan had the distinct impression that at any moment he was going to see his big first mate begin to caper about the deck like a great lumbering bear.

"She did it!" Chapin exclaimed gleefully. "By God, I'd never have believed it!" Suddenly, as if he could not contain his excitement, he was vigorously pumping Glenmorgan's hand. "You're a lucky man, Michael. Damn me, if it ain't the luck of the Irish."

"What the devil are you ranting about?" growled Glenmorgan, plainly convinced his first mate's sanity was in doubt.

Chapin had the presence of mind to appear chagrined at behavior that ill suited the *Raven*'s second in command.

"Er—sorry, Michael." Again the huge grin spread irresistibly across his face. "But you can't deny this has been a remarkable day. We showed 'em, by God!"

"Very well, Dick," Glenmorgan sighed. "If you say so. However, I suggest you get the t'gans'ls off her. In this soup we could find ourselves thrust on to the *Barracuda*'s main deck before we knew what was happening."

He had almost to grope his way to the binnacle through the thick curtain of mist. He studied the compass points as if he were seeing them for the first time, and he had to force his tired mind to make the necessary calculations to put them back on a course to Antigua. When that was done and he had relayed his orders to Brindle, he would go below and assure himself that all was well with Meg, he told himself, feeling the weariness dragging at his body.

Now that the danger was past, he was suddenly aware that he was laboring under an almost overwhelming desire to see her, to hold her near—indeed, to have her for a little while all to himself.

Fifteen

As the *Raven* rounded James Island and began the final approach into Charles Town Bay, Meg's eyes went to Glenmorgan's still figure at the taffrail. He was gazing forward at the bustling harbor, filled with vessels of every kind. More than twenty merchant ships lined the wharves projecting from the river front, while perhaps five times that many rode at anchor farther out in the bay. Along the east bay, mule-drawn freight wagons carried cargo to and from the great warehouses lining the waterfront, and the shop-lined street fronting the harbor from north to south was swarming with people.

In that instant she seemed to glimpse behind Glenmorgan's careful mask to the powerful emotions underneath. He was drinking it all in, the bustle and commotion, the teeming crowd involved with the daily comings and goings of a great seaport. She could read it all in the stern lines of his face, in his stance, ramrod straight, his hands clasped rigidly behind his back.

After seven years of forced exile from the place of his birth, Michael Glenmorgan was coming home to friends and family—and unfinished business.

And *she* had no part in any of it. This was Clarissa's world.

Meg fought the urge to flee below decks to the safety of the stern cabin, her initial feelings of excitement and eager curiosity suddenly eclipsed by other, stronger sensations. She had to force herself to smile and nod as her grandfather called her attention to various landmarks—the old fort on Sullivan's Island, the broad span of marshland that separated the north end of the island from Haddrell's Point on the mainland, the wide mouth of Cooper River, Comings Point, and finally the town itself, the wall with its bastions and small forts at the corners, the tree-lined streets and tall, stately houses glinting in the sunlight. She was conscious only, however, of a mounting nausea in the pit of her stomach.

Her discomfort was due, no doubt, to the unfamiliar feeling of constriction around her middle, she tried to tell herself. Never in a hundred years would she grow used to being encased in layer upon layer of clothing. The silk underthings that confined and clung to her limbs were bad enough, but to be forced into an inverted wicker basket, flattened on opposite sides to form an oval and strapped about the waist, had brought her almost to the point of rebellion. She had finally submitted to it and to the torture of soft-leather shoes only because Glenmorgan had gone to all the trouble to purchase them for her at St. John's on Antigua. That, and because the blue silk gown that went over all the other things had hung shapelessly about her slender hips without it.

Even so, she was acutely aware of feeling absurd and hopelessly awkward in all her new finery, a feeling that had been dramatically reinforced when she hobbled into the main cabin that morning to present herself for Glenmorgan's critical inspection.

It had not helped that her grandfather had fallen suddenly into a violent fit of coughing as she made her appearance in the doorway. Or that Glenmorgan had apparently been stricken dumb at the sight of her. Miserable and blushing with embarrassment, she had stood rigidly under his frozen scrutiny.

"Well?" she had at last been forced to demand when the silence stretched to unbearable limits.

"I'm afraid," her grandfather began in a voice that sounded suspiciously strangled, "that I should have foreseen the desirability of engaging a lady's maid for you. The captain did mention it, but I . . . well, no matter. The thing is, my child, there are—er—certain complexities to a lady's wardrobe that you may need to have explained to you. The—ah—er—gown isn't quite right, you see. And the—"

"Not right?" she exclaimed, realizing all in a second that she must look every bit as foolish as she felt in the accursed dress. "Not right? It is a horrid thing, obviously designed to torture and torment its wearer. And these *shoes!* Surely they cannot be meant for human feet! I should rather go naked than submit to such atrocities. I should rather die than be seen at all. Oh, I wish the sea would rise up and swallow me—now, this very instant."

Only then, as tears of humiliation threatened, had Glenmorgan at last taken command of the situation. "No doubt you will excuse us," he said curtly to Pippin and, without waiting for an answer, took Meg's hand and led her firmly back into the sleeping cabin.

No sooner had the door closed behind them than she found herself suddenly clasped in his arms, his mouth covering hers in a kiss that had silenced her protests and taken her breath away.

A long sigh breathed through her lips when at last he released her.

"And now," he murmured, smiling a little at the dazed look in her eyes, "while I admit to finding a certain charm in the notion of having you go naked, at least in my presence, I've no intention of sharing that very special privilege with the rest of the world. With a few minor adjustments, I think you will find the gown tolerable."

His expression perfectly sober, he undid the tiny fastenings down her front, which should have been more properly at the back, and helped her out of the sleeves. "There," he said as he slid the dress around so that the plunging square neck fit over her shapely breasts where it belonged. "That's better, don't you think?"

"Perhaps," she admitted grudgingly. She let him help her slip her arms once more through the elbow-length sleeves, ending in graceful froths of lace, and tried not to fidget as he redid the fastenings, this time down the back where they belonged.

His hands came to rest on her shoulders when he finished. "And now for the panniers," he said, turning her to face him. A wry gleam of humor flickered in his eyes. "I'm afraid it is more fashionable at present to wear the flat sides fore and aft rather than broadside to broadside."

Meg blushed with embarrassment. "Well, how was *I* to know? I daresay *you* have dressed a great many women before."

"Oh, any number," he agreed with only the slightest twitch at the corners of his lips. Helping her to hitch up her dress, he embraced with a glance the delectable picture of femininity posed fetchingly with skirts clutched above the waist. "But none," he remarked feelingly, "with such exquisite attributes."

The necessary adjustments made to the wicker frame so that she no longer appeared to be wearing a canoe underneath the gown, he at last led her to the cot and bade her to sit down. Kneeling, he removed the offensive shoes. "You will observe," he said, holding the footwear up to show her the soles, "that shoes are designed to fit the shape of the foot. There is one for the left and one for the right. Unfortunately, they are not interchangeable."

Holding the slippers so that she could slide her feet into them, he helped her to stand.

The difference was astonishing. While it would take her some time to become accustomed to the novelty of wearing shoes, she at least did not have to suffer the discomfort of having them on the wrong feet when she did so.

When at last she stood before him for a final critical appraisal, Glenmorgan had taken his time, standing back from her and commanding her to pirouette slowly before him two or three times—as though he were having difficulty making up his mind, she fumed resentfully. Not until she turned on him with a dangerous sparkle in her eye had he relented. Then, laughing, he brought her hand to his lips and lightly kissed her knuckles.

"The gown," he remarked, suddenly serious, where before he had been teasing, "is only adequate. But I can assure you that Charles Town will never have the honor of welcoming a more beautiful woman."

She had not really believed his lavish praise, but the warmth in his eyes had been enough to sustain her until that actual moment of rounding James Island to find herself face to face with an uncertain future.

The slow approach to the harbor was accomplished without mishap, and at last the *Raven* rode at dock before an imposing structure fronted by its own private wharf. GLEN-MORGAN & SON was painted in bold letters across the building's facade, obviously the offices for what had once been the Glenmorgan family shipping business. Surprisingly, they appeared to house a thriving enterprise. Through the large windows in the front, Meg could see numerous men inside, seated at desks, and before the ship had even pulled up to the wharf, a well-dressed man somewhere in his middle to late twenties came rushing excitedly out the door and down to the dock.

As the *Raven* came alongside and men eagerly caught

and made fast the mooring lines, he shoved his way through a gathering crowd of curious onlookers. A wild grin broke across his face as he spotted Glenmorgan at the nettings. "Michael!" he shouted, waving his hand over his head. "By God, it *is* you!"

"Aye, Thomas," Glenmorgan grinned back at him, making no attempt to hide his own pleasure, "as you see. Come aboard, man. We've a lot of catching up to do."

As if afraid that Glenmorgan would vanish the moment he took his eyes off him, the elated Thomas half ran, half stumbled toward the gangway which was being lowered. When he came aboard, Glenmorgan was at the entry port, waiting to greet him.

Their hands clasped in a crushing handshake. "Thomas, it's *good* to see you."

"And you, Michael. By God, I see you still have your great bear of a first mate with you," exclaimed Thomas as he saw Chapin looking on with obvious satisfaction.

Glenmorgan's free hand went to the other man's shoulder, gripped, and held. "Tell me about everyone. Mother and Kate. Brigida and the boy. He must be a strapping, fine lad by now."

"He is that," Thomas beamed. "He has five years under his belt and an infant sister to keep him company." Suddenly his fingers gripped Glenmorgan's arm hard above the elbow. "Kate never gave you up. Not even when Clarissa put into port with Tharp and her father and began spreading it about that you'd bought it at Antigua. But Brigida and your mother took it hard. You must go to them *at once,* Michael. Kate's been fretting herself sick with worry over you."

"Rest assured, Thomas," Glenmorgan answered gravely. "I will, just as soon as I've seen to things here. But first, there's something I'd like you to do for me."

Thomas was beaming again. "Anything, Michael. Just name it."

Glenmorgan's gravity gave way before a gleam of amusement. "The same old Thomas. Ready to leap into the fire without so much as a question. Come. There's someone I want you to meet."

Taking him by the arm, Glenmorgan led him aft toward Meg and her grandfather, who had retreated into the shelter of the poop, away from curious eyes.

Meg, who had witnessed what was obviously a momentous reunion for the two men, studied the newcomer with curiosity as he came near. Not above average height, he was slender and well made, with a youthful face, which was both pleasant and well to look upon. He had brown hair, tied into a queue at the nape of his neck, and brown eyes, which regarded her with frank admiration as Glenmorgan began the introductions.

"Thomas, shake hands with Joseph Pippin, the man who saved my life at Antigua. And his granddaughter, Meg, to whom I owe a great deal more than my life." The captain's hand went to Thomas's shoulder. "I have the honor of presenting to you both a man who is my friend and my business partner, but more importantly, the man who had the extremely good foresight to win my sister Bridgida's warmest affection. My brother-in-law, Thomas Sutton."

"A pleasure, Mr. Sutton," Pippin said, shaking the other man's hand.

"The pleasure is all mine, sir," Sutton replied with sincerity, his curiosity intensified as much by what Glenmorgan had not said as by what he had revealed about the two. "I am in your debt for saving Michael's neck." He grinned, taking the sting from his next words. "For some strange reason the women of the Glenmorgan family place a very high value on this ruffian's continued existence, though for the life of me I cannot see why. If ever you or your granddaughter need anything, I hope you will not hesitate to come to me."

"As a matter of fact, Thomas," Glenmorgan smoothly interjected, "that is what I wanted to discuss with you. I'd like you to inquire about for a house suitable for their needs. Mr. Pippin is something of a scholar who prefers his privacy. A place on the bay, secluded from curious neighbors and having access to a private bathing beach. Money, of course, is no obstacle, but their needs are simple—something cozy and comfortable rather than elaborate or grand. They will require no more than three day-servants—a cook and serving maid, and a housekeeper to see to the smooth running of the household. We will pay well for their services, and in return they must be completely trustworthy. Oh, and one more thing." He paused, his eyes thoughtful on Meg. "Miss Pippin will require a lady's maid. A level-headed woman whose discretion can be depended upon. Do you think you can do all that?"

Sutton frowned thoughtfully.

"The house should not be too difficult. In fact, I have one in mind that might be just the thing—it was built by a gentleman a few years back for his—er—niece, I believe. The girl ran off with an artist, and the old gentleman has since returned home to England. In the meantime, a caretaker has kept it up. I think it very likely that it could be made ready to receive occupants almost immediately. The servants, however, might take a little longer."

Especially the lady's maid who could be depended on to hold her tongue, thought Sutton, suddenly worried what Kate and Brigida would think if they knew their brother was arranging a cozy little nest for a dazzling beauty who looked to be younger than themselves. Immediately he caught himself, ashamed at where his thoughts were leading. Michael had said he owed Miss Pippin more than his life. That was all that was important. Anything else that lay between them was nobody's business but their own.

"Do what you can," said Glenmorgan, well aware what

Sutton must be thinking, what everyone would think. Not for the first time he toyed with the idea of declaring Meg to be his intended bride and, as before, discarded it. Meg was as stubborn as she was beautiful and every bit as maddeningly elusive. She was all too capable of openly disavowing any intention of becoming his wife.

His thoughts went back over the past two weeks at sea, the shared intimacy of life on shipboard with Meg at his side—long, blissful days spent on the weatherdeck, talking and laughing or being silently content with one another's company as they watched the slow passage of the sea beneath the stern. It had seemed at such moments that they might go on sailing forever across an ocean without end. Only at night as she made love to him or lay spent in his arms afterward had he sensed the quiet desperation beneath her outwardly calm acceptance of reality. Time *was* passing, and every day brought them closer to Charles Town.

Gradually, it was borne in on him that she was treating each moment they spent together as if it might be their last. And yet whenever he had tried to broach the subject of marriage, she had proven as elusive as quicksilver, putting him off with a shrug or a sudden change of the subject or, if he proved too persistent, silencing him with lips that teased and tormented him until he forgot everything but his need to possess her.

In some ways they had drawn as close as two people could, and in others he felt that he knew her even less well than he had before. Only one thing was certain. While she was as adamantly opposed as ever to marrying him, *he* was just as grimly determined to make her permanently his.

She would be his wife. He would settle for nothing less.

At present, however, he found himself at an impasse. If he could not openly declare his honorable intentions, then he must do whatever else he could to protect her from slanderous tongues.

Offering the excuse that they had a matter of some import to discuss, he took Thomas aside.

"Michael, you devil!" exclaimed Thomas as soon as they were out of ear shot of Meg and her grandfather. "You're the only man I know who could contrive to have himself saved by the most beautiful creature I've ever laid eyes on."

"I'm glad you approve," Glenmorgan smiled humorlessly, "since she and her grandfather will be staying as my guests for the time being—either in the Town House or elsewhere, Thomas. It's up to you."

"Then it will be the Town House, of course, Michael," Thomas answered without hesitation. "Was there ever any doubt of it?"

Glenmorgan gripped his arm hard. "Not where your loyalty is concerned—never, Thomas. But it isn't as simple as that. There are Brigida and the children to consider, as well as Kate and my mother, which is why I think you better let me finish what I was about to say before you commit yourself to anything. Pippin, I'm afraid, is a fugitive. His real name is Belding. Perhaps you've heard of him. He's wanted for mutiny against the King's Navy."

Thomas struck a fist to his palm. "Good God, I remember. He was on the *Argonaut*. But that's impossible. No one survived the shipwreck."

"You're wrong," Glenmorgan replied. "Belding did. And until I can clear his name, he is a danger to anyone who takes him in. The worst of it is that he was a physician here in Charles Town for several years before he shipped out on the *Argonaut*. He was well known, Thomas, and might be recognized. Do you still want to welcome him into your home?"

Glenmorgan looked away, unable to watch the struggle in the other man's face. He could hardly blame Thomas for having his doubts. It was a lot to ask of anyone, let alone a man with a family. But for Meg's sake, he had had to try.

His hands tightened on the deck rail as his brother-in-law's quiet voice broke into his somber reflections. "Your friends are welcome. Surely you must know that."

Thomas smiled sadly, seeing the surprise in Glenmorgan's eyes. "You forget, Michael," he said with compelling simplicity. "It's your home, too. Hell, we wouldn't have the Town House, or anything else, if it hadn't been for you."

It was a short distance from the pier to the wide steps, which led from the quay to the entrance of a small courtyard paved with flagstones. As they came to a wrought iron fence covered with wisteria, Meg hung back, feeling dwarfed by the towering three stories of the house, the graceful portico with its twin tiers of marble columns, the marble steps rising to a great, carved door beneath a stained-glass fanlight. She had never seen anything so grand. To her, it loomed grander, even, than the house on Antigua, and far more intimidating.

Her grandfather's hand beneath her elbow urged her toward the double-wide gates in the fence. Before she could stop herself, she heard herself gasp, "I—I can't!"

"You can. And you will." Pippin's arm went bracingly around her shoulders. "It's only a house, Meg. I won't let you fling it all away now. Surely we've come too far for that."

Meg could only shake her head. More than anything she wanted to go back to the ship. She would suffocate inside those walls, cut off from the sea. She saw Sutton turn to stare at her in sudden concern. Then Glenmorgan was beside her. With a casual nod of the head, he sent the others ahead.

"Sometimes, when I was a boy," he remarked conversationally, taking her hand in his, "if I couldn't sleep, I used to sneak out onto the terrace at night. Up there," he said, pointing to the vine-covered balcony, hugging the front of the house, which faced the bay. "From there you can see all the way to the sea. I used to pretend it was a ship's quarterdeck, and I was its captain. Using the stars, I plotted my course to the West Indies, or sometimes to places a great deal farther away than that. That will be your room, if you like, the one that opens on to the terrace. There's a stairway that leads into a garden. It was one of my favorite hiding places when I was a boy and had to get away to be by myself. You'll find that the doors are never kept locked, and the windows are always left open to let in the breeze off the sea."

Meg frowned uncertainly, gazing up at him. "And now that you are all grown up," she said, "and have been to see all those places you dreamed about as a boy, do you think you will still feel the urge occasionally to get away by yourself?"

Glenmorgan smiled. "You may be certain of it." His fingers brushed a stray lock of hair from her face. "Especially if I know a girl with hair the color of moonlight will be there waiting for me. You will be there, won't you, Meg?" he murmured, his look quizzing her. "Waiting for me?"

They had been walking as they talked, and suddenly, though she could not remember having climbed the marble stairs, Meg became aware that they were before the great carved door, standing open as though it, too, were waiting for an answer to a question. As indeed it was.

Gravely she lifted shadowed eyes to his face, knowing she dared not tell him the truth and that she couldn't lie.

"Always," she answered, in a voice hardly above a whisper. "In my heart."

Then without another word, she turned and stepped through the doorway.

Glenmorgan frowned, troubled by her answer. Only a fool or a blind man would have failed to see the sadness in her eyes or sense the vagueness of her reply. He would have called her back to demand an explanation or at least to pin her down to a more satisfactory response. But then a low cry issued from the far end of the hall.

"Michael?"

He glanced up to see a slender female in a rose-colored gown staring at him from the foot of the stairway. She was no taller than the last time he had seen her—she had reached, then, to his shoulder—but instead had filled out in that lovely, mysterious way of a woman. Before, she had seemed all arms and legs. Now, she was all soft, feminine curves. And her hair, as raven black and unruly as his own, was no longer parted in the middle and worn, subdued, in severe pigtails down her back. Gathered neatly back from the forehead, it fell in soft curls from the crown down to her shoulders. No longer the freckle-faced tomboy he had taught to fish and sail a boat, she was a strikingly beautiful woman with the determined chin and wide-set intelligent eyes, reminiscent of their mother's.

Unable to recognize in this full-bodied young woman the kid sister who seven years before had begged him to take her pirating with him, he felt a harsh sting of emotion in his throat.

"Kate?" he ventured at last as he watched her start uncertainly toward him.

The next instant she was in his arms, laughing and crying, as he picked her up off her feet and swung her around.

"Kate, how you've changed," he rumbled, setting her down and holding her from him so that he could take a good long look at her. "What are you? All of twenty now?"

"I'm one and twenty, but I feel older. Faith, Michael, I've waited so long for you to come home." Lifting a hand to the side of his face, she stared at him with eyes of the same penetrating blue as his own. "You've changed, too," she murmured with a hint of sadness. "I believe if I didn't know you, I could almost be afraid of you." A rueful smile broke suddenly across her face. "On the other hand, I am quite *certain* that if I were not your sister, I should fall instantly head over heels in love with you! I almost pity the unsuspecting females of Charles Town, young and old alike."

"Wretch!" exclaimed Glenmorgan wryly. "Rest assured, the ladies of Charles Town are safe enough from me."

"Mama will be sorry to hear that," warned his sister with dancing eyes. *"She* hopes to see you settled with a wife and children of your own—a son, at the very least, to carry on the family name."

Meg, who had been an unwilling witness to the intimate exchange between brother and sister, felt a blush sting her cheeks as Glenmorgan's eyes pointedly went to hers.

"Then our mother will be glad to know," he drawled with cool deliberation, "that I am in complete sympathy with her hopes for my future. Unfortunately, I have yet to convince the lady."

Meg shot him a darkling glance, which Glenmorgan parried with the grin that had devastated more than one female's heart.

Kate, who had until then had eyes only for her brother, was brought suddenly to an awareness that she was being remiss in her duties as a hostess. From the piercing quality of the look bent over her shoulder, moreover, she could not doubt that the personage who awaited her attention was one of no little importance. Following Glenmorgan's gaze, she turned to survey the young woman waiting uncertainly a few feet away.

Her initial impression was of an ill-fitting gown, the hem too short and the style slightly outmoded. Good heavens, was her horrified thought, this was hardly the sort of female she had envisioned for her brother. That was before, however, she took a good look at the girl it adorned. Slowly she exhaled a long breath. It was little wonder if Glenmorgan seemed smitten! Not even the gown could detract from that face and form. She was breathtaking, and yet even that was not enough to describe the overall effect. Even at a glance Kate could sense there was a great deal more to the child than met the eye. Hard upon that thought came the realization that her visitor *was* obviously very young and more than a little apprehensive.

The next instant Kate was striding across the hall to take the girl's hands warmly in her own.

"My dear, you must excuse me for leaving you standing at the door," she exclaimed contritely. "What a very poor opinion you must have of our hospitality. Please, do come in. I'm Kate, well, Caitlin, actually. But everyone calls me Kate. And you must be Meg. I seem to recall, even in the excitement of the moment, that I met your grandfather upstairs—Mr. Pippin, isn't it?—and that he mentioned you would be along shortly. My mother and sister have taken the children on a short outing, so Thomas is keeping your grandfather company in the drawing room. We can go and join them, if you like. Or if you prefer, I could show you to a room where you could freshen up before dinner. You must be tired after your voyage."

"Yes, I—I would like that," Meg murmured, grateful for the opportunity to escape to someplace where she could be by herself. "I am a little tired."

"Of course you are, my dear," replied Kate sympathetically. "I'll take you right up."

"I've promised Meg my old room, overlooking the bay," Glenmorgan smoothly interjected. "I hope that's convenient."

"But of course it is." Kate smiled. "You can take Papa's room. It's just as he left it." Reaching out, she took her brother's hand tightly in her own. "It's like a miracle. You'd hardly guess someone else had ever lived here. Oh, Michael,

I'm so glad you're home. Everything will be all right now. I know it."

"You may be sure of it," Glenmorgan said. Giving Kate's fingers a squeeze, he released her before turning to Meg. "Go with Kate." His hand touched the side of her face. "I'll be nearby if you need me."

Wordlessly, Meg nodded, but inside, she felt a weight settle on her heart. She had seen behind his calm mask, if his sister had not. Things were a long way from being all right, and here, in this place that was so foreign to her, she felt powerless. Feeling the house closing in on her, she turned to follow Kate up the staircase. It was as if the time she had shared with Glenmorgan on board the *Raven* had been only a dream, she thought, and felt it slowly slipping away from her.

Keeping up a steady flow of inane observations, which required nothing of Meg but that she nod occasionally or smile, Kate ushered her brother's guest up two flights of stairs and down a hall with rooms on either side. Meg had a fleeting impression of walls painted dove gray and hung with family portraits, of straight-backed mahogany chairs, a small table with a porcelain vase, and underfoot, a floral carpet, until at last they came to a door painted white.

"Here we are," said Kate, opening the door and stepping back to let Meg enter before her. "We took all of Michael's things with us when we had to move out of the house. Mama and I did our best to put everything back the way it was."

Meg, stepping into a bright pool of sunlight streaming in through French doors, hardly heard her. In awe, she slowly let her eyes travel about the room, taking in at a glance pale blue walls with neat white trim and, underfoot, a thick Aubusson carpet. She had never seen anything like the mahogany bedstead, the mattress covered with an indigo-colored satin comforter. Beside the bed was a night table with a brass oil lamp, and in addition to a chest of drawers and a wardrobe, the room contained a dressing table and a wash basin and stand, while in one corner, conveniently sided by a small table with a reading lamp, stood an overstuffed armchair, upholstered in rich brown leather, and a secretary filled with leather-bound books.

Never in her wildest flight of fancy could she have imagined such a room. And yet somehow she had little difficulty picturing Glenmorgan, sitting in the armchair reading, or standing at the French doors gazing out at the ships in the harbor. For the first time it was borne in on her just how wide was the gulf separating them.

As from a distance, she heard Kate say her name and tried to overcome her sense of hopelessness to answer her.

"Meg, dear, what is it?" Kate tried again, her arm going about the other girl's shoulders. "Are you ill? You have gone quite pale."

"No." Meg pulled herself free and stood with her back to Kate. "No, I am simply hopelessly out of place. This room, this house." She came about to face the older girl with a wildness in her eyes. "They are as foreign to me as my grandfather's one-room hut would be to you. Or the islands I grew up on. Until this morning I had never had shoes on my feet. I can't eat your food or pretend that I'm not different from you. I don't even know how to dress myself. I don't belong here, and if I stay, I shall only cause you and your family embarrassment. Surely you must see that."

"I see nothing of the sort," answered Kate, as moved by the other girl's distress as she was startled by her sudden outburst. "I see a very lovely young woman who, Thomas has told me, helped to save my only brother's life. Michael cares a great deal for you, that much is obvious. Do you truly believe I could do any less? Or that my mother could, for that matter? We can teach you how to dress, Meg. Or how to take tea with the governor's wife, if need be. The rest will take care of itself, if you only give it a chance."

Meg stared speechlessly at the other girl. Obviously Kate meant what she said. The warmth in her eyes was undoubtedly genuine, and there seemed nothing of the haughty disdain of the females Meg had glimpsed in the house on Antigua. She was not at all what Meg had expected in Glenmorgan's sister. "You are very kind," Meg murmured at last, feeling disarmed and helpless before such generosity. "I—I shall try not to disappoint you."

"Nonsense," Kate smiled. "It isn't kindness. You will be doing me a great favor if you can achieve what no other female has been able to do." The child would have her eternal gratitude, Kate thought grimly to herself, if she could banish Clarissa Tharp from Michael's heart once and for all. But aloud she said, "Above all things, I want my brother to be happy. And seeing you and the way he looks at you has made me hope . . . But enough said for now," she added hastily, seeing the look of dismay in the other girl's eyes. "Here, why don't you let me help you out of your dress. Perhaps you will see things differently when you have had a good rest."

It was hardly likely, thought Meg bleakly as she allowed Kate to undo the fastenings at the back of her gown. If anything, Kate and her unspoken hopes for Glenmorgan's future had only complicated matters more than they were before.

278

Sixteen

Meg did not really believe that she would be able to sleep in her strange surroundings, but she nevertheless allowed herself to be dressed in one of Kate's sleeping gowns of flowing white gauze and afterward tucked into the huge bed beneath the down comforter.

The gasp of startled delight that burst from Meg's lips as she sank down into the luxurious depths of the feather mattress brought a bemused smile to her hostess's lips.

"There," exclaimed Kate, laughing. "We will spoil you so that you would not dare dream of leaving us." But to herself, she wondered what sort of a life Meg must have led to be in ignorance of so many things she herself took for granted. Like an infant, discovering the world for the first time, she had had to finger practically everything in the room, and she had done it with the same sort of innocent wonder Kate had seen in her nephew and niece. Yet Meg's speech was genteel and her manner pleasing, and she carried herself with an easy, unconscious grace that many well-bred young girls acquired only after years of training.

Meg Pippin was a definite enigma, thought Kate, who decided right then and there that she had a great many questions to put to Michael Glenmorgan as soon as she could corner him. Wishing Meg a restful repose and bidding her to ring if she needed anything, Kate left the room, closing the door quietly behind her.

Perhaps she was worn out after all the excitement and trepidation of arriving, or perhaps it was something else—a growing heaviness of spirit of which she was only vaguely aware. Whatever the case, Meg went to sleep almost as soon as her head hit the pillow and slept without stirring through dinner and long into the night.

The dream, when it came, was fragmented and terrifying—shifting images of a sealess land, a cell with iron bars for windows, and herself, staring wild-eyed and grief-stricken, into the depths of the gemstone at the image of Glenmorgan, lying bloodied and still as death—the gemstone, falling from her hands and shattering.

She came awake with a start, her heart pounding and her body cold with sweat. Bolting upright in the bed, she shivered and stared blankly into the muted glow of the oil lamp beside the great mahogany bed, and on the bedside table, a bowl of fruit, the likes of which she had never seen before. Vaguely, she realized that Glenmorgan must have brought it to her and felt an insane urge to giggle. Sternly quelling the impulse, she clutched her knees to her chest and waited for her heart to cease its hammering.

She was assailed by a sharp pang of disappointment accompanied by a perverse feeling of pique that Glenmorgan had stolen into her room and left without bothering to arouse her. In the magical days aboard the *Raven,* she had grown used to awakening snug in his arms, his lean body warm against hers. How unbearably lonely it was in the great bed without him!

Still more than a little shaken by the dream, she suddenly could not bear to remain in bed another second. Impatiently, she flung aside the bed covers and slipped her legs over the side. The feel of the thick wool carpet beneath her bare feet was new to her, and for a moment she curled her toes into the deep pile, savoring the novelty of it. Then, fitfully, she picked up a round, red piece of fruit and bit into it. It was juicy and sweet, and it crunched delectably between her teeth. She took another bite and, chewing absently, was drawn at last to the French windows, which had been left ajar to admit the cool breeze off the bay.

A crescent moon stood overhead, shedding a pale light over the harbor, and from the terrace, she could see the tall masts of the ships, like a forest of bare trees. Stepping out to the railing, she leaned over it, glorying in the wind as it played through her hair. She drank in deep draughts of the night air as, longingly, she gazed out over the wharves toward the sea beyond, her senses alive to the smell of salt air and the gentle lap of the waves against the dock pilings.

For a moment she lost herself in a waking dream of swimming, gloriously free, through clear waters. She could almost feel the revitalizing strength flowing through her, the sensuous flow of the water against her bare skin. She returned with a jerk to an awareness of herself standing, gazing out to the sea, her whole being suffused with a yearning to plumb its watery depths.

Then at last she knew what afflicted her spirit. Yearnings were awakening in her that had remained dormant and appeased somehow, so long as she lay in Glenmorgan's arms. She was being drawn to the sea. And little wonder. It had been over three weeks since her last dive to the *Argonaut,* and she had not been in the water since!

Her mother could never have survived so long, denied the sea, and Meg knew she owed her own present well-being to her human half—and to the strength she had drawn from Glenmorgan's sustaining presence. On the ship, too, she had not felt separated from her natural element, for it had always been there, beneath her and all around her. It was only here, in this house, that her spirit had become depressed. She shuddered to think what it would be like someplace far removed from the sea. Nevertheless, she could not go forever without renewing herself. Another week, perhaps two, if Glenmorgan was with her to distract her from her physical and spiritual needs. But Glenmorgan was not there with her. She was alone and vulnerable, and the sea was only a short distance away.

But no, she told herself, it was far too dangerous. She was sure to be seen. And yet if she were, what did it really matter? she asked herself, her earlier feelings of hopelessness returning stronger than before. She could not keep up the deception forever. The longer she stayed, the more certain it was that Glenmorgan would find out the truth about her. And to complicate matters even more, now there was Kate to think about, and Glenmorgan's mother, who wanted a wife and family for her son. She should go before she disappointed all their expectations. Even her grandfather would be better off without her, now that he was with friends who would look after him.

Angrily, she stopped herself. She had gone over all this before, she reminded herself, and she had decided to stay until Glenmorgan was safely out of danger. It was only that the dream had upset her, and her head was throbbing so that she could not think at all clearly. Then it came to her that the dream had come as warning, a glimpse of what could happen if she continued to deny her mermaid half— the shattering of the gemstone, the image of Glenmorgan lying dead. Faith, it was too horrid to contemplate.

The half-eaten fruit fell, unnoticed, from her hand, and blindly she took a step toward the wooden stairs leading to the garden below.

Glenmorgan's voice reached out to her from the shadows: "If the apples are not to your liking, there are other fruits in the kitchen to choose from."

Meg froze, her heart pounding.

"A-apples?" With an effort, she realized he must be referring to the red fruit she had dropped. "No, I did like it. I—I wasn't hungry." She turned and probed the shadows, till at last she saw him at the far end of the terrace, his shoulders propped against the wall. The scent of tobacco smoke drifted to her, and in the darkness she could see the red glow of a cheroot in his hand. Then he was leaning forward, crushing the cigar beneath his bootsole.

"It's just as well you're up," he said. "I wanted to talk to you."

She backed a step. "I couldn't sleep," she hedged, her body half-turned, unconsciously poised for flight. "I was going down to the garden."

"That can wait." Straightening, he held out his hand to her. "What I have to tell you cannot."

"No." Meg stayed where she was, her spirit in rebellion, her mind in turmoil. With all her heart she wished to go to him, to fling herself into his arms and pretend they were on the *Raven* once again. But snatches of the dream kept flashing through her mind, and her head hurt abominably. Only one thought was clear to her. The sea was where she belonged, and it was calling her.

In torment, she clapped her hands over her ears as if by that she might shut it out of her mind.

"What do you want from me?" she cried in a strangled voice. "How long have you been there, watching me? Making sure I won't escape." There was a roaring in her ears like the pounding of the surf, and she felt herself sway. "Why can't you leave me alone?"

"Meg!" Strong fingers closed about her arms to help steady her. "What is it?" came Glenmorgan's voice, sharp with concern. "Tell me what's the matter." But she was beyond reason.

"Don't!" she gasped. Furiously, she broke into a struggle. "I don't belong here. You cannot keep me against my will."

With a muttered oath, Glenmorgan pinned her against his

chest. *"Listen* to me, Meg. You are not a prisoner here. My room is next to yours. It shares the terrace. I was standing guard, but *not* to keep you in. *Look*, Meg. Down there, in the shadow of the house across the street."

As if compelled, Meg's eyes went where he was pointing. At first she could see nothing. Then a furtive movement caught her attention. Suddenly she stilled. The roaring receded from her ears, and she could think again.

"I—I see him." She ran her tongue over dry lips. "A man—watching this house."

"Aye," Glenmorgan said. "And he's not the only one. There are at least two others."

Slowly Meg felt her knees giving way beneath her. If she had succeeded in slipping out of the garden, in all likelihood she would never have made it to the pier.

Glenmorgan's arms tightened, as he felt her sag against him.

"Easy," he murmured, drawing her deeper into the shadows. He held her, his face grim, until at last he felt her trembling cease.

"Tell me about them," Meg said when she had herself in hand again. "Who are they?"

"They're from the *Fortuna,*" he answered, loosening his hold as he felt her stir in his arms. "Tharp's schooner. They followed us from the ship. I've already warned Thomas to keep a close watch on Brigida and the others. And now I'm warning you. You will not go out alone. Not for any reason. I want your promise, Meg."

"But why?" Meg evaded, knowing full well she could not keep such a promise, not even for him. "What could they possibly want from me?"

"To use you to get at me. Tharp's dangerous, Meg—more dangerous than you can possibly imagine. He'll stop at nothing to do what he came here to do, and right now I'm the only one who stands in his way." His hands rose to cradle her face. "I'm asking you to trust me, Meg," he said, his eyes probing hers. "Now and in the weeks ahead—no matter what you may hear or see."

Startled, Meg hastily lowered her eyes. Trust went both ways, and she, who had deceived him from the very first, must go on deceiving him, until in the end, it inevitably drove her from him, just as it almost had this night. But she could not tell him that.

"I—I don't understand," she answered at last, forcing herself to meet his piercing scrutiny. "But I will—I—I do trust you."

She saw the pale flash of his eyes in the starlight. Then he kissed her, his mouth open, his lips moving hungrily over hers.

His kiss somehow frightened her. And she clung to him when he released her, her eyes, wide and questioning, on his face.

His harsh bark of laughter jarred in the stillness.

"My poor, sweet Meg," he muttered strangely. "They'll eat you alive in the Assembly Rooms. They'll lure you out to the garden walks so they can fill your ears with pretty compliments. What will you do, I wonder, when they try to turn you against me?"

"Who?" she gasped, her cheeks going pale. "Who would do such things?"

His teeth gleamed whitley in his face.

"Your admirers, my love," he answered, and sweeping her up in his arms, carried her in to her bed. There he laid her down among the pillows and, leaning over her, studied her face.

"Someday," he said, his expression peculiarly wry, "perhaps I'll be able to make you see that the last thing I'd ever want is to hurt you. Then maybe you'll tell me what you were really doing out on the terrace tonight."

Meg's breath caught in her throat. Then, before she could

summon the wit to answer him, he kissed her again, this time with a slow, sensuous tenderness that awakened a deep, melting pang inside her. A soft groan escaped her lips when he lifted his head to look at her out of dark eyes that smoldered with barely controlled passion. Then the mask dropped in place, and she could read nothing in his face.

With his finger, he traced the curve of her neck down to the pulse throbbing at the base of her throat. There he stopped and, lightly flicking her chin, drew away. "Try and sleep," he murmured huskily. "You needn't worry that I'll bother you again."

There was a finality in his words that bewildered and filled her with dread. He had said it as if there would be no tomorrows. And he was leaving her, just as she had begged him to do only moments earlier.

"No!" Her hand caught his wrist as he started to rise from the bed. She saw his glance narrow sharply on her face. She stared back at him, making no attempt to hide her panic. "Don't go," she whispered. "I cannot bear it if you go."

Silently he cursed. Then he was beside her, his face grim as he put his arms around her. "Tell me what's bothering you. Dammit, Meg. How can I help you if you won't talk to me?"

Meg clung to him, her eyes clenched tightly shut.

"Lie with me tonight," she answered. "It's all I ask of you." All she'd ever ask of him, she added silently to herself, as he lowered her shoulders to the bed.

There was an urgency to their lovemaking that had never been there before, and yet a strange tenderness, too, that communicated itself in the lingering caress of hands and lips—of eyes, shadow-cast and smoldering with desire.

With aching deliberation, Glenmorgan undressed her and

then quickly himself. And at last he was with her in the great bed.

As if sensing his mood, Meg lay quiescent. Her arms flung above her head against the pillows, she gave herself to him, to his hands trailing liquid flame over her body. Slow and deliberately sensual, his touch seemed meant to drive her to madness. Then at last he sought the moist warmth between her thighs.

Shivering with delirious pleasure, she groaned and arched upward against him, her head moving aimlessly back and forth against the pillow. With a gasp, she uttered his name, willing him to come into her, pleading with him to end her torment. Rolling quickly over on his back, he guided her to him, lifting her with his hands about her slender waist, until she was poised above his proud manhood, her legs astraddle his hips.

Slowly, he brought her down on top of him.

A keening sigh broke from Meg as she felt herself filled by him. Then with arms of steel, he lifted her again and once more drew her down, a sheath to his blade. Over and over, he guided her, controlling her, teaching her the rhythm of slow-building rapture, until she was moving instinctively on her own, carrying them both toward the final fulfillment.

His hands cupped her breasts as she arched above him, her head thrown back so that her long hair fell in silken waves down her spine. His eyes glinting blue flames between slitted eyelids, he beheld her, a beautiful creature of supple strength and liquid motion. She was a marvel, he thought distractedly, a lovely, mysterious sea-sprite. And tonight he had almost lost her. He had seen it in her face as she stared out to the sea, had read it in her eyes as she turned on him in anger. She had meant to run away, his maddeningly elusive and hopelessly naive Meg. He had been prepared for it tonight. If only he could make sure of her in the weeks of uncertainty ahead!

Then at last he forgot everything but his overpowering need.

Spanning her waist with his hands, he pulled her down hard on top of him, thrust savagely into her flesh. A shuddering gasp broke from her depths as his seed burst forth inside her. Then her flesh was constricting in exquisite waves about his, intensifying his own pleasure. Spent at last, she collapsed weakly on top of him, her face turned into the strong curve of his neck.

"Michael," she breathed, without realizing she had spoken out loud.

Glenmorgan stilled, a fierce light in his eyes. Smiling faintly, he ran his hand over her hair in long, steady strokes, till at last she fell asleep.

Glenmorgan had already gone when Meg awakened to the songs of birds that were unknown to her, and to the perfume of flowers she had never smelled before. Glenmorgan's scent lingered on the pillow next to her, and she hugged its feathery softness to her, burying her face in it. For a moment she lay still, savoring the memory of him in the bed with her. A long sigh breathed through her lips. She had been mad to give in to her desire, and yet she knew she would do it again if he were to come to her then, at that very moment. By the faith, she was hopelessly, utterly lost.

Fitfully she flung off the covers and, dragging the discarded nightgown on over her head, wandered restlessly across to the French doors.

It was early morning, the scent of dew still fresh on the breeze. She stared out over the unfamiliar huddle of buildings, her ears assaulted by the rumble of cart wheels already plying the streets below. Suddenly the walls seemed to press in on her, and she wondered crossly if everyone in the house had forgotten her.

The day before, Kate had taken the blue silk dress away, saying she would have it freshened for her young guest, which meant that, except for the nightgown, Meg literally had nothing to wear. Personally, she wished never to see the hated silk dress again with its absurd wicker basket frame underneath.

With a sigh, she turned desultorily back into the room. Plopping down on the bed, she retrieved the comb and the gemstone mirror from under her pillow, where she had hidden them the day before, and busied herself freeing the tangles from her hair. Then she poured water into the basin from the large pitcher on the wash stand and, disrobing, sponged her face and body clean as well as she could. Drying herself with a linen towel, she dressed once more in the nightgown.

Hungry in earnest now after her long fast, she next set about devouring the contents of the bowl on the bedside table. When she had consumed everything in its entirety, save for the yellow peelings of three bananas, she felt a trifle less hollow, but a great deal more restless with nothing left to occupy her.

Fitfully, she began to pace up and down the room, her eye straying more often than not to the white beveled door. At last, unable to bear another moment confined where she was, she crossed resolutely to the door and, after a brief struggle with the handle, managed to get it open.

The deserted hall was bathed cheerfully in sunlight, which streamed in through tall arched windows on the east. There the stairway descended to the floors below. She was acutely aware of the silent stares of the Glenmorgan family portraits as she padded noiselessly past them. Not a sound came from the rooms behind the closed doors on either side of the hall, and she began uneasily to wonder if the whole house was deserted.

Cautiously, she descended the mahogany stairs to the next floor below. Here, somewhere, was the drawing room in which Thomas had entertained her grandfather, she realized. She wished she had thought to ask Glenmorgan in which room her grandfather was staying. Surely he, at least, must be somewhere in the seemingly vast confines of the house.

As if in answer, she heard the familiar rumble of a deep-throated chuckle coming from one of the rooms ahead. With a heart-felt sigh of relief, she hurried forward toward an open door.

She had a brief impression of a spacious room, made to seem larger still with great mirrors that reflected images of tables and chairs, a blue brocade settee, a crystal chandelier and tall windows with a southern exposure, and her grandfather standing with his elbow propped on a white Georgian mantlepiece like one she had seen in a picture book once long ago.

"Grandfather," she blurted as she burst into the room. "I've been looking everywhere for you—"

Realizing too late that he was not alone, she blushed and came to an abrupt halt.

"Meg," Pippin said after the initial split second of startled silence. "Come in, child, and meet our delightful hostess. Mrs. Glenmorgan, allow me to introduce to you my grand-daughter. Meg, say hello to Captain Glenmorgan's mother."

"How do you do, ma'am," murmured Meg, staring quite frankly at the older woman who rose from one of the over-stuffed chairs fronting the fireplace.

In her youth, she had undoubtedly been a great beauty with guinea gold hair and eyes the deep blue of a clear summer sky. Now, in her late forties, there were silver streaks in the gold locks, and about the eyes, fine lines, which crinkled when she smiled. Nevertheless, she remained a strikingly attractive woman with fine-boned, delicate features, belied somewhat by the firmness of the chin and a mouth which showed a distinct tendency toward humor. Dressed in a loose, flowing gown of pale yellow, she was neither tall nor short, plump nor thin, and carried herself with a calm self-assurance.

"I am doing very well, thank you. And please call me Mary," she answered with a wry glimmer of amusement at the girl's unaffected stare. If she felt any surprise at being accosted in her best drawing room by a young lady who was barefooted and attired in a nightgown, she gave no indication of it.

"*Now* I understand why he named it Marigold," blurted Meg. "The plantation, I mean. You are even more beautiful than Captain Glenmorgan said you were."

She said it with such simple candor that Mary Glenmorgan could not doubt that it was meant with utter sincerity. Indeed, Michael had warned her that her young guest would be prone to freely express her thoughts.

"Why, you have no idea," she replied, smiling merrily, "how pleasant it is to hear you say so. I believe I may return the compliment. You are everything my son said you were, and more. I'm glad you've decided to join us at last. We were beginning to worry when you did not ring for the maid to bring up your dress. I should have sent up Hannah long before this, but Michael made me promise not to disturb you till you were ready."

"But I have been ready ever so long," Meg declared. "And as for my dress"—she gave a wry grimace—"I wish never to see it again. I would much rather wear this," she said, making the flowing fabric of the nightgown swirl about her long slender legs. "I cannot believe females were meant to be bound in garments designed to squeeze the breath out of them. Or to be strapped into cages that make it impossible to sit or to move without knocking into things. It's

291

cruel and unnatural. And yet even you submit to it. Why? Maybe you can explain it to me. I cannot make any sense of it."

At this juncture, Pippin noisily cleared his throat and opened his mouth to speak, when Mary Glenmorgan silenced him with an almost imperceptible gesture of the hand.

"I'm afraid sense has very little to do with it, my dear," she replied. "It's the look that counts. The silhouette is femininely delicate and calls attention to the slenderness of the waist, which is aided by the corset underneath. When I was a girl, I was able to cinch my waist in to a mere seventeen inches. Now, I'm afraid, I am limited to a rather larger twenty-four. Observe, now, the movement of the skirt as I walk. One must appear to glide. It is a graceful, fluid motion, rather like a swan on a lake, and the gentlemen, I promise, find it altogether feminine and provocative. Would you not agree, Mr.—er—Pippin, is it not?" she asked, her eyes dancing as she gazed at the gentleman over the top of her ivory-handled fan.

Meg stared askance as her grandfather rose gallantly to the occasion.

Bending at the waist, he saluted the dainty knuckles of the hand which Mary Glenmorgan gracefully extended. "On you, my dear lady, it could only be everything that is charming."

Mary Glenmorgan's eyes lifted with suddenly renewed interest, quickly camouflaged behind a mask of gaiety.

"La, sir," she gurgled, rapping him lightly across the wrist with her fan, "you flatter me. I begin to think you have been something of a lady's man in your past, something I never suspected when you used to call on us in the old days."

Pippin's still gray eyes returned her look steadily.

"I confess to having been many things in my past,

ma'am," he said, "but never that. I'm afraid it is you who bring it out in me."

To Meg's startled amazement, Mary Glenmorgan appeared actually to blush.

"You intrigue me, Mr. Pippin," Mary replied with a seriousness that had been previously lacking. "Perhaps you will tell me sometime about this curious past of yours." Then she laughed, and the spell was broken. "In the meantime, I believe I must get better acquainted with this young lady. Come, my dear," she said, taking Meg's arm in her own. "Perhaps you and I can take a look at your blue silk dress and see what may be done to make it more suitable. You will excuse us, won't you, Mr. Pippin?"

Meg had to stifle a startled giggle as she beheld her grandfather present an elegant leg. "Your wish will ever be my command, madam," he pronounced with solemn gallantry. "And thank you—for your kindness."

Mary smiled conspiratorially at Meg. "Nonsense," she retorted. "I have the feeling the two of you have been sent expressly to liven up my existence. And I'm quite certain things will never be the same for at least one other member of this household."

She did not specify who that other member was, but chuckling as though pleasantly amused at the thought, she whisked Meg out of the room.

At the stairway, they were met by Kate and a younger version of Mary Glenmorgan, who eyed Meg with open curiosity.

"You're Meg," she said without waiting for an introduction. "Kate's told me all about you, or at least all she knew, which was actually very little. I'm Brigida, and I could not be happier to meet you." Then, without waiting for Meg to reply, she exclaimed, "Mama, I was just coming to look for you. There's no time to lose if we are to have Meg properly fitted out in time for the St. Cecilias' opening concert, not to mention the Dance Assembly, the new play at the Dock Street Theatre, and Mrs. Pinckney's soiree a week from Saturday."

"Heavens, child," admonished Mary Glenmorgan with a meaningful glance at her older daughter. "Meg has only just arrived. You'll overwhelm her with so many promised treats at once."

"That's just what I tried to tell her," Kate interjected with a comical grimace. "But you know how she is when she sets her mind on something."

Brigida gave a small gasp. "Now I've heard everything. I suppose you are going to say next that it wasn't your idea Meg should be brought out as soon as possible—*before* a certain female has the chance to get her claws into Michael again."

"But of course it was," laughed Kate. "It's just that I distinctly remember saying we should go easy, so as not to frighten our guest away before she has had the opportunity even to make her first curtsy in society."

"I'm afraid, Brigida dear," soothed Mrs. Glenmorgan, "that Kate is right. The St. Cecilias will just have to open their concert season without Meg. And as for the Dance Assembly or Mrs. Pinckney's soiree—*they* are clearly out of the question. Meg will do much better if we bring her out slowly."

"But Mama," Brigida insisted, "I've just come from Mme. Debray, who has agreed to take on the challenge. She's below right now with her assistants, and you know how greatly in demand her services are. I cannot simply turn her away."

"Then don't, my dear. By all means bring her up to Meg's room. Only leave the assistants below. Mme. Debray will understand when you tell her our guest is visiting here incognito and wishes to remain so. There is nothing like a mystery to intrigue the interest of the Mme. Debrays of the world. She will trade on it for weeks to come, you may be sure of it."

Meg, who hadn't the least idea what they were talking about, was not sure she trusted the sudden look of understanding that passed between Brigida and her mother.

"Mama is right, Kate," said Brigida, a decided gleam in her eye. "Why, Mme. Debray was just telling us that she had the honor last week of making up a dress for no less a personage than Mrs. Rawlston of Meadows."

"Clarissa Tharp's aunt?" queried Mrs. Glenmorgan with the barest arch of an eyebrow. *"That* must have been a feather in Mme. Debray's cap."

"Where the hen goes, the chick may soon follow," Kate commented sagely. "I believe she is to pick the gown up tomorrow or the next day."

"Then I suggest you send Mme. Debray right up. Anyone as busy as she is must have little time to waste." Turning to the unsuspecting Meg, Mrs. Glenmorgan smiled bracingly. "Come, my dear. I'm afraid you may find the next few hours a bit trying, but you must just try and remember it is in a good cause. It is the price every woman must pay to appear her best."

It was to be a great deal more than "a bit trying," Meg was soon to discover. Nearly from the moment Mme. Debray was ushered into her presence until the woman left six hours later, Meg was forced to stand almost continually on a stool in her silk underthings while the modiste studied her from every angle, turning occasionally to discuss the merits of fabric, color, and dress styles with Mrs. Glenmorgan and her two daughters. She was measured, poked, pinned, prodded, and forced to endure having fabrics and patterns held up to her until she was driven to the verge of calling a storm down on the merciless dressmaker and her three accomplices. Not until it was nearly time for something called "three o'clock dinner" was she allowed to sit down for a tray, which was brought to her room.

As this was accompanied by her grandfather, who had overseen the choice of dishes, she was somewhat comforted after her ordeal, which, she had been told, was to continue on the following morning and for two days afterward, until a complete wardrobe had been plotted, designed, and made ready for the seamstress and her assistants to actually begin sewing. It was not a pleasant prospect, and not even fruit salad, tossed vegetable greens, and an extraordinary concoction called "chocolate custard," which looked a little like mud but tasted so exquisitely sweet that the first mouthful sent cold shivers of delight coursing through Meg's entire length, could wholly make up for it.

"I cannot bear it," she said, pacing the floor like a caged animal. "Grandfather, they want to cut off my hair. You know I cannot allow that. And where is Glenmorgan while I am forced to endure having myself made over into a swan? What *is* a swan anyway?"

"Well, it's a—"

"I haven't laid eyes on him all day," she continued, cutting him off before he could give an answer to either of her questions. "Kate says he has gone on business and doesn't know when he will return. He might be facing Tharp at this moment, or lying wounded somewhere, and I am trapped here where I can do nothing to help him. I am blind to what is happening. I can see nothing of him in the gemstone. The bond between us is weakening. It is because this house drains my powers and robs me of my strength. I am *dainoan*, Grandfather, or I am nothing. When the old ones angered the god and lost the City of Three Circles, they could only exist in the sea. The part of me that is *muirsiol* must drink in the life-sustaining properties of seawater. It is *bethuinmuir*—'life in sea.' The part of me that is *lanncridhe*, 'land-heart,' or 'that which yearns for

296

the land,' is sustained only by the power and strength of my other half. I will be unable to live in this form if the power is drained from me. I will die." Dropping to her knees at Pippin's feet, she laid her head in his lap. "You said we should have a house on the sea away from everyone. You said I would be free to come and go as I pleased. Grandfather, you promised."

"And so we will, child," he answered, his brow creased in a worried frown. "It's only a matter of time."

Meg breathed a long sigh. "I'm running out of time, Grandfather. It must be soon. Very soon."

Pippin, who had been wondering for some days how she had gone as long as she had without renewing herself, soothingly ran his hand over her hair. "You must have patience, child," he murmured, his expression grave. "I'll think of something, I promise you."

297

Seventeen

Glenmorgan did not come to her again as he had on that first, memorable night, and Meg, left to her own devices, found herself struggling against a host of fears. She was haunted with images of the captain lying wounded or dead by Tharp's evil hand, or being lured into one exotic trap after another by the treacherous Clarissa. Perhaps inevitably, as her thoughts gradually became more tormented, her mood more despondent, she was at last plagued by the suspicion that Clarissa had won him back again.

Those were her blackest moments, and she fought valiantly against them. She told herself that she was being foolish and clung desperately to the sweet memories of the magical days aboard the *Raven*—to no avail. In the dark hour before dawn, the spectre of Glenmorgan lying in Clarissa's arms would rise up to haunt her.

Sorely tried by her sessions with Mme. Debray during the day and endlessly pacing the room after dark or tossing fitfully in her bed each night, she was growing increasingly hollow-eyed and withdrawn into herself, a condition that did not go unremarked by the other members of the household.

"I'm worried about her, Mama," Kate confided to Mary Glenmorgan over breakfast one morning. "She eats hardly

298

enough to keep a bird alive, and she's not sleeping. I know it."

"She was asleep when I looked in on her this morning," offered Brigida. "And little wonder. I heard her moving about in her room when I went to check on Baby Elizabeth late last night. I didn't have the heart to awaken her for breakfast."

"Then it's time we did something to distract her," said her mama, sitting down before a plate of sliced tomatoes, cold shrimp, and hominy topped with butter. "She is obviously out of sorts, and I can't blame her. It's bad enough that Michael has taken himself off to heaven knows where, but she has been shut up in this house as well with nothing to divert her since she arrived. It's time we took our young guest on an outing—something intimate, I think. A family affair with Thomas and the children. Until her new wardrobe is ready, we don't want to call attention to ourselves."

"Then," said Pippin from the other side of the table, "might I suggest a picnic on the beach?"

"Heavens, sir," exclaimed Mary Glenmorgan, turning to regard Meg's grandfather with astonishment, "it is the beginning of February. Hardly the time of year for going on picnics."

"But that's why it would be ideal," replied Pippin. "The good people of Charles Town are hardly likely to be flocking to the beaches, which means we shall have the privacy you wish. I might point out as well that the weather has been unusually fine of late and that there is nothing like the ocean to bring the bloom back into my granddaughter's cheeks. You might say it is her natural habitat, since she has lived all her life in the Caribbean."

"But of course, Mama," Brigida exclaimed. "We should have thought of it before. Meg is obviously homesick for her islands. It will do her good to walk along a beach, and little Tommy will be in alt. I'm afraid he has more than a little of his Uncle Michael in him."

"Well, I suppose it could do no harm," Mary Glenmorgan conceded. "It's a shame Michael will very likely be nowhere around when he's needed. But Thomas, of course, can be counted upon to come with us, and you, Mr. Pippin. I will not hear of leaving you behind."

"I shall consider it a pleasure, ma'am," Pippin responded, relieved that he had achieved the first step in solving Meg's problem.

Pippin's suggestion of a picnic having been agreed upon, Brigida immediately sent for Thomas to inform him of their plans. Entering into the spirit of things, he proposed they go by boat and meander along the coast perhaps as far as the Isle of Palms. It was a fine day for it, more like April or May than February, with a fair sky and a light, steady breeze.

"Oh, but that would be perfect," agreed Brigida, her face lighting up at the prospect. "So much easier than trying to pack everything into two carriages. And I enjoy nothing so much as an afternoon of sailing. Thomas, you are a genius!"

"Nothing makes me happier than to make you think so, my dear," replied her husband, grinning at her enthusiasm.

It was a merry party that set out from the wharf on board the sloop Thomas had rented for the day. To ensure the safety of the women and children, he had taken the precaution of enlisting Dick Chapin to serve as skipper over a crew borrowed from the *Raven*. They were further accompanied by the children's "Mauma," who had ruled the nursery from the time Glenmorgan and his sisters had occupied it, and a nursery maid to help her look after young Tommy and the infant Elizabeth.

Meg, especially, appeared to blossom as soon as she stepped aboard. Her cheeks were becomingly tinged with color and her eyes sparkled with excitement. She did not even mind that she had been forced to wear the hated blue silk. It was enough that she was at sea once again. Glenmorgan's absence was the one bitter drop in her cup. Still, it was good to see an old familiar face, she thought as she gravitated quite naturally toward Chapin, who greeted her with the lopsided grin she remembered so well from her days aboard the *Raven*.

"Mr. Chapin," she exclaimed, "how glad I am to see you!"

"It's good of you to say so, miss," drawled the first mate, looking bigger than ever in the stern of the boat. "I expect I can return the compliment. You're a sight for sore eyes, Miss Pippin, and that's no lie."

"Then your eyes deceive you, for I have been told I have become quite pale and far too thin," she said with a grimace of distaste. "Which is why you have been persuaded to forsake your beloved *Raven* for this far less impressive vessel. I hope they did not take you away from some more pleasant pursuit in town."

"Not likely, miss," Chapin laughed. "Towns and sailors don't generally mix. I've plenty to occupy me aboard ship without going where I'm sure to find trouble."

Meg's glance went to Chapin in surprise. "But I understood Charles Town was your home. Surely you have been to visit your family?"

"Well, as to that," Chapin replied gravely, "I was orphaned when I was a lad of twelve. The small pox took my folks and two older brothers."

Meg's eyes filled with sympathy.

"I'm sorry. I didn't know."

Chapin shrugged massive shoulders. "It was a long time ago. Though I expect your grandfather remembers."

"Grandfather?" Meg echoed in surprise.

"Aye. He was there when it happened. They came all the way from Charles Town to our little settlement up the

Ashley—he and Turlough Glenmorgan. Never saw anyone care so much or try so hard. But there wasn't much anyone could have done. The pox wiped out nearly every man, woman, and child before it was finally over. Turlough took me in and raised me like one of his own." His glance strayed to Kate, who was laughing as she struggled to keep little Tommy cornered long enough to button his coat. "I reckon the Glenmorgans are my family now."

Suddenly it came to Meg, seeing the look in his eyes, that what he felt for Kate was not exactly a brotherly affection. Tucking that discovery away for a later time, she returned to the subject uppermost in her mind. "But you knew my grandfather back then?" she prodded gently.

Chapin nodded.

"Aye, though he's changed some since those days. I couldn't place him at first, not till I saw him tending the lads after the fight with the galleys. But everyone in these parts knew Doc Belding." He glanced sideways at Meg. "Except for the cap' n, of course. He never met your grandfather in those days. Turlough had sent him off to school in England about the time the doc hung up his shingle here. And afterwards, he was away at sea on one ship or another. Turlough never could get him to settle down."

"Any more than he could you, I suppose," Meg said, smiling a little.

Chapin gave her an answering grin.

"Well, someone had to look after him, the cap'n, I mean."

"Tell me what he was like—my grandfather. He's never told me about himself, except that he had ruined his life and Turlough Glenmorgan gave him the chance to redeem himself."

"That much is true, I expect. Turlough was always trying to help someone or other. The doc was never the same after that time on the Ashley. I heard later his wife died while

302

he was away fighting the pox. She was sickly, and maybe he blamed himself for not being there when she needed him. Anyhow, he took her loss real hard. Turlough did what he could to snap the doc out of it, but it was like he just didn't care about anything anymore. Or maybe he'd cared too much." Suddenly, as if he decided he had said too much, he shook his head. "But what do I know about anything? I was away at sea most of the time with Michael. Maybe you should ask your grandfather about all this, Miss Pippin."

"Won't you call me Meg?" she answered, smiling up at him. "And I'll call you Dick, if that's all right. You did say we should be friends, didn't you?"

Chapin's grin expanded to fill his face.

"Aye, that I did," he said. "Meg it is then."

As Chapin's attention was taken up with maneuvering the boat out of the harbor after that, Meg left him alone. Leaning her elbows against the side, she studied the ships at anchor as the sloop sailed past them. There were vessels of all kinds—brigantines and schooners, barques and fishing smacks, and the great ships that plied the Atlantic. Having made their way from England and Europe to the Azores and from there, carried by the trade winds, to the West Indies, they had come at last on the Gulf Stream to Charles Town to unload goods and take on the harvested crops, which they would transport back to their home ports, thus completing a great circle. In the winter months from November until March, when the hurricane season began anew, it was always the same, Meg knew. She had seen them often enough in the Caribbean, had wondered about the lands from which they came, and though her grandfather had given her books to read about England and Europe, they had served only to whet her curiosity all the more.

303

With something of envy she imagined Glenmorgan sailing, as these ships had, to countless exotic places. How small was her world compared to his! she thought, then froze, her heart pounding, as she was given further proof as to just exactly how small that world was.

Drago's frigate, the *Sea Hawk*, still showing the scars of battle, was tugging gently at its anchor just off the starboard!

"Meg, you should be wearing your bonnet, dear," said Kate, coming up behind her. "Has no one ever told you the sun will ruin your complexion?"

"What? My complexion?" repeated Meg, tearing her eyes away from the pirate ship. "No. No, the sun never bothers me." She looked from Kate to Chapin in the stern. From the grim cast of his jaw, she knew he, too, had seen Drago's *Sea Hawk*. But it was too late to avoid the other ship, and Chapin knew it.

If he suddenly tried to change course, he would only draw attention to the sloop. As it was, he could only hope the very innocence of their appearance would be enough to allay any interest in their passing. It was what Glenmorgan would do. Only Glenmorgan wasn't there. By God, he wished he were, thought Chapin, as he steered dead ahead on a course that would take them within a few feet of the frigate.

Meg held her breath as the sloop passed slowly down the frigate's side. But no alarm was sounded, no cry of recognition. In another few minutes they would be hidden from view by the next ship. It was then that Meg saw the three men on the weather side near the entry port deep in discussion. One was Drago—she could never mistake that slim figure—and one was a stranger with bold, haughty features. The third man had his back to her. Then suddenly he turned, and she felt the blood drain from her face as she recognized Logan Tharp.

For an instant their eyes met. Then the ship vanished from view behind a great hulking freighter.

Only then did Meg become aware that Kate had said something to her, her voice edged with concern.

"I—I beg your pardon. What did you say? I'm afraid my mind was elsewhere," Meg stammered.

"Well, I should say so," replied Kate, her eyes, unnervingly like the captain's, scrutinizing Meg's face. "What is it, Meg? And don't tell me it was nothing. You went positively white back there. Something about that ship frightened you."

Meg opened her mouth to deny it then, realizing that Kate would not be put off, closed it again.

"That ship," she said at last, "is the *Sea Hawk*. It's commanded by Captain John Drago." She could not quite stop a shudder at the memory of Drago's hands on her. "He's a pirate. I've run into him before."

"And so, I have the feeling, has my brother." Kate's hand closed on Meg's wrist. "That was Logan Tharp on deck."

"Yes." Meg smiled mirthlessly. "I have seen him before, too. When he tried to kill your brother."

Turning without another word, she went below ostensibly to see to her grandfather, who, for obvious reasons, had chosen to remain below decks until they should be safely out of the harbor. But her real reason had been to put off the questions that Kate had obviously been on the point of asking her.

Meg did not venture topside again until the boat was well clear of the harbor. Then, in spite of the brisk sea breeze and the dazzling sunlight, she was aware that there was a blight on the day. She shivered, remembering Tharp's soulless eyes on her, like the touch of a cold hand upon her heart. And not for the first time she wondered where Glenmorgan was.

"Are you warm enough, Meg?" queried Thomas Sutton,

305

coming up beside her as she stood staring at, without seeing, James Island off the starboard. "I'd be happy to fetch a boat cloak for you."

"No, I'm fine, thank you."

Turning, Meg smiled at the picture of little Tommy perched happily on his father's shoulders. It was the first time she had seen the children since her single visit to the nursery one afternoon in the company of their mother. Then, Tommy had seemed instantly taken with her. He had even gone so far as to show her his favorite toy, a small wooden boat, which his Uncle Michael had carved many years before. The boy had it now, clutched in one plump hand.

"Tommy and I like it on the boat, don't we, Tommy?" she said. "We're having too much fun to be cold. I don't think I've ever seen so many big boats in one place before."

The boy's brown eyes gazed frankly into her own.

"They're not boats," he informed her in a gruff little voice. "They're ships. I'm goin' to be captain of a ship someday. Just like Uncle Michael. He has the best, most fastest ship in the whole world. Doesn't he, Papa? There's not a ship in the King's Navy that could catch him if he didn't want 'em to."

"You bet, Tommy," laughed Thomas Sutton, swinging the boy down and setting him on his feet. "Though you'd better not let your mama hear you talking like that. You know how she feels about the subject. You're to be a planter someday, my lad."

The boy's face screwed up into a stubborn scowl, but before he could utter a childish protest, Meg quickly intervened.

"Look, Tommy," she said, pointing. "There, coming around the point. That's a fine, big ship. I wonder where it comes from."

"Aw, that's easy. It's a Dutchman," Tommy replied importantly. "Anyone can tell that. See how broad she is? They make 'em broader and heavier than most. Didn't you know that?"

"I'm afraid," Meg tempered, "that I don't know very much about ships."

"I do. Papa taught me. He knows everything. He used to sail with Uncle Michael."

"Did he?" replied Meg, properly grave, though there was a suspicious twitch at the corners of her lips.

Sutton gave a wry grimace.

"Tommy, my lad, I'm afraid you talk too much," he said. "But I suppose there's no harm in Meg's knowing. It was six years ago—nearly seven now. I was being transported for debt to Jamaica as an indentured servant when the ship I was on was raided by Lavoillet's pirates. Given the choice of signing on or walking the plank, so to speak, I happily turned to pirating." He shrugged. "I might have enjoyed it, too, if I hadn't earned Lavoillet's displeasure in Kingstown. He'd have killed me, but for Glenmorgan. Michael purchased my freedom with a handful of black pearls and six months later bought me passage to Charles Town. Gave me enough money to pay my debts and made me his business agent here in Charles Town. But more importantly, he gave me a letter of introduction to his mother. Otherwise, I'd never have met Brigida." His hand rested unconsciously on his son's blond curls. "Everything I have I owe to Michael Glenmorgan. I expect there's nothing I wouldn't do for him."

"Are you going to marry my Uncle Michael?" piped up Tommy, tugging at Meg's skirts. "Mama and Aunt Kate say you are."

Sutton, seeing the hot blush stain Meg's cheeks, hastily clamped a hand on the back of the boy's coat.

"Oh, no you don't," he said, swooping the boy up in his arms and tickling his belly. "Now you're meddling in something that's none of your business, my lad. It's time Mauma Tillie took you in hand again."

Sutton carted the boy off, still kicking and giggling in delight, and once more Meg was left to herself.

Shortly after two in the afternoon, Chapin sailed the sloop to an island crowded with palmettos and dogwood. As soon as the mooring lines were secured to a pier protruding into a small bay, the party, accompanied by Chapin, disembarked, leaving the crew on board to enjoy a lunch Mary Glenmorgan had ordered brought along for them.

For the first time since she had stared into Logan Tharp's eyes, Meg relaxed and managed to put the unpleasant incident from her mind. Little caring what anyone thought, she kicked off her shoes and raced Tommy up the beach. She let him win, then plopping down beside him, she helped him fashion a lopsided ship out of sand while the others laid out the lunch on linen cloths spread out on the ground.

Meg pretended to eat with as much relish as the others, but she could not help feeling a trifle left out. Her grandfather seemed wholly taken up with entertaining Mary Glenmorgan with stories of his seafaring days, while Thomas lay on a quilt with his head in Brigida's lap and listened indulgently as she prattled on about Elizabeth, who was cutting her first tooth. It was not long before Chapin and Kate wandered off along the beach together, and as Mauma Tillie was busy laying Tommy and Elizabeth down for a nap, there was no one to notice when Meg finally rose and slipped quietly off by herself.

Meg nearly ripped the gown in her haste to undo the infuriatingly small fastenings at the back of the bodice. But at last she was free of the hated gown and all the things underneath. Leaving them in an untidy heap behind a pile of driftwood, she ran into the surf and dove headlong into a rolling wave.

A gasp broke from her lips as the chill water closed over her body. Then electrifying currents of energy surged through her, transforming her from human to mermaid. She drew deep draughts of water into her altered lungs and felt a slow warmth spread through her as the temperature of her body became equalized with that of the sea around her. The sensation of weightlessness after being earthbound and forced to carry the burden of her own body on two legs made her feel giddy, and for the first time she realized how greatly she had missed the exhilaration of gliding effortlessly through the water with slow, powerful strokes of her marvelous tail. On land, it would be the difference between walking like a human or soaring through the air like a bird, she mused whimsically.

In her first overpowering joy at being free, she swam wildly, heedlessly, little caring where her mad burst of energy might take her. But eventually a measure of caution returned, and reminding herself that she had only a short time before she must return, she amused herself by exploring the ocean bottom.

How different from her burgeoning Caribbean waters, she thought, delving the thirty feet or so to the ocean floor. She found oysters, shrimps, and crabs, but none of the brilliant schools of fish that inhabited the warm waters of her native islands, no coral reefs, no manta rays, no dazzling displays of color. In comparison, the ocean floor was dull and drab, and she suddenly felt more homesick than ever before.

Realizing she would be missed if she did not return to the island soon, she rose reluctantly toward the surface.

The skiff seemed to come out of nowhere. It was almost upon her before a frisson of warning caused her to stop where she was and look up. The black hull loomed above her, then passed over her head, followed shortly by another. Suddenly her stomach clenched with an overpowering feeling of wrongness.

Her heart pounding, she followed the boats to the island and watched from beneath the surface as men leaped out to drag the vessels ashore—twenty sailors at the very least. She surfaced to get her bearings.

There was no sign either of the men or of Chapin and the others, and she realized suddenly that she was on the opposite side of the island from the pier where the sloop was moored. The sense of danger was stultifying.

The strangers were cutting across through the trees. They were going after Glenmorgan's family.

She knew at once that she could not reach the sloop in time to give a warning. But she could take the strangers' boats and leave them stranded.

Without stopping to consider further than that, she swam toward the shore.

Chewing thoughtfully on a blade of grass, Kate glanced sidelong at Chapin's stolidly impassive features.

"So you have stayed by him all these years," she said, leaning her back against the trunk of a palmetto tree. "Guarding his back whenever he rushed headlong into danger. Mad Mike Glenmorgan's ever faithful lieutenant. Oh, yes. I've heard the tales told of you and Michael. Did it ever once occur to you that you might be killed?"

"The thought crossed my mind a time or two," Chapin admitted, grinning wryly. "But I'm still here."

Kate tossed the blade of grass away with an impatient gesture. "Yes, you're still here. But for how long, Dick Chapin? You know Michael better than anyone. How long do you think he'll be content to play the role of a gentleman merchant? How long before he'll be off again to the Orient or some other place just as exotic and dangerous?"

"No longer than it takes to finish his business here, I expect," Chapin answered, his eyes on Kate. Even in the plain gown of gray serge, which had seen better days and which she had chosen for the outing for that very reason, she was breathtakingly beautiful. Too lovely and too fine for a rough-hewn bear of a man like Dick Chapin, he reminded himself. It was all right to love her. God knew, it was impossible not to. But only from a distance, as he had from the first time she had come to him, a five-year-old imp of a girl with roguish blue eyes, and laid her small hand in his. "You're going to be my big brother, just like Michael," she had confided. "And I'll always love you and look after you so that you won't miss your mama and papa so very much." She had captured his lonely heart in that single moment and had held it ever since, though he had been careful never to let her know it. He had in the only way he knew how done his best to help and protect her after her father's death—he had gone with her beloved Michael and kept him alive for her.

"You didn't really expect to keep him here, did you, Kate?" he asked gently, wishing there was some way he could save her the pain of losing her brother again.

"No." Flinging away from the tree, she moved restlessly a few paces away, then stopped with her back to him. "No, Michael will always be Michael. And I doubt that even his mysterious sea-sprite, as he calls her, can change him. He'll go his own way as he always has," she said half-bitterly. Then, turning, she impaled him with eyes that shook his defenses. "That doesn't mean that you have to go with him. Michael's soul was claimed long ago by the sea. We've all learned to accept that. But you're not like him, Dick. I remember you in the old days at Marigold. You'd come home with the dirt under your nails and your shirt soaked with sweat because you'd been out with the field hands. You were happy working the land. You can't deny it, can you, Dick?"

Chapin smiled whimsically.

"I expect not," he said. "I come from a long line of farmers. I reckon we've got the soil in our blood. It's kind of funny when you think about it. Old Turlough tried his damndest to make a farmer out of Michael, and all the time he was making plans to send me to sea, I'd have given my soul to run Marigold for him."

"Then why didn't you say something?" demanded Kate. "Why didn't you tell Papa?"

"Because it wasn't my place to. Michael was his son. Not me. I'd have done anything Turlough asked of me. I owed him that for taking me in."

"You owed him nothing! And even if you did, surely you've repaid it a dozen times over." Going to him, Kate clasped the lapels of his coat with her hands and shook them as if by that she might shake some sense into him. "Why have you stayed away, Dick Chapin? Why didn't you come to see me? Answer me. I have a right to know."

Chapin shifted his feet uncomfortably.

"I was going to come, Kate, believe me. I just figured it'd be better to wait for a while. I didn't want to butt in."

"Didn't want to 'butt in'?" echoed Kate incredulously. "Good God, did you think you wouldn't be welcome?"

"To tell the truth, I wasn't sure," admitted Chapin, his blue eyes stubborn. "You made it pretty plain the night I left that you never wanted to see my ugly face around here again. Or something pretty close to that."

"And you accepted that?" Kate demanded, her face paling to a pearly white. "Of all the thick-skulled, impossibly mule-headed men. I was fourteen, a lonely, frightened girl who was about to lose the one person upon whom I could always depend. How do you think I should have reacted? I was in love with you, Dick. I've always loved you. And if

312

you don't kiss me very soon, I'm going to become even more shameless and kiss *you*. So what do you think of that?"

For the first time Chapin's reserve appeared to break.

"Enough," he rumbled, pulling her hands away from his coat. "You can't mean that."

Stubbornly, Kate held her ground.

"Dammit, Dick Chapin. I'm not a child anymore. Stop treating me like one."

"Then stop acting like one," he came back at her, his voice unwontedly harsh. A shadow of pain flickered across his face, quickly hidden. "You don't know what you're saying, Kate," he said hoarsely. "What you're suggesting is impossible. What do you think your mama would do if she knew?"

"She'd congratulate me for having had the sense to fall in love with a man who is as good and generous as he is strong," Kate declared, her head up and her eyes flashing. "She took you in and raised you as if you were her own son. What in heaven's name do you think she would say?"

Chapin uttered a short bark of laughter.

"That you were meant to marry a fine educated gentleman," he answered, "not a big dumb ox like me. And she'd be right. Good God, Kate. Can you see me at one of your fancy parties? I'd make a fine picture stumbling over my own big feet."

"Stop it!" Furiously, she faced him, her slender frame bristling with indignation. "I won't listen to you belittle yourself, do you hear me? You're as good as any man I know—better! I'll not let anyone say you're not, not even you, Dick Chapin."

Chapin's big hands knotted into fists at his sides. At any moment Kate half expected Mad Mike Glenmorgan's fearless lieutenant to break and run.

With a sigh she leaned her hands against his chest and

313

lifted her eyes to his. "You are the most impossible man I have ever known, but I won't let you throw away my happiness simply because you think I'm too good for you. I can't believe you could even suggest such a thing!" Suddenly she hesitated, a frown darkening her brow. "Unless, of course, you don't feel about me the way I feel about you," she said. Slowly the color drained from her face. "Seven years is a long time, after all. And I was only a child. Good God, that's it, isn't it? That's why all this nonsense about my being too good for you—why you didn't come to see me. There's someone else!"

Chapin made a helpless gesture.

"Now wait just a minute, Kate."

"Oh, you needn't bother to deny it." Stepping back, Kate drew herself up to her full five feet seven inches in height. "I'm afraid I owe you an apology," she uttered in frozen accents. "You might at least have had the decency to tell me the truth. Faith, what a fool I've been! Throwing myself at you like a-a—!"

"Dammit, Kate," sputtered Chapin, his face reddening. "It's nothing like that." He took a step toward her.

The scream, when it came, froze them both where they were.

"What the devil?" muttered Chapin.

Kate's eyes flew to his. "Mama and Brigida!"

As a shot rang out, Chapin drew the pistol from his belt and, with a curt order for Kate to stay close, broke into a run back the way they had come.

They had wandered farther than they realized. By the time they reached the party on the beach, the fighting was over. Mary Glenmorgan knelt beside Sutton, who lay sprawled on the sand, blood streaming from a gash on his forehead. Mauma Tillie held the screaming infant Elizabeth in her arms, while the nursery maid huddled in the sand, groaning in fright.

314

"Dick, thank heavens!" exclaimed Mrs. Glenmorgan. "They've taken Brigida and Tommy. And Meg is nowhere to be found. There," she said, pointing toward the trees. "Pippin and the others have gone after them."

With a muttered curse, Chapin lumbered away, leaving Kate to look after Sutton and her mother.

Hoarse shouts and the clang of steel against steel drew him deeper into the trees, until at last he burst out of the tangle of underbrush and forest onto a clear stretch of beach. With a sweeping glance, he took in the scene of fighting—his own lads from the sloop, outnumbered two to one, wielding cutlasses in a pitched battle for their lives, Brigida, half-swooning, with Pippin standing in front of her, a smoking gun in his hand and a corpse sprawled on the sand at his feet. And in the channel, rounding the headland, a ship's barge, making for the beach.

Chapin cursed. More of Drago's cutthroats. He allowed himself a single, despairing thought of Kate. Then deliberately he drove everything from his mind but the madness of battle.

Pippin saw the big first mate wade into the mass of heaving bodies, saw him ram his fist into the jaw of a bearded lout and, without pausing, hack another across the back of the neck with his sword. Then the old man's attention was taken up by other, more pressing matters.

Moffit, Drago's second-in-command, yanking his blade from the squirming body of a sailor, stalked toward the old man. His face split in a malicious grin at sight of Pippin, unarmed, save for an empty pistol. In a last desperate gesture, Pippin flung the useless gun at the pirate's head. Moffit knocked it away with a contemptuous sweep of the cutlass and lunged toward him. In dread fascination, Pippin watched the blade, waited for it to plunge into his body.

A tall figure blotted out his sight, struck Moffit's cutlass aside. With a sense of unreality Pippin saw the two men

315

come together, chest to chest, while all around him, Drago's men, faced with the *Raven*'s reinforcements swarming from the barge, were dropping their weapons.

Moffit's eyes bulged in his head as he stared into a pair of steel-flecked orbs.

"Captain Bloody Mike Glenmorgan," he rasped, the sweat pouring off his brow. "How in hell—"

Glenmorgan's lips stretched in a mirthless grin. "I followed the stench," he ground out between clenched teeth and thrust the other man backward. As Moffit stumbled and caught himself, Glenmorgan's sword slashed out and down.

The pirate gaped with disbelief at the front of his shirt, neatly slit down the middle.

"You've developed a nasty habit of meddling in my affairs, Moffit," observed the captain. "I suggest you drop your weapon. Now, while you still can."

Moffit's jowls turned a livid red beneath their whiskers. "You can bloody well go to hell!" he growled. Wildly he lunged at Glenmorgan, the cutlass slashing the air before him.

Glenmorgan sidestepped, bringing the flat of the sword hard across the pirate's buttocks. With a bellow, the pirate hurtled headlong, his face plowing a furrow in the sand.

Rolling over on to his back, Moffit froze at the kiss of cold steel against his throat. "Now," drawled the captain. "Tell me why Drago sent you after my family."

"Your family!" blustered the pirate, his tongue darting out to lick dry lips. "No one said nothin' about your bloody family. It were the girl we was after. Only, the lads nabbed the wrong one. It weren't till we got back here that I got a look at her an' seen the error."

"What girl?" growled Chapin, stepping forward. His stomach clenched at the thought of Kate and her mother left unprotected on the other side of the island.

"The old man's granddaughter," Moffit rasped, shoving

himself backward away from Chapin's menacing front. "Keep 'im away from me, Captain. We never meant any harm to your family. It were the girl from the island we wanted, I swear it."

"He's lying!" said Brigida. "They took Tommy." Pippin caught her and held her as she flung herself toward the pirate. "Make him tell you what they've done with my son!" she cried, straining to break free. Her eyes, wild with anguish, flew to Glenmorgan's. "It's all your fault. None of this would have happened if you'd stayed where you belong. But you had to come back, and now I've lost Tommy. Oh, God, my baby," she groaned, sagging against Pippin. "My baby."

Grim-faced, Chapin snapped out an order for two men to accompany the old man and the woman back to the others. "In the meantime, Captain, why don't you leave Moffit here to me. I'll make him bloody well talk."

"I doesn't know anything about any boy," Moffit choked, his eyes darting nervously from Glenmorgan's granite-hard features to Chapin's. "When we got back here, the boats were gone, or you'd never caught us. The boy's here, I tell 'ee, less'n he turned fish and swam."

Grabbing Moffit by the tattered remains of his shirt, Chapin dragged the pirate halfway to his feet.

"You don't see him anywhere, do you?" Chapin growled. "A little tyke, no bigger than my arm? Why, you miserable excuse for a human being. I'll—"

"Wait!" At Glenmorgan's low-voiced order, Chapin stopped, his big fist drawn back, his intent written plainly in Moffit's frozen attitude of cringing expectation. "Leave him be," Glenmorgan said strangely, his attention fixed on a point down the beach. "It would seem he's telling the truth."

"By heavens," rumbled Chapin, letting the pirate fall unceremoniously to the ground. "It's Tommy, or I'm dreaming."

Brigida, too, had seen him. Calling out his name, she was already running toward him.

"My God, Michael," Chapin uttered feelingly as he came up beside Glenmorgan. "That was a close thing. I'd never have forgiven myself if anything had happened to that boy—or any of the others. Dammit, it's all my fault. I should have figured Drago would pull something like this. I should have seen it coming. But somehow I never figured Drago for a low-down job of kidnapping. What in hell did he hope to gain from it?"

Glenmorgan gave him a long, cold look. "Meg," he said curtly, and turning on his heel, stalked away.

Eighteen

Glenmorgan clenched and unclenched his hand on his sword hilt as he fought to contain his impatience. Ill-humoredly, he cursed the sloop and its crowded deck, which made it impossible to walk about. He needed to walk, if only to relieve the pent-up pressure in his chest. Good God, he would rather take on a dozen pirates single-handedly than be forced to wait and do nothing.

Nevertheless, he stubbornly refused to leave the boat for the greater freedom of the dock, a perversity of character which he found cynically amusing about himself. It was undoubtedly conceit that made him stay where he was. He was Michael Glenmorgan, after all—a man with a reputation for a cool head and cold-blooded daring. Only he knew what it was costing him to maintain the pretense, when in reality he was chafing to be on the move, to do anything but remain idle while Meg was out there somewhere, hurt, or perhaps, worse.

Bloody hell, Brigida had been right to condemn him. He had brought them all into danger, and Meg most of all.

His mouth hardened at the memory of Brigida, white-faced and shaking. Her bitter words of accusation seemed still to ring in his ears. She was his sister, but it had seemed suddenly as if he had never known her. And perhaps truly

319

he never had. And what of Kate, who had always tagged after him as a child, her eyes filled with hero worship for the elder brother who had had about him an aura of romance and adventure? Good God, what a fool he had been never to have given a thought as to how they might be affected by his return! They were Glenmorgans. He had taken it for granted that they, no less than he, would want to see their father's murderers brought to justice. It had never occurred to him to take into account the possibility that, being women, they might view things differently.

He turned at the sound of footsteps on the companionway.

"How are they?" queried Glenmorgan as Sutton emerged from the cabin hatch and joined him aft in the gently pitching sloop.

"Tommy's asleep. Brigida, too, thank God. Kate and your mother are looking after them." Sutton sighed and settled heavily on the stern bench, grimacing a little as the movement awakened the dull throb in his head. Wryly he fingered the bandage wrapped around his forehead. "He could tell us very little more about what happened—nothing about Meg, I'm afraid. When the bloody bastards started to drag Brigida off, Tommy ran after them. The plucky little bantling hit one of them in the shin with a piece of driftwood, and that's when they knocked him unconscious." The normally good-natured features took on a granite hardness. "Maybe they thought they could ransom him back to us, or sell him on the white slave market. Whatever the case, they picked him up and carried him off with them. The bugger who had Tommy apparently became separated from the others, because when the boy came awake, there was no sign of anyone else." Sutton allowed himself a grim smile. "The bastard was more than a little put out to find his boat had drifted into the channel and washed up on to a sand bar. Tommy said the fellow threw him over his shoulder and started to wade out to the boat. And that's when everything gets pretty hazy and wild. All that nonsense about a shark. The poor lad must have been scared half out of his wits to imagine such a thing."

"Aye," agreed Glenmorgan, his eyes singularly grim. He had seen men attacked by sharks in waist-deep water before, but never one that knocked the feet out from under its victim and then allowed him to swim ashore unscathed. Even more incredible, however, was the notion of a shark coming about to assist a drowning child to safety. No shark had done it, but a girl, capable of salvaging a ship full of gold, might have been able to pull the thing off. Was it too farfetched to think that a child, terrified and struggling for his life, might confuse a girl for a large fish? From all accounts, Tommy had never really seen what or who saved him from drowning. He had lost consciousness and awakened alone on the beach, his fear assuaged by the memory of a beautiful lady who had sung to him in his dreams.

Glenmorgan's mouth thinned to a hard line. There wasn't a doubt in his mind that Tommy's beautiful lady was Meg. The question was, what had happened to her afterward?

"Go below, Thomas," said Glenmorgan wearily, noting the tinge of gray about the other man's set features. "Try and get some rest. You look like the devil, old friend."

Sutton gave a wry grimace. "I feel like I've been kicked in the head by a mule. I hate to think how this would have turned out if you hadn't come after us. How in hell did you know?"

"It was all over the harbor that you took a boat out. When I heard Drago was in port, I didn't care for the odds." His look sent a cold chill down Sutton's back. "We'll weigh anchor as soon as Dick's finished securing the prisoners."

"We're leaving?" Sutton blurted, then stopped, his hand moving in a gesture of futility. "But surely there's something more we can do. We can't just leave without knowing if she's—"

"Meg's alive," Glenmorgan cut in in hard accents. "I don't know how, or where she is, but I do know she's alive."

"Good God, Michael, I know how you must feel. But you can't possibly be sure of that."

"Can't I?" murmured Glenmorgan. "Look at him," he said, nodding toward Pippin's tall, stooped figure in the bow of the boat. "Would you say he had the look of a man who has just lost his granddaughter?" The old man stood with his elbows propped on the gunwale, his expression thoughtful, as he stared toward the island. A thin tendril of smoke curled lazily into the breeze from a pipe clenched between his teeth.

"He doesn't appear overly worried," Sutton ventured doubtfully. "You think he knows where she is?"

Glenmorgan thought of the way Meg had looked that first night in the Town House. The haunted expression in her eyes—the longing. He had sensed then that she was slipping away from him and that somehow her need to be free and near the sea was at the heart of it. It was why he had left the next morning. Now it appeared that he might very well have returned too late. "I think," he said to Sutton, "that he knows she is well able to take care of herself when she is in her own element—here, with the sea at her doorstep. If she wanted to be found, she would be here with us now."

"And you think she doesn't wish to be found?" Sutton stared at his brother-in-law as if he suspected Glenmorgan had lost his mind. "Think what you're saying, man. What the devil would she do out here all by herself?"

"How the hell should I know?" snapped Glenmorgan, a crack in his iron composure showing at last. But almost immediately he caught himself. "Forgive me, Thomas," he said, gripping his friend's shoulder. "I shouldn't have taken my ill-temper out on you. But if I'm right, Meg might be nowhere near this cursed island." And what if he was wrong? he thought. Drago might have her, or her luck might have run out and she could be dead. Silently, he cursed. Tommy's would-be abductor was the only man who could have shed any light on what had really happened out there today, and he had died in the fight on the beach.

Whatever Sutton might have replied was silenced by a sudden shout from the end of the pier. Both men turned to see Chapin lumbering toward them.

"Captain, I think you'd better come," called the first mate, panting a little from his recent exertions. "The lads have found something."

"Wait here, Thomas," Glenmorgan ordered curtly. "Look after the women."

Sutton opened his mouth to protest, but Glenmorgan had already bounded lightly on to the pier and was making toward Chapin with long swift strides.

Oblivious to the uneasy stares of his men, Glenmorgan stepped over the pile of driftwood to the discarded articles of feminine attire. His face was hard-cast and unreadable as he knelt to examine first the gown, then the delicate silk underthings and soft leather slippers.

From behind him, Chapin said quietly, "There was no sign of a struggle, Captain. Just the clothes, lying there— like, well, I know it sounds crazy, but it would be just like Meg to go for a swim."

Glenmorgan's fist clenched in the fine silk fabric of the gown, crushing it. A swim off the Carolina shores in February? It was insane, and yet that was exactly what he was thinking. In fact, he'd bloody well wager his life on it.

He came to his feet. "I doubt any further search of the island will yield us anything. Call in the rest of the men, Dick. We'll weigh anchor within the hour. In the meantime, ask Mr. Pippin to join me here, if you will."

"Aye, Captain," Chapin rumbled, turning to leave. "You heard him, lads. Let's be about it."

When Pippin arrived several moments later, he found Glenmorgan, standing with one booted foot propped on a piece of driftwood, his stern features devoid of emotion as he appeared to contemplate one of the leather slippers held in his hands.

"I have the distinct impression," Glenmorgan began, lifting his eyes to study the other man's face, "that Meg's disappearance has not come as a great surprise to you. I have even entertained the possibility that the two of you engineered this outing for that very purpose."

"Then you would be mistaken," replied the old man quietly. "Meg needed some time away from the house. A picnic on the beach seemed an ideal diversion for her, that's all. It's obvious she took advantage of the opportunity to go in for a swim. I'm hardly surprised by that. In fact, I was sure that she would."

"I see, and naturally it does not alarm you that she has not returned from her swim, never mind that it is February and the water is a good deal colder here than she is used to. In which case I must assume that you know something that I do not. Because I *am* concerned, Mr. Pippin. I am concerned very much by it. And furthermore, I am hard put to explain it."

Glenmorgan was not sure what reaction he had hoped to elicit from the old man, but it was hardly a gleam of amusement in the gray eyes. "Perhaps," Pippin suggested, his voice tinged with the barest hint of irony, "you are making too much of Meg's disappearance. For what it's worth, Captain, I suggest you think what *you* might do if you were a female caught out without your clothes on."

Meg watched with a sinking heart as the sloop, heeling lazily to the breeze, vanished around the tip of the island.

Now what was she to do? she wondered morosely as she left the water and walked along the beach. Swim the seven miles back and then try to explain how it was she had managed such a feat dressed in panniers and silk? Perhaps she could claim she had signaled a passing vessel to come and pick her up. And then what? She had slipped and fallen into the drink as she attempted to step into the boat and that's why her clothes were wet? It sounded a feeble excuse at best, but the alternative was to try and make her way through the streets of Charles Town stark naked, and that, she thought, might attract a deal of unwanted attention to herself.

The sun was dipping behind the horizon, taking with it the warmth of day. Shivering in the cold, Meg hurried toward the pile of driftwood in which she had hidden her things. For a long incredulous moment, she stared at the bare ground, unable to believe her eyes. The gown, the hoop, her shoes—everything was gone. Thinking at first that she must have come to the wrong place, she glanced up and down the beach. But no, there was the low sandy knoll covered with bracken, and there, too, was the lifeless remains of a palmetto, which had at some time been struck by lightning. She could not be mistaken.

Suddenly she stilled, her head cocked, listening for something in the quiet of gently lapping waves and the rustle of wind in the trees. She felt the blood quicken in her veins, the tingle of nerve endings along her spine.

She knew that Glenmorgan was there before she turned and saw him, his tall frame draped in a long, billowing cloak.

Deliberately he came up to her. His eyes, glittery in the half-light of dusk, swept her from head to toe. She could not stop herself from shivering as a cool breeze explored her bare skin, still wet from the sea. Instinctively her head came up as she saw Glenmorgan's lips thin to a grim line.

Then wordlessly he swept the cloak from his shoulders and, wrapping it around her, bent to lift her in his arms.

"You insane little fool," he muttered gruffly. "It's time I took you home."

Meg sat huddled in the stern sheets and watched as Glenmorgan effortlessly maneuvered the sloop's small skiff into the channel. He had not said a word to her since he had tossed her a bundle containing a sailor's blouse and loose-fitting trousers and curtly ordered her to put them on. Wordlessly she had dressed, too cold to put up an argument. Even then, in her borrowed clothing, she was grateful for the added warmth of Glenmorgan's cloak wrapped around her, though she was not sure what chilled her more—the brisk Atlantic breeze or Glenmorgan's unnerving silence.

He sat at the stern, his hand on the tiller, his gaze fixed straight before him.

"You might at least tell me if everyone is all right," she ventured testily when she could not bear the suspense any longer.

Glenmorgan leaned forward to trim the boom, sending the little boat skimming across the wind on a new tack, then settled back on the stern seat, his arm hooked over the tiller, before bothering to answer.

"We lost two men," he said shortly. "Other than that, everyone is fine, except for Thomas, who will have a head-ache for a day or two." At last he looked at her, an odd look that made her feel strangely queasy inside. "Thanks to you, neither Tommy nor Brigida was harmed. And don't bother to deny it. You're the only one who could have set the boats adrift and rescued Tommy from his kidnapper. By the way, he's convinced he was saved by a particularly large and benevolent fish—a shark, no less. I don't suppose you could explain why he should have come up with such an idea?"

Meg, feeling the blood steal into her cheeks, was grateful for the concealing darkness. "No, but how—how very odd," she stammered.

"*I* thought so," Glenmorgan agreed with just the slightest emphasis on the "I."

"But then, he—he's very young and impressionable. And there was a lot of confusion," Meg suggested helpfully.

"Oh, undoubtedly. Especially," he added with only a hint of dryness, "when you knocked the feet out from under the villain who had him."

"Yes, especially then," Meg concurred, with a great deal of feeling. The pirate had not frightened easily. He had fought until she had been forced nearly to drown him before he finally made a break for shore. Which meant that by the time she got back to Tommy, he was already near death's door. It had, in fact, taken the "Song of Id" to call the child back into his body before he could wander too far, something which she had dared only as a last resort. The idea of planting the suggestion in his unconscious mind that a great fish had saved him had been an inspiration. It should confuse matters enough so that no one would question him further. Even so, she had had no choice but to leave him as soon as she sensed him coming awake. Otherwise, he would have seen her and guessed the whole. Fortunately, by then Glenmorgan had miraculously arrived and defeated the pirates on the beach. "You're sure he's all right?" she queried, remembering her frantic attempts to revive Tommy.

"He's home by now, safe in his bed," Glenmorgan assured her. "Which is where you should be."

"I'm not tired," retorted Meg, impatient with the strangeness of his mood. She could feel the tension in him and his eyes on her as if they were trying to bore holes through

327

her. "Who were they? Why did they want Brigida and Tommy?"

"They were Drago's men from the *Sea Hawk*. As to why, I can't answer that yet. But I intend to find out," he replied, keeping to himself the knowledge that Meg had been their real target. The less she knew, the less likely she was to fling herself recklessly into danger.

"Drago's men," Meg repeated. "But I thought . . ."

"You thought what?" prodded Glenmorgan.

Meg shook her head. "I don't know. It's just that I can't see what Drago could hope to gain by such a thing. It doesn't seem right somehow that he would go to such lengths just to get even. I mean, where would be the profit in it? And since we saw him with Tharp and that other man on the *Sea Hawk,* I thought perhaps—"

"You saw Tharp with Drago?" Glenmorgan queried sharply.

"Yes, when we were leaving the harbor. Didn't Kate tell you?"

"Doubtlessly it slipped her mind. She had her hands full with Tommy and Brigida. The other man, what was he like? Had you ever seen him before?"

Sensing Glenmorgan's sudden, keen interest, Meg struggled to recall her fleeting impressions of the stranger. "He was dark, like you. And taller than the other two." She frowned, unable to remember his face. "It's no use. I didn't get a very good look at him. He was missing an arm—his left, I think. That's all I really remember about him." She sensed Glenmorgan's frame go suddenly taut. "You know him," she said with sudden certainty.

"Aye," Glenmorgan answered, steely-voiced. "I've been waiting for him to show up. I was beginning to think perhaps I'd missed him."

"Well?" Meg prompted impatiently. "Who is he?"

"His name is Jean Freneaux, and he is a very dangerous

man. It would be better if you have nothing to do with him should you ever run into him again."

Meg stared speechlessly at Glenmorgan's stern silhouette. "And that is all you mean to tell me?" she demanded incredulously when it was obvious he did not intend to go on.

"It's all that you need to know."

"But it isn't fair," she exclaimed. "I could help you if you would let me."

In the darkness, his hand found and curled around the back of her neck.

"You *have* helped me," he said in a low, thrilling voice. "More than you know. Now the rest is up to me. Stay out of it, Meg. I won't have you hurt."

Meg bit her lip to keep from flinging back a sharp retort. There was no use arguing with him. She had learned that much in the past few weeks. Irritably, she wondered if all landsmen were as hopelessly stubborn as this one. Very well, she thought. If he refused to trust her, she would just have to find out about this Jean Freneaux on her own.

They lapsed into silence after that. Glenmorgan seemed absorbed with guiding the boat through the maze of ships anchored in the harbor, and Meg, preoccupied with her own thoughts, did not even notice that the skiff veered away from the lights of the city or that they were heading north away from the wharf up the mouth of the Cooper. It was not until Glenmorgan gave the curt order to take the tiller that she became aware that they were nowhere near the docks where the *Raven* was moored. Looming out of the dark was a wooden jetty lit by the eerie glow of a lantern.

Hastily Meg did as she was bidden while Glenmorgan eased the jib, then posed, ready with the bowline for the boat to come alongside the jetty.

"I thought," commented Meg doubtfully some minutes

later as, with the boat secured, Glenmorgan helped her disembark, "you said you were taking me home to my bed."

"Aye," he replied, maddeningly noncommittal. "So I did." Taking her hand firmly in his, he led her across a short stretch of sandy beach to a lush lawn, which was deliciously damp and cool underfoot. Recently cut and obviously well tended, it had almost the feel of a carpet beneath her bare feet.

Piqued and more than a little mystified, Meg tried again. "You might at least tell me where you're taking me."

"Did no one ever tell you that it was ill-mannered to be overinquisitive?" countered the captain. "Or that curiosity could cut short your existence?"

"I thought," Meg retorted, "it was felines that suffered from that particular malady. At least that is what Grandfather's always telling me."

"Aye, felines and females. But then, they have so much in common, it's hardly surprising. Their refusal, for example, to do what they're told. Like wandering off by themselves so that no one knows where they are. At least a cat would know better than to go swimming in the middle of winter, which is more than I can say for a certain female I know."

Meg struck a whimsical pose. "I wasn't aware cats swam. But then, I've never had the privilege of knowing one. They sound like perfectly charming animals."

"Do they?" responded Glenmorgan ironically. "Remind me to get you one. No doubt the two of you would get along famously."

They had come, as they talked, to a flagstoned walk, which wound through a spinny of moss-draped trees, swaying contentedly in the sea breeze. It was an enchanting place, permeating a feeling of peace and contentment, and momentarily Meg forgot her pique at Glenmorgan's impenetrability.

Then they emerged from the grove of trees, and a cottage loomed out of the dark, small and cozy, its windows aglow with a friendly light.

"Oh, but it is perfect!" exclaimed Meg, delighted. "Whose house is it?"

"Yours," replied Glenmorgan, lifting the brass knocker and letting it fall.

A flash of startled surprise crossed Meg's face, followed by a dazzling smile. In another moment she would have flung her arms about his neck, but just then the door opened to reveal a plumpish middle-aged woman dressed in gray serge and wearing a white cap perched on top of neat brown curls.

"Captain Glenmorgan!" she exclaimed in a pleasingly low-pitched voice. "Come in, won't you please, sir. And you, miss. It's a brisk night in spite of the fair weather we've been having." In short order she ushered them into a cozy parlor made cheerful by a fire crackling merrily in the fireplace. "I had almost given you up," she confessed to Glenmorgan as she bent over to stir the embers and add a log to the flames. "And this must be the young lady you told me about. Come in by the fire, miss. Here, let me take your cloak. Yes. That's better," she crooned, seeing Meg comfortably settled in an overstuffed armchair placed close to the fire. She showed no surprise at seeing the captain in the company of a young woman garbed in male attire. On the contrary, she exuded a motherly warmth toward her young guest.

"Can I get you anything?" she asked, smoothing out the folds of her apron. "A bite to eat? Or perhaps some brandy, Captain?"

"A spot of supper, here before the fire, should do nicely, Mrs. Clagg. And a decanter of brandy would not be amiss, thank you. Afterward, you may feel free to retire. We'll clean up after ourselves."

"You'll do no such thing, Captain," exclaimed Mrs. Clagg, clearly scandalized at such an idea. "I'll not have you doing my chores for me. They'll keep till morning, don't you worry." Crossing to a cabinet, she removed a decanter of brandy and two glasses and setting them on a tray, carried it to a small occasional table near where Glenmorgan stood by the fire.

"How do you find it here at Cherry Orchard, Mrs. Clagg?" queried the captain with more than polite interest. "Now that everything is in place. It's not too remote, I hope?"

"Oh, not at all, sir. But then, I've never really been one for the city. I was raised in the back country. I expect Cherry Orchard is about as close to heaven as I've ever been, sir. And that's something else I have to thank you for. Heaven knows I can never repay you for all you've done for me since my man Jesse was lost at sea. You must know how grateful I—"

"I'm the one who is grateful, Mrs. Clagg," Glenmorgan interrupted before she could finish what she had been about to say. "Your husband was a good man and a valued friend. He's greatly missed, I assure you." He had taken her hands in both of his as he spoke, and now, giving them a squeeze, he released them. "It's worth a great deal to me to know Miss Pippin will have someone like you to look after her."

"Likely we'll never agree as to who owes who what." Mrs. Clagg gave a quick dab at her eyes with the corner of her apron. "Men like yourself are leery of being reminded of their good deeds. I know. My Jesse was just such a one. But there it is. And now if you'll excuse me," she said, brisk once more as she crossed to the door, "I'll go and see to your supper."

"Jesse Clagg was the *Argonaut*'s first mate," Glenmorgan said in answer to Meg's questioning look. "His wife was left with four children to rear on her own. Now that they're all grown, she was glad enough to take the position of housekeeper here. A daughter, Emma, will come during the day to help about the house."

"And Grandfather?" queried Meg, who was just beginning to grasp that Glenmorgan, far from courting Clarissa's affections, had spent the past week preparing this surprise for her—Meg.

"I've made arrangements for him to join you here tomorrow," he informed her as he filled one of the glasses. Meg shook her head in refusal as he lifted the decanter inquiringly in her direction. "I had planned to bring you both here this evening. But circumstances dictated otherwise." He replaced the decanter on the tray. Then, glass in hand, he leaned his elbow on the mantlepiece and gazed somberly into the flames.

He was silent so long that Meg nearly jumped when he spoke. "You enjoyed your little swim, I hope?" Meg had to fight not to squirm as his eyes lifted to survey her with a sudden piercing intensity.

"As a matter of fact, I did—until the men came," she responded uncertainly. He did not sound in the least as if he had meant it. If anything, she had the distinct feeling that he was about to give vent to whatever had been seething inside him all evening.

"And that's it," he stated. "No explanations. No excuses. No matter that you had everyone believing you'd either perished on that accursed island or been taken captive. I don't suppose you mean to tell me what the devil you were doing in the water all that time or how you managed to keep from being chilled to the bone?"

Meg's eyes flashed with resentment at his insinuating tone.

"Perhaps," she blurted, "I hid in the pirates' boat. Or perhaps I turned into a fish and swam until it seemed safe to return. Maybe even Tommy's shark. What does it matter?

333

I was not harmed and I was able to help in a small way. I don't understand why you're upset. One would almost think you are sorry I wasn't drowned."

"Oh, that was excellently done," Glenmorgan applauded with a cynical curl of the lips. "I have spent the last several hours contemplating any number of dire explanations for your disappearance. And now I'm supposed to feel a heartless brute for being just a little bit 'upset,' as you put it. Well, it won't work, Meg. I *am* upset. I have every reason to be. And what's more, I'm well aware that you have not really answered my questions. But that's all right. Keep your precious secrets, if you must. I can't, however, have you pulling any more stunts like this. I can't afford to be distracted from what brought me here, and I will not have you placing yourself in danger. If I have to, I'll send you back to the West Indies."

Bristling with indignation, Meg shot to her feet.

"I am not a child to be sent home for misbehaving," she countered furiously. "You do not have that power over me, Captain. I have money. I'll find my own place to live. Dick will help me."

"Oh, he will, will he?" queried Glenmorgan dangerously. "I wasn't aware that the two of you had become such fast friends."

"There are a lot of things you don't know," Meg retorted bitterly. "About Dick and about me—about your family. There are things going on all around you that you're too blinded by your precious vengeance to see. Well, go and get yourself killed if that's what you want, and just see if I care. You needn't worry that *I'll* trouble you anymore. I'll find a way to survive without you."

It was not what she had meant to say. Only minutes earlier she had been filled with a warm, tender feeling for him because of the cottage and the knowledge that she should have trusted him more. She could not understand what had happened to change all that. The last thing she had wanted was to quarrel with him. But now that it had happened, she would not back down. She had rescued his nephew and saved his sister, even made it possible for Glenmorgan to trap the pirates on the island. And what was the thanks she got—a lecture and a threat to send her back where he had found her!

Hurt and angry to think he could so easily cast her off, she never once considered that he might be undergoing a reaction to the strain and anxiety of the day's events. But then, she could not know that, deep down, he had thought her lost to him, not dead, perhaps, but vanished forever from his life. Or that no matter how often he had told himself his fear was totally irrational (after all, where was she to go or how achieve her escape without clothes or a boat?), he had not been able to shake the fact that each time he had hurt her, she had demonstrated an uncanny ability to disappear without a trace, just as she had done this day and on one particularly memorable occasion in the Caribbean. It had never occurred to him that, far from being devastated by his lengthy and unexplained absence, she might turn to Dick Chapin for solace.

For the first time in his life he experienced searing pangs of jealousy, like red-hot coals in his belly, something he had not felt even when he discovered Clarissa's betrayal. Not that he could blame Chapin. No man could have resisted Meg's cursed sweet innocence. He himself was proof of that. All along he had been deluding himself into believing that she loved him when in truth she had only been untutored and unworldly, a child of nature whose generosity and beauty enthralled and captivated without her even being aware of it. And worst of all, her heart had remained untouched. Or had it? Perhaps Dick had in truth succeeded where he had failed.

His hand clenched on the glass with the thought, even

as it came to him with bitter clarity, that she could have picked no better man than Dick Chapin. Solid and dependable, and with the heart of a lion, he would never let her down.

Deliberately he tossed off his brandy and set down the empty glass. If the wind lay in that quarter, then he would do nothing to stand in their way. Far from it. He would make sure that Dick was removed from any chance of danger. Ironically, it only made what he had to do a hell of a lot simpler.

"It would seem," he uttered with a weary sense of finality, "that we have said all there is to be said. You may inform Mrs. Clagg that I could not stay for supper. Regretfully, I find that I have pressing business elsewhere." At last he looked at her out of eyes that chilled her somehow. "You will, of course, keep the cursed house. You've bloody well earned it. I hope you and Dick will be happy in it."

Meg let forth an involuntary gasp. She and Dick? Whatever in the world had he meant by that? Then it came to her that, having tired of her and all the trouble she had caused, he was giving her to his first mate. As if she were a possession to be passed from one to the other. How dare he!

He was already to the door, his hand on the door handle, when she recovered her wits enough to answer him.

"We shall do very well without you, thank you. *He* at least will never break his word to me."

Meg winced as the door slammed emphatically shut. Involuntarily, she took a step forward, her hand outstretched as though to bring Glenmorgan back to her. Then she stopped and let it drop to her side again.

When Mrs. Clagg came back into the room a few moments later, she found the captain gone and her new young mistress standing uncertainly in the middle of the floor, a peculiarly stunned expression in her lovely eyes. Sensing all was not as it should be, the housekeeper carefully set down the tray she was carrying.

"Now, now, miss," she murmured, her voice deep with sympathy. "You mustn't take it to heart—whatever's passed between you and the captain. He'll be coming back again when he's had time to think things over. I know. You learn a thing or two when you've had a husband and reared a son and three daughters. Besides, Captain Glenmorgan's plainly in love with you, it's that obvious."

"Obvious?" repeated Meg, sounding as lost as she looked. "I'm afraid you're mistaken, Mrs. Clagg. He doesn't even like me very much."

"How can you say so when there's this cottage to prove otherwise," said Mrs. Clagg. "He had Mr. Sutton purchase it outright from the old gentleman who owned it, or at least from the old man's agent. Then he moved out all the old furnishings, except for a small piece or two, and replaced the lot with fine, new things. All week he's had workmen painting and repairing, till the old place is better than new. And that's only the beginning. The carpets and drapes, the wines in the wine cellar and the victuals in the pantry, the fixings for the kitchen, right down to the dishes and cooking utensils, are all brand spanking new. Now if that's not the work of a man in love, then I don't know a thing about it."

"I see," said Meg slowly, staring around her at the twin chairs with high backs and padded arms, both upholstered in a heavy fabric of the kind Brigida had called brocade. They were lemon yellow in color as was the snug couch, cozily designed for just two people. Four wooden armchairs of a dark polished wood stood about the room in varying attitudes seemed meant to promote quiet conversation. Next to the tall wooden mantle, painted blue and bearing a portrait in a golden frame, stood a high wooden cabinet with polished brass handles. A silver tea set on a low table and various brass candlesticks added to the simplicity of the room, which, unlike those of the Glenmorgan Town House, seemed warm and cozy rather than grand and somehow daunting.

And then suddenly she *did* see what Mrs. Clagg had been trying to tell her. It was not really the things themselves, either their richness or their numbers, that served as a measure of Glenmorgan's regard for her. It was what he had achieved with their careful selection and arrangement. He had gone to a great deal of trouble to create a cozy little nest in which she could feel snug and safe. Though small, the room did not make her feel closed in the way the grand Town House had. From the moment she entered, she had pictured herself and Glenmorgan together, there before the fire, and had known instantly she could be happy here.

But not now. It was all ruined now, thanks to her hasty temper. Glenmorgan was gone. She had driven him away, and she did not see how she could ever win him back again. But then, that was the way she had wanted it, was it not? she told herself bitterly. At all costs, she had sworn Glenmorgan must remain free.

Suddenly weary and wishing only to be left alone, she allowed Mrs. Clagg to lead her upstairs.

Nineteen

After leaving Cherry Orchard, Glenmorgan made his way to the wharf, and from there to a seedy establishment on the waterfront which bore the unlikely name of the Crystal Palace. He took a table off by itself in a dark corner and, trying in vain to banish from his mind the image of a pair of blue-green eyes scintillating sparks of anger, proceeded to steadily down a full bottle of rum, followed in due course by another. He was in no mood for company and in even less of a humor to tolerate the boisterous arrival of half a dozen sailors, who elbowed aside the handful of patrons at the bar and monopolized the attentions of the scantily clad females. Nevertheless, it was not until one particularly loud and persistent ruffian placed two beefy hands on Glenmorgan's table, his two hundred fifty pounds of hardened muscle leaning against them, that the captain was at last moved to accept the inevitable.

"My mates, here, have been tellin' me that you be Captain Bloody Mad Mike Glenmorgan," jeered the sailor, his lips baring large uneven teeth in a sneer. When Glenmorgan failed to react with even so much as a grunt, the sailor lowered his head to peer more closely at the still, shadowy figure. "Maybe you didn't hear me. I'm Billy Barlowe," he persisted, "and *I* says you don't look half big enough, or mean enough, to've done all the things that's been said about you." Giving a loud belch, Barlowe winked over his shoulder at his sniggering mates before turning back to Glenmorgan again. "I reckon you take after your papa. I hear tell he shot himself before they could hang him for a thief and a yellow dog of a traitor."

"Is that what you hear?"

Slowly Glenmorgan's head lifted. A pale shaft of light from a shaded lamp fell in a narrow band across his eyes.

Barlowe frowned, the grin fading from his lips—just before steely fingers clamped in his hair and slammed his face down hard against the table top. Yanking the sailor's head back again, Glenmorgan smashed the half-empty rum bottle over the top of his skull.

Without so much as a groan, Barlowe slumped across the table and slid to the floor.

Hardly had the dust settled before Glenmorgan was on his feet. The neck of the bottle with its jagged remains clutched ready in one slender hand, he squared off before the gaping seamen.

"All right," he announced in soft, chilling accents, "who's next?"

No one noticed a seaman's slight figure steal to the door or realized when he slipped out into the night. A low rumble slowly crescendoed to a roar as the maddened sailors closed in around Glenmorgan—with the result that sometime well after midnight, Sutton received word that his brother-in-law had set himself up to take on all comers.

Without hesitation, Thomas gathered up a small force of his own dock workers and marched to the rescue. It was obvious he had come to the right place when a human projectile shattered the front window and landed at his feet. Ascertaining at a·glance that the unconscious wretch was not his brother-in-law, Sutton entered at the head of his men to find the alehouse in a shambles and Glenmorgan in the

process of polishing off a two-hundred-pound longshore-
man with a bone-crunching right to the jaw.

Glenmorgan, catching sight of his brother-in-law, stepped
indifferently over the various bodies littering the floor.

"What the devil are you doing here?" he demanded.

"Rescuing you, or so I thought," Sutton replied, grinning
crookedly. With a nod of the head, he dismissed his men.

"You thought wrong," growled Glenmorgan. Rubbing the
bruised knuckles of his right in the palm of his left, he
shoved past Sutton and ordered the tavernkeeper to fetch
another bottle.

"Make that two," spoke up Sutton, leaning his elbows
against the bar next to the captain. "Since I'm here, I might
as well make a night of it. Like old times, eh, Michael?"

"The bloody hell it is." Glenmorgan eyed his in-law with
a noticeable lack of humor. "What do you want, Thomas?
I neither need nor want a bloody nursemaid. If it's Meg
you're concerned about, you may rest easy. I left her at the
cottage—safe and unharmed."

"Then why—"

"If I had wanted conversation," Glenmorgan pointedly
interrupted, "I would have gone to the club. You're a married man, Thomas. Go home to your wife and family."

"I might remind you that it's your family, too," Thomas
persisted. "And that they're worried about you. Why not
come along with me now? They'll rest easier knowing
you're home."

"They'll rest easier knowing I won't be troubling them
with my presence," Glenmorgan rejoined cynically. "And
we both know it. Go away, Thomas. I've a different sort of
companionship in mind."

Closing his fingers around the neck of the bottle, he
shoved away from Sutton and made for a garishly dressed
female of indeterminate years who had been eyeing him for
some time from the far end of the bar. "Now," he said,

341

taking her hand unceremoniously in his, "you may show me this room of yours."

Sutton moved to block his way. "Michael, don't do this. Whatever is bothering you is better dealt with among friends."

"And who's saying he isn't among friends?" demanded the woman. Leaning provocatively against Glenmorgan's lean, masculine frame, she gazed up into his face with what was meant to be a sultry look from beneath fantastically long eyelashes. "Claudette Beauchamp knows how to ease a man's troubles. Just you ask anyone."

"There, you see?" Glenmorgan's lip curled in cynical amusement. "I am in excellent company, and so you may inform my mother and sisters. I expect they will be vastly amused."

"Dammit, Michael," exclaimed Sutton, torn between hurt and concern at his friend's odd behavior. "What the devil are you up to? The man I know would never dishonor either himself or his family in such a manner—and with such a woman. If you care nothing about them, you might at least think what it'll do to Meg when she finds out you prefer the company of a—a—"

"A whore, Mr. Sutton?" supplied Madame Beauchamp.

Sutton nearly backed before the sudden hard leap of anger in Glenmorgan's eyes.

"You're a fool, Thomas," murmured the captain with chilling deliberation. "Worse than that, you're a bore. Go home, while you still can. And in the future I suggest you stay out of my way."

White-lipped, Sutton moved stiffly aside, his eyes never leaving Glenmorgan's face. Then turning abruptly on his heel, he stalked out the door.

"That was cleverly done, Captain," murmured the woman, loosening her hold on Glenmorgan's arm. "The men with whom you wish to make contact would think nothing of killing you or your friend if he proved trouble-some. You have chosen a curious way to make yourself known—a tavern brawl is hardly what I would have expected. Still, it has a certain flair that might appeal to the Frenchman." She laughed. "He is a backwoodsman, that one."

"He's a soldier," Glenmorgan corrected. "It would be a mistake to underestimate him."

The woman's eyes glittered coldly. "Be sure that you do not. I've seen what he can do to a man with a knife—even with only the one arm." She relaxed, letting the warning stand for itself. "When you came to me before, you said you wanted to meet the Frenchman and that you would pay well if I could arrange it. I will take nothing less than the amount upon which we agreed, Captain."

Glenmorgan retrieved a plump purse from his coat.

"It is yours." The woman's eyes sparkled as she reached up to take it. Then Glenmorgan closed his fingers around it. "When I have met the Frenchman," he said coldly.

The woman shrugged a scantily clad shoulder.

"If it's true that he's in Charles Town and has met with Tharp, I believe we may expect him to show himself here anytime now. He has a particular fondness for the entertainment my girls provide. He will come, Captain, and then I'll make sure he learns the notorious Captain Glenmorgan has grown disenchanted with honest pursuits." The woman's fingers clenched on the fabric of his shirt, crumpling it. "In exchange, you must keep your promise to me." Her heavily painted eyes took on a fierce expression. "You'll make Thornton and his little witch of a daughter *pay* for what they've done."

Deliberately, Glenmorgan pulled her hand from his shirt front.

"I'll keep my promise," he said coldly. Holding her wrist in a hard grip between them, he studied her face for a long moment. "What did they do to you to make you hate them so much?"

The red lips parted on a harsh burst of laughter. Contemptuously, she jerked her wrist free. "I was not always a whore, Captain. Ask *her*—ask Clarissa Tharp how Claudette Beauchamp came to be the madame of a bordello."

"Perhaps I will," said Glenmorgan, thrusting the bottle of rum in her hand. "In the meantime, you can reach me at the Planters' Hotel."

It was a short walk from the Crystal Palace to the Planters' Hotel, a block off Dock Street. The brisk night air served to clear Glenmorgan's head and relieve him of the lingering odors of sweat and stale beer. Nevertheless, his mood had not improved by the time he reached the hotel's two-story piazza with its ironwork arches and balustrade. As he entered the ground floor, he gave a curious glance around the spacious room. Everything was exactly as he remembered—the great marble fireplace with the two tall windows side by side next to it, the oak desk and two wing chairs, the brass chandelier. Even the reception room, which was frequented between acts by those attending the Dock Street Theatre directly behind the hotel, had the same two armchairs ranged before the fireplace and the same picture hanging over the mantle. Both rooms were deserted, except for the night clerk at the desk, who handed Glenmorgan a quill to sign the register.

"Will you be staying long, sir?" queried that personage, glancing curiously at the name on the register.

"Perhaps," Glenmorgan answered shortly as he picked up the room key. Ordering a bottle of brandy to be sent up, he took the stairs two at a time. Twenty minutes later, he lay on the bed, his stockinged feet crossed at the ankles and his rumpled shirt opened to the waist as he made indentures on the bottle of brandy and brooded on the course of action to which he had committed himself.

His contact in Antigua had advised him to approach Madame Beauchamp, and he had done so some days earlier. But something about her had not rung true. His well-honed sense of self-preservation had triggered an instinctive distrust of the woman. He had decided against using her. But Meg had changed all that. Damn her!

Bloody hell! He had been aware for some time that without Meg his life would not be worth the living. And with the bitter certainty that he had lost her, he had leaped at the prospect of immediate action with the added spice of danger to sweeten the pot. So be it, and to hell with the consequences. The sooner he was able to conclude his business in Charles Town, the sooner he could weigh anchor and be gone from the cursed reminders of a girl with silvery hair and eyes that could bewitch a man's soul.

In a quick motion, he tossed off his drink. Then closing his eyes, he leaned his head back, felt the brandy, like liquid fire, explore his empty belly, waited for it to dull his senses. To no avail. His thoughts returned stubbornly to Meg, along with an image of her silken body clasped in the arms of Dick Chapin. Cursing, he refilled the glass.

He awakened late the following morning with bleary eyes, a throbbing headache, and a less than amiable disposition. If he had discovered any truths the night before, he couldn't remember them. What he did remember, with bitter clarity, was Meg's avowal that she and Chapin would survive well enough without him.

Disgusted with himself, he thrust himself from the bed and fortified himself with a stiff drink.

An hour later, feeling somewhat better after a bath, a shave, and a late breakfast, he left the hotel and, hiring a chaise, directed the driver to proceed along Broad Street to the shops on the east side of town.

As a boy, he had heard his father boast more than once that a man could buy anything in the shops of Charles Town, if he had either the money or the credit. It soon proved that things had not altered in the seven years of Glenmorgan's absence. If anything, the goods were even more varied and plentiful than he remembered them. In short order, he had purchased suits, shirts, stockings, and footwear enough to satisfy even a lord, a pearl-handled pocket pistol and ammunition, a saddle, a harness and chaise, and he even hired a groom and a driver to go with them. A Chickasaw stallion and a team of four already awaiting his pleasure in a stable on the outskirts of town, he left instructions for the groom to fetch them to the hotel.

Three o'clock dinner had already come and gone by the time he returned to the hotel. Having ordered a decanter of whiskey and a cold collation to be brought up to his suite, he sprawled in a wing chair some minutes later, his long legs stretched out before him, and savored the Bourbon, taken neat as it should be. It had been a long time since he had enjoyed a good whiskey. In the Caribbean he had had, more often than not, to be satisfied with rum, a spirit that he considered only just palatable.

At last he ate hungrily, washing the cold peas, sliced turkey, oyster patties, and Beaufort rice bread down with whiskey. His hunger satisfied, he lit a cheroot and stood staring out the window over the harbor, while in the other room, a hotel servant put his newly acquired wardrobe neatly away.

In an hour or two, he would dress and put in an appearance at the theatre. No doubt his presence in the box Thomas had reserved for him for the season would excite a deal of attention, especially from the occupants of the neighboring box. Clarissa would be there. She never missed an opening night.

The knock at the door brought a wary glint to his eye.

346

Picking up the small handgun he had purchased that day, he held it, ready, in the palm of his hand.

"The door's open."

Chapin's big frame filled the doorway.

"Expecting trouble?" he queried mildly, his look registering the gun in Glenmorgan's hand. The plain, honest face, Glenmorgan noted grimly, held a faintly guarded expression.

"It pays to be careful." Laying the gun down beside the tray that held the remains of his meal, he picked up the decanter and filled two glasses. "Did Drago's men give you any trouble?"

"Not so you'd notice. Naturally they were none too happy at their changed circumstances. I can't say that I blame them. A career in the King's Navy is hardly what I'd choose for myself. They grumbled more than a little when they saw the *Sea Hawk* weighing anchor. Drago's gone, Michael. Pulled out and headed south. Moffit said to Sainte Augustine."

"Sainte Augustine. Are you certain?" Glenmorgan handed Chapin the glass.

"Aye. I thought it was odd, too—Drago making up to the Spaniards. But Moffit seemed eager to talk as soon as he saw Drago was pulling out without him. His way of getting even, I expect, for Drago leaving him to the mercy of the British Navy."

"Aye, no doubt." Glenmorgan turned back to pick up the other glass. "And the British captain. I trust he was properly grateful to have eighteen prime seamen dropped into his lap?" he asked, wondering how and when Chapin would finally broach the subject of Meg.

Chapin grinned. "Captain Stuart was happy as Christmas." Sobering, he studied the grim cast of the other man's expression. "What's happened, Michael?" he asked. "Is it Meg? Good God, man, don't tell me she's—"

"She's safe and well," Glenmorgan answered shortly. "I took her to the cottage."

Chapin frowned. "Then what . . ."

"You might as well know that she told me everything," Glenmorgan stated flatly, staring into the amber liquid in his glass. He tossed off the drink and set the glass on the table. "In case you're wondering, I don't hold it against you. Where women are concerned, a man's at the bloody mercy of whatever fate throws his way. I ought to know that better than anyone. I could only wish you had told me which way the wind lay."

Chapin, understandably confused, shifted his weight uncomfortably. After releasing the captured seamen into the care of the British captain, he had returned to the ship, where word awaited him that he was to report to Glenmorgan at the hotel. He had come straightaway to his captain. Consequently, he had not heard the news about Meg or about Glenmorgan's falling out with Sutton. Uneasily he wondered if Glenmorgan knew what had passed between Kate and himself. And then it came to him that Meg must have seen him with Kate on the island. Maybe she had even overheard what passed between them. "Bloody hell, Michael," he blustered, his face turning a dusky red. "I never meant for it to go so far. It just sort of happened. I've loved her since the first time I set eyes on her, and though you and I never talked about it, I always figured you knew how I felt. Not that it matters now," he added, Kate's white face and blistering condemnation etched in his memory. "I told her nothing could ever come of it. And nothing ever can."

"Don't be a bloody fool," Glenmorgan uttered harshly. "She's expecting you to come to her. Do you think I'd be here if she hadn't made it clear that it was you she wanted?"

Chapin stared at Glenmorgan with a dull sense of disbelief. "She told you that?" he demanded gruffly.

"I said she did, didn't I?" Glenmorgan answered, heartily

weary of the entire affair. Good God, he had made it plain that he would step aside, leaving Chapin a clear field. What more did the man want from him?

"Aye, you did," Chapin said ponderously. "But it doesn't change a bloody thing." The big man's jaw hardened in grim determination. "She deserves better than me. I expect you know that as well as I do."

"Good God, you tax my patience too far!" Glenmorgan swung around to face Chapin with light, piercing eyes. "She loves you, and by heaven you're going to marry her!"

"I'm afraid," Chapin answered, his gaze stubborn and fixed on a point beyond Glenmorgan's shoulder, "that this is one time I can't oblige you. With all respect, Captain. This is a *private* matter. Not even you can order me to do what goes against my conscience."

"Curse your blasted conscience. You should have thought of that *before* you led her to believe you meant to set up housekeeping with her."

At last Chapin's stolid front appeared shaken.

"That's a bloody lie," he declared hoarsely, his cheeks flaming red. "I never promised her any such thing. For God's sake, Michael, you can't believe that I'd do or say anything to dishonor Kate."

"Kate?" Glenmorgan stared at him with a thunderous expression. "What the devil has Kate to do with any of this?"

"She has everything to do with it," Chapin declared heatedly. "Who the hell have we been talking about?"

Then it came to him with blinding certainty. "Good God, you don't think that *Meg* and I . . .?"

"What I *think* has nothing to say to it," Glenmorgan answered coldly. "It happens to be what Meg told me. Are you saying she made it all up?"

Chapin gave a dismissive wave of the hand.

"No, of course not. Not Meg. She could never do anything like that." Stubbornly, he lifted his eyes to Glenmorgan's. "For Christ's sake, Michael. You can't honestly believe there could ever be anything between Meg and me. Hell, the idea is preposterous. You must have misunderstood her."

"If I did, then I'll ask your pardon for it—and hers," Glenmorgan answered in soft, chilling accents. "If, on the other hand, I find out you've been making up to Meg and playing fast and loose with my sister, by God, friend or not, I'll bloody well put a pistol ball through your heart."

Chapin's face went as white as it had previously been red. "I never thought I'd see the day when Michael Glenmorgan would doubt my word. *Or* when he'd believe me capable of being so lowdown as to trifle with a female's affections, let alone Meg's or Kate's. The only thing keeping me from calling you out right now is the reminder that you're Turlough Glenmorgan's son and that we used to be closer than brothers."

Glenmorgan smiled frostily. "Don't let sentiment stop you. Or my father's memory. You may be sure that I won't. Anytime you think you're man enough, I'll be ready to oblige you."

Chapin took a step toward the captain, his big hands clenched into fists at his sides. His eyes clashed with Glenmorgan's and held. Then the anger gave way to a puzzled look. Shaking his head, Chapin backed away.

"You'll be needing a new first officer," he said stiffly, the hurt and bewilderment plain to read in spite of the stubborn pride of the man. "I'll be leaving the ship and taking what's rightfully mine."

Glenmorgan turned sharply away. "Take it and be damned. I don't give a stone's toss in hell what you do."

He was still standing, staring out into the night, when the door slammed firmly shut.

* * *

Clarissa Tharp sat at her dressing table, watching with a critical eye as her maid performed the finishing touches to her mistress's hair.

She did not even bother to turn her head when Tharp, entering through the door separating his rooms from hers, stopped to observe her with cynical detachment.

"A new gown," he mused aloud. "And the Rawlston diamonds. It would seem you have in mind a conquest, my dear. Do you really think Glenmorgan will fall for it? You did shoot him, after all."

Clarissa impatiently waved the maid away. "That's enough, Hettie. Leave me now." At last she turned to regard her husband with cold dislike. "I'm not afraid to show myself, if that's what you mean. It's opening night at the theatre, and I don't intend to miss it."

"No, I did not imagine that you would. I regret that I shall not be present to observe the touching reunion. As it happens, however, I have business elsewhere."

"You've spoken with Freneaux," said Clarissa with an air of finality. "Well? Are you going to tell me about it, or must I worm it out of you?"

"As entertaining as I should find your methods of persuasion, my dear, I'm afraid I haven't the time. A pity, really," he murmured, smiling in sardonic amusement, "to allow Glenmorgan all the fun." Extracting a plump purse from his coat pocket, he dropped it with a heavy, metallic clunk on the dressing table. "The Frenchman was generous. There will be a great deal more of this when the cargo has been delivered. Drago has already sailed, and Freneaux will follow in a week or two. In the meantime, I have business at the plantation. I suggest you keep your father on a short tether while I'm gone. Glenmorgan will make use of him if he can."

"Father has used up his credit in Charles Town," Clarissa replied with an indifferent shrug. "Without credit or money,

I doubt he will be much abroad. Besides, I shall be keeping a very close watch on Glenmorgan. Father still believes the good captain has Freneaux's cursed letters. If he does, I intend to have them back."

"If he had them, I sincerely doubt that your father would still be walking the streets of Charles Town. He would be swinging from the gallows for a traitor. How unfortunate that old man Turlough had to find out about our little smuggling enterprise. All this business with Glenmorgan might have been avoided otherwise. You might even have married him instead of me, my dearest Clarissa."

Clarissa glared at his reflection in the mirror as he trailed his fingers down the side of her neck and over the bare skin of an ivory shoulder.

"Enjoy your little game while I am gone," Tharp continued, observing the prickle of goosebumps rise on her flesh. "Only make certain you do not mistake lust for something else. What I have always admired most about you, my dear, is your utter lack of sentimentality." His hand stopped its caress. In the looking glass, his eyes met hers. "I should be disappointed if you persuaded yourself you were actually in love with the gallant captain."

"Don't be absurd." Contemptuously, Clarissa jerked away from him. "Love is for fools and innocents. And I am neither."

Neither one of them paid any attention to Thornton, who, giving a light rap on the outer door, entered the room.

"I hope not," murmured Tharp. He smiled coldly. "Our relationship has been mutually profitable until now. It would be a shame to spoil it."

Without bothering to acknowledge Thornton with so much as a nod, Tharp left the room.

"What the hell was that all about?" demanded Thornton of his daughter.

"Nothing." Clarissa shrugged and rose from her dressing

352

table. "Except to warn me to keep you out of the gambling rooms." Picking up her mantle from where it lay slung in readiness across the bed, she crossed to the door. There she paused, her hand on the doorhandle. "You will heed that warning—won't you, Father."

It was not a question. And she did not wait for an answer. Exiting, she left Thornton staring at the closed door.

"Damn," he cursed aloud. He had come hoping to squeeze some funds from his daughter, his own resources being somewhat strained at the moment. And while he seethed with resentment at Tharp's cavalier treatment, it had not surprised him. Tharp made no bones about the fact that he had no further use for his father-in-law. Nevertheless, things had come to a sorry pass when his own flesh-and-blood treated him like a bloody hanger-on.

Who were they to begrudge him a few hundred pounds now and then, he thought. He was the one who had doctored the books and kept Turlough in the dark about the gradual draining of funds from the company. He and Tharp had needed the money to invest in rum and munitions for the more profitable venture of smuggling arms to the French-allied Indians. It had been beautifully simple, especially when Freneaux had provided the last link in the circle, paying gold for the guns and transporting them from Sainte Augustine to New Orleans and, from there, inland up the Mississippi to the Choctaws. The newly organized Georgia colony had made the Upper Creeks allies of the British, which left the Choctaws and Alabamas the sole friends of the beleaguered French. With the French ships harried by the British Navy, he, Thornton, had been the one to see the possibilities and to recruit Tharp to his little scheme. His mistake had been in allowing Tharp to deal directly with Freneaux. It had allowed them both to cut him, Thornton, out when they had outgrown the need for Glenmorgan shipping as a front for their operation.

Damn them all to hell, he thought. And damn Freneaux's carelessness in allowing a courier to be intercepted by Turlough, not once, but twice. Those cursed letters were the only tangible evidence linking him to Freneaux, but even more importantly, there was nothing in them to indict Tharp. That put Thornton in the unenviable position of being a scapegoat, if one were ever needed, and gave Tharp damned little incentive to make good his promise to put Glenmorgan once and for all out of the way. Especially now that Glenmorgan had apparently retired from pirating and seemed no longer a threat to Tharp's smuggling activities. Perhaps Tharp was right in believing Glenmorgan had lost the taste for vengeance or that the letters were not in the captain's possession. But Thornton did not believe it. Not for a moment. Glenmorgan had them, and he meant to use them. The question was how and when.

Bloody hell! He could not sit around in Tharp's cursed town house with nothing to occupy him but the bitter certainty that Glenmorgan was biding his time, waiting for the right moment to come after him. He needed diversion. Perhaps Ashton would extend his credit. The proprietor of the Blue Dolphin had been surprisingly generous in accepting Thornton's promissory notes in lieu of actual capital. It was the only gambling establishment, in fact, where Thornton was still welcome.

Deciding it would not hurt to try, Thornton's eyes fell on the plump purse, which Clarissa had apparently in her haste forgotten to place in her wall safe. Thornton licked his lips and glanced nervously about the empty room as if expecting to find prying eyes spying on him from behind the drapes or the tapestried screen near the fireplace. Clarissa might never notice the purse was just a trifle lighter, he thought, reaching to undo the pursestrings.

* * *

Clarissa, in the company of her Aunt Rawlston and two male cousins, trained her opera glass on the curtained alcoves across from her. The usual Charles Town contingent were in attendance, she noted, nodding to Mrs. Pinckney in the company of Mr. and Mrs. Laurens. Young Henry must still be in England, she heard her aunt remark, along with Christopher Gadsden. The youths were about twenty now, fine young gentlemen from all accounts.

Clarissa, only half attending to the flow of conversation around her, was conscious of a keen disappointment. The only gentleman that interested her had apparently decided not to put in an appearance.

For one of the few times in her life, Clarissa found it difficult to lose herself in the drama going forth on stage. She was, in fact, tempted to plead a headache at intermission and return home. She was in no mood for small talk or gossip. Unfortunately, her Aunt Rawlston would not hear of it. A glass of ratafia would do wonders for her, she was told as the foursome made their way across to the Planters' Hotel.

Clarissa, who detested ratafia, wanted a stiff brandy. "Oh, a glass of white wine, then," she snapped peevishly when her aunt insisted that in public a lady never touched anything stronger. She could not afford to alienate her aunt or her influential uncle. Not until she was certain she no longer needed them. Perhaps when Tharp gave her her share of the money. Then she could leave Tharp and the detestably provincial Charles Town behind her once and for all. No doubt London or even Paris would suit her nicely, she thought.

When the servant returned, however, a snifter of brandy resided on the tray, along with her aunt's ratafia and her cousins' Madeira. "Pardon me, ma'am, but the gennelman tole me to bring it," said the servant, gesturing with his chin toward a curtained alcove beyond the fringes of the milling crowd. "He said you'd know who'd sent it."

"Really," exclaimed Mrs. Rawlston, her plump face registering a mixture of inquisitiveness and scandal. "What sort of gentleman would order a lady brandy? I'm not surprised he chooses not to show himself."

"Never mind, Aunt," said Clarissa quickly, a gleam of triumph in her eyes. "I know the gentleman. I beg you will excuse me."

Without waiting for an answer, Clarissa made her way through the crowd to the alcove and slipped inside. She blinked, blinded by the contrast between the bright lights of the reception room and the murky shadows of the curtained recess.

The next instant strong fingers closed about her throat and thrust her ruthlessly back against the wall.

"I could choke the life from you, here and now," murmured a soft, chilling voice. "Give me one good reason why I shouldn't."

Sternly Clarissa quelled her rising panic.

"I—I can't, Michael. God knows, you have every reason to punish me as you would. My only excuse is that I loved you."

"Loved me." His low bark of laughter was hardly comforting. "By God, love like yours could prove damnably fatal."

"I meant you to die. I would do it again. You hurt me. But in spite of that, I could not bear to see you tortured." At last she clung to him with her hands, willed him to believe her. "Think. Can you imagine Logan would have granted you so merciful a death?"

He did not answer her, and for one dread moment she felt sharp claws of fear. Then his hands forced her head back and his mouth closed sensuously over hers.

Clarissa groaned when he released her lips to explore the tender flesh below her ear.

"Where's Logan?" Glenmorgan murmured, pressing his lips to the base of her neck where it met the shoulder.

Clarissa gasped and arched against him, her hands seeking the lean hardness of his muscled body.

"Gone," she answered, her breath shallow in her throat. "To the country. He won't be back for days." Hungrily she drew him to her. "We have all the time we need."

Glenmorgan smiled to himself. Tharp had left Antigua with a hold full of powder and guns. The admiral had been certain of that. And Thomas had been equally certain that they had never been unloaded on the docks of Charles Town. Either Clarissa was lying about where Tharp had gone, or just maybe he knew now why Drago had sailed for a Spanish port. With Spain allied to France, Sainte Augustine would be the logical point of exchange for the smuggled goods. He'd wager his life the guns were on their way there at this very moment.

Clarissa's insistent lips brought him back to the present. A hard sardonic gleam in his eye, he returned her kiss. The game had begun in earnest.

Twenty

"There," pronounced Kate, stepping back to give her protégée a final, critical inspection. "Meg," she exclaimed softly, "you are every bit as stunning as I knew you would be."

Meg stood in front of the oval looking glass in her old room at the Town House and stared in bemused wonder at her own reflection. She hardly recognized herself in this strange creature dressed in—what had Kate called it?—a Watteau gown, the bodice fitted at the front, but the back falling in box pleats from the neckline to the hem. It was every bit as uncomfortable as had been the blue silk, which had been permanently relegated to a closet somewhere, but she had to admit it was a great deal more attractive. It was, in fact, an exquisite creation of cream silk embroidered with seed pearls, the overdress opening at the front to reveal a delicate tiered petticoat of ruffled lace. From her feet clad in white satin slippers to her hair caught up at the crown and allowed to cascade down the back of her head in soft curls, she little resembled the half-human, half-mermaid who preferred somewhat scantier apparel. Unwittingly she found herself wondering what Glenmorgan would think if he were to see her in such a gown. Then immediately she caught herself.

It had been two weeks since that last bitter exchange of words, and in all that time, he had not once been back to Cherry Orchard. He had, in fact, removed from the Town House and taken up residence in the Planters' Hotel, Kate had informed her on one of her frequent visits to the cottage. Meg did not have to be told that he was seeing Clarissa. She guessed it from all that Kate did not say.

More than his younger sister wondered if Glenmorgan had taken leave of his senses. There had been a heated exchange between Sutton and Glenmorgan, so bitter that afterward Sutton refused to discuss the nature of their disagreement even with Brigida. But even that did not compare to what came next. It was all over the city that Glenmorgan and Dick Chapin had had a falling-out.

Strangely enough, the one person who should have been most upset by these startling events appeared to demonstrate a calm acceptance. Mary Glenmorgan, to the amazement of her loved ones, maintained a cheerful attitude, admonishing her daughters to be patient and have faith in their brother. She was joined in this by Pippin, who seemed singularly unmoved by Meg's account of the disastrous evening at Cherry Orchard. He even went so far as to break out in laughter at one point in her narrative.

"Let me get this straight," he rumbled, the gray eyes positively dancing with amusement. "You told him Chapin would help set you up in a house? Good God, no wonder our iron-nerved captain has apparently gone off half-cocked. And poor unsuspecting Chapin. Faith, that must have been an encounter to try men's souls."

"Stop it!" Meg stared at him with a darkling expression. "You're laughing at me. Why? What have I done?"

"What indeed," chuckled her grandfather. Then sighing at the troubled hurt in her eyes, he folded an arm about her shoulders and pulled her close. "It's nothing, child—only the mating ritual of humans. Of all God's creations, only the human makes what should be a relatively simple matter something so complex that even the gods must laugh at it. Rest assured, your captain will come back to you. In the meantime, go with Kate and Brigida to the concerts and balls. Enjoy yourself. You have always wanted to learn about your father's world. Now you will have your chance."

"Come, dear," murmured Kate, bringing Meg back to the present. "Everyone is waiting."

Meg felt her mouth go suddenly dry as Kate turned her gently, but firmly, toward the door.

"It's only a small gathering," Kate added, feeling Meg's hands, cold as ice, in hers. "Only twenty couples for dinner and perhaps thirty more for the dancing afterwards."

"So many?" Meg swallowed dryly. "If that is a small gathering, I cannot but wonder what you would consider a large one."

Kate laughed and squeezed the other girl's hands. "I have seen as many as four hundred at the governor's ball. Now quit worrying. You'll do fine. Just remember to smile and flutter your fan the way we taught you."

Mary Glenmorgan, Brigida, and Thomas were waiting for them when the two girls finally descended the stairs to the receiving hall on the second floor. Amid the exclamations over her dress and her appearance in general, Meg was relieved to glimpse Dick Chapin, standing a little apart from the others. She smiled to herself. Somehow it made her feel a little better to realize that, though Chapin's stalwart frame showed to advantage in new white breeches and a dark blue evening coat, he looked to be just as miserable and out of place as she did.

"Dick," she exclaimed softly as he came to bow gallantly, if a trifle self-consciously, over her slim white hand. "How fine you look!"

"In a pig's ear," he rumbled back, running a finger expressively around the inside of his cravat. "I'd sooner ride out a hurricane on a ship's deck than put in an appearance at one of these fancy dress parties. But you, Meg. You're going to dazzle them all." Holding her at arm's length, he studied her face. "The truth, now. How have you been?"

"Lonely. Worried. Afraid." Her eyes searched his. "I heard what happened, and it is all my fault. Please, I must talk to you—later, when there is more time."

"Put my name on your dance card." He grinned wryly. "It'll be one dance I'll have a good excuse to sit out."

After that, Kate came and, acknowledging Chapin's presence with the barest hint of a cool nod, whisked Meg away. The receiving line was forming to greet the arrival of the first guests.

Meg, placed between Mary and Thomas, soon forgot to be nervous as she concentrated on making her curtsy, just as she had practiced it time and again under Kate's critical eye. As for the guests, *they* varied in their greetings from a sincere warmth to friendly politeness, but on the whole seemed a congenial gathering. She could not know that she herself gave a most favorable impression of freshness and naivete, combined with a disarming frankness that did her no harm in their eyes. She breathed a sigh of relief when at last Mary Glenmorgan announced it was time to go into dinner. Somehow she had managed to get through the ordeal without disgracing herself.

As she entered the dining room on Chapin's arm, Meg felt her heart sink. Confronted with the reality of the long table covered with white damask and sumptuously laid out with East India china, old-world silver, and fine cut glass that sparkled in the light of a magnificent crystal chandelier, she suddenly could not recall the first thing about the proper use of the bewildering array of tableware. All of Kate and Brigida's patient coaching was for naught. She would make a complete and utter fool of herself.

"Don't stare, lass," Chapin murmured softly, nodding and

smiling at the other guests. "It's not so hard. Just watch and do what everyone else does."

Meg, grateful to find herself seated between Thomas on her left and Chapin on her right, soon discovered that no one appeared to notice whether she used the right fork or not. They were too busy emptying their plates and conversing with those on either side of them. Meg herself ate little, merely sampling the okra soup, rice, cabbage palmetto, and leafy greens. The smothered veal, chicken tartare, and stewed crabs she did not touch at all, and her grandfather had warned her against the tall glass of champagne before her plate.

All in all, she would rather have spent the evening at home with her grandfather, she reflected, wondering what the others found to talk about. Thomas's attention had been monopolized almost the entire evening by a stout matron on his other side, who, adorned with a long, bobbing feather, dyed purple to match her dress, resembled some exotic bird. Meg watched, fascinated at the woman's ability to stuff her mouth with food and still carry on an uninterrupted flow of chatter.

"He was at the theatre opening night, most unfashionably dressed in a suit of unrelieved black," Meg heard her say between mouthfuls of stuff Dick called Dutch blumange. "Although I must confess it became him most admirably, what with that raven black hair of his. His chaise is black, too. Everyone is talking about it and his matched set of four, all perfectly white. He is making a sensation everywhere he goes. And you say you have not seen them, Mr. Sutton?" she asked, reaching for a rice cake upon which she spread a liberal amount of thick, creamy butter. "Why, I believe every woman in Charles Town has fallen in love with Glenmorgan. He exudes such an irresistible aura of mystery and danger. I am surprised I do not see him here tonight. It is, after all, his mother's house. But then, I did hear something about bad feelings between you. Naturally I discounted it, knowing how you all stood up for him during his unfortunate fall from grace. Of course that is all past history now. I understand the King himself offered him a knighthood for his heroic endeavors against those dreadful pirates. Certainly Mrs. Tharp finds nothing to discredit him in *her* eyes. Quite the contrary, she has been seen with him on any number of occasions. I wonder that her husband does not object to so marked attention from the gallant captain."

"I'm afraid I couldn't comment on that, Mrs. Gladden," Thomas replied stiffly.

Under cover of the table, Dick squeezed Meg's hand. "Never you mind what the gabblemongers say," he growled beneath his breath. "The captain's up to something, I know it. I only wish I could be sure what."

Meg ducked her head to hide the sudden shimmer in her eyes. Dear, faithful Dick. He was still loyal in spite of everything. She wished she could be as sure as he, but the truth was, she didn't know what to think or feel. During the day, she played the part of a human girl and was overcome with doubts. At night she returned to the sea and knew only loneliness and a terrible yearning nothing could assuage. Day *and* night, she was tormented with worry. In her heart she knew Glenmorgan was courting danger.

She lifted troubled eyes to Chapin's. "It is my fault that you and he have argued. It was because of something I said. I was hurt and angry. I didn't mean it the way he—"

"I know." He grinned wryly. "Believe me, I *know.* And so will he one of these days. If I know Michael, he's decided you'll be better off without him—you and Kate and everyone else who's ever meant anything to him. But don't you give up on him. Not yet. I've got the feeling he's going to need all his friends."

Meg felt her heart grow sick with fear. Her lips parted

to ask Chapin what he meant, but Mary Glenmorgan had risen to signal dinner was at an end. Chapin smiled crookedly and patted Meg's hand.

"Now don't you worry," he said, sorry he had said as much as he had. "The captain can take care of himself. This is your night. Don't let anything I've said spoil it for you."

Meg glanced helplessly back at Chapin as Kate came to lead her away.

"What has he been saying to you?" Kate demanded on the way upstairs to freshen up before the other guests arrived. "You look pale as death. He's told you something about Michael, hasn't he?"

"No, not much." Meg faltered, confused by Kate's anger. "He was only trying to be kind. It was that woman, Mrs.— Mrs. Gladden. She was talking about your brother and Clarissa. I couldn't help but overhear."

Kate's fine eyes hardened. "I should have known. I don't know why Mother insisted on having her. Amelia Gladden delights in fomenting trouble. You may be sure she meant you to hear every word." Stopping in the middle of the hall, Kate turned earnestly to Meg. "You mustn't pay her any heed. Or any of the others. You were bound to find out about Michael and Clarissa. I'm only sorry it had to be tonight. But you must not let anyone see that it means anything to you—especially Clarissa. Do you understand? You must simply act as if you could not care less what anyone says or does. If you don't, Meg, they will tear you into little pieces."

Meg gasped. "Who? Who will do such a thing?"

"Those who feed on the misery of others," Kate answered grimly. "Not everyone is like that, but there are those who, in spite of their fine manners and smiling faces, would like nothing better than to see you fall flat on your face—or anyone else connected to this family. Believe me, I have seen it all before."

"It is what they did to you when your father lost everything and your brother was forced into piracy," Meg said, reading the remembered hurt in the other girl's eyes.

Kate smiled mirthlessly. "It is what they tried to do, but our real friends stood beside us. We kept our heads up, and so must you." Suddenly she gripped Meg's hands hard. "I wish Michael had come tonight. Damn him! How very like him to leave us all in the lurch just when we need him the most. I'm so sorry he's let you down, Meg. No matter what happened between you, he should have been here. He owes you that much at least."

"No, you are wrong. He owes me nothing, and he has not let me down." Meg shook her head sadly. "You mustn't be angry with him for some imagined hurt you think he has done to me. I couldn't bear it if you did. He has done nothing to be ashamed of. You, better than anyone, must know how much he loves his family—what he would do to protect any one of us if he thought we were in danger."

"Oh, yes," Kate rejoined bitterly. "Michael would risk his life for us. It's what he does best. Never mind that we should much rather have him home with us—alive and well." Kate, seeing the distress on the other girl's face, instantly relented. "Oh, never mind all that for now. Hear that? It's the musicians tuning up for the dance. This is your coming-out party. And whether Michael is here or not, you're going to be a grand success, I promise you."

Meg was not so sure, especially when, fifteen minutes later, she found herself at the top of the stairs looking down on the crowded ballroom.

She was all alone. Insisting that she would only ruin Meg's grand entrance, Kate had already gone down. Meg could see her now beside Chapin, both of them smiling their encouragement up at her. Soon everyone would be staring at her, waiting for her to trip on her dress, maybe even hoping to see her fall ignominiously down the stairs. She would rather descend into shark-infested waters than place herself at the mercy of these landsmen who would tear her into shreds if they sensed the least sign of weakness in her. This was not at all as she had imagined it would be in those distant days when she had lain, dreaming, on the beach, of the world beyond her little island. Indeed, nothing was.

At the last moment, her courage failed her, and she wanted nothing more than to be as far away from the sounds of music and gaiety as possible.

She froze, her heart pounding, as she sensed a tall figure loom suddenly at her side. She felt her heart stand still for a single, breathless moment, and vaguely, she was aware that a hush had fallen over the ballroom below. Then she looked up into Glenmorgan's blue, piercing eyes.

"I thought you had forgotten your promise," she murmured, her face grave. "I thought you would not be here tonight."

Silently Glenmorgan studied her. She was even more beautiful than he could possibly have imagined. He detected Mary Glenmorgan's influence in the simplicity of the hairstyle and in the gown, unadorned by an excess of ribbons and bows. The lack of jewelry, too, was a wise choice. Meg would appear to be what she was—one of nature's perfections, a creature of beauty and innocence.

Holding her eyes with his, he offered her his arm.

"You were wrong," he said. "I would never break a promise to you."

He led her in the minuet that Kate and Mary had taken such pains to teach her. She did not miss a step even though she was hardly aware the whole time of anything but the tall figure of the man leading her through the intricate motions of the dance.

366

How different he looked with his hair tied back at the nape of his neck with a ribband—colder somehow, harder, and yet so handsome, she thought her heart must break just looking at him. Dressed all in black, except for the snowy white of his shirt and cravat, he was a stranger to her. Only his eyes were as she remembered them, she thought with a shiver. Eyes of blue fire that had always had the power to hold her spellbound.

They did that night, too, until the music stopped and Glenmorgan stood motionless, holding her hands in his.

"My mother and my sisters are to be congratulated," he murmured. "You *are* beautiful. The most beautiful woman ever to grace Charles Town." He smiled mirthlessly. "But it will be the old Meg, barefooted and untamed as a sea-sprite, who will haunt my dreams at night."

"What are you saying?" Meg gasped, alarmed by the note of finality in his words. Her face pale, she moved toward him.

Glenmorgan stopped her. "It's no use," he said. "Go home, Meg. Back to the West Indies. There's nothing for you here."

Meg opened her mouth to protest, to somehow bring him to his senses. Then surrounded by clamoring admirers, eager to make the acquaintance of the new young belle of Charles Town, he released her and walked away.

The rest of the night was a blur to her. Glenmorgan, merely by making an appearance at her coming out, had ensured her instant success, just as he had meant to do. Why? she wondered bitterly, when he so obviously wanted her out of his life. He might as well have taken a knife and plunged it through her heart.

Not even her grandfather could persuade her otherwise when, later that night, she fell on her knees before his chair and laid her head in his lap.

"It is over," she whispered. "I was a fool to think I could

make a difference. He has gone back to Clarissa. And now it is time that I went back to the sea, where I belong."

"Not yet, child. It's too soon to give up." Grasping her hands in his calloused palms, he forced her to look up at him. "Trust me, Meg. Have faith. He will have need of you yet, I promise you."

Meg, yearning for the solitude of her island, took refuge in long walks along the riverbank with Kate or sometimes Chapin. At night she sought solace in the sea. But nothing eased her aching torment of doubt. Glenmorgan was lost to her, and nothing would bring him back again.

"I don't understand you, Meg," Kate declared one afternoon, flinging up her hands in exasperation. "Michael made his appearance at your coming-out party. He danced the opening minuet with you. For heaven's sake, he made certain no door in Charles Town would be closed to you. And what do you do but hide yourself here, at Cherry Orchard. Why, Meg? It has been a whole week since the party. What are you afraid of?"

Meg turned away from the window through which she had been staring out at the steady drizzle of rain. How could she explain to Kate that the night of the party Glenmorgan had finally convinced her that she had no part in his life?

"I'm not afraid," she said. Crossing to the sofa in front of the fireplace, she flung herself down on it. "I simply cannot seem to find the desire to go out."

Kate studied the other girl for a long moment before plopping down on the cushion next to her.

"It's because of Clarissa, isn't it?" It was a statement, not a question. "You're afraid you'll see them together. And well you might. He's making a fool of himself over her all over again. And the really dreadful thing is that you could put a stop to it if you wanted to."

"Could I?" Meg smiled gravely. "I'm afraid you don't understand his obsession. Clarissa nearly killed him, and it hasn't stopped him. Nothing will. My greatest fear is that she will try again, and this time she will not fail." As if she suddenly could not bear to remain still, Meg got up again and crossed fitfully to the fireplace. "If only there were some way I could find out what he is doing," she fretted, more to herself than to Kate. Whatever it was, it was dangerous, and he would not thank her for meddling where she was not wanted, but not knowing was driving her mad with worry.

"Well, you may be sure of one thing," Kate said, interrupting Meg's train of thought. "You will never find out anything cooped up in this house. If you really want to know what is going on, you must get out and mingle with other people. Come with us to the theater tonight. Mama has her own box. Heaven knows, you might even find you enjoy Shakespeare."

Meg smiled whimsically. "I already know how I feel about Shakespeare. He captured my heart and my mind long ago," she confessed, tempted in spite of herself. "Grandfather made sure of that."

"Then it is settled. Dick will call for you in the carriage at seven. Oh, don't look at me that way," Kate grimaced at Meg's quizzical expression. "It was all Mama's doing. I should have preferred to go unescorted, but she wouldn't hear of it."

Meg frowned in perplexity. "Surely you are too hard on Dick," she ventured, wondering what Chapin could have done to turn Kate so thoroughly against him. "You must know that he cares deeply for you, Kate. Even I can see how greatly he suffers at your coldness."

"Can you?" Kate countered with an indifferent shrug of the shoulder. "I, on the other hand, cannot see it at all. Wear your new robe battante," she suggested without pause, ef-

369

fectively dismissing the subject of Dick Chapin from further discussion. "Emma will know which gown it is. And have Emma put your hair up. Nothing frilly. Simply have her pull it back from your face." Slipping on her cloak, she pulled the hood up over her dark curls. "Remember—the carriage at seven," she admonished, reaching for the door handle. "Don't disappoint me."

Meg hardly noticed Chapin's dumbfounded expression as she descended the stairs that evening, breathtaking in shimmering blue silk, the gemstone about her neck, and her hair, dressed plainly, pulled back from the forehead and caught up in loose curls at the crown. Eager for information, she hurried him to the carriage.

"Tell me about Glenmorgan," she said almost before he had time to settle his weight on the seat beside her. "Have you seen him? Have you talked to him?"

"Aye," Chapin rumbled, "I've seen him. Hobnobbing with the sort that'd look better hanging from the yardarms by the neck. Which is where *he'll* end up if he doesn't watch it. It's like he doesn't give a damn anymore what anybody thinks." Especially the way he was carrying on with Clarissa, Chapin thought gloomily. He was flaunting the affair in public, flinging it in Tharp's face. If it was a duel he wanted, it could not be long in coming.

"Who did you see him with?" Meg asked, her hands clinging to Chapin's arm. "Was it the Frenchman? The man with only one arm?"

Chapin looked suddenly grim. "How do you know about *him?*"

Meg gave an impatient gesture. "Never mind how I know, just tell me."

"He *could* be the one Glenmorgan's angling for," Chapin admitted reluctantly. Michael had not mentioned the Frenchman after seeing the British admiral on Antigua. But then, he had confided damned little in his first mate. "I haven't seen Freneaux around, but then, you never do. The Cherokees call him Fire-Claw because he strikes out of nowhere with the suddenness of lightning."

"Cherokees?" Meg asked.

"An Indian tribe friendly to the British, when they're not fighting the colonists hereabouts. So far they've been useful against the French in King George's blasted war, and Freneaux would like nothing better than to stir up trouble among them. A few years ago he tried the same thing with the Chickasaws, another friendly tribe to the west of us. He helped incite a band of Shawnees to attack the Chickasaws south of the Tennessee River. The Chickasaws proved a mite tougher than he expected. They beat off the French and the Shawnees. And now it's rumored he's here, bent on starting a war between the Creeks and Cherokees. His mother was Huron, and he's got no use for the British. If Michael's after him . . ."

Seeing the look on Meg's face, Chapin broke off what he was going to say.

Meg did not seem to notice. She had not understood a word he had said about French Indians and British allies. She understood one thing only—that Glenmorgan was involved in something far more dangerous than simple revenge.

Gripped with fear, she turned her head to stare blindly out the carriage window.

Curse him! she thought, the tall Georgian houses with their columned piazzas and vine-covered balustrades blurred in her vision from more than the rain. He had made it plain that she had no part in his world, that indeed, she never would. And now her heart was breaking, not only from the curse, she knew, but from the impossible love she bore the man who seemed bent on his own self-destruction.

She was in truth dying for Glenmorgan, slowly, bit by bit, and soon there would be nothing left of her.

The realization filled her with a sudden, terrible anger. Her spirit rebelled at the prospect of so ignoble an end. She was the last of her mother's line, a creature of magic and rare gifts of power. If die she must, she would do it fighting to help her chosen life-mate whether he wanted it or not.

The Meg who stepped regally down from the coach before the Dock Street Theater was a far cry from the tormented girl who had climbed into it at Cherry Orchard. Even Dick, lost in his own misery occasioned by Kate's disaffection and Glenmorgan's worrisome behavior, was struck by the change in her. She might have been accustomed all her life to finding herself the cynosure of attention. A faint, cool smile on her lips, she casually inclined her head to Charles Town's fashionable elite, who instinctively parted to let her pass. Mary Glenmorgan or the queen herself could not have pulled it off better, he thought.

More than a few of the gallery craned their necks in order to see what was creating such a stir in the boxes above them. Meg, however, who greeted Thomas Sutton and the Glenmorgan ladies with genuine affection, appeared oblivious to the number of monocles and opera glasses being trained on her. Nor did she notice, as she drew back her hood to reveal her hair, shimmering silvery in the subdued glow of candlelight, the fixed regard of a slender, solitary figure in the box directly across from her. Chapin, however, slipping the cloak off her shoulders, noticed it, as did Thomas; and neither of them liked it.

Meg, sitting between Kate and Chapin, exerted herself to contribute to the flow of conversation around her. To all appearances, she seemed to be enjoying herself, but Kate was not fooled. More than once she caught Meg's glance straying to the boxes across the way.

At last Kate was moved to lean toward her. "You may relax," she whispered. "He isn't here tonight, and neither is Clarissa. However, Logan Tharp is, and apparently you've made quite an impression. He's hardly taken his eyes off you since you arrived."

Meg felt her stomach clench sickeningly at the thought of Tharp's black soulless eyes on her, though outwardly she remained composed. Waving the feather fan before her face in imitation of Kate, she whispered back, "Where? I don't see him."

"That's hardly surprising. He's seated back, away from the light, in the box across from us."

Meg, stealing a look, could just make out an indistinct form partially concealed in shadow. Unwittingly her breath caught as deliberately he leaned forward, letting the light play on his pale, handsome features. In the instant before the houselights were doused, signaling the curtain was about to go up, she looked into his eyes and felt cold fingers of fear touch her heart.

Clarissa, Glenmorgan observed upon entering her private sitting room, appeared something less than pleased about something. Not only was her maid in tears as she went about sweeping up the shattered remains of a perfume bottle that had been recently smashed against one wall, but the lady returned his embrace with a noticeable lack of fervor, almost an impatience, which was not at all in keeping with what he had come to expect from her.

"Is something wrong?" he murmured against her hair. "You seem upset."

"It's nothing. Only a trifle of a headache." She pulled away and moved fitfully to the grog tray, started to pour a

373

brandy, then changing her mind, set the decanter down. "You are late," she said, crossing to the fireplace.

"I was unavoidably detained. A previous engagement I could not break." He watched her as she roamed here and there about the room, straightening a picture on the wall, fingering a glass vase on a side table, rearranging a small grouping of figurines on the mantlepiece. His glance rested briefly on a purse, obviously empty and lying on the back of the settee, where it appeared to have been flung. "There is still a quarter of an hour before the concert," he pointed out. "Plenty of time if we leave now."

She paused in her nervous perambulations and shook her head. "I really don't feel much like going out tonight. I know the symptoms. I'm afraid I shall only get worse before I am better."

"Are you sure?" Glenmorgan studied her from beneath drooping eyelids. The crease between her delicately arched eyebrows might indeed indicate a headache, but he had the distinct impression that something else was bothering her. "You were looking forward to the Mozart. Perhaps you could take something."

"No! It's no use, I tell you." She stopped, her hand going to her forehead. "Forgive me. It's just that I—I have had a trying day. My father and Logan between them seem determined to drive me to my bed. I simply cannot face the prospect of having to smile and be charming tonight."

Glenmorgan crossed to her, his hands framing her face. "Then of course I shouldn't dream of asking you to," he said softly. With his fingertips he massaged her temples in slow, sensuous circles until a long, shuddering sigh breathed through her lips and her eyes drifted closed.

"Yes, that's better," Glenmorgan murmured. "You have been doing too much. You should rest. Shall I call your maid to you?"

"No. She's a fool. She would only annoy me." A low

moan sounded deep in her throat as his fingers found and began to massage the taut muscles at the back of her neck. "You have no idea what I have been through with Logan. And now my father. *Damn* him! The old fool is at some gambling hall this very moment, plunging us deeper into debt. I could almost wish him dead for all the trouble he has caused me." She stiffened beneath Glenmorgan's touch, realizing, no doubt, that she was being rather too confiding in the captain. "But enough of my problems." She laughed a trifle shrilly and started to pull away. "I'm keeping you from the concert. You'll miss the overture."

Glenmorgan pulled her firmly back again. "Don't talk," he said, noting the glazed look of pain in her eyes. The headache was real. She had, he recalled, been subject to them even when he had known her as a young girl. It might suit his purpose very well. "I've no intention of leaving just yet." A grim smile touched his lips as he felt her relax beneath the slow movement of his fingers over her neck and shoulders. She did not offer so much as a protest when he began to undo the fastenings at the back of her bodice or, later, when he laid her down on the bed, the bedcovers flung back so that her naked body shone palely in the dim light of a single lamp. A shuddering sigh breathed through her lips as he settled beside her, his hands moving over her soft skin, caressing the silken smoothness of her back, the feminine curve of her waist and hips, the rounded firmness of her buttocks.

Glenmorgan leaned his elbow on the mantlepiece and stared into the fire on the stone grate. He thought of the woman lying asleep in the other room. It was past midnight. He had been closeted with her for five hours. Time enough for the servants to wonder, for the seeds of rumor to be planted. It did not matter that nothing had happened save

375

that he had soothed the tension from her body until she had at last given in to sleep. It was enough that he had been with her, here, behind closed doors. Tongues would wag, and imaginations would do the rest. Tharp would know he had been with her, and so would the rest of Charles Town. So would Meg!

His fingers clenched on the glass in his hand as he saw in the leap of flames the sweet face that never ceased to haunt him. Bloody hell! It was what he wanted, wasn't it? Tharp would have to fight him now. Dragging his eyes away, he drained the brandy from the glass.

There was a rustle behind him, and the cloying scent of jasmine filled his nostrils. He turned to see Clarissa standing in the doorway to the bedroom, a satin sheet wrapped about her nakedness.

"You're awake," he said. "Is the headache back? I thought you would sleep till morning."

Her amber eyes studied him with a sort of baffled wonder.

"No, I—I feel better than I have for weeks. Thanks to you." She crossed to him. Her small white hand moved possessively over the muscled hardness of his chest beneath his shirt, open to the waist. "I'm glad you're still here," she murmured, pressing the soft fullness of her woman's body against him. "I can show you how grateful I am." She ran the tip of her finger lightly over the outer rim of his ear. "Until tonight, I was beginning to suspect that you were only using me to get at Logan."

"Were you?" He laughed mirthlessly. "And now you've changed your mind, is that it?"

"Yes. Oh, yes, Michael. Now I can tell you that I've been waiting for you, waiting an eternity. I want to make love to you. Now, my darling. Tonight."

Glenmorgan smiled coldly.

"What you would grant me has nothing to do with love. To call it that, Clarissa, *would* be an obscenity."

"How *dare* you!" Glenmorgan's fingers clamped about her wrist before she could slap his face. She gasped in pain.

"I dare," he said, sickened by this night's work, "because I know the difference."

Releasing her, he shrugged into his coat. "The game draws to an end, Clarissa. You've served your purpose. When Tharp learns what has passed this night—and he will, won't he, Clarissa, you'll make sure of that—he'll have no choice but to call me out. As for you, you'll be wise to leave Charles Town—now—before it is too late."

Clarissa stared at him, her eyes hard and opaque with sudden, dawning comprehension. "You set me up! All these weeks. You never cared anything about me. *Damn* you! If all you wanted was a duel with Logan, you hardly needed to go to so much trouble."

Glenmorgan's eyes flashed cynically.

"No, not just a duel. But payment for what you took from my mother and sisters. I think you will find your welcome has run out in Charles Town, just as it once did for them. At least you have your life, which is more than I can say for my father." Ignoring her gasp of outrage, he strode quickly from the room. He did not look back, even when the brandy decanter crashed against the door he closed behind him and Clarissa shrieked, "I hope Logan kills you! Do you hear? I hope he kills you!"

He paused at the outer door to receive his hat and cloak from the butler, to whom he remarked that Mrs. Tharp was not feeling well. "Is Mr. Tharp or Mr. Thornton expected in this evening?"

"Mr. Thornton has gone out for the evening, suh. And Mr. Tharp—I believe he was to attend the theatre. Howsoever, I'm sure Mrs. Tharp will be properly looked after."

Giving a nod, Glenmorgan stepped out onto the stoop,

where he drew in a long, cleansing breath. He was free of Clarissa, once and for all. To his surprise, he felt little satisfaction in what he had done. It was more like finding an oppressive burden had been lifted off him. Briefly he let himself conjure up an image of Meg. Then smiling cynically at himself, he descended the steps and set out at a brisk walk for Dock Street and the Blue Dolphin.

Giles Thornton mopped the sweat from his face with a square of white linen before reaching for the stack of gold coins at his elbow, the stack that had been growing steadily smaller with each passing hour of play. Clarissa would be furious with him for having come to the Blue Dolphin tonight, he thought dourly, and more furious still when she found out the extent of his losses. His mouth felt suddenly and inordinately dry. Damn all females, he mused ill-humoredly. They were a curse on a man's existence. He reached for the shot glass of whiskey by his hand and tossed it down at a single gulp. Impatiently he snapped his fingers at the Negro waiter to bring him another.

Through an alcohol-induced haze, he heard his name. "Eh? Whaz 'at?" With an effort he focused his eyes on the figure across from him. Recognition, like icewater tossed in his face, momentarily sobered him. "Glenmorgan. Bloody hell. What're you doing here?"

"It's fairly obvious, isn't it?" came the reply, couched in accents of boredom. "I'm dealing faro."

"Hellsfire!" sputtered Thornton, his face reddening. "I can bloody well see that. What's happened to . . ." He stopped himself just in time. He had been about to demand what had happened to Clarissa. It would hardly do to acknowledge publicly that his daughter was supposed to be entertaining Glenmorgan that evening. Quickly he covered. "What's happened to whassisname—Ashton?"

Glenmorgan eyed Thornton with a steely glint of amusement, which left little doubt he knew exactly what Thornton had been about to blurt. "Ashton," he said, "has retired for the night. I'm sitting in for him."

"The devil you say." Thornton swallowed dryly. In spite of his advanced state of inebriation, he sensed a warning alarm go off inside his head. Something was not right. The Blue Dolphin catered to the rich landowners and merchants. Fortunes exchanged hands on these premises, and the house had to be prepared to cover all bets. Why would Ashton entrust the bank to an outsider? "Would you have me believe the bloody fool went off to bed, leaving you with the bank? This isn't baccarat, it's faro. The bank stays with the house dealer."

Glenmorgan's thin-lipped smile did little to ease Thornton's sudden premonition of impending disaster. "You're right, of course. However, since I own the house, the bank is obviously mine. I thought you knew: Ashton works for me."

Thornton had the feeling the walls were closing in on him as he absorbed this information and its ramifications. He had signed numerous bills of credit over to Ashton. Vaguely he realized he owed a substantial sum to the gambling establishment. Good God—owed Glenmorgan! The last of the gold he had stolen from Clarissa's wall safe would not have begun to pay for it. And now even that was almost gone.

"The bets are laid," observed one of the gamesters, a Goose-Creek man and a cousin to the governor. "Are you in, sir, or not?" he demanded of Thornton.

"Well, Thornton?" murmured Glenmorgan with a slight mocking edge to his voice. His cold eyes flicked to Thornton's dwindling pile of coins. "I understood you were a gambler. Surely you don't intend to quit now?"

Thornton dabbed again at his face and neck with the

square of linen. It was true. He was a gambler to the core. Still, he was not such a fool that he didn't realize his luck was out, had been ever since he had come back to this accursed town. He knew he should call it a night, knew as well that Glenmorgan was deliberately prodding him to stay. He hated Glenmorgan with something akin, in his shallow nature, to a passion, just as he had hated Glenmorgan's father. There was nothing he would not have given to turn the tables on the cursed captain. With just a few winning turns of the card, he could have enough to buy back his bills of promise. With a whole string of them, he could even break the bank. He had seen it happen before, to a few lucky bastards. It might happen to him with the very next turn of the card—the beginning of a run of luck, like a vein of gold, that every gambler dreamed of.

"A hundred on the deuce," he announced, slamming the coins down on the two of spades pictured on the velvet layout.

Thornton did not see the faint, sardonic curve of Glenmorgan's lips. His eyes were on Glenmorgan's slender fingers. In dread fascination he watched them slide the top card, a four of diamonds, from the shoe and discard it. He felt queasy with relief as the next card stood revealed, a jack of clubs.

"Damn the luck," muttered one of the players, echoing the sentiments of the four gentlemen who, like him, had bet on the jack.

Thornton leaned back in his chair. The worst was over. If he had not won, at least he had not lost.

But he had won, he discovered, as Glenmorgan, discarding the jack, uncovered the two of hearts.

Richer by two hundred pounds, Thornton expanded. Ordering a round of drinks to celebrate his change of luck, he laid his bet on the four. A five of clubs and a queen of spades left him neither poorer nor richer than before, and emboldened, he next ventured a hundred on the ten. He won. Doubling the bet, he chose the trey and won again.

Convinced his luck had changed for the better, Thornton increased the amounts of his wagers. The pattern remained constant: he either won or he didn't, but he did not lose—for a time, at least. It was well into the wee hours of morning when it gradually bore in on him that not only was he practically the only one left in the house, but his stack of coins was once more growing steadily smaller. Desperate to make up the difference and convinced that he had suffered only a temporary setback, he plunged deeper, betting recklessly, until at last he was reduced to a paltry two or three hundred. He was sweating profusely, and he no longer experienced the exhilarating effects of the alcohol he had been steadily consuming. He felt numb with the realization that he was staring ruin in the face.

He put everything on the seven, a card which had won for him more often than not.

The first discard immediately quashed all hopes of a turnabout. In dazed disbelief, he stared at the seven of clubs, followed by the winning nine of spades.

Bitter with hatred, he watched Glenmorgan rake in the winnings. The bank was richer by two thousand pounds of Thornton's money—Good God—Clarissa's money! He quelled the insane urge to giggle.

Dully, he shoved back his chair and lurched unsteadily to his feet. He was finished. Clarissa had long ago closed her pursestrings to him, and Tharp would be only faintly amused to learn his former partner was ruined. Tharp no longer needed Thornton. No, there would be no help from that quarter.

"Before you go," murmured Glenmorgan, watching Thornton from beneath drooping eyelids, "there is the matter of some bills of promise you owe me. I have taken the liberty of adding them up."

Thornton stared at the sum written in a bold hand on a slip of paper. Good God, he had not dreamed it could possibly be so large. It was more than a fortune. It was a bloody king's ransom!

"I don't carry that much on me," he said, feeling his cravat, stifling, around his neck. "I'll need a few days."

"Naturally." Glenmorgan's lips curled faintly. "Or perhaps you would care to play again for higher stakes." Thornton stared at the slender packet of letters Glenmorgan laid on the table. He knew with awful certainty that they were Freneaux's. In a daze he heard Glenmorgan say, "Win, and you will have these and the bills of promise. Lose, however, and I have your signature on this."

Thornton's hand trembled as he picked up the sheet of paper covered with writing that Glenmorgan laid on the table. He had to read the opening lines twice before he understood the full significance of what he held in his hand.

"Good God." His knees gave way beneath him, and he dropped heavily into a chair. "I *can't* sign this. You might as well put a gun to my head."

As through a haze he saw the cold glitter of Glenmorgan's eyes. "Now you begin to understand," Glenmorgan murmured softly.

Glenmorgan let the words hang in the air like an epitaph. "Of course, there is always the possibility that you won't have to do either. You could win." Thornton winced at the hard edge of steel in Glenmorgan's voice. "Either way, it's more of a chance than you gave my father."

"Bloody hell, it wasn't me," Thornton blustered. "I didn't kill Turlough. I couldn't. I don't have the nerve for killing." The flesh quivered on his face as Glenmorgan's eyes stared dispassionately back at him.

"It's your bet, Thornton," Glenmorgan said. "I'm waiting."

Moments later, Thornton stared with a sense of inevitability at the cursed queen of hearts peering up at him. He choked on a rising wave of laughter. It was over. Even if he'd had the money to flee the country, he could not have run far enough or fast enough. Freneaux would find him— Freneaux, whose reputation for cold-blooded savagery filled his heart with terror.

Thornton shook with a mindless sort of laughter. At least he would not go down alone.

Taking the quill from the waiting servant, he dragged the paper toward him.

It was strange to think that he was signing his death warrant. Indeed, he felt oddly buoyant when it was done. Laying the quill with careful deliberation on the table, Thornton leaned back in his chair.

"And now," he said, "the final turn of the card."

Glenmorgan acted reflexively. Seeing the gun in Thornton's hand, he threw himself to one side out of the chair just as a blinding flash, followed by the deafening crack of a shot, filled the room. He landed hard on his shoulder and rolled. His hand drew the pearl-handled pistol from his boot. The next instant he fired.

Glenmorgan stared down at Thornton's body, slumped lifelessly in the chair, and felt nothing. Faced with the realization of his own ruin and the utter certainty of Freneaux's brand of retribution, Thornton had chosen the only way out left to him. Glenmorgan had been the instrument of death, but Thornton had brought it all on himself.

Leaning over, Glenmorgan pulled Thornton's signed confession from beneath the dead man's arm. It would ruin Tharp in Charles Town and clear Turlough Glenmorgan's name once and for all. It would even give the admiralty what they needed to disrupt Freneaux's line of supplies. But it would not give them Freneaux himself.

It wasn't finished—not by a long shot. It never would be if Freneaux walked free. And so far Freneaux had proven as elusive as a trail of mist.

Bloody hell, he was through waiting for the Frenchman to nibble at the bait. If Freneaux would not come to him, then he would go where Freneaux would be sure to show himself.

Twenty-one

With the "gay season" in full swing, Meg found herself being invited to a dizzying round of balls, soirees, and other entertainments, the culmination of which was to be the much-talked-about Race Week.

Practically everyone came in from the outlying farms to participate in Race Week. It was then the rice crop was sold and business matters dispatched. But when that was done, there was plenty of time for socializing. The horses and jockeys were looked over and their chances of winning discussed. Wagers were laid, and past races reminisced. And everyone mingled, exchanging the latest news and gossip. Aside from the races, there would be dinners and dances and, most importantly, Kate informed her, the Jockey Club Ball.

Meg, listening to Kate talk, was filled with conflicting emotions about the great event. She was both surprised and gratified that she had attracted enough attention for Kate to predict that she would be the belle of the ball. And indeed, in spite of Kate's warnings and Glenmorgan's fears for her safety, she had found that she liked and enjoyed the people she met. The men, young and old alike, flattered her with their attentions and endeared themselves to her with their gallantry and acts of generosity. With them, she could laugh and enjoy the lighthearted banter that seemed the accepted behavior between male and female. It was different with the women. With them, she was never quite sure where she stood. Not that she was not treated with kindness and overt offers of friendship. She was. But beneath it all, Meg sensed an aloofness and occasionally even a certain amount of hostility. It was not until the rumor began to circulate that her heart had been pledged long before she arrived at Charles Town that the ice began to thaw. She was not to know that Kate had deliberately fostered the rumor. She knew only that women who had previously regarded her with something akin to suspicion now tolerated her presence among them.

On the other hand, Meg knew all too well that she was in reality an outsider who could never really be a part of the society in which she found herself. She simply could not feel the same enthusiasm for Race Week that Kate did. Far from it. The prospect of finding herself among so many people was more than a little daunting. If anything, it only intensified her sense of being isolated and different from everyone else. How strange that she could feel lonely in a crowded ballroom! And yet she did. The truth was, she was lonelier than she had ever been before; and worse, more and more, she felt cut adrift from her true self and from everything that had previously given her life meaning.

But then, Glenmorgan had been her one real link with this teeming, bewildering world of landsmen, and her sole motivating force for being there. And now Glenmorgan was gone.

Everything seemed suddenly to be happening so fast. Thornton was dead. Clarissa had left Charles Town some days before without leaving any word where she was going. And Glenmorgan had mysteriously sailed aboard the *Raven*. Not even Chapin knew where. And as if that were not enough to occupy her thoughts, Logan Tharp, apparently

386

unmoved by his wife's disappearance, had begun to show a marked interest in Meg.

Meg shivered, just thinking about it. Not that he had been so bold as to leave his card at the Glenmorgan Town House the way so many other of her new admirers had done. He hadn't. Nor had he sent her any invitations, implored her to dance with him, or done any of the other things she had grown to expect from the young men who tried to court her. He was much more subtle than that. Wherever she went, whether it was a dinner, dancing, or the theatre, Tharp was there more often than not, watching her. Though he invariably acknowledged her with a languid nod of the head, he had never made any attempt to openly accost her—until today.

They had come to Mrs. Gladden's to a music recital and had been listening for some time to their hostess's niece and a few other marriageable young ladies of the town sing to the accompaniment of the pianoforte or harp. Meg, feeling the need for some air, had stolen out onto the balcony.

For a moment she let her guard down as she lifted her face to the breeze flowing inland from the sea. Silently she sent her thoughts outward to Glenmorgan, willing him to return with the evening tide. Consequently, Tharp was almost upon her before she heard the sound of a light step behind her and turned.

"Ah, a pity," he murmured with an almost convincing regret. "I had no wish to disturb you. I should, in fact, like to paint you as you were, the wind in your hair and your whole being expressive of some indefinable yearning. You intrigue me, Miss Pippin. I cannot but wonder what you were thinking before I intruded."

"My thoughts, sir, are my own," she replied, "and shall remain so. And now perhaps you will excuse me."

"No. Stay." Tharp stepped in front of her as she started

387

to move past him. "I think you enjoy the entertainment as little as do I. Do you sing, Miss Pippin?"

Meg went cold as she felt his eyes on her, deriving some obverse pleasure from the rapid rise and fall of her breasts. "When I am alone and there is no one else to hear. But I am not alone here, Mr. Tharp," she pointedly observed.

He smiled quizzically. "Can you truly think I mean you harm?" His hand reached up as though to touch her.

Meg lifted her head. "Do you not, sir?" she demanded, a warning light in her eyes.

As though snatching back an impulse, Tharp closed his fingers lightly in a fist. "No, Miss Pippin. I do not. I believe you are something rare and exquisite, a treasure beyond price any man might give his soul to possess." Deliberately he let his hand drop to his side. "You see, *I* have heard you sing."

She knew at once that it must have been on that fateful morning on Antigua a seeming lifetime ago, when she had summoned the storm to save Glenmorgan from him. A warning sounded within her. He *knew*.

"I am neither a treasure nor something to be possessed, Mr. Tharp," she replied coldly, every inch of her scintillating with a fearless pride. "And whatever you think you may have heard or seen, I promise you know nothing about me."

A hard gleam of admiration leaped in Tharp's eyes.

"Perhaps not, Miss Pippin," he said. "But I shall. You may depend on it."

Kate, coming out to look for her, provided the excuse she needed to escape. Meg could feel Tharp's eyes on her back as she murmured to Kate that she was not feeling well. Together they gave their excuses to Mrs. Gladden and left. Henceforth, Meg vowed as she followed Kate outside to the carriage, she would keep the gemstone about her always.

* * *

Glenmorgan crouched on the shores of Anastasia Island and stared across the still waters of the bay to the fort of San Marco. In the moonless night, its massive walls, the corners, like great arrowheads pointing outward, were little more than a dark mass blotting out the lights of Sainte Augustine behind it. Everything appeared peaceful.

He switched his gaze to the *Sea Hawk,* riding at anchor little more than a cable length from where he stood. A little after dusk, the ship's boats had crossed the sound to the Spanish town, leaving a skeleton crew on board. It should be easy enough to take her. The trick was to do it without arousing the fort.

Motioning his men to follow, he slipped noiselessly into the water.

John Drago headed back to his ship in a foul mood. He had been amused at the prospect of dropping anchor in a Spanish harbor. The bloody Spaniards had been after him for years and would have liked nothing better than to string him up and reclaim the frigate he had pirated out from under their noses. Drago would have given a great deal to see Colonel Villanueva's face when the commander of San Marco beheld the signal break from the *Sea Hawk*'s mainmast, the signal that had ensured Drago safe passage. That satisfaction and Tharp's assurance that he would be cut in on the Carolinian's profitable smuggling enterprise had been all that persuaded Drago to leave Charles Town without the prize on which he had originally set his sights. That and the fact that Moffit's miserable failure to abduct the girl had made it practical to put some distance between himself and Glenmorgan. For the time being at least.

He felt a reluctant admiration for Glenmorgan whenever he thought of their encounter on the island off Antigua. The captain's bluff had been masterfully done. Glenmorgan had

389

fooled him completely. A sardonic smile played about the thin lips. No wonder Glenmorgan had been willing to risk so much. The girl was worth a hundred times what Tharp would pay for transporting his precious guns to Sainte Augustine.

Thought of the guns brought him round full circle to the thing that had caused his ill humor. Another day had passed without the Frenchman's putting in an appearance, and while Drago was left cooling his heels in this godforsaken place, it had suddenly come to him that Tharp might have guessed what the girl was, that Tharp might this very moment be after her for himself.

Silently he cursed. He should have slit Moffit's throat long ago. Not only was the man a bumbling fool, but he was cursedly loose with his tongue as well. He might have known Moffit would spill his guts to Tharp about the girl. Now Tharp knew all about Gates and Phillip Belding, and how the purser had raved to anyone who would listen that Belding had been saved by a mermaid. Drago cursed. He had tried to laugh it off. Everyone in the West Indies knew Gates was bloody insane, he told Tharp. But Tharp's interest had been sparked. After all, mermaid or not, any female who could salvage a shipload of treasure was a curiosity worth delving into.

As the boat drew up alongside the ship, Drago was still mulling over his failure to snatch the girl for himself. Consequently he failed to note the ship's unnatural silence. He had climbed through the entry port and stepped on deck before the hairs at the nape of his neck prickled a warning.

The night watch, he thought. Where was the bloody night watch? There should have been a man at the entry port to acknowledge the captain's arrival on board.

His fingers curled around the butt of the pistol in his belt, and slowly he started to back toward the entry port.

He froze at the touch of cold steel against his spine.

"Careful, Drago," murmured a soft, familiar voice. "I suggest you do nothing to alert the boat crew. There's damned little profit in dying."

"I'm afraid, Captain," said Drago a few moments later as he sprawled carelessly in a chair in his quarters, "that I cannot tell you when Freneaux will arrive. I am beginning to wonder if he will come at all. Frankly, I find it odd that *you* are here. What the devil are a few guns to you, when you have the beautiful and accomplished Meg Pippin in Charles Town?" He paused ever so slightly. "Or were you wise enough to bring her here with you?" he queried, his eyes suddenly keen beneath heavily drooping eyelids.

"Meg is safe." Glenmorgan, standing with his booted foot propped on the edge of the window seat, turned his head to look at the pirate. "Why?" he demanded flatly.

"Oh, no particular reason." Drago toyed with the telescope that lay on the table, his fingers tracing the heavy, ornate casing. He had stolen it off a Portuguese trader. "I was just thinking, that's all. If I had a treasure as rare as the one you possess, I'd not leave it where anyone could steal it. Especially the man I hated most in the world. And especially when it's already been tried before."

Glenmorgan felt a vise close on his innards.

"I'm in no mood for games, Drago," he murmured, his voice cold-edged and steely. "What are you saying? That Tharp ordered you to kidnap Meg on the Isle of Palm?"

"On the contrary." Drago laughed. "The idea was entirely my own. I detest Logan Tharp almost as much as you do, though perhaps with less reason. Can you truly think I should choose to share a prize with him, any prize, much less one that is so utterly priceless?"

Glenmorgan was careful to keep his features schooled to reveal nothing of his startled reaction to that admission.

Drago was a man who used women and then discarded them. He did *not* value them. And he was hardly the type to become enamored of one. What about Meg, then, made her "priceless" in his eyes? "I always knew you were clever, Drago," he drawled, dropping his foot to the deck. "So you know all about Meg. I'm surprised, in the circumstances, that you let Tharp in on it."

Drago waved a careless hand. "It was Moffit—the fool. I should never have let him live after Antigua. But you have been as careless. You should have killed Tharp when you had the chance. I may save you the trouble yet. Any profit in helping Freneaux to start a war between the Chickasaws and the Cherokees is negligible compared to what your precious Meg could bring me. The possibilities, after all, are practically limitless. Not only can she fetch riches from the depths of the sea, but she could sink whole navies or disable whole fleets of traders. She could reduce coastal towns to rubble or hold them hostage for ransom. Whoever rules her could rule the sea. But then, you must know these things as well as I. You have already seen what she is capable of doing." He leaned forward, suddenly eager. "Tell me, Glenmorgan. Are there others like her? I have heard the legends but never before seen one, never dreamed they actually existed—mermaids with the power to command the elements. I thought Gates was insane until I saw her, goading the whales to attack us."

Somehow he knew what Drago was going to say before the pirate actually voiced it aloud. Perhaps he had known it all along. He had simply refused to accept the evidence. Meg, a mermaid—it was too farfetched by half. And yet, with sudden, blinding certainty, he knew it was true. It explained everything—the air of mystery surrounding her, her ignorance of the land except for what she had gleaned from the old man's books, the coincidences of the attacking whales and the concealing storm when they had been most

392

needed, her ability to do what should have been impossible for a mere mortal. Even her steadfast refusal to marry him. It all added up. And then it hit him.

No wonder Pippin had been so protective of her. She must inevitably become an object of greed or envy, even fear and hatred, once the truth became widespread. So far Drago had guessed—and Tharp. A cold chill coursed down Glenmorgan's back. Chapin was a good man and brave, but he was no match for Tharp. Somehow Glenmorgan had to get back to her, to Charles Town, before it was too late. But Drago must not know that. Drago must be made to believe that Glenmorgan did not care what happened to her.

As if bracing himself for the inevitable, he had turned to stare blindly out the stern windows as Drago talked. Now, with a supreme effort at self-command, he quelled the turmoil of emotions seething within.

He laughed incredulously. "Good God, you're not serious?" He turned to look at Drago. "Faith, you are, aren't you? And I suppose it would be pointless to deny it. You wouldn't believe me. But the fact remains that, no matter what you believe you saw, Meg is only a girl," he lied glibly. "A remarkable one, I agree, but a human girl nonetheless. Her mother was a pearl diver who trained her daughter in the art. I myself watched her salvage the chests from the *Argonaut* and can attest that there was no magic involved. Only a great deal of courage and human fortitude. As for the whales, their kind have attacked boats before. Meg was fortunate they took no interest in her after your men chased her from her grandfather's ketch. Which brings up an interesting speculation. How does Belding fit into the scheme of things? Is he one of these mer-creatures, too?"

"Who gives a damn what he is?" Drago growled irritably. Then after a moment, he noticeably relaxed. "Oh, bravo, Glenmorgan." He laughed, leaning back once more in his chair. Still, it was enough to convince Glenmorgan that the seeds of uncertainty had at least been planted. "I see what you're trying to do. And you're right," Drago continued. "I don't believe you. And neither will Tharp. When you come right down to it, he's the only one who will profit from any of this. He's there, and we're here, fools that we are. Why? What is your bloody interest in Freneaux?"

Glenmorgan crossed to the wine cabinet and poured himself a brandy. "There were three of them—Giles Thornton, Logan Tharp, and Freneaux. Together, they ruined my father and then killed him."

"Ah," Drago murmured. "I begin to understand you, Glenmorgan. I am surprised you have let Tharp live so long, if what you say is true."

Glenmorgan shrugged. "Killing Tharp is too easy. I intend to make him suffer everything he made my father suffer. Before I'm through, I'll have stripped him of everything—his name, his honor, his fortune— even the woman he stole from me. Then, and only then, will I deprive him of his life. Thornton has paid the price. Now, it's Freneaux's turn." In a few hours either he or Freneaux would be dead, thought Glenmorgan. Suddenly in light of what he had just learned about Meg, he wondered if he had been playing a fool's game.

He looked at Drago, a hard, steady look. "If you help me get your ship and your cargo past the guns on San Marco, I'll return your ship to you—on condition that I have your word you'll head back to the West Indies when this is over."

"And if I don't?" Drago queried, with an indifferent lift of a crimson clad shoulder.

"Then I run you through, here and now, and take my chances with San Marco. I'll not leave you behind to come after me. That, you can depend on."

Their eyes locked across the distance, Glenmorgan's cold-flecked and steely, Drago's, crafty and measuring. In the end, Drago's gave way.

"If I did not find you so entertaining, Captain," he sighed, "I should be very greatly annoyed. Very well, you win—this time. But I promise there will come another."

Meg walked barefoot along the sandy bank of the river, her fingers absently toying with the gemstone on its woven chain around her neck. Her eyes were distant, unseeing, as she stared across the broad expanse of water to the low, wooded bulge of land, distant and hazy, on the other side. Her lonely retreat, on a sheltered cove along the river and secluded by woods on three sides, had become as familiar to her as the island cliffs and turquoise bay at home. Here, she came to be alone with her thoughts and the terrible longing of her heart, to gaze into the gemstone for a glimpse, no matter how brief, of a beloved face.

Like snatches of a dream, she had seen him on the rolling deck of his ship in the night, or below, poring over his charts, and then again in darkness, only this time on the shores of an island. With a cold prickle of her skin, she had sensed the danger all around him. And then Chapin had come to find her and the image had been lost to her. Nevertheless, the bond that had been forged between them a seeming eternity ago remained unbroken, so she had comforted herself with the knowledge that Glenmorgan was still alive.

As she stopped to stare blindly out over the water, a groan seemed torn from her. Tightly, she closed her fingers around the gemstone and pressed it to her breast. She did not know how she could bear it much longer. With her whole being she yearned to see Glenmorgan come striding across the lawn to her, to have him clasp her to him and crush her lips beneath his.

It was only a dream, she thought. He would not come, not for her. Her head lifted. But he *would* come for Tharp. And when he did, it would be the final confrontation, the day of reckoning for them all. It would be soon, she thought. Very soon.

"Meg!" As from a distance, she heard her name shouted and, turning, saw Kate coming toward her, her cheeks glowing from the briskness of the breeze and her walk from the cottage. "Meg, thank heavens! I've been looking everywhere for you. Emma brought me your message. Meg, dear, what is it? It sounded so urgent."

Meg let the other girl take her hands in hers. "Forgive me," she said, smiling apologetically. "I did not mean it so. It's only that I've wanted to talk to you for a very long time, and now I know I cannot put it off any longer." She paused and, freeing her hands, walked a pace before turning back to Kate. "I shall be going away soon—back where I came from. And I could not leave without—"

"Leave? But Meg, you can't! Not now. Not when you've come so far! Michael will come back to you. He will, Meg. You must believe that!"

"He won't. Indeed, he mustn't. It can never be, Kate. You must accept that, as I did from the very beginning. But it doesn't have to be that way with you and Dick. No, *listen* to me," she said as she saw Kate visibly draw away. "You love each other. I knew it the first time I saw you together. And I will not let you throw your happiness away over a misunderstanding."

"A misunderstanding?" Kate echoed, her eyes widening in disbelief. "What do you know of it?"

"Dick told me what happened. He couldn't help it. I wouldn't leave him alone until he did. He's coming here today, Kate. I told him to. Indeed, he is here now." Kate turned sharply, a gasp exploding from her lips as she saw Chapin coming along the curve of the river toward them.

Meg laid a hand lightly on Kate's arm. "Talk to him," she said softly. "Let him explain. Surely you owe him that much at least."

Then, gathering up her skirts, she turned and fled, leaving Kate to face Chapin's determined advance alone.

Kate, flinging a glance after Meg, then back to Chapin, spun on her heel and started grimly toward the gravel path that led to the cottage.

"Kate," Chapin called. He quickened his pace till he came abreast of her. "Dammit, Kate. Wait," he panted, falling into step beside her.

"We have nothing to say to each other, Dick Chapin," Kate declared, her chin in the air.

"Oh, yes we do." Halting in his tracks, Chapin caught her by the arm and spun her around to face him. "Ever since the Isle of Palm, you've treated me like I had the plague. Maybe I deserve it, but not for what you accused me of. I think it's time we cleared up a few things."

"I think you have already made yourself patently clear," Kate retorted, disdainfully jerking her arm out of his grasp. "Your interests are obviously fixed elsewhere."

"That's not true, Kate Glenmorgan." Chapin's jaw hardened ominously and he took a step toward her. "There's no one else, and you bloody well know it."

"Do I?" Warily, Kate retreated before Chapin's grimly determined advance. "Don't come any closer, Dick Chapin, I warn you. I'll—I'll scream if you come any closer."

"Then scream and be damned, Kate Glenmorgan," he growled, making a grab for her. With a squeal, Kate darted out of his reach and fled behind a palmetto tree.

Undeterred, Chapin lunged after her. His fingers snatched a fold of her gown just as his foot caught on a snag. The next instant he was hurtling forward to sprawl full length with Kate on the ground beside him.

"Kate, for God's sake," he gasped, feeling the slender body next to his begin to shake. "Tell me you're not hurt."

"You b-brute," uttered Kate in a strangled voice, her hands over her face. "You—you bully."

"Aye," he answered, a hard gleam of suspicion springing to his eyes. "And you're a heartless jade," he countered, dragging her hands down to reveal her dirt-smudged countenance convulsed in laughter. "You deserve a beating for scaring me half to death, but I'm of a mind to give you a far worse punishment. I'm going to marry you, Kate Glenmorgan. And God help me. I doubt there's another man alive who could put up with your foolery."

In answer, Kate cradled his face tenderly between her palms. "Stoopid," she murmured fondly. "It was all your fault for making me go to such lengths to win a declaration from you. I was afraid you would never get over your absurd sense of honor long enough to ask me."

"Kate," he whispered brokenly. "I never dared dream you could ever care for me. I still can't believe it."

"And I have been so frightened, all these years, that you would never come back to me." Suddenly she flung her arms around his neck. "God forgive me," she groaned. "I almost hated Michael for taking you away."

It was a good deal later before Chapin at last bestirred himself enough to suggest that Kate's mama would send out a search party to look for them if he did not soon return her daughter to her.

Kate, smiling dreamily up at him, reluctantly allowed him to pull her to her feet and dust off her rumpled gown.

"This is all Meg's doing," she reminded him, entwining her arm in his. "I think it is only right that she be the first to hear the good news."

When they reached the cottage, however, Meg was nowhere to be found. Neither Pippin nor Mrs. Clagg had seen her. Only then did Kate remember Meg's strange mood earlier, when she had found her wandering alone along the riverbank. Suddenly anxious, she related all that had passed between them before Chapin's arrival.

"There's nothing to worry about, Kate," Pippin consoled her. "Meg's around somewhere. When she comes in, I'll have a talk with her. In the meantime, give her a day or two to work out whatever is bothering her. She'll be ready to accompany you to the races day after tomorrow. Mrs. Clagg and I'll see to it."

Freneaux was smaller than Glenmorgan had expected— scarcely above average height, but powerfully built, with strong, muscular thighs and a barrel chest. The empty left sleeve of his buckskin coat was tucked into a wide leather belt about his waist, along with a long-barreled pistol and a deadly-looking hunting knife in a fringed sheath. He was somewhere in his middle forties, yet his hair was black as a Huron's, his mother's people. So were his eyes, glittering coldly in the impassive hardness of his narrow face, tanned to the color of brown leather.

True to his reputation, he had arrived unseen and unexpectedly. It was the night following the *Sea Hawk*'s capture, and not even the lookout had spied the single-man canoe slip noiselessly beneath the stern. Glenmorgan, keeping vigil with Drago in the stern cabin, had been the first to detect the shadowy figure limned against the open stern window.

"Why don't you come in?" Glenmorgan had said, coming casually to his feet. "And join us in a glass, Freneaux."

"So," grunted the Frenchman some moments later, "you are Glenmorgan. Your reputation has reached even into the backwoods, *Capitaine*."

399

"And *I* have heard of you, Freneaux," replied Glenmorgan, who had to brace his legs against the sudden rise and fall of the ship pulling against its anchor. His mind registered the fact that the wind was quickening—the wind that would take him back to Charles Town and Meg, if he was not already too late. Sternly he quelled the thought. "Thornton told me all about you."

Freneaux's dark features remained impassive, though Glenmorgan was certain he detected a brief flicker in the expressionless eyes. *"Vraiment?"* said the Frenchman. "And what has he told you, this M'sieu Thornton?"

"All about you and Tharp and Lavoillet," Glenmorgan said. "How at first it was only a matter of using my father's ships to smuggle guns past the English blockade. It was, of course, easier to supply your Indian allies that way than to wait for the chance one of your own ships might slip past the British Navy—and so much more dependable. Thornton set it up. He contacted you through Mme. Beauchamp, with whom he had once been on intimate terms. Then he brought Tharp in on it. As my father's agent in the West Indies, Tharp was in a better position to purchase the goods through the Dutch with Lavoillet as an intermediary—he picked the contraband up from a Dutch free port and transported it to a point of rendezvous where it was transferred to one of my father's ships."

Glenmorgan paused. "You'll tell me if I'm leaving anything out?" When Freneaux showed no signs of favoring him with an answer, Glenmorgan continued. "It was all very profitable for everyone concerned, until Tharp decided to expand the operation. Why not sell information as well as guns? After all, he was in a perfect position, not only to observe the British fleet in King's Harbor, but to glean information of a more pertinent nature from the officers, whom he was in the habit of entertaining on a lavish scale. Not many men can resist a woman as beautiful as the charming Clarissa. Unfortunately, my father accidentally intercepted two letters meant for Thornton, which were enough to expose Thornton for the thief and the traitor that he was." Glenmorgan let a steely note creep into his voice. "That's why you killed my father."

Freneaux's hand came to rest casually on the haft of the knife. "An interesting story," he commented. "But it does not concern me. I had no reason to kill your father. I am a soldier, not a spy. I risked nothing from exposure."

"Are you so sure?" Glenmorgan said. "What about the loss of your supply routes? Lavoillet is dead, along with his lieutenants. Drago, here, is the only one left of Tharp's confederation of smugglers and spies. Isn't that right, Drago?"

"Aye," nodded the pirate, "it's true enough. We've been a trifle depleted of late."

Freneaux shrugged contemptuously. "You English are a mercenary people. There will always be smugglers who will do anything for the profit. I suggest, *Capitaine,* that you look to the one who had the most to gain from the death of your father. There you will find his murderer. But as I said before, it does not concern me. I am here for the cargo of guns, nothing more. You have them, yes?"

"Aye," Drago affirmed.

Freneaux looked at him. "I promised Tharp ten thousand."

Glenmorgan's arm moved. Freneaux's glance rested expressionlessly on the drawn pistol in Glenmorgan's hand, then shifted to Drago.

"You have only to unload the guns at the fort," he said, "and the gold is yours."

Glenmorgan thumbed the hammer back. The metallic click sounded loud in the close confines of the cabin. "The guns stay here," he said flatly. "And you're not going anywhere, Freneaux, except to a British jail."

"I think not, *Capitaine."*

The Frenchman moved without warning. The knife blade flashed in the lamplight. Lunging to one side, Glenmorgan squeezed the trigger, as he felt the blade slice through his shirtsleeve, drawing blood. Then a leaded weight glanced off the back of his skull and struck between his shoulder-blades. His shot went wild, and he staggered, deafened by its report and blinded by an explosion of lights inside his head. He dropped to his knees. From somewhere he heard Drago's voice. "Sorry, Glenmorgan. But business is business, and I simply couldn't let ten thousand slip through my hands, now could I?"

Through a red haze, he saw the pirate standing over him, the Portuguese telescope clasped like a club in his hand. "I'll have my pistol back now," Drago said, dragging the gun from Glenmorgan's belt.

"The shot will have aroused the crew," said Freneaux, his black eyes no longer impassive but glittery with antici-pated danger. "How many men has the *capitaine* aboard your ship?"

"I saw perhaps a dozen. More than that I couldn't say," Drago answered as the unmistakable pound of feet on the deck and along the companionway carried to the men in the cabin.

"Captain!" a voice shouted down from the skylight. "Captain, are you all right?"

"Answer him," growled Drago, pressing the muzzle of the gun against Glenmorgan's temple. "Tell him it was noth-ing, an accident, d'you hear me?"

"Tell him yourself, Drago," Glenmorgan gasped, his en-tire body clenched against the throbbing pain in his head.

He heard Drago curse and braced himself for the pistol ball that would splatter his brains. Out of the corner of his eye, he saw a flash of movement, knew it was Freneaux, making for the stern window.

"Where the hell do you think you're going?" Drago

growled. Glenmorgan felt the pistol waver and, gritting his teeth against the pain, rammed his shoulder hard into Drago's side. The pirate slammed into the table. Glenmorgan rolled and kicked at Drago with both feet, knocking the legs out from under him. As the pirate crashed to the deck, Glenmorgan scrambled for the Frenchman's knife, left imbedded in the bulwark. He turned, saw Drago twist and bring the pistol to bear. His arm went back and the blade snaked from his hand.

There was the sickening thud of metal striking flesh. Drago jerked. The pistol clattered to the floor, and his hands clawed at the blade lodged in his throat. His eyes filled with terrible certainty, then rolled backward in his head. With a hideous gush of blood, he was dead.

The next instant, the cabin filled with men. "Are you bad hurt, Captain?" rumbled a voice, harsh with concern.

Glenmorgan, recognizing Brindle, the sailing master, shook his head. "Get me up," he gasped. "There isn't time." Rough hands pulled him to his feet. Grimly he fought down his nausea and struggled to order his thoughts. "Freneaux escaped," he said as someone tore his sleeve and used it to stanch the blood flowing from the deep cut high up on his arm. "Some of you lads, get Drago's men over the side. Tell them the ship's going to blow and they've only barely enough time to reach shore. Brindle, you set the fuse to the powder magazine—fifteen minutes, no more. The rest of you, get the boats over the side. Shoot anyone, other than our lads, who try to come anywhere near them. We've blessed little time before they come for us from the fort."

In moments the cabin emptied, and Glenmorgan himself lurched unsteadily for the door. Instantly a strong hand caught his wrist, and a burly arm went about his waist. "Here, Captain," said a gruff voice. "Lean on me. You're fair out on your feet."

A blaze of anger rose up in him, and he cursed. "Mind your own business, damn you."

"Aye, Captain," cheerfully agreed the sailor, "just as soon as we have you topside."

Glenmorgan glared at the homely face, angry with himself for taking his ill-temper out on the other man. It was Tollet, the wounded sailor whom Meg had helped nurse back to health. Instantly the anger went out of him, and he leaned gratefully against the sailor's burly strength. "Very well, Tollet," he rumbled, "since you seem set on playing nursemaid. For God's sake, get me out of here!"

It would be a close thing, Glenmorgan realized as he glanced quickly along the decks to make sure he was the last one left on board. He looked out over the swelling sea. He could just barely make out the *Raven*'s crew in the two boats making with all speed for the island and, toward the mainland, the bobbing heads of Drago's men swimming for the fort. Then, gritting his teeth against the persistent throb in his head, he lowered himself over the side and down the rope ladder, dropping the last few feet into the pitching boat that waited for him. He felt hard hands grasp him ungently to keep him from tossing overboard, then he was thrust unceremoniously amidship among the crowded bodies of his men as the boat shoved away from the abandoned ship.

"Pull, lads," Brindle rasped. "Pull as if your lives depended on it."

Less than five minutes later, the hull scraped against sand, and Glenmorgan scrambled with his men over the side on to the island. Running, they had hardly put the island between themselves and the frigate when a tremendous blast ripped the heavens. Orange flames and billowing smoke marked the *Sea Hawk*'s death passage to the bottom. Then, just as quickly, there was nothing.

"She's gone, lads," Glenmorgan heard Brindle rumble. "Swallowed up by the sea. But yonder lies the *Raven*. I'll not be sorry to feel her decks beneath my feet."

Glenmorgan's feelings echoed that sentiment as, some twenty minutes later, he climbed wearily up the *Raven*'s entry port. He opened his mouth to order Chapin to get the ship under way as soon as the boats were made secure, then stopped and closed it again, made to feel empty with the sense of loss that had ridden him all the way from Charles Town. Chapin was gone, it was time Glenmorgan accepted that. The former first mate was out of harm's way, and that's the way it must stay, for Kate's sake as well as the man upon whom her happiness depended.

He barked the order to Pritchard, Chapin's replacement, and made his way quickly to the quarterdeck.

"Put on all the canvas she'll carry, Mr. Pritchard," he shouted above the strengthening gale. "I want to see Charleston Harbor by this time tomorrow."

Twenty-two

There was a haunting sadness in Meg's eyes that even her pretense at laughter could not quite camouflage. Kate and Brigida noticed it and attributed it, quite accurately, to Glenmorgan's continued absence. For a while the look gave way to eager curiosity as the horses were led to the starting post. Meg demonstrated an unabashed pleasure at the sight of the beautiful, long-limbed creatures as well as a keen appreciation for the small figures of the jockeys, decked out in brilliant colors and clinging with apparent ease to the backs of the spirited animals.

"Oh, but they are marvelous!" she exclaimed. "I can think of nothing in the sea to which I might draw a comparison. I daresay that horses are quite singular creatures."

"Aye," muttered Dick Chapin, who preferred the stolid dependability of oxen or mules. "Singularly flighty and lacking in any great degree of intelligence."

"Oh, no, how can you say so?" retorted Kate. "Why, I should liken them to Michael's beloved sailing ships—always pining to be free to race with the wind and just as spirited and lovely."

The general consensus was with Kate, and laughing, Dick politely declined further comment.

Meg, who had never seen a horse race before, demanded

to know why they must always run inside a track and why always around in a circle. Indeed, she did not see why they must have riders who beat them with sticks and kept them from racing freely as they were meant to do, like the black-and-white whales, she said, or the dolphins who raced for the sheer joy of it.

Thomas answered that that might be fine out in the wilds where there were no spectators to be trampled, but if one wanted to watch them or lay wagers on the winners, it was necessary to do so within a confined area and under the control of jockeys.

"Wagers?" echoed Meg, who obviously had not the least idea what he was talking about.

"Aye," said Chapin from the other side of Kate. "Putting money on a horse you think will win." He went on to explain about odds and paying off when one lost.

"I should like to place a wager," Meg said when he had finished. "On that horse." She pointed to a long, lean Chickasaw stallion who shone a marvelous blue-black in the afternoon sunlight.

Thomas gave a low whistle.

"You've an eye for horse flesh, I'll grant you that," he remarked with a wry glint in his brown eyes. "That's Raven's Wing, Michael's entry. And over there, the sorrel with four black stockings—that's Tharp's Lucky Chance—the favorite to win. The final race will be between those two, if I don't miss my guess."

Meg, following his gaze, felt her heart grow suddenly cold as she picked out the sleek reddish brown stallion and saw, standing a short distance beyond it, a tall, familiar figure in conversation with an elegantly dressed woman. Meg pressed the back of a fist to her lips as though to stifle the cry that rose inside her at the sight of his left arm, held stiffly in a sling across his chest.

Still, she must have made some sort of sound, because

Kate leaned suddenly near. "Meg, what is it?" she asked, her voice vibrant with concern. "You're white as a sheet."

Meg, unable to voice an answer, merely shook her head. Then Kate saw them, too.

"Faith," she exclaimed beneath her breath. "It's Michael! And he's with that—"

"Easy," Chapin warned, closing his hand on her arm. "It'll do no one any good to make a scene, least of all Meg."

Kate knew he was right. Still, she could not restrain herself from commenting on Clarissa Tharp's brass. She was not sure what damned the woman more—the fact that she had the indelicacy to appear in public so shortly after her father's death, or that she did so on the arm of the man who had killed him. Either way, she was ruined among the polite circles in Charles Town.

And what of Tharp? she wondered. A cold chill coursed down her spine as she spotted him, giving some last-minute instructions to the jockey who was to ride Lucky Chance. Slim and elegant as always, he appeared oblivious to Michael and Clarissa, but Kate had the feeling that he was perfectly aware of them. Then in disbelief, she saw Clarissa fling her arms around her brother's neck and kiss him with wanton abandon. Instinctively, her hand clutched Meg's as she felt the other girl stiffen. A groan welled up inside Kate.

Michael would have his duel, if that was what he was after. Clarissa had just made sure of that.

The *Raven*'s arrival in Charles Town Harbor twenty-four hours after setting sail from Sainte Augustine excited little notice. From the wharf, Glenmorgan went straight to the Planters' Hotel. It was well after dark, and still the streets teemed with people, some, he knew, from as far away as the back country, fifty miles inland from the town. No sooner had he reached his lodgings than he sent for his groom and a stable lad whom he had entrusted with a special assignment.

Stripped to the waist, he endured the clumsy efforts of his servant to cleanse and rebandage the wound on his arm while he listened to the groom's report then issued orders for the next day's race. Not until he had dismissed both the groom and the servant did he question the boy, Joshua, about Meg.

Assured that she was presently at home, where she had remained for the past two days and nights, and that she was even then under the observation of Joshua's confederate, Nick, he sent the boy back to his room over the stables, then flung himself facedown on his bed. He was asleep almost before his head hit the pillow.

When he awoke late the next morning, he dressed, ate breakfast, and caught up on the latest gossip from one of the chambermaids who had a gleam in her eye for the tall, handsome captain. He was hardly surprised by the news that Clarissa had gone into retirement somewhere in the country. He had hoped in this one instance she would bow to convention. He did not analyze his reluctance to meet her again. He told himself he did not want the complication of a vindictive female, not now, when he was about to confront Tharp. But he knew it went deeper than that. For the first time in seven years he had doubts about what he was doing, about where it might inevitably lead him.

It was not something he wanted to think about, any more than he wanted to think about Meg and what he had discovered in Sainte Augustine.

Impatiently he set out in his chaise and turning on to Meeting Street, came eventually to the curtain wall and Sir Nathanial Johnson's Half Moon Battery with its moat and two drawbridges, which served as the town gate. He passed through to the farmland outside the town limits and took the well-traveled road that led to Newmarket.

The race grounds, set on a broad green amid stands of oak, magnolia, and pine, were congested with carriages, wagons, and carts of every kind. Glenmorgan, leaving his chaise to go the rest of the way on foot, nodded to the gentlemen on horseback and touched the brim of his hat to the ladies in their carriages as he passed. His eye was caught by a woman in green satin who drove past him in a chaise painted bright red and trimmed in gilt. He recognized Mme. Beauchamp's bold features, saw her wave. He nodded, then immediately forgot her. There was only one gentleman whom he was interested in seeing, and only one female—a girl with blue-green eyes and silvery hair.

Certainly he had no wish to see Clarissa emerge from an enclosed carriage and make purposefully toward him.

"So, you decided to come back," she hissed, making no attempt to hide her loathing. "Under the circumstances, I'm surprised you didn't keep going. Do you have the least idea what you have done? You murdered my father. *Damn* you for that. I trust it has given you a deal of pleasure. And as an added spice to the gravy, Logan has turned me out and threatens to divorce me. I'm ruined and penniless, Glenmorgan, just as you intended. But it's not over yet, I promise you. Logan is watching, though he pretends not to. And see your little strumpet, sitting in the Grand Stand? Well, she sees *you*. I mean to give them both an eyeful."

Before Glenmorgan could stop her, she flung her arms about his neck and pressed her lips to his.

Her eyes were hard and glittery with triumph when Glenmorgan forcefully dragged her arms down and disengaged himself from her. "Goodbye, Michael, my darling," she murmured, her smile ugly. "I don't think we shall ever see one another again. I pray Logan kills you. Revenge would be sweet. Still, as Logan's widow, everything, including

410

Marigold, would be mine. Think about that when you go up against him. Either way, I come out the winner."

She laughed and started away, glancing back over her shoulder to blow him a last, mocking kiss.

The carriage seemed to come out of nowhere. Glenmorgan glimpsed a flash of red out of the corner of his eye and bounded for Clarissa—too late. The woman at the reins pulled back. The startled horse reared, its forefeet striking out. Clarissa's scream was cut short by a glancing blow to the temple. Limply, she dropped to the ground.

Glenmorgan caught the bit and dragged the frightened horse down.

The glance with which Mme. Beauchamp met his was singularly devoid of remorse. "It was an accident, Captain. You saw it," she said, her look challenging him to deny it. "She stepped in front of my carriage. I did everything in my power to stop it."

Glenmorgan had no time to spare her. Dropping to a knee beside Clarissa's still form, he felt at the base of her throat for a pulse. It was a pointless gesture. He had known she was dead as soon as he looked into her eyes, fixed and staring, like the sightless glass eyes of a doll.

"A pity," murmured a dispassionate voice behind him. "Her mistake was in letting herself fall in love with you. I did try to warn her."

Anger, like bile, rose in Glenmorgan's throat. His eyes lifted to Tharp's face. "This is your doing," he said. With cold deliberation, he came to his feet. "You corrupted her, Tharp, like everything else that you touch. Whatever she became was because of you."

Tharp smiled, faintly amused. "I wonder if Mme. Beauchamp would agree with you." He glanced musingly at the woman in the carriage. "How old was Clarissa when she publicly branded the lady a whore? Twelve or thirteen? And all because it displeased her to have her father marry

411

again. A stepmother, after all, might not have been so easily manipulated as poor Thornton. I've always wondered which one of them actually held the gun to your father's head. Not that it matters. Either way, it was Clarissa who pulled the trigger."

All in an instant Glenmorgan knew Tharp was telling it the way it had really been. He knew, too, why Freneaux's words of advice had continued to haunt him all the way back to Charles Town. It all fell into place. As a woman, Clarissa had had the most to lose from her father's exposure. With Thornton ruined and either dead or in a British jail, she had faced the loss of name, fortune, and position, even the chance for an advantageous marriage. She had been willing to kill in order to protect those things that she could have only through a man.

"Clarissa has paid the final price for whatever she might have done," he said grimly. "Now there's only you, Tharp. You might be interested to know that I've been to Sainte Augustine. Drago's dead, and Freneaux won't risk showing his face around here again. It's finished, Tharp. The admiralty knows everything."

A crowd had gathered round them. Chapin could be heard, shoving his way through the packed onlookers. Tharp glanced around at their curious faces.

"It seems," he said, "we shall not be racing after all. A shame. I was looking forward to winning. Ah, well. Another time, eh, Glenmorgan?"

The next instant Tharp had stepped back and melted into the crowd.

Cursing, Glenmorgan lunged after him, but hampered by his wounded arm and the press of the crowd, he soon lost him. At last he halted, panting, at the corner of the Grand Stand and waited for Chapin to catch up to him.

"Michael, what the devil? Good God, man, you're bleeding!"

It was Thomas, vaulting lightly over the rail. He reached for Glenmorgan's arm.

"No, never mind that now. Tharp," he gasped. "Did you see which way he went?"

Sutton shook his head. "After what happened—well, Brigida and the others were pretty upset. I hurried them to the coach. Mary thought they would be better there, where they didn't have to see. . . . You know, dammit," he blurted. "Hell, that was no sight for women's eyes."

"I'm obliged," said Glenmorgan. "You were right to send them home. They should be safe enough there. I doubt Tharp will chance going back to Charles Town."

As Sutton's face paled, Glenmorgan experienced a sudden queasy sensation in the pit of his stomach. "But I didn't," Thomas told him. "Kate and Meg wouldn't hear of it, not until they were sure you were all right. I left them in the coach. They're still there, waiting for word from me."

Glenmorgan's glance, suddenly grim, met Sutton's. As of a single mind, they both broke for the carriage, Sutton leading. Halfway there, they met Chapin, coming toward them.

"Michael, thank God," he gasped, his barrel of a chest heaving from his exertions. "Tharp got away. Made it to his bloody carriage. He must have come upon the coach and seen Meg and the others waiting for Thomas. Bloody hell, he shot the coachman, poor devil."

Sutton blanched. "Good God, Brigida—"

"She's all right," Chapin hurried to inform him. His hand gripped Glenmorgan hard by the arm. "It's Meg, Michael," he said huskily. "Tharp took her with him."

Meg awakened slowly, as though surfacing from a bottomless sea of darkness. She was vaguely aware that her head hurt and that she felt somewhat sick to her stomach— rather the way she had felt the one and only time she had

413

drunk too much wine, she thought, reluctant to leave the darkness, reluctant, even, to open her eyes.

Then, like snatches of a nightmare, she remembered. The taut silence of the coach and Kate clinging to her hands. The rumble of carriage wheels and the sudden crack of a gunshot. The hollow thud of a body striking the ground. Brigida's scream.

Meg opened her eyes. Faith of her fathers, it had not been a dream! She remembered being dragged from the coach by a black man, who must have dwarfed even Dick Chapin in size, and being thrust bodily into a waiting carriage. She remembered Tharp's loathsome presence and having some vile drink forced down her throat. And then she remembered nothing.

Tharp had abducted her, that much was clear. But where had he taken her?

Her heart pounding, she sat up and took stock of her surroundings.

She was in a room about the same size as her bedroom at Cherry Orchard, with a four-poster bed, a wardrobe, a cherrywood commode, and a dressing table with a mirror and bench. An overstuffed chair stood before the fireplace, fronted by a plain white mantle. The walls were a rich coral, and on the floor was a thick flowered rug. The room brooded in muted sunlight seeping through gold damask drapes across a single window.

Bolting from the bed, Meg ran to the window and flung the curtains wide.

A groan broke from her lips, and in the sudden throes of despair, she curled her hands around the iron bars lodged in the casing. Slowly she sank to her knees. It was the window, just as she had seen it, weeks ago in her dream.

She did not know how long she remained on the floor, sunk in despondency. It was long enough for her limbs to grow stiff and numb, and at last she forced herself to get

414

up. Only then did she notice that she was no longer wearing the green velvet walking dress she had worn to Newmarket, but a flowing nightgown of white gossamer and silk. Instinctively, she reached for the gemstone and, with a sigh of relief, discovered that it, unlike her clothes, had not been taken from her. Her comb, too, lay on the dressing table beside the silk purse she had carried with her to the race grounds.

Clasping the comb to her, she went to the door and reached for the handle. Instantly she snatched it back again at the sudden metallic click of the key in the lock. She fell back a step, then another. As the door opened, she stood her ground, her head lifted in instinctive defiance.

A hard gleam of admiration leaped in Tharp's eyes at the sight of her. Whatever else she was, she was magnificent. He did not doubt that Glenmorgan would move heaven and earth to find her. How unfortunate that his efforts would be wasted. Only Clarissa had known about the plantation. He had purchased it through an agent months before it became obvious his West Indies ventures were no longer prudent or viable. And now Clarissa was dead.

He had worked it all out days ago—the abduction and the escape to the plantation. From there, an Indian guide would take them safely through the swamp to the sea, where a coaster waited to pick them up and carry them north to Nova Scotia. After that, they would have all the time in the world to book passage on a Dutch trader to anywhere he wished to go.

In the meantime, the last place Glenmorgan would think to look was Marigold, and by then, it would be too late. The guide would be here before the week was out. It was all that was keeping them there.

* * *

Glenmorgan grimaced wryly as he eased his bandaged arm into the sleeve of his coat.

"It's a nasty cut, and you waited long enough to have it properly looked after," remarked Pippin, observing him with a caustic eye. "You're lucky it's not inflamed. Tear open those stitches again, and you might not be so lucky. You might even lose the arm."

"I'm obliged," Glenmorgan grunted. "But I didn't come here for a lecture. I've already lost enough time, thanks to my former first mate. I should be out there, looking for Meg."

"Maybe now you can," Pippin retorted, "without falling into a faint, or worse, a fever. You can thank Chapin for *that,* at least."

It was true, Glenmorgan knew. He had been reeling on his feet with pain and exhaustion when Chapin had literally overpowered him and delivered him to Cherry Orchard. He owed Chapin, but that and everything else would have to wait. Whatever strength he had must be spent in finding Meg.

Pippin, reading that and so much more in Glenmorgan's strained features, understood the torment that drove him. "It's been four days," he said gravely. "Where can you look that you haven't tried already?"

"I wish I knew," Glenmorgan admitted wearily, hating the feeling of helplessness that grew stronger with each passing hour. "Bloody hell! Tharp *must* have been expecting trouble. Or maybe he had planned to abduct Meg all along. Whatever the case, he got away too cleanly for it to have been mere chance. He had a plan of escape already laid out and waiting, right down to his horse and groom. By the time we got around to looking for them, the man, the horse—everything—had simply vanished. No one saw them leave. No one even knows where Tharp keeps his stable."

Pippin eyed him with a strange intensity. "You may be sure he has taken Meg out of Charles Town." Dropping his eyes, he picked up a square of white linen. "My guess," he said, looking up again, "is somewhere inland. I doubt that he'd trust himself at sea with a mermaid."

Glenmorgan turned sharply, his eyes piercing on the old man. "So it's true," he said softly.

"Aye, it's true," Pippin nodded. "Now, hold *still,* Captain. Before you ruin all my work."

Glenmorgan was silent as the old man secured the wounded arm in the sling of white linen and ordered him to keep it there. When he finished, he looked up to find Glenmorgan watching him.

"It's time we talked," Glenmorgan declared flatly.

So, it was here, Pippin thought, wondering if Glenmorgan was prepared for the answers. Quietly, he said, "What do you want to know?"

Glenmorgan clenched his left hand in a fist, felt the sharp backlash of pain from the wound help steady his thoughts.

"You tell *me,*" he said. "A mermaid, good God, I don't even know what that is. I made love to her, and now you tell me she's not even human."

"She's half-human," Pippin answered, crossing to the window to stare out over the lawns. "My son was her father. As to what a mermaid is . . ." He ran a hand through his hair. "I'm not sure how to answer that. I can tell you what Sheela, Meg's mother, told me, that the sea-dwellers are a race almost as old as time, a people steeped in knowledge of things we cannot begin to understand. Perhaps it is magic, or maybe it's something else, an ability to utilize forces of nature we simply know nothing about. Sheela could assume human form and for brief periods was able to walk on the land. It's different with Meg. Oh, she can shift from one form to another at will, but I have noticed since coming here that the more often she assumes her hu-

417

man shape, the longer she is able to remain on land. It's as if she is gradually attaining a balance between her two halves." Or as if she were becoming with each passing day more human and less a mermaid, he reflected, but did not voice that troubling thought aloud. "Still, the sea remains the source of her strength," he said warningly, "and the gemstone she wears is both the receptacle and the mirror of her true essence, a kind of medium through which her powers can be channeled. Meg once called it the crystallized song of herself."

"What the devil are you talking about?" Glenmorgan snapped. "What powers?"

"The power to command the elements, create storms, see glimpses into the future, to name a few. I don't know how to make it any clearer than that. Don't you see, Captain, it isn't necessary to understand who or what she is. It is enough to know that her motivating force is love. Though she has powers at her command that you and I cannot even imagine, she is sworn never to take a life. She will not violate that oath, not even to save herself."

Glenmorgan's expression was grim in the extreme. "How long?" he said. "How much time before she must renew her strength?"

Pippin shook his head. "I wish I knew," he answered gravely. "I only know that she cannot survive away from the sea indefinitely. And if anything should happen to the gemstone . . . well, I'm afraid that Meg's song would be permanently silenced."

Glenmorgan walked to the window looking out over the cherry tree orchard from which the house derived its name. Something about Clarissa's death had been nagging at the back of his mind, something he sensed was important, but for the life of him he could not pin it down. He tried to put aside the weariness and the aching torment of uncertainty about Meg, tried to clear his mind of everything but those last moments before Clarissa had been struck down.

The image of her face contorted with hatred seemed indelibly etched in his memory, but what was it she had said? Something about a duel and hoping that Tharp would be the victor. He remembered that plainly enough, she had said it once before. What else then? That even if Tharp died, she would still come out the winner. Why? He felt a sudden leap of excitement. Because then everything would be hers—everything, including . . .

"Marigold," he said softly. "It *has* to be." Eagerly, he turned to Pippin. "It's too late to get word to Dick. He's on the *Raven* by now, hunting down Tharp's schooner. But you can tell Thomas when he gets here that I couldn't wait. I'm on my way to Marigold!"

"I'm afraid not, Captain Glenmorgan," announced a clipped voice at the doorway. "You won't be going anywhere except to see the admiral." The two men turned as one in time to see a British naval captain push Mrs. Clagg to one side and step into the room, a pistol held trained and ready on Glenmorgan. Three marines were quick to enter after him.

"I tried to stop them," said the housekeeper, "but they just shoved their way in."

"It's all right, Mrs. Clagg." Glenmorgan turned to the officer. "You could do with a lesson in manners, Stuart. But now that you've forced your way in, what do you want with me? The admiral should have had my written report by now."

"Aye, he got it. Apparently he did not find it satisfactory. He wants to see you, Glenmorgan—immediately. Either you can make it easy on yourself, or we can take you in irons. It's strictly up to you."

Silently, Glenmorgan cursed. "Tell Thomas," he said bitterly to Pippin. "I'll want Raven's Wing ready and waiting when I get back. And pray that it won't be too late!"

Meg stared coldly at Tharp's slim, elegant figure.

"Why have you brought me here?" she demanded. "By what right do you hold me against my will?"

"By the right of might, Miss Pippin," Tharp replied, "if, indeed, that is your name. And because I conceived a desire to have you to myself. After all, how many people can lay claim to having a real, live mermaid? I find I am quite fascinated at the mere concept of such a creature's existence. You do not appear different from us. I confess I was disappointed. I expected gills at the very least."

"You jest, surely," Meg answered, an angry flush tinging her cheeks at the realization that he had examined her naked body while she lay unconscious and vulnerable. "I am as you perceive me—a human with two feet and two legs. I cannot conceive why you should imagine me to be other than I am."

"I do not imagine it, Miss Pippin. I know it to be true. There is hardly any other explanation for what I myself witnessed."

"Indeed, sir. And what exactly did you see?"

"I saw you leave your cozy little cottage and enter the water. You never surfaced, though I kept vigilance for well over six hours—until the sun came up, as a matter of fact. I confess I was somewhat concerned that you might have drowned, until I encountered you the very next afternoon at Mrs. Gladden's recital. Most peculiar, would you not agree?"

Meg gave him a look of cold dislike. "What I find peculiar, Mr. Tharp, is that you saw fit to spy on me. I often swim at night. I am not sensitive to the cold, and under the cover of darkness I may swim unfettered by clothing. If you did not see me leave the water, it is hardly remarkable. It *was* dark after all."

Tharp smiled. "It was the night of the full moon, Miss Pippin," he countered, apparently enjoying the exchange of wits. "However, if I concede that it is possible I missed you that night, I still remain convinced that you are no mere human. I am curious about your pendant. It is most unusual. May I?"

Meg had to exert tremendous self-control as Tharp lifted the gemstone to examine it. "I cannot recall having ever seen a stone quite like this. What, may I inquire, is it?"

"I haven't the slightest idea, Mr. Tharp," Meg answered. "I do not pretend to any great knowledge of gems. For all I know, it may be no more than glass."

Meg felt cold fingers of fear as Tharp studied her with his soulless black eyes. "I wonder," he murmured.

She nearly sagged with relief when there came a knock on the door.

"I apologize, Miss Pippin, for the necessity of having to keep you drugged during your journey here. You have slept a full night and most of a day and must be quite famished." Turning, he opened the door to admit a black woman with a tray of food.

Meg did indeed feel weak with hunger. Stubbornly, however, she refused to show it as the woman whispered something for Tharp's ear only.

Tharp's expression, as he turned back to Meg, was as unruffled as ever, but Meg thought she sensed an undercurrent of emotion behind the facade—irritation, perhaps? She didn't know.

"I shall leave you to enjoy your meal," Tharp said, bowing at the waist. "Regretfully, I find my presence is needed elsewhere. Good afternoon, Miss Pippin. We shall talk again soon."

Alone again in the room, Meg remained standing where

she was, dazed by the bitter knowledge that the worst had happened. She had revealed herself, no matter how unwittingly, to one not of her blood. She would pay dearly for breaking that most ancient of taboos. She was already the prisoner of a man who would hesitate at nothing, a man who would attempt to break her and use her to his own ends. She would destroy the gemstone herself before she allowed that to happen, she fiercely vowed.

Then immediately she swayed, a bitter laugh welling up inside her. She would undoubtedly be beyond his manipulation or anyone else's before many more days passed. Cut off from even the sight or smell of the sea and without food suitable to maintain her, she would quickly lose strength. She felt light-headed and unsteady on her feet already, the result of the drug Tharp had forced on her.

Ignoring the tray of food, she sank down on her knees beneath her attic window and stared out over fallow fields, copses of pine and oak, and in the distance, silvery glimpses of the Ashley. It was all as Glenmorgan had described it once in those faraway days on the island, even to the moss-draped trees touching branches over the lane leading up to the house Turlough Glenmorgan had built for his bride.

She had come to Marigold! Meg knew it in her heart. How strange, she thought, that her journey should end here, and yet, perhaps somehow fitting, too.

Twenty-three

Like practically everyone who had ever been reared on a Carolina plantation, Glenmorgan had learned to ride almost as soon as he could walk. In his youth, he had come to know, even love, more than a few horses, but he swiftly discovered that Raven's Wing was in a class all by himself.

The Chickasaw stallion quickly outdistanced Sutton on his rented hack, and though Glenmorgan kept him at a hard run, the black showed no signs of flagging. He was swift and seemingly tireless, and Glenmorgan was in no mood to spare either his mount or himself.

In spite of their unrelenting pace, the miles seemed to Glenmorgan to stretch endlessly before him. He was gripped with the fear that he might already be too late. Tharp was no fool. He would know that he could not tarry long at Marigold. Sooner or later his presence at the deserted plantation would be noticed, and that was something he could not risk. He would vanish into the wilderness, making his way north, or he would make a break for the sea and a ship to carry him south, to Sainte Augustine maybe, or even back to the West Indies. He might already be out of Glenmorgan's reach and Meg with him.

Bitterly Glenmorgan cursed the British admiral, who had kept him fretting in Charles Town, when he should already have been at Marigold. *Damn* Captain Stuart of His Majesty's Navy and the luck that had brought him to Cherry Orchard just as Glenmorgan was on the point of leaving!

There had been certain questions regarding the loss of the guns and Freneaux's escape for which the admiral had had to have answers, and those Glenmorgan had given in his written report had not been the ones that he wanted.

He had lost two nights and a day before he at last convinced the admiral that the guns had had to be destroyed to keep them from falling into the hands of the Spaniards. As for Freneaux, the *Raven* was hardly equal to the task of taking on San Marco in a foolhardy attempt to get the Frenchman back again. Finally, his patience at an end, Glenmorgan had pointed out that, thanks to himself, the king had a healthy addition to his war chest, the smuggling and spy ring in the West Indies and Southern colonies had been disrupted, and the munitions meant to incite a war between Britain's Indian allies had been destroyed. If these accomplishments did not warrant the pardon he had been promised, then they could either bloody well hang him and be done with it or let him go. They had, after another hour of deliberation, let him go.

At least Sutton had met him on the dock with good news. The *Raven* had run down the *La Fortuna*. They had been making south along the coast when Chapin took the schooner off Stono Point. Neither Meg nor Tharp had been aboard.

Glenmorgan, spying a farmhouse before him, eased back on the reins. He begrudged every moment that kept him from Marigold, but it was necessary to breathe the stallion and perhaps fortify himself with food and drink. Anxious about Meg and in a fever of impatience at the admiral's vacillations, he had had no appetite for food aboard the flagship.

The farmer, Jedediah Longacre, it soon developed, had

known Glenmorgan's father and remembered his son. Calling in to his wife to bring meat and bread, he helped Glenmorgan tend to his horse. He had carved a modest farm out of the wilderness and, lacking the monetary resources of his neighbors, made no pretense at opulence or leisure. Consequently, he had little difficulty in recalling the luxurious travel coach that had stopped four nights before to breathe and water the horses. He remembered the gentleman, too. A cold, inhospitable man with eyes that were not easily forgotten. Longacre had not seen a woman, but there could easily have been one, as the coach was enclosed and the windows curtained.

Twenty minutes later, revitalized by the food in his belly and buoyed by the certainty that Tharp had come this way before him, Glenmorgan mounted and urged the stallion to even greater efforts. Marigold lay less than an hour away— Marigold and hopefully Meg.

Meg sat on the floor beneath the window, her head propped on her knees hugged to her chest. She had watched the dawn of another day, the sixth of her captivity, with a peculiar sense of detachment. Soon the woman would come with her breakfast tray. She would find Meg's supper left untouched, and after trying to cajole the captive to eat, she would leave the tray and take the uneaten meal away.

Tharp had not repeated his first visit, and Meg did not question why he had not come. She was only glad that she had not had to see him. The long, empty days had become a ritual of untouched meals, with the woman Meg's only visitor. Consequently, Meg did not even glance up at the sound of the key in the lock.

Vaguely, she heard someone enter, heard the rattle of the tray being set on the table. She waited for the sound of departing footsteps and became aware instead of a lengthening silence. A cold prickle of nerve endings served as a frisson of warning. Deliberately she lifted her head.

Tharp drew in a long, slow breath. Even weakened by hunger, she exuded the same aura of proud unassailability that had first drawn his attention the moment he glanced down from the *Sea Hawk*'s deck and caught sight of her. Now, looking into the marvelous blue-green eyes, he had the oddest feeling that she, not he, held the upper hand, that though she might be his prisoner, she was beyond his reach. It was a feeling that made her all the more desirable in his eyes.

"I am told," he said, "that you refuse to eat."

"I cannot help what you are told," Meg answered.

"And yet it's true, is it not? You have not eaten the food brought to you."

"The truth is that I *cannot* eat it and that, even if I could, I wouldn't. I have no need for food."

Tharp's interest quickened. "Why?" he said. "Because you aren't really human after all?"

"Because I am dying." She said it with such finality that Tharp was forced to believe her. And yet, in her eyes there was a gleam of mockery. Why?

"I am prepared, Miss Pippin," he said after a moment, "to treat you with a certain amount of tolerance. I am not, however, prepared to see you die. Tell me what I can do to save you."

"Return me to the sea and set me free."

"You know I cannot do that."

"Yes," she replied.

Tharp marveled at her total acceptance. She knew something that he did not. What? He had to know. "You belong to me now. If the sea will save you, I can and will take you to it. I'm afraid, however, I should have to have your word that you would come back again. Otherwise, you are no use to me."

426

"I *am* no use to you," Meg breathed, passionate at last. "And I can never belong to you. I give myself freely or not at all. And that I have already done!"

"To whom? Glenmorgan?" Tharp yanked her to her feet. Her hand pinned to the small of her back, he held her against him, his free hand fondling her breast. "That is no obstacle," he murmured, baring her shoulder to his touch. His eyes bored into hers. "Believe me," he muttered thickly, and forced his mouth down over hers.

Her lips remained cold and unresponsive beneath his— like her body, like her eyes, staring back at him. He pulled back, obsessed with his desire to possess her.

"I'll kill him," he said softly.

"Then you will kill me, too. A mermaid gives her heart only once." Her marvelous eyes met his. "To a lifemate," she said.

At last he understood, even if he could not bring himself to accept it. Like the eagle that mates for life, she had bound herself to Glenmorgan. He felt the blood surge to his brain. Glenmorgan! The name was like a curse. Wherever he turned, Glenmorgan was always there. But this time he would make sure of the captain. This time nothing would stand in the way of what he desired. His eyes focused on Meg. He *would* have her, even if it destroyed her.

"I suggest you overcome your distaste for food," he said, "if you want to see your captain again. He will be coming for you, you may be sure of it. I have received word that he has already cut off my escape route to the south. It will be only a matter of time before he looks inland." What she didn't know, however, was that they would already be on their way across the swamp.

"No, not for me," Meg murmured. She lifted her head in proud defiance. "He's coming for you. You would do well to run, Mr. Tharp—now—while you still can."

Tharp's gaze narrowed sharply. Nearly flinging her from

him, he walked from the room, locking the door behind him.

Meg sank to the floor, grateful to be left alone. Taking up the gemstone, she peered into its surface. Glenmorgan's face appeared to her in the blue-green depths, but blurred and indistinct, as if seen through a fog. She blinked her eyes and tried again. It was no use. The image was already fading, along with her small store of strength. "Michael," she whispered.

Closing her eyes, she slid into a deep well of darkness.

She awakened to a hand on her shoulder, shaking her. A voice shouted in her ear.

"Wake up, damn you! I do not intend to let you die. At least not yet. You will see me kill your precious captain first."

Frowning, Meg opened her eyes. "Michael?" she whispered. "Here?"

Tharp, leaning over her, smiled coldly. "Oh, yes, my dear. Does that cheer you? He is even now at the foot of the lane. I can only presume that he managed somehow to kill or elude the man I left to guard the road. Now get up. I haven't time to exchange pleasantries."

Hauling Meg to her feet, he dragged her, resisting, from the room.

Glenmorgan glimpsed the flash of sunlight against metal and reacted instinctively. Drawing the sword from its scabbard, he drove the stallion straight for the figure crouched behind the thicket. Glenmorgan heard the pistol go off, felt the bullet fan his cheek. Then the stallion leaped.

Glenmorgan's sword slashed out and down as the stallion sailed cleanly over the thicket. He saw the man fall back

428

with a scream, his hands clawing at his face where the blade had cut. Then the stallion was on the ground and running.

Glenmorgan did not look back. Cutting across the corner of the field, he broke onto the road again where it curved to meet him. Ahead of him he saw the tree-lined lane, a quarter of a mile long, that led to Marigold. He leaned forward in the saddle, urging the stallion to greater speed.

The house at the end of the lane little resembled the sprawling white mansion he had carried in his memory. Ghosts were known to haunt many country houses and some in the town, and no one had wanted the house in which Turlough Glenmorgan had met a violent end. Now, with the paint peeling and the windows boarded up, it clearly showed its seven years of neglect. At least now he knew why Sutton had been unable to buy it at any price. He should have realized Tharp was behind it.

A slow rage grew in him as he thundered to the end of the lane. Pulling the heaving stallion to a plunging stop, he leaped from the saddle.

He felt his scalp prickle as he climbed the steps to the wide porch and saw the heavy oak door left slightly ajar. He stepped back, drew the pistol from his belt, and kicked the door open. Meg's scream shattered the silence.

"Michael—no!"

He saw her, held like a shield in front of Tharp, on the gallery overlooking the hall. Then Glenmorgan dove head-first through the doorway, slammed to the floor, and rolled. As Tharp's shot missed, gouging splinters from the floor, Glenmorgan came to his feet.

"Let her go, Logan." His eyes on Tharp, he walked toward the foot of the stairs.

"She's bound to you, Glenmorgan," Tharp called down. "Did you know that? Her life to yours. If you die, she dies, too. I find that singularly ironic."

"Don't listen to him, Michael! He's trying to distract you!"

Glenmorgan's eyes flickered to Meg. One of the boards had been pulled loose from the window to one side of her, and through the gap a shaft of sunlight glanced in, falling across her. In the light, dancing with dust motes, she appeared to shimmer. She was pale and thin, her face and form delicate-seeming and insubstantial. A fierce pain shot through him at the sight of the change in her.

He reached the bottom of the stairway and started up the first step. "Move away from him, Meg."

The creak of a board at his back warned him, and he spun around—too late. He saw the gleam of white teeth against a black face just before a fist slammed, like a battering ram, into his ribs. The man towered above Glenmorgan, three hundred pounds of sheer muscle. Glenmorgan gagged, the breath knocked from his lungs, and clenching his teeth, drove his shoulder hard into his assailant. The force of the impact carried them both, careening into the wall. Glenmorgan gasped as his wounded arm struck. Then he was being crushed in a bear hug that lifted him off his feet. Bright lights burst inside his head and he struggled against the haze of darkness closing in on him. He brought his arms up and slammed the heels of his hands hard against the other man's ears. He was released with a bellow, the black man clasping his hands to the sides of his head. Dragging in painful gasps of air, Glenmorgan reached for the pistol, lying on the floor beside him.

Meg clutched the gallery rail to help steady herself. She saw Glenmorgan raise the gun and fire, saw the black man stagger as the pistolball struck him in the chest then, with a roar of rage, lunge toward the man who had shot him. In a horrified daze, she saw the wounded giant snatch Glenmorgan off the floor and slam him bodily into the wall— again and again.

430

She screamed at Tharp. "Stop him!" In despair, she saw Glenmorgan claw at his sword, saw him drag the blade free and plunge it into his attacker. The big man staggered back. A look of surprise on his heavy face, he swayed and slowly toppled forward.

Even as the resounding crash of the body slamming into the floor echoed and died away, Meg saw Glenmorgan drop to his knees. A shuddering gasp broke from her lips as she realized his sleeve was blood-soaked, his arm hanging limply at his side. As if in a nightmare from which there was no awakening, she watched him pitch forward and lie still. Then a terrible cry welled up inside her.

"No!" The cry was torn from the depths of her soul. Her grief was inconsolable, as was the rage, like a swelling floodtide within her, a rage such as she had never felt before. *"You!"* she cried, turning on Tharp. The gemstone leaped in her hand, a terrible thing of white, burning light. The song of power came, unbidden, to her lips.

Tharp backed before her, his eyes awestruck and staring. Darkness fell like a curtain over the house as black, roiling clouds blotted out the sunlight. A deep rumbling shook the earth, causing the house to tremble around them and beneath their feet. Tharp stumbled backward and fell, his hand up before his eyes to ward off the gemstone's fierce light. And still the forbidden song poured forth from inside her, gathering force, drawing from her grief and rage, channeling them outward until the gemstone glared a dazzling white brilliance.

"Meg!" Strong hands clasped her roughly by the arms and shook her. "Meg, stop it, before you kill someone!"

The gemstone flared in a single blinding flash of brilliance, which, as if suddenly doused, vanished. Meg gasped and stared in stricken disbelief into Glenmorgan's face.

Again Glenmorgan shook her, gently this time. "Meg,

431

it's all right. Do you hear me? I'm here, and you're safe now."

A sigh shuddered through her lips. "Michael, you're alive! I thought . . ."

Glenmorgan caught her as she sagged limply against him. Made awkward by his wounded arm, he lowered her to the floor and felt frantically for a pulse at the base of her neck. He let out a slow breath as he found it, faint to his touch but steady. She was alive, but for how long?

Her hand, clenched in a fist, lay against her breast, and gently, he pried her fingers open.

A low gasp broke from his lips at the sight of the thing in her hand.

What had Pippin called it? The receptacle and mirror of Meg's essence? The crystallized song of Meg herself? It had shone with a clear translucent beauty, its heart of blue-green flame pulsating and vibrant with color. Now its core was riven and shot through with a multitude of thin spidery cracks, as though it had been forcefully shattered from within. What had once been a marvelous transparency was obscured now and clouded so that the gemstone's inner flame was reduced to little more than a frail glimmer deep at its center.

Glenmorgan groaned. "Good God, Meg. What have you done?"

The clatter of hoofbeats outside, plunging to a halt, broke through his anguish. He reached into his pocket for the pearl-handled pistol and came up empty—the gun was gone. Realizing he must have lost it in the fight, he shoved himself to his feet and lurched to the rail. Bitterly he cursed. If these were Tharp's men, he was in a damnably tight spot.

An image flashed in his mind of a crouched figure against the wall, and it came to him like a sudden premonition that he had, in all the confusion, forgotten about

Tharp. He turned. And saw Tharp bent over Meg's inert body.

"Don't move," warned Tharp, "if you value her life." Glenmorgan froze at the sight of the knife at Meg's throat. The blade flashed and Tharp came to his feet. "I shall be leaving now," he said. "I suggest you don't follow." He dangled the gemstone in front of him. "I should hate to have to destroy this, it makes such a fascinating souvenir."

He had been backing warily toward the end of the gallery, and now he turned and ran to the window. From the hallway below came the shout: "Michael, what the bloody hell?" Then Tharp vanished through the gap in the boarded window.

"Thomas, up here!" shouted Glenmorgan, lurching for the stairway. He reached the hall and clasped Sutton hard by the arm. "It's Meg. Take her to Pippin. He'll know what to do. And Thomas, be quick about it. Pippin's her only hope."

"Aye, Michael. But what about you?" Sutton called after Glenmorgan's retreating back.

"I've a race to run. Pray God Raven's Wing has the heart of a champion!"

Tharp thundered into the lane on his long-legged sorrel as Glenmorgan clapped heels to the stallion. The rangy black leaped into his long, gliding stride. Glenmorgan, riding recklessly, his cheek nearly pressed to the stallion's neck, grimly assessed the odds. While the black had already been ridden twenty-five miles at a heartrending pace, the sorrel was fresh, and his rider was forty pounds lighter than Glenmorgan's hundred-eighty pounds. Still, the black was more powerfully built, with the deep chest and long rangy build of an athlete, and he had the heart of a lion.

It seemed as they pounded out of the lane onto the road that the Chickasaw stallion was gaining on the sorrel.

Tharp must have realized it, too. Lashing the sorrel about the shoulders and neck with the reins, he once more began to draw away.

Glenmorgan's heart swelled as he felt the black's stride lengthen in answer to the sorrel's challenge. The Chickasaw stallion had been bred to race, bred to win. He was gaining again, the black straining every fiber of his body to overtake the horse in the lead. Glenmorgan saw Tharp turn and look back over his shoulder. There was less than a length between them. Glenmorgan willed the stallion on, knowing that even the black's great heart could not carry them at that gruelling pace much longer. Then the black was drawing even with the sorrel's heaving hind quarters. Steadily he gained, passing the flanks and finally the shoulders, until at last the two stallions ran neck and neck.

"Pull up!" Glenmorgan shouted. Leaning outward from the saddle he snatched at the sorrel's reins. Tharp's hand with the knife slashed out at him. Cursing, Glenmorgan snatched his arm back, blood welling from a cut across the back of his wrist. Then kicking his feet free of the stirrups, he launched himself bodily at Tharp.

The force of the impact carried both men toppling from the saddle. They hit the ground hard, Glenmorgan on top, and rolled in a twisted tangle of arms and legs. Glenmorgan heard the sickening crunch of bone. Then they landed in a heap, neither man moving.

Irritably Glenmorgan moved his head away from the soft warmth, like moist velvet against his face. It moved with him. And at last he opened his eyes to Raven Wing's inquisitive muzzle.

"Hello. So you decided to hang around, did you?" He

grimaced, his body awakening to a multitude of aches and pains. Groaning, he shoved himself up. And then he remembered.

Tharp lay beside him, dead, his neck bent at an unnatural angle. And a few feet away, the sorrel grazed unconcernedly. Conscious of a tightness in his chest, Glenmorgan searched the dead man's pockets for the gemstone. He found it and, heart pounding, held it up to the sunlight.

He exhaled a long breath. The flame at the heart of the gemstone still glimmered.

Wryly he saw his hand shaking and closed his fingers around the stone. Meg was alive. It was all that mattered.

Glenmorgan ran his hand over the black's lathered neck, then handed the reins to Longacre.

"I'd be obliged to you if you take good care of him," he said. "He's earned that and more today."

"We'll see to it that he's fit as a fiddle when you come for him. It's yourself you'd better worry about," said the farmer, watching Glenmorgan pull himself wearily onto the sorrel's back. "My wife did the best she could for that arm, but riding isn't likely to help it."

"It'll do." He ached in every part of his body, and the cuts on his arm and wrist hurt like the devil. Lifting the reins, he nodded to Longacre. "I'll send someone for the black when I can." Then he touched heels to the sorrel's flanks.

It was long after dark when Glenmorgan dismounted before the cottage at Cherry Orchard. Wearily he turned the sorrel over to Emma's young son, who had come running out of the house to meet him. "Look after him, lad," he said, pitching the boy a coin. "Make sure that you cool him

435

down properly before you feed and water him. Can you do that?"

"Yes, *sir*," exclaimed the boy, his eyes round at the sight of Glenmorgan's stained clothes and rough appearance. "I've a pony of my own. I know what to do."

Nodding, Glenmorgan limped past the boy and up to the house. Entering without knocking, he found Pippin in the parlor with Dick Chapin.

"Thank God," exclaimed Chapin, coming hurriedly to his feet. "Any longer, and I was going out after you. You look like the devil, Michael. Can I get you something—a-a drink?"

"Later." Glenmorgan's glance went to Pippin. "Where is she?"

He felt a sharp stab of fear at the look in the old man's eyes. Nervously, Chapin shifted his feet.

"She's gone," said Pippin, moving toward him in a businesslike manner. "Back to the sea. Now sit down and let me have a look at that arm."

"To hell with the arm!" Glenmorgan growled, impaling the old man with light, piercing eyes. "Will she live?" The words seemed dragged from his depths. "Will she come back again?"

"The sea will revive her and give her strength. But she'll not come back here again, not on her own. If you want her, you will have to go after her—to the island more than likely. Come now and sit down. Meg's body may already be on the way to mending, but only *you* can make her heart whole again. She will need you, well and strong, if she is to find the will to go on living."

With the bitter certainty that Meg was gone and that there was nothing he could do to call her back again, Glenmorgan felt the last of his strength desert him. He sank heavily into the chair to which Pippin guided him and, drawing the gem-

436

stone from where it hung on a chain about his neck, gazed into it.

Was he dreaming? Or did the web of tiny cracks already seem less pronounced, the interior less cloudy? A long breath escaped his lips. No, he could not be mistaken. He did see it, and it was more powerful than before—the depths of the gemstone scintillated a blue-green heart of flame.

The gemstone was mending. And with it, Meg. He would give her all the time she needed. But when the stone shone with a clear, unmottled transparency, he would be there. There was not a storm or a sea too savage to keep him from her.

Epilogue

Meg perched on a boulder atop the windswept cliffs looking out over the lonely stretch of sea. It was the end of April. The beginning of the hurricane season was fast approaching, but today the sky was a clear, deep blue, unmarred by anything more sinister than a few white drifts of cloud. The island looked just as it had when she left it to follow Glenmorgan and her heart to Charles Town seemingly an age ago, and yet she was painfully aware that it was irrevocably altered.

Or perhaps it was only that she had changed, she thought, feeling her aloneness like an unbearable weight upon her heart. The island was crowded with memories, like ghosts, haunting her wherever she wandered.

She had known as soon as she emerged from the jungle into the clearing in which her grandfather's hut stood, solitary and vacant, that that was why she had shunned coming back. The hut, the cave, the cove with its white, sandy beach—the island itself—brought everything she wished to forget flooding back again. And not even the wondrous thing she had discovered in the hidden depths of the sea— her mother's people—could banish the sense of incompleteness that she felt without Glenmorgan—without her chosen lifemate.

She had shattered the gemstone, but even had she not, the song of power would still be silenced within her. Only Glenmorgan could ever bring it back again. Only Glenmorgan could completely heal her heart.

It was that truth which had driven her at last to this lonely place. Here, she had used to watch the ships pass by and dreamed that one day she would go to all the far places of the earth where they touched port. Those days seemed an eternity ago, those dreams empty now.

With a heavy heart she stood, her slim body limned through the thin fabric of the gown she had donned one last time simply for the memories it evoked. It was time she left this place. The whales waited, the whales and the vast unexplored depths of the sea. She would never come back again.

Her eyes stinging, she lifted her arms above her head.

"It's a long way down," remarked a deep voice musingly at her back. Meg gasped and lowered her arms, her eyes fixed and staring on the white sails of a ship just rounding the headland. "And though I should be both amazed and thrilled at seeing you make such a dive, I'd really prefer that you put it off for another time."

Slowly, she turned, her heart pounding beneath her breast. She struggled to control the heady surge of joy that coursed through her at sight of Glenmorgan, looking just the way he had the first time she had seen him—tall and lean, his powerful figure garbed in a flowing white shirt and black leather breeches, his hair, black as a raven's wing, falling unbound to his shoulders. "Why?" she said.

Glenmorgan smiled crookedly. Straight and slim, her silvery mane flowing about her shoulders and small, willowy waist, she was even more thrillingly beautiful than he remembered her. He felt an old, familiar hunger awaken and stir.

"Frankly," he replied softly, "I don't relish the thought of having to jump in after you."

Impatiently, Meg shook her head. "No. Why did you come?"

"You didn't think that I wouldn't?" murmured Glenmorgan, quizzing her. "A Glenmorgan mates for life, I thought you knew that. Besides, I had to return this to you, didn't I?"

A misty smile trembled on her lips as she beheld the gemstone—whole, translucent, and dazzlingly beautiful.

"You got it back," she said, her eyes shining with the same glorious sheen as the stone dangling from its chain. Then almost instantly they darkened, troubled. "I meant to use it as it was never meant to be used—to kill. I would have done it, too, if you hadn't stopped me. I could not bear it when I thought you were dead because of me. Because of . . ." She stopped, her cheeks paling. "Tharp," she whispered hoarsely, "is he . . ."

"Aye," Glenmorgan answered grimly. "He'll never trouble anyone ever again. The funny thing is I would have let him go. When you collapsed so limply in my arms and when I saw the gemstone, shattered and blackened, I forgot all about Tharp. My only concern was for you. If he hadn't stolen this," he said, draping the chain around her neck so that the stone lay between her breasts, "I'd have left him to skulk away like the miserable creature that he was."

"And Clarissa?" she asked, not wanting to but unable to stop herself.

"Clarissa was a boy's fantasy, a dream without substance. She ceased to exist for me the moment I looked into eyes as marvelous and mysterious as the depths of the sea itself. I warned you once that things would not always be what they seemed. At first I distanced myself from you because I thought you were in love with Dick and later, when I realized the truth—that you had spoken out of anger and innocence and that there was nothing between the two of you—then I thought you would be safer if everyone believed I was still obsessed with Clarissa. I hadn't taken into account that Drago and Tharp would discover what I was too blind to see—that the woman I loved was rarer and more wonderful even than I imagined her to be." Framing her face between his hands, he gazed deeply into her eyes. "It's over, Meg. The past is dead and buried. Marigold is Kate's now, and Dick's. Aye. They were married weeks ago. And with Thomas to run the shipping business, I am free to go where I choose, do as I please."

"And—and Grandfather?" Meg stammered, wanting somehow to prolong the magic of this moment, to put off reality just a little while longer.

"The admiral was finally induced to clear your grandfather's name. And if I'm not mistaken, Pippin won't be alone at Cherry Orchard much longer. It seems the 'old man' isn't as old as we might have thought him to be. But then, you probably realized before I did that he's in love with my mother. Kate did, and she claims Mary Glenmorgan is just as taken with him." His dark head went back at the startled look in Meg's eye, and his laughter rolled over her like a joyful caress. "Don't tell me they had you fooled, too," he said, his eyes yet brimful of mirth. But almost immediately he sobered. "There's just you and me now, Meg—and the *Raven* to take us anywhere you say. Tell me you love me and that you'll be my wife, and it's done. Say it, Meg. Say that you love me."

"I love you," she murmured, her face deeply troubled. "More than you can possibly know."

A flame leaped in his eyes as he clasped her to him. "Meg!"

She drew back as if she could not bear his touch. "No, don't!"

441

A cold hand clutched at Glenmorgan's heart. "Dammit, Meg. What foolishness is this?"

"I'm a mermaid," she cried, her voice filled with anguish. "Don't you see? It isn't enough that I love you. I have to know, Michael. Why did you come after me?"

"Good God, why do you think I came?" he demanded, his face grim. "I came because I'm bloody miserable without you. You haunt not only my dreams at night, but my every waking hour. Dammit, Meg. I love you."

Meg gazed at him with shining eyes. "Do you?" she said, afraid to believe. "How much do you love me?"

Glenmorgan's glance pierced her through. "So much that my life wouldn't be worth the living without you."

"Are you sure?" she insisted. "I was willing to kill for you, and that is the same as dying, for one of my kind. Are you willing to become as one with me? To know what I know, feel what I feel? I will not live with you as my mother lived with my father. I cannot, not now, when I have found my mother's people. I want you to come with me, to see them and experience all that they have to offer. And to do that, you must become as I am. You will not be giving up what you are," she hastened to assure him. "You will still be free to walk the land, to sail your ship, live wherever you choose. And if I am one with you, I'll be free to go with you. Together, joined in the way of the old ones, we will be able to live in either or both worlds." It was why the rite of *hrum* had been forbidden between a mermaid and a landsman. She knew that now, after talking with her mother's people. She knew, too, that Glenmorgan had proven himself worthy, or he would not be there on the Island of the Mermaids, which was hidden by magic from outsiders. The protective spell had been breached by Drago only because Meg had opened the way, so that Glenmorgan would be free to leave whenever he chose. She had sealed it once more when she left with Glenmorgan.

442

And now he was here, led by his heart and the gemstone, or perhaps by the god. Her own heart shining in her eyes, she gazed up at him.

"It is your choice, Michael," she said, her voice husky. "But you have to understand that the joining is forever. Once done, it cannot be undone. You will be bound, no less than I, for as long as we both shall live. But more than that, you will be bound by the strictures of my people never to use the knowledge and the power that will become yours against another living creature."

Glenmorgan was looking at her gravely, his face unreadable, and Meg felt a sudden stab of fear. She was asking too much of him, she thought, and unable to bear the anguish of losing him again, she turned her head away to hide the panic in her eyes.

She froze at the touch of Glenmorgan's palm, warm against her cheek. "Meg." Gently, he forced her to look at him. "I don't begin to understand what you're trying to tell me," he answered slowly, as if measuring his words. "I can't promise I will never lift my hand against another. God knows I'm weary enough of killing, but I'm not a bloody saint. I would always fight to defend what is mine." He smiled wryly. "And I'm afraid I'll never be satisfied living off fruit and seaweed." The smile faded as his eyes probed hers, willing her to understand. "I can't change the world or what I am, any more than I can change what you are. But I can and will swear that I will never violate your trust in me. This power, whatever it is, will never become an instrument of destruction in my hands. If it will make it possible for us to be together, that's all I want from it." He paused, a suspicious glint in his eye. "There's just one other thing. I'm used to having two legs and—well—certain other parts of my body that I've grown pretty attached to. Just how much of a physical transformation are we talking about here—if I'm to become 'as you are'?"

She was in his arms almost before he had finished.

"You will never have a fishtail, if that's what you're worried about," she laughed, flinging her arms about his neck. "You will always be as you are now—a human and a man—and our children will be more human than sea-folk, though they will have powers other human children do not. You, like them, will be able to extract from the sea what you require to live—air from water, strength from the energy contained in the sea. With the power will come the knowledge of how this is done." She cocked her head to one side, her mouth quirked in a mischievous grin. "Did you truly think I would allow anything to alter that part of you that gives me such great pleasure? I promise I am far too selfish for that."

"Minx," he growled with obvious feeling and clasped her savagely to his chest. "Seductress," he muttered, drinking in the flushed loveliness of her face. A kindling fire leaped in his eyes. "Meg," he groaned. "My sweet love."

Then his lips were devouring her, weaving their spell of magic over her, and his hands were awakening the tempest that would carry them both to the heights of rapture. And suddenly she knew what her mother had never really known—that their love would never be a prison. Together they would truly be free. Through him, she would come to know all the places she had ever dreamed of seeing, and through her, he would learn the secrets of the sea, even the wonders of her mother's people, whom she had discovered still living in a marvelous place, far below, in the watery depths. They would join now, first in the way that she had come in the beginning to love him, then again, later, in the way of her people.

"Michael," she breathed, losing herself to the ecstasy of his embrace. "Oh, Michael, I have been waiting so long."

It was all either of them said for a very long time.

PINNACLE BOOKS HAS
SOMETHING FOR EVERYONE —

MAGICIANS, EXPLORERS, WITCHES AND CATS

THE HANDYMAN   (377-3, $3.95/$4.95)
He is a magician who likes hands. He likes their comfortable shape and weight and size. He likes the portability of the hands once they are severed from the rest of the ponderous body. Detective Lanark must discover who The Handyman is before more handless bodies appear.

PASSAGE TO EDEN   (538-5, $4.95/$5.95)
Set in a world of prehistoric beauty, here is the epic story of a courageous seafarer whose wanderings lead him to the ends of the old world — and to the discovery of a new world in the rugged, untamed wilderness of northwestern America.

BLACK BODY   (505-9, $5.95/$6.95)
An extraordinary chronicle, this is the diary of a witch, a journal of the secrets of her race kept in return for not being burned for her "sin." It is the story of Alba, that rarest of creatures, a white witch: beautiful and able to walk in the human world undetected.

THE WHITE PUMA   (532-6, $4.95/NCR)
The white puma has recognized the men who deprived him of his family. Now, like other predators before him, he has become a man-hater. This story is a fitting tribute to this magnificent animal that stands for all living creatures that have become, through man's carelessness, close to disappearing forever from the face of the earth.